He knew that once he ▓▓▓▓▓▓
her, would not be able to ▓▓▓▓

Almost as though she had no choice, she slowly lifted his knuckles to her mouth, pressed her lips to them.

His blood surged to where her lips met his skin. He took his hand from her. He slid it up through her hair.

"Evie," he said hoarsely. "Evie."

There was no preamble, no finesse. Just a slow, incinerating, unleashed hunger when he kissed her.

By Julie Anne Long

A NOTORIOUS COUNTESS CONFESSES
HOW THE MARQUESS WAS WON
WHAT I DID FOR A DUKE
I KISSED AN EARL
SINCE THE SURRENDER
LIKE NO OTHER LOVER
THE PERILS OF PLEASURE

Coming Soon

IT HAPPENED ONE MIDNIGHT

ong

A
Notorious
Countess
Confesses

AVON
An Imprint of HarperCollins*Publishers*

AVON BOOKS
An Imprint of HarperCollins*Publishers*
10 East 53rd Street
New York, New York 10022-5299

Copyright © 2012 by Julie Anne Long
ISBN 978-0-06-211802-8
www.avonromance.com

First Avon Books mass market printing: November 2012

Avon Trademark Reg. U.S. Pat. Off. and in Other Countries, Marca Registrada, Hecho en U.S.A.
HarperCollins® is a registered trademark of HarperCollins Publishers.

Printed in the U.S.A.

10 9 8 7 6 5 4 3 2 1

Acknowledgments

My DEEPEST GRATITUDE TO MY EVER-DELIGHTFUL, supportive editor, May Chen; to my endlessly clever agent, Steve Axelrod; to my darling sister, for cheerfully submitting to having ideas bounced off her; to the hard-working, talented staff at Avon Books; and to all the lovely friends and readers who let me know what my books mean to them.

Chapter 1

SHE WAS CONFIDENT NO ONE WOULD EVER EXPECT to find her in a church. After all, it was too late to save her soul. It was as black, they said, as the widow's weeds she'd shed with the same unseemly haste she'd hoisted her skirts for the Earl of Wareham. Whom she'd then *killed* with unseemly haste. But then, what did one expect from someone of her . . . origins?

This was, of course, all nonsense. Evie had worn black for precisely as long as her etiquette book (her name had been engraved in gold inside the cover—how the earl had loved his extravagances!) proscribed. She'd in fact pored over every word in that book as if they were spells that would roll away the stone blocking the door of societal acceptance.

And . . . well, if anything could be said to have *killed* the earl, it was . . . enthusiasm.

She'd been naïve (a word she'd first learned from an exiled French prince, who had been quite *naïve* to think that *she'd* ever been naïve). This still galled. Before she'd married the earl, she'd been certain her epitaph would read: *Here lies Evie Duggan. No one ever got the better of her.* After she'd married him, she'd indulged in a bit of laurel-resting and even a daydream or two: *"Here lies Evie Duggan . . . devoted wife and mother, a more beloved woman never lived . . ."*

Ah, and that . . . *that* had been her mistake. If not for that, she might have been able to anticipate what happened next. Reveries made one soft. She never should have forgotten that the world was on the side of the planners, not the dreamers.

At the moment, she was too weary to be terribly concerned about the color of her soul. She was unaccustomed to weariness; it sat on her like a heavy, itchy blanket.

She kept her hands piously in her lap, steepling her elegantly gloved fingers in an unconscious imitation of the ancient, squat, little church. She'd always learned by imitation. Henny, her maid, shifted uncomfortably next to her. The pews had been built centuries ago, when all men and women were smaller, which Evie supposed had made it easier to scurry into the trees and shrubbery like so many squirrels when marauders descended. Such a violent past, England had, or so she'd learned from one of the earnest bloods who'd appeared backstage at the Green Apple Theater, where her career, such as it was, had begun. He'd brought offerings of wildflower bouquets and his passion for history. This, of course, meant he hadn't a prayer of earning more than a crumb of her attention—she was a practical girl above all else—but Evie was a great respecter of passion of any kind, and a listener, and both qualities had served her well.

The ton had turned the infamous Evie Duggan into a squirrel when the world had once been her oyster. She wasn't here by choice, but she was certain Pennyroyal Green, Sussex, would cloak her to some degree. After all, it was home to the Everseas, one of whom had once disappeared from the gallows in an explosion and smoke before a crowd of thousands. Surely she was dull compared to that?

It was just a bloody pity the nickname the ton had foisted upon her was so irresistibly vivid.

Her life had just been yanked out from beneath her, leaving her wobbling and directionless as a spun top for the first time ever, which was perhaps what had made her susceptible to the ringing church bells as her carriage rolled through Pennyroyal Green just after the sun rose. The bells seemed to beckon, and so she'd followed. Perhaps in this new life, she'd be the sort of person who went to church, rather than the sort of person who caused other riders to topple from their horses in an attempt to get a look at her when she rode in The Row with an admirer. Perhaps the women here would be her friends since she'd recently discovered she had none, when she'd once thought she'd had dozens.

"*Must* you wriggle so, Henny?" she hissed.

"Beggin' yer pardon, m'lady, but these pews are hard as a hangman's heart and narrow as a rat's bunghole. Me petticoat has crawled *right* up me ar—"

Two women in front of them swiveled to stare at them, jaws swinging wide in outrage.

They stared at Evie. In swift succession, impressions ticked over their faces, settled in, moved on: they took in the fur-lined pelisse, the hat that cupped her face like a lover, elegantly highlighting her cheekbones and green, green eyes. Astonishment, suspicion, envy, confusion joined the parade; at last, bald curiosity settled in.

But not, thankfully, recognition.

Evie gave them a small, serene smile.

Henny leaned over and said *sotto voce* to Evie, "Why, the townspeople hereabouts are *so* kind, my lady, to leave their mouths open to catch any flies afore they can trouble the likes of their *betters.*"

Their heads whipped back around to face the front of the church. One of the silk flowers atop one of the bonnets continued to shiver, as if cowed. Henny had that effect upon nearly everything.

There immediately followed a soughing sound, like wind bending meadow grass. A moment later, Evie realized it was the sound of dozens of heads turning toward the altar, of wool-covered bums shifting on polished wood.

She turned her own head.

Her first thought was: *Well. He's certainly tall for a vicar.* But then Eve couldn't recall ever before seeing a vicar in captivity—perhaps intimidating height was a requirement of the job. She was struck by the width of his shoulders, a great shelf tapering elegantly into a lean frame. In his hands rustled sheets of foolscap upon which he'd no doubt written the words meant to improve their collective souls. Bent over his notes as he was now, he looked as if he were supporting the weight of invisible wings

She could have sworn that every pair of feminine shoulders rose and fell in a sigh when the vicar looked up, a smile, faint but warm, inclusive but impersonal, ready on his face, before he dropped his gaze again to his notes. The perfect vicar smile. She'd spent enough time in a theater to admire stagecraft. She'd spent enough time with men to be cynical about all of them.

She had no use for *any* of them anymore. *That*, of a certainty, was part of her new life.

Henny by no means shared this conviction.

"*Cor!*" she whispered, gripping Evie's arm. And then slowly, "Would ye *look* at that bloke! 'e can warm me bed anytime 'e wants—"

Evie elbowed her hard.

"Good morning. Thank you for coming."

Oh. His voice surprised her: a baritone with the depth of a bell and deliciously frayed at the edges, it was like stumbling into a patch of sunlight on a relentlessly gray day. Her eyes closed; the temptation was to bask in it.

Her sense of self-preservation propped her eyes open again. She'd once heard that an Eversea had fallen asleep in church, tipped forward, and cracked his chin on the pew in front of him before toppling to the floor.

She couldn't wait to hear him say more things.

"Goats," is what the vicar said next.

The congregation stirred—or some of it stirred—uneasily. She heard a cough that might just as easily have been a laugh.

Evie stirred, too, worried now, but still hopeful. Surely . . . surely she wasn't about to be subjected to a homily about *goats*? Perhaps he'd said . . . ghosts? . . . instead, which would have been infinitely more interesting?

"Many of us keep the horned beasts, so we know they usually butt heads for two reasons: to play . . . or to assert dominance."

Goats it was! Christ! If ever there was proof she wasn't in London anymore, surely this was it. Somehow she'd failed to anticipate she might be tortured to death by boredom. She had a horror of boredom. She was positively *gifted* at avoiding it. Likely some instinct for self-preservation had kept her from churches until now.

She threw a desperate glance at the entrance. She could hardly bolt down the aisle, and she doubted she could get the big ancient door of the church open without throwing her body at it like a battering ram, although Henny might be able to.

But Henny appeared enraptured.

Eve swiveled back toward the altar and discovered that the sun was now high enough to shed a beam on the vicar. She was arrested: Nice bit of celestial theater, that. In his face, curves and angles seemed united for the purpose of breaking hearts: a jaw clean-edged as a blade, cheekbones that rose like battlements, between them the sort of hollows sported by poets, all deepened and defined by strategic shadow and light. It somehow contrived to be both sensitive and implacable.

Her heart could not be broken, of course, for the simple reason that it was beyond the reach of any man. But it hardly seemed necessary for a country vicar to look like that, or to have such *presence,* that air of calm command, that comfort in his skin. And because she knew men, she knew it was this, more than his looks, that kept all of the eyes in the room on him.

She could feel herself tensing. She suddenly felt trapped. But she was in a church, not a *cell.* As there was no hope for escape, she would stoically endure by watching him the way one might watch scenery unfurling outside a carriage window, and listening to his voice the way one might listen to, oh, birdsong or the sea. And for a time it worked. But Henny's enormous thigh was flush up against hers, which was a bit like being pressed up against a hot bombazine pillow, and the same sunlight illuminating the vicar shafted through one of the austere, stained-glass windows and threw a perfect rectangle of heat on her. And she was weary, so weary. Her thoughts drifted, became diffuse.

Evie's last thought before she fell asleep was: *If he were an angel, surely he'd be the fallen sort.*

She suspected he was a man with secrets, and she ought to know.

WHEN MR. ELDRED'S goat attacked Mr. Brownwell and sent him flying five feet across his garden, it had been nothing short of an answered prayer. Adam had been in a foul mood that morning, brutally gnawing his quill, slashing out flaccid, uninspired sentence after flaccid, uninspired sentence and hurling crushed wads of foolscap across the room until they stacked like snowballs against the wall. He'd thrust his hands up through his hair (it was useful to keep it a little too long for precisely this reason) and rued again his choice of the church over the military, for being shot at seemed preferable to being stared at by dozens of eyes when he had nothing, absolutely nothing to say to them on Sunday.

A typical Saturday, in other words.

But then Mr. Brownwell had stopped in at the vicarage, vibrating with outrage and gesturing at a gaping hole in the seat of his trousers. The incident (a boundary dispute, as it so happened) lit the touch paper to inspiration, and at the eleventh hour (it was *always* the eleventh hour) the Goat Affair evolved into a sermon about loving one's neighbor. Granted, a few of his parishioners already did this rather too literally and quite surreptitiously. This he knew because after a year in Pennyroyal Green, many of them had begun confiding in him with something approaching abandon.

"He has a way about him," they told each other. "Such a good man. So calming, so *certain*. One *wants* to tell him things, and he always knows just what to say."

He didn't always know what to say. He sometimes had no *idea* what to say until a parishioner laid a trouble at his feet and looked up at him with hope—or challenge—in their eyes. In the year since he'd arrived to take up the modest living in Pennyroyal Green at the behest of his wealthy uncle, Jacob Eversea, he'd learned that his job was like carrying a torch through a long tunnel where he could only see a few feet in front of him at a time, and occasionally bats flew at him, or he stumbled across alcoves full of treasure, or just missed stepping in something foul. He felt his way through.

Fortunately, he liked surprises. Even unpleasant ones held a certain appeal, for he was secretly a conqueror by nature and the youngest of six competitive children and could in fact, on occasion, be positively bloody-minded. All of which meant he would in fact be damned if anything defeated him, whether it was his exams at Oxford or the things that mattered most to his impossible father, like shooting, or a sermon that refused to write itself, or how to make sure the impoverished O'Flaherty family who lived on the edge of town didn't starve. Since he was a boy, he'd driven himself with a quietly cheerful mercilessness to excel. His Eversea cousins had recently discovered this quality when he had calmly, without fanfare, surprised the devil out of everyone by shooting the heart out of every target in the yearly Sussex Marksmanship Contest. He took home a big silver cup and the respect of the men of Pennyroyal Green, who instantly decided they didn't care what a vicar looked like as long as he knew his way around guns, horses, and dogs. He most certainly did.

For his arrival in Pennyroyal Green to take up the living at the vicarage *had* been greeted with a certain amount of skepticism. He was related to the Everseas, after all (on their mother's side), and certainly looked like it, what with the height and the steal-your-breath looks. Both of which filled the church with parishioners on Sundays and the hearts of women with yearning, though he knew some of his parishioners half dreaded (or half hoped) he'd bound impulsively into the congregation midsermon and begin ravishing women. Not *all* of the Everseas had been rogues. Still, those were the ones that people tended to remember.

He knew he'd need to be faultless beneath their scrutiny. So he was. He'd charmed them; he liked people, so he did this effortlessly, in the way of all Eversea men. He sent not so much as a wayward twinkle or lingering glance toward any of the town's young ladies (and there were dozens of comely ones); each of them received an equal measure of regard. He'd decided to be the best bloody vicar in creation. Which was comical, he saw now in retrospect. For unlike target shooting, this turned out to be *quite* out of his control, formidable though his control was. He hadn't anticipated that his duties—immersion in the joys, griefs, deaths, births, weddings, secrets, poverty, and petty concerns of his parishioners—would tumble him like a gem, knock the corners from him, humble him, distill him to his very essence. Thus uncluttered with expectation, somehow he could now see even more clearly into the heart of their concerns. He worked ceaselessly. He scarcely had time to even *daydream* about ravishing anyone. Somewhere along the way he'd stopped wanting to be the *best* vicar and simply prayed to do as much good as possible. He'd begun to feel equal to the job, but privately, he didn't know if he would ever truly feel worthy of it. He just knew he would never stop trying to be.

And at least he now dreamed less often of standing stark naked at the altar before his congregation.

His female parishioners continued to have this dream with regularity, however.

And now he stood in the sunlight outside the church while his parishioners filed by to thank him and shake his hand. Mrs. Sneath, that worthy woman, now stood beaming before him. She'd raised five sons who'd gone on to be spectacularly successful both in marriage and in trade, as they wouldn't dare be anything else under her watch. She now headed a battalion of women known as the Society for the Protection of the Sussex Poor, dedicated to good works and reformation of lost souls, whenever she was able to get her hands on one. Her fondest wish, she'd told Adam, was to witness a miracle, a true miracle, one day. She'd privately pronounced his character "exemplary," which was all that was needed to remove any lingering doubt about his *tendencies* in the minds of the remaining skeptics.

"Marvelous sermon, Vicar. Loving thy neighbor is *always* wonderful advice, and often such a challenge. I hope you plan to come round to supper this week so we can discuss plans for the auction and the rest of the Winter Festival?"

A series of events to raise funds for the local poor were planned—an auction, a small assembly, a larger ball—and she and her committee were coordinating them, but his approval and opinion was solicited. The ladies were indispensable, really, given the endless nature of parish duties.

Indispensable *and* maddening. A piquant combination.

"I wouldn't miss it for anything, Mrs. Sneath," he assured her.

"My niece will be visiting from Cornwall and joining us for supper." She added this slyly.

Ah, but of course, she would. "How lovely it will be to meet another member of your family."

"Her needlework is *unparalleled.*"

"You must be very . . . proud."

Because that was when he saw her: the petite woman flanked by another woman roughly the size of a bear. She was blinking in the sun, like a creature emerging from a cave. And well she might. An accusing shaft of celestial light had illuminated her during the sermon, and that's how he'd noticed she'd been fast asleep, slightly slumped against the bear of a woman. Not only that, but *snoring* a bit, too, if the fluttering of the net on her hat was any indication.

Not *once* before had anyone slept through one of his sermons. He'd directed nearly the entirety of it to her, out of incredulity and indignant pride.

Fragments of their low and heated discussion floated to him as Mrs. Sneath spoke.

"Funny how you're suddenly an etiquette expert, Henny, when the vicar looks like . . ."

" . . . 'aven't the faintest idea what a 'donnis' might be, but fancy words aside, I've been starved for *scenery* since we've arrived, if ye take me meaning, me *lady*, so if ye'd be so kind as to . . ."

" . . . don't want to make myself conspicuous, Henny, and you *know* . . ."

"Did you enjoy the honey, Vicar?" Mrs. Cranborn had slipped past Mrs. Sneath and was now aiming a radiant smile at him.

"The hon—oh, yes, thank you so much again for the kind gift."

He was forever being given jars of things, honey and jam and apples and ointments, which he supposed was a way of reminding him how much more pleasant his life would be should he ever decide to give a woman the run of it. He remained "dangerously unmarried," or at least this was how his aunt Isolde Eversea put it. But then she would, given the nerve-taxing his cousins Colin and Ian had given her. *Mercifully* unmarried was often how Adam viewed it. The dreams of standing naked at the altar had been supplanted by dreams of swimming through the vicarage up to his neck in blackberry preserves, only to find the door neatly embroidered shut by the word "Bless Our Home."

To his surprise, the small woman and the bear approached.

Mrs. Cranborn glanced up at the large woman in dark bombazine, recoiled in rank astonishment, and reflexively stumbled a few steps back.

And so Adam took his first look at the woman he'd clearly bored. She seemed comprised entirely of vivid contrasts: black curls at her temples and alabaster cheeks and eyes like the proverbial jewels, so green, they seemed, even through that scrap of net that fluttered from her hat. Her pelisse hung and swung and clung flawlessly, a fit only the most exclusive of seamstresses could accomplish—this much he knew about women's clothing. She seemed unreal, like something out of a storybook. He supposed she was beautiful. But he was moved by women who seemed touchable, unwrappable, like Lady Fennimore's daughter Jenny, whose soft hair was forever coming out of its pins. This one seemed entirely contained, as sealed and gleaming as a jar of preserves.

"I hope you don't think it inappropriate, Reverend, since we haven't been properly introduced. But I wanted to thank you for the sermon." The glance she slid over to her bear-sized companion said *Satisfied?* as clearly as if she'd spoken it aloud. "I am the Countess of Wareham. This is my maid, Henrietta La Fontaine."

The Countess of Wareham . . . the name echoed in the recesses of his mind. He was certain he'd been told *something* about her. Given her appearance, he was unsurprised by both the title and her

accent—he secretly thought of those etched con-
sonants and indolently elongated vowels as The
London Ironic Dialect. It was as though nothing,
nothing in the world could ever possibly divert her
again, so she indulged the world by viewing it with
detached indulgence.

He *was*, however, surprised a countess would introduce her maid. There had in fact been the slightest hesitation before the word "maid," as though
the countess wasn't entirely certain *what* to call her.

He bowed graciously. "A pleasure to meet you,
Lady Wareham. I'm the Reverend Adam Sylvaine.
How kind of you to attend the service."

Henrietta dipped a graceful curtsy. "Yer sermon
was a balm to me soul, Reverend."

She had a very fierce gaze, did Henrietta. Eyes
like bright little currants pressed into dough.

"As soothing as a lullaby, some might say,"
Adam said pleasantly.

Lady Wareham stiffened. Her eyes narrowed so
swiftly one might almost have missed it.

He didn't.

But then a distant little smile drifted onto her
face, the sort a queen might offer a peasant child
who held a daisy out to her.

"Thank you, again, Reverend, and good day.
Come along, Henny."

"Good day to you," he said politely, and bowed
elegantly.

He bit back a wry smile. He suspected she'd
exhausted the novelty value of church, and he
wouldn't be seeing her there again.

Henrietta winked at him as she walked away.

Chapter 2

In the carriage, Evie gloomily entertained the possibility that her soul really was impermeable to moral repair or renewal. Clearly it was resistant to sermons. An inauspicious start to her exile—that was, *new life*—in Sussex.

Cheeky vicar. The nerve. Lullaby, indeed.

"You were *snoring*," Henny said.

"Surely not," Evie said idly.

"*Quiet*-like," Henny conceded. "But you were."

And then Evie listened with half an ear as Henny planned aloud about supper "—cold roast, I think there is, and didn't you ask Mrs. Wilberforce to get in some cheese?" She'd hired a housekeeper by the name of Mrs. Wilberforce, but Henny was in charge of her staff, as her capabilities were far-ranging, her roles and titles as diverse and subject to change as Evie's had been: maid, housekeeper, abigail, advisor, scolder, dresser at the Green Apple Theater (which was where Evie had met her), frightener of unpleasant suitors, visitor of apothecaries in the dead of night. She viewed Pennyroyal Green as penance, of a sort. For Eve had all but saved Henny's life many years ago by employing her as her dresser when Henny was penniless. She would follow Eve to the ends of the earth, but she reserved the right to complain.

Suddenly, the coach lurched to a halt, and they were both thrown forward, nearly knocking their heads together.

The coach rocked a bit as the driver clambered down. Eve unlatched the door and peered out just as he was about to peer in.

They both reared back.

"Beggin' yer pardon, m'lady, but seems summat is awry wi' one of the horses. Team's gone balky. We beg a moment to have a look to see if we may find the trouble."

And thus the utter disintegration of my life continues, Eve thought wryly.

"Certainly. If I may just step out for a moment . . . ?"

Because all at once she wanted air. Being transferred from the enclosed little church to the enclosed carriage merely enhanced the sensation of her life shrinking to the size of a cell.

He assisted her down from the carriage, and she landed lightly on the road, bordered by low grass and other greenery not yet killed by frost.

She inhaled and inspected what was now her new view and would be for the forseeable future: soft hills mounded like a messy blanket; stubby, needled trees, oaks, some of which still sported leaves despite its being the brink of winter. Smoke spiraled from the chimneys of the few cottages scattered in the middle distance. She moved off the road and stretched and peered: The gray line on the far horizon was the sea.

Henny followed her out of the carriage and stretched and inhaled mightily.

And then her driver returned to her and gave a little bow.

"Lady Wareham, I fear we may have a dilemma. One of the horses has lost a shoe, and it would risk laming him if we continue on the journey."

Of *course* they had a dilemma. Life had become nothing but dilemmas of late. "How far are we from Damask Manor?"

"A good twenty minutes or so by carriage."

Which meant at least double the time walking. She wasn't incapable of it—God only knew she'd been a country girl a lifetime ago—but it was unthinkable for a woman of Henny's age and size to undertake that journey on foot.

Henny took command. "There's smoke from that chimney." She pointed. "I'll see if I can fetch some help, will I? Perhaps a farmer will lend a cart. I'd like to stretch me legs, anyhow, after those torture pews."

Evie hesitated. "Well, if you insist. I suppose it couldn't hurt."

Henny insisted and trudged off, crested a rise, then disappeared over one of those small hills into the little valley, following a narrow beaten path to one of the picturesque little houses with the inviting chimney smoke.

All was silence. Apart from the shifting hooves and murmurs of her driver and footman, they were entirely alone. Evie scanned the trees again and gave a start.

Alone apart from a small blond boy leaning out

from behind a tree. He was staring solemn-faced and unabashedly, the way children do.

She crossed her eyes good and proper, taking care to make her expression hideous. Little boys *loved* that sort of thing, and she wasn't above reaching for an easy laugh.

He quite gratifyingly giggled. His front teeth were missing, which for some reason charmed her to her core. He must be seven or eight years old, then, she thought. Seamus at that age had been a devil in short pants. Then again, long pants hadn't done much to reform him.

"Spiders aren't pretty," the boy said.

She was accustomed to small boys and non sequiturs. "Well, I don't know about that. I suspect girl spiders are pretty to boy spiders."

This the boy found uproarious. His eyes vanished with mirth when he laughed.

She smiled along with him.

"Are girl cows pretty to boy cows?" he wanted to know.

"Undoubtedly."

"And are girl dogs pretty to boy dogs?"

She pretended to consider this. "In all likelihood, yes. Some girls dogs to some boy dogs, anyhow."

"All dogs are pretty to me, too," he confessed.

"*And* to me," she agreed solemnly.

The boy went silent, bashful and delighted with their accord.

"Have you a dog?" she asked.

"Oh, yes. A hound. Her name is Wednesday."

"A fine name for a dog. A fine day of the week as well. Why is she called Wednesday?"

" 'Twas the day our neighbor brought her to me to keep forever."

"It must have been a special day."

"*Pauuuuuuuulie!* Paul! Where the devil *are* you?" A frantic woman's voice echoed all around them suddenly.

"Ah. And you must be Paul," Evie guessed.

" '*Twas* a special day," the boy agreed, without even blinking, evidently entirely deaf to his mother's voice.

The woman huffed up the hill and sighed with relief when she saw him. "Paulie! What have I told you about running off? Your blessed dog is chasing the chickens and Grandmama is expecting us for—"

She clapped her mouth shut when she saw Evie. She froze midwalk, stiff-legged as a hunting dog pointing out prey.

Then her eyes frosted, and her mouth became a tight, horizontal line.

"See, Mama?" Paulie said cheerfully. "She doesn't *look* like a spider. She's pretty. And spiders aren't."

Oh God.

Evie's breath left her in a painful gust.

She stood, cold in the gut, hot in the cheeks, feeling foolish and utterly blank.

That hated, *hateful* nickname. But how would a boy have known unless he'd overheard his mother talking?

Which meant that his mother had learned it from someone else.

Who had learned from someone else.

Which means they must know about her after all.

So much for refuge in Pennyroyal Green. So much for a new life here.

"What did I tell you, Paul, about bothering strangers?" She said this to her son, but the woman still eyed her unblinkingly.

"But *Mama*, she's very nice and she likes dogs and she said that boy dogs think girl dogs are pret—"

The woman latched her fingers about his arm and gave him a tug, dragging him behind her. He protested something on an unintelligible whine.

"Because I'm your mother, and you will do as I say without questioning it, that's why. She simply isn't *our* sort, Paul."

Ah. The staggering self-righteousness of it.

Evie couldn't move. Her bones had turned to stone.

It was the sort of thing that once would have bounced from her as gaily as guineas flung down on a gaming table. For years, nothing ever dented her; she had shaped the world to suit *her*, as surely as though she were a signet ring and the world sealing wax.

But it was then she realized her hand was flattened protectively, right over the velvet frogs closing her expensive pelisse, one of the earl's many—one of his last, in fact— gifts to her. Exactly as if a dart had entered just there.

She dropped it instantly.

"And she's not *that* pretty, Paulie," drifted back to Evie.

This, at least was predictable, and made her snort softly.

It was a moment longer before she could toss her head insouciantly. And then for good measure, she stuck her tongue out at their retreating figures before whirling on her heels.

And nearly bouncing off the chest of a man cresting the hill behind her.

Chapter 3

She leaped back with a stifled shriek, clapping her hand to her heart.

"*Sweet Merciful Mary Mother of God*, ye shouldna sneak up like that! Ye creep like a cat ye bloody big . . ."

She stopped.

A very ripe Irish accent, long dormant but apparently healthy and whole and frisky and unleashed by shock, echoed across the countryside. *Bloody big bloody big bloody big . . .*

Ohhhh. The *shame* of it.

She wanted to close her eyes and sink deep, deep into the earth.

Instead, she forced herself to look up—*very* up—at who proved to be the Reverend Adam Sylvaine, the vicar.

He appeared entirely unruffled. Apart from his eyes, that was. They fair danced like flames with wicked, wicked, downright un-Christian mirth.

One of her horses whickered into what threatened to be a never-ending silence.

Be a gentleman, she silently willed him. *Leave it lie. Pretend you heard nothing at all.*

Up his eyebrows went.

"Biiiig . . ." he prompted.

She eyed him stonily. *Bastard,* she was tempted to complete. Why not? In for a penny, in for a pound.

He waited. Patient as Job. Wicked as Lucifer. Amused as hell.

"Vicar," she completed inanely, finally, on a mumble.

His head went back as though this was almost too good to be true, then came down on a nod.

"I suppose I am," he agreed thoughtfully, though his voice held a suspicious tremble. Stifled laughter. "I suppose I *am* a big . . . *vicar* . . . Though no one has ever before accused me before of creeping like a cat. Something to do with being . . . well, *big,* I suppose."

The vicar was taking the piss out of her, as her brother Seamus would say, and quite effectively, too.

She looked full into his face then. His eyes were such a disarming blue—the color of deep, still water, of Lough Leane in Killarney—they made her strangely restless. It was as if the weather inside him was always clear and temperate. Like his conscience and unblemished soul, no doubt, she thought sardonically. An unprepossessing black wool coat—Weston hadn't stitched up that one, she knew this for *certain*—whipped behind him in the stiffening wind, which was also doing its best to pluck a carelessly knotted cravat from the confines of a gray, striped waistcoat of no discernible pedigree.

And as though they were a beckoning road, her eyes followed the line of longer, finer, harder thighs than a vicar had any business possessing down to the dusty, creased toes of his boots. Which most definitely had not been made by Hoby.

Her eyes stayed safely on the ground. She took advantage of a moment of unexpectedly necessary composure gathering in the wake of the revelation about his thighs.

"I thought vicars were supposed to wear dresses." She said this almost testily. At least she had gotten control of her accent.

"Oh, a dress is optional."

Ping! Insults bounced from *him,* it seemed.

"And by 'dress,' I suppose you mean 'cassock'?" he added helpfully. "Difficult to creep like a cat in a cassock, you see, Lady Wareham. It swirls about one's ankles, flaps noisily in the breeze. One needs *stealth* to stop iniquity in its tracks."

In . . . iquity?

The word was a slap.

But . . . perhaps he was jesting? Surely he was? Did *he* know about her? Was the whole of this horrid village going to take turns plaguing her in turns? Would they turn out with boiling oil?

"Is that why you've suddenly appeared? Did you scent *iniquity* on the wind then, Reverend Sylvaine? Do you roam the Sussex countryside sniffing for it, like a truffle-hunting pig?"

He didn't reply for so long she finally turned to look at him.

To find he'd gone as rigid as if he'd been driven into the ground.

Something about that stillness made her think that angering him would be very unwise, indeed. Which seemed a peculiar thought to have about a vicar. But despite the fact that he wasn't blinking, he didn't *seem* angry. He was studying her the way one might study a lock about to be picked. The only movement was his hair. The breeze lifted it, let it fall, lifted it, let it fall. Hidden in the dark blond were dark gold or copper threads or strands sunbleached to silvery fairness. In the silence and stillness it was absurdly fascinating.

"I've dozens of cousins and a number of siblings, Lady Wareham. If you've siblings, you won't be surprised to learn that my hide is quite callused. It's nearly impossible to offend me."

Well.

He said it evenly. As if he hadn't just seen right through her and neatly incinerated her defenses, as surely as if she were a petulant child.

"Some might interpret that as a challenge, Reverend."

Which was precisely how she was acting, and she couldn't seem to stop.

He went quiet again. And then he smiled. Very, very faintly. Just enough, it seemed, for her to notice the elegant shape of his mouth. To tease out one dimple at the corner of it. And when at last he spoke, again she felt his voice more than she heard it, like fingers brushed along the short hairs at her nape. It had gone soft, so soft. But somehow it wasn't gentle.

"Oh? Did you come to Pennyroyal Green for challenge, then, Lady Wareham?"

She stared at him.

He stared back.

And to her astonishment, heat slowly washed the back of her neck, the backs of her arms, and it was suddenly more difficult to breathe. It occurred to her that she'd never seen a man who was so . . . contained. Yes: That was precisely the right word. As though something in him, some potential, *required* control. And whatever it was, whatever *he* was, pulled at her. The way earth pulled water into it. It felt stronger than she was, and her entire life had depended upon her being stronger than anyone.

She turned abruptly away. She inhaled in the hopes of clearing her head, but the traitorous air had turned to wine or some such; her thoughts staggered like foxed heirs at a gaming hell.

He was only a vicar, she reminded herself. The man had caught her in a rare moment of weakness amidst a particularly vulnerable episode in her life. That was all. And she was very weary, of course. After all, the church nap had hardly been the restorative kind.

She tugged her pelisse about her more snugly and stared toward her halted carriage with a little frown. Where the devil was Henny?

"It seems one of our horses threw a shoe," she said finally. Her voice was fainter than she would have preferred.

She wondered if she'd disappointed him.

He'd been watching her. She half suspected he knew the number of her eyelashes now.

"I see," he said easily enough, after a moment. "I was on my way to visit a parishioner when I saw your stopped carriage. And as there's no worry about brigands on this road since One-Eyed William haunted these parts a few decades ago, and as this isn't precisely one of the more scenic parts of Sussex, I feared something might be amiss."

One-eyed William? Was he *jesting*?

She said nothing.

"I'll just have a word with your driver then, shall I?"

When she didn't reply—for she couldn't seem to find her voice—he turned. She listened to him take one step, then two steps away, and somehow the sound of his footsteps seemed like the sound of failure.

"Reverend Sylvaine . . ."

He stopped, turned back toward her, his brows raised in a query.

The surest way to regain her power was to deploy what made her powerful.

"I must ask your forgiveness. I fear you startled me from my manners, and . . . I've never before met a vicar, you see, and it seems like such an interesting, important role. Pray, how does one become a vicar?"

She, possibly better than any other woman in England, knew the way beneath any man's ramparts—whether he was the Home Secretary or the King of England or a coal monger: It was flattery, served up with flirtation and innuendo.

She was startled when Reverend Sylvaine drew up visibly, instantly almost comically wary.

"One of the best ways, I've learned, to become one is to be related to the family who owns the living," he said shortly. With just a hint of irony.

And said nothing more.

"Must one be faultless of character? Entirely . . . free of vices?" She folded her hands before her and aimed her gaze up at him through her lashes with the precision of a rifleman.

The vicar glanced down at her demurely folded hands as though she'd unlocked a pistol. And then he slowly looked back up into her face.

He hesitated.

"I suppose it depends on how one interprets the word."

A masterpiece of circumspection, that sentence.

His eyes were now unreadable as an empty sky, shuttered. Hers, she was fairly certain, thanks to some collusion between her thick black lashes and the color of her eyes and the angle of sunlight and the sheer *intent* to charm, were sparkling.

"Have *you* any vices, Mr. Sylvaine?" Her tone implied that she sincerely hoped he did, that she would be understanding and forgiving, would indeed find them fascinating, and that her own would *nicely* complement his.

The vicar was now as tense as a bunched fist.

And then a faint dent appeared between his eyes.

Alas, by no stretch of the imagination could she interpret this expression as "bewitched."

"None, I'm certain, that would interest you." He said it gently, and turned his head just slightly back toward the road, where his duties apparently awaited. As though, of all things . . .

. . . he was *bored.*

She was speechless.

"I should think it's safe enough to walk alone along this part of the green, Lady Wareham, but perhaps you oughtn't go far until you know the country better. Perhaps you'd prefer to wait inside your carriage out of the cold?"

She knew when she'd been dismissed. Pride—and astonishment—prevented her from flailing.

"Seeing to the safety of your flock, are you?" she managed almost lightly. Her voice was faint from the jostling her pride had taken.

He smiled politely. "And to my duty as a gentleman." More of that peculiar, distancing gentleness. "I apologize for startling you. It wasn't my intention."

To her horror, heat bloomed in her cheeks again.

"My maid is very nearby," she said shortly, struggling to hide her embarrassment. "And I don't mind the cold."

"I'll just see if I can be of some assistance to your driver then, shall I?"

When she said nothing, he made a very elegant bow and turned away from her. She stood still as a stone, watching as he hailed the driver and her footman, who greeted him cheerily. All those male heads gathered together, the powdered one and her stocky, hatless driver and Mr. Sylvaine's fair one, conferring in low voices. While the driver gently held the horse's head, the vicar bent and lifted up the glossy animal's hoof and inspected it. Evie watched in astonishment as he tugged his cravat free of his waistcoat and carefully, almost tenderly, wrapped the horse's hoof to the evident approval of her staff.

And then he turned and waved a farewell, striding up the road, no doubt toward his original destination. Cravatless.

She watched him go.

At last she heard the huffing of Henny's breathing before she saw Henny, then Henny crested the hill, skirts lifted in her hands, exposing a few inches of thick, sturdy ankle decorously covered in thick, sagging woolen stockings. "I fear no one answered me knock at the door, m'lady."

She dropped her skirts and froze in place when she saw her mistress's face.

Her eyes went wide.

Then she narrowed them shrewdly and swiveled her great head about and raised a hand to shade her eyes when she saw Adam Sylvaine walking away, posture like a soldier's, stride long and easy.

Silently, they both watched him.

They in fact watched long enough for it to become ridiculous.

He never once looked back.

"Now *that* one is a *man*," Henny pronounced finally. As though they'd been debating the topic.

Evie snorted. "The country air has curdled your brain." She tossed her head and strode toward the carriage. Henny followed on her heels, still huffing.

"Now ye listen to me. Ye think ye're worldly and grand now and that ye've known every sort of man there is to know. But if ye've too many flowers in your garden, they all start to smell the same, dinna they? Ye canna tell one from another. And I tell you, that one is better."

"Because he's a *vicar*? For heaven's sake, Henny," she said wearily, "he's . . . *just* a man." It was easier to use the word "just" to describe Adam Sylvaine when he wasn't standing near enough for her to count the colors in his hair. "Beneath their clothes, under the skin, they're all the same. It always becomes evident eventually. It matters not whether they look like angels or gargoyles."

"I didna say he was *saintly*, or even good. I said he was better," Henny maintained obstinately.

With the maddening air of superiority she liked to adopt when she couldn't support an argument.

In her weakened state, the word "better" for some reason cut Evie too close to the bone. She'd no hope of being *better,* it seemed. Life had seen to that, and it had taken on a momentum of its own long ago. Still, she hadn't any regrets. Regrets implied she could have made other choices, and she wasn't certain she could have. Certainly, she'd viewed her life as a triumph of planning until recent events had exploded it like a cue taken to racked billiard balls.

"It might behoove you, Henny, to remember that *age* doesn't necessarily bequeath wisdom."

"Ye only use words like 'behoove' when you know I've the right of it. And mind you, better means he isn't for the likes of *you,* rag-mannered chit that ye are."

"A rag-mannered chit who has tolerated *your* cheek for much too long."

They bickered with comfortable familiarity all the way back to the carriage.

The driver and footman had just finished reharnessing the horses and scrambled upright when the two of them approached.

"Why did the vicar wrap the horse's hoof?" she asked the footman.

"He said he should hate for us to ruin our livery, m'lady. He insisted upon it."

"But . . . I'm not certain I understand. Why would anyone need to ruin anything?"

"As a precaution, m'lady, to protect it until he can be shod again, we needed to wrap his hoof. Shoe came off cleanly, like, so no damage done yet, and we're fortunate he wasn't lamed. Vicar knows his horses!" he said admiringly. "If we take the drive slow, we should reach home without harming him. Vicar said he'd send the farrier out to us straightaway."

It was the sort of report one's servants didn't usually trouble a countess with. But there was no man of the house, and her budget, settled upon her by Monty's estate, could scarcely justify keeping the horses and carriage and the footman as it was, and the health of something as valuable as a horse was of paramount concern. And she had no doubt that everyone below stairs knew it.

And livery was costly, too. Likely the vicar knew it. She imagined what the cost of a cravat meant to a vicar, and his kindness threw her own churlishness into stark relief.

"Thank you," she said gently to the footman. "We shall take the drive home slowly, then, and come to know the lovely scenery of our new home a little better."

"Very good, my lady."

She'd made him smile, and this lightened her mood a little. It was such an *easy* thing for her to do, normally, to charm, to ease, to make things better, to take *care* of things, and she felt her failure with Reverend Sylvaine bleakly. She was an *expert* at identifying the thing that made a man feel most proud and the thing that made him feel most inadequate, and she would praise the one and bolster the other. Of course, once captivated, she could tweak his vulnerabilities and strengths the way a skilled driver used ribbons to steer horses, should the need arise.

"Now, Lord Asquith, *he* could by no stretch of the imagination be compared to a flower," Evie concluded inside the carriage, continuing the argument with Henny, determined to win it.

"Lud, but isn't that the truth of it," Henny agreed, sighing and leaning back into the well-sprung seats. "The man stunk like a shop in Seven Dials. 'Twas an ointment 'e bought in the dead of night at McBride's Apothecary and used for a masculine complaint."

Evie was fascinated despite herself. She knew McBride's well, in large part because McBride could be relied upon to pawn things, something actresses often needed to do. "How would you know a thing like that?"

"I ken a thing or two. I might 'ave been a tart in my day, too," Henny said smugly. "Given arf a chance."

Evie was too weary to object to the word "tart," especially when it was said with genuine affection. Henny had known her in every incarnation. And Henny had surprising success with men. "Perhaps you ought to give it a try, Henny. Mayhap you can land an earl, too, and the two of us can retire in style."

Her maid gave her thigh a delighted slap. "I may do that very thing."

Evie looked out the window, out upon the soft hills unfolding endlessly, to the smoke spiraling up into the sky from cottage chimneys of houses filled with people who would in all likelihood be gossiping about her within days and would never welcome her, to the flat silver line of the sea in the distance, and knew a moment of disorientation:

The view could have been her past or present or future. She felt anchored to nothing.

For some reason she found herself craning her head in the direction Adam Sylvaine had disappeared. As if he, of all things, was the star she could navigate by.

Chapter 4

ADAM WAS SURPRISED TO FIND HIMSELF AT LADY Fennimore's door. He paused and fished out his pocket watch; he was only ten minutes later than usual. He frowned, surprised, and stuffed it back into his coat. He could scarcely recall the walk at all, and he'd taken it once a week for nearly a year now. Time had suspended as two images overtook all other thought.

Lady Fennimore's daughter greeted him at the door, as usual.

"How is she this morning, Jenny?"

Jenny gave a start. She took an infinitesimal step backward, eyes widened.

It was then he heard himself as she'd heard him: curt, preoccupied, irritated. Very unlike him. The sort of voice that might make anyone take a step back.

He added a smile to apologize for it. Jenny forgave him with a melting smile of her own and twined a finger in a stray curl that had escaped its pins.

"She's about the same, Reverend, but she's always so much better after she sees you. You can go straight up if you like. I've just put the kettle on, and I can hear it about to boil. I thought you might like some tea after your long walk."

"You're always so thoughtful, Jenny. Tea would be wonderful. And the walk is one of my favorites."

Pleased pink moved into Jenny's cheeks and throat and collarbone, and she touched a hand to a wayward tendril of fair hair and floated to the kitchen, buoyed by his smile and kind words and her own daydreams about the vicar, which involved her serving tea and rubbing his wide shoulders and propping one of her own needlework pillows beneath his head when he napped.

She was *certain* the "love thy neighbor" sermon had been directed to her.

He watched her go, her softness and simplicity and eagerness to please balm after his last little encounter. And as she disappeared into the kitchen, and Adam strode through the foyer, past the gilt-edged mirror nailed up over a small table struggling under the weight of roses stuffed into a Chinese urn. Lady Fennimore kept a hothouse, though it sometimes seemed as though the hothouse kept her, so profuse were the blooms and so prevalent the scent of them in her house.

Just as he was about to launch himself up the now-familiar flight of marble stairs, he froze.

Then turned, and as cautiously as if he were about to accost a burglar midcrime, returned to the mirror.

To discover his expression was dark and abstracted; his jaw was tense. His eyes were brilliant, with some fierce emotion, something perilously close to anger but not quite.

No wonder Jenny had taken a step back.

He'd best do away with that expression before the astute Lady Fennimore got a look at it and somehow worked out that a woman had caused it.

A thoroughly baffling, *unpleasant* woman.

Who had gone from sleeping in church to shrieking in what sounded very much like gutter Irish (which had perversely amused him) to prickly and difficult, to flinging flirtation at him—she'd quite alarmingly *sparkled* at him—like a soldier hurling boulders with a trebuchet.

Despite all of this, two impressions surfaced through all the others. And these were the ones that dogged him all the way to Lady Fennimore's house.

How he'd first seen her: standing utterly still, two hot pink spots on her cheeks, hand flattened against her rib cage. Then squaring her shoulders, like a pugilist shaking off a blow.

Something Maggie Lanford had said hurt her.

And then there were the freckles.

He'd seen them as they stared each other down—a faint scattering, only slightly darker than dried tears, on each cheek. And something about them, and her green eyes, made him think of bird's eggs, and summer days, and from there he'd found himself wondering what that smooth cheek might feel cradled in the palm of his hand. What it might be like to drag his thumb softly over those pale spots which, if he knew women, were the bane of her existence, to soothe away whatever hurt had put the hot pink in her cheeks.

He'd never had a thought like that in his entire life. Let alone about a woman he disliked.

He inhaled deeply, exhaled, and turned his back on the mirror.

LADY FENNIMORE WAS propped in bed, engulfed by a night rail and topped by an enormous frilly cap from which her cobweb-fine gray hair escaped. She was layered over with great heaps of blankets. Her hands lay frail as lace gloves atop the counterpane. The sun had full run of the room and poured emphatically through the enormous windows, and Adam could see every one of the thousands of wrinkles that comprised her now-tissue-fine complexion.

"Ah, there you are at long last, Vicar. I don't know what should keep you. Come and sit by me and savor my last moments on earth. Perhaps you ought to record my thoughts for posterity. I had a few new ones this morning though demmed if I can remember them now. God knows no one else says anything worth remembering these days. Though your predecessor had one or two moments of profundity. I'm awaiting yours."

A combative glint lit her eyes.

"Doubtless if deathless prose ever occurs to me, I'll owe it *entirely* to your inspiration, Lady Fennimore."

He and Lady Fennimore rather enjoyed each other.

Now they did, at least. At first she was one of the things that had helped knock the corners from him. One of the proverbial bats that flew out at him from the tunnel.

She smiled. And then she squinted at him. "Young man, you look distracted," she accused.

"Enthralled by your company, that's all."

She snorted. "And I do believe you're getting a wrinkle. About your left eye."

This little observation was an example of why she terrified Mrs. Sneath's battalion of women and why he was the one who visited most often.

"Your eyesight is remarkably good for a dying woman," he said dryly.

"A pity, isn't it? I'd rather use up all of my faculties before I meet my Maker, and yet some of them work brilliantly yet. You oughtn't think so much. Do more praying than thinking. You'll wind up with fewer wrinkles. I was a thinker, and look at me now."

"Perhaps I'll pray that my Maker forbears giving me any more wrinkles, lest you point them out."

She laughed again. It devolved into a cough, and she lay back with a sigh and closed her eyes briefly. He waited with her.

She sighed and opened her eyes.

"I've been giving things away, you see, in preparation for my next . . . oh, let's call it my little journey, why don't we. Reverend Sylvaine, will you be so kind as to open that box on the table there?"

She angled her chin toward a tiny, hinged wooden box on the table next to her bed.

He leaned forward to retrieve it and levered it open.

Inside was a tiny gold cross, a necklace. He lifted it up on one finger; the fine chain pooled in his other palm, cool and smooth.

"It was mine when I was a girl. It was given to me by my uncle, and he told me to wear it for good luck and protection, and I did for years until my neck grew too fat for it. Jenny wanted it, but she'll inherit a good deal when I go, and I told her I wanted to give it to *you*. And you might be the only person she wouldn't begrudge such a thing. It's not valuable, mind you, but I'd like you to have it, Vicar. I expect you'll encounter many a soul who might benefit from a little protection. Give it to someone who needs it."

He went motionless. He didn't trust himself to look up just yet. He was swamped by the full knowledge that his visits here would soon cease.

His day-to-day life was marked now by moments like these. Without warning, something a parishioner said or did would unaccountably move him. He knew these moments were both expanding and reshaping him, the way the sea shaped a continent. They made him better—better able to help, to understand, to see—but not always without a bit of pain.

He cleared his throat and looked up.

"Thank you, Lady Fennimore. I'll cherish it. I wish I'd known you then."

"Ah, Reverend. If you think I'm a delight *now* . . . Now, if you'll close the door, I've something to confess. And I shouldn't like my Jenny or anyone else to hear."

Ah! So more surprises were in store. He stood and closed the door and returned to the chair.

"You may be surprised, young man, to know that I was a Diamond of the First Water in my day."

"I don't doubt it at all. Your eyes are magnificent."

"Face like yours, flirting with an old woman like me." She snorted. "Shameless, and you a man of God."

"I'll do penance for my moment of weakness, of a certainty."

She laughed again, and he waited when the laugh became a cough that shook her, and she reached for her handkerchief again. She cleared her throat.

"A pity it is you'll marry one of these village milksops, and have a dozen dull and pretty children."

"Now, Lady Fennimore, consider that it's possible that you do the young ladies of Pennyroyal Green a disservice."

"That is, unless something goes awry. Like with that Redmond chit," Lady Fennimore continued.

"She's married to an earl, now, Miss Violet Redmond is." There was no use debating which Redmond chit she referred to; everyone knew Violet had once threatened to throw herself down a well over an argument with a suitor and had needed to be pulled back by her elbows. "She's a countess."

Were *all* countesses difficult? he wondered.

"He's not a proper earl, though, is he? He's part savage or some such. American," she sniffed.

"The Earl of Ardmay is truly an earl according to the King, Lady Fennimore."

"The king," she snorted, as if the King had a questionable birth, too. "But as I was saying, Reverend, it's marriage, and the marriage bed that will open any milksop's eyes and turn her into a woman."

Given the events of the day so far, and of his life in general, he was somehow unsurprised to be discussing the marriage bed with Lady Fennimore.

"Oh, they're all milksops. So tediously easy to

frighten. I'd like challenge, now and again! Then again, every well-bred young woman ought to be a milksop if her mother does her job right," she said authoritatively. "My own Jenny, she's a milksop."

He thought of Jenny and her softness and seeming pliancy. But another woman had embedded herself in his awareness like a splinter. He thought of that accent with the "r's" rolled tight and round and the "bloody" and knew definitively *she'd* never been a milksop. Though he hadn't the faintest idea who might have raised her. Or what precisely she *was*, if she wasn't a milksop.

"And now I will tell you something, young man, and it has been preying upon me. I'm not long for this world, as you know."

"So you tell me," he said lightly.

Her fingers wandered the counterpane and found his hand. He gripped hers. Her hand felt like a scrap of silk stretched over hard ivory; no flesh remained. But it was still strong.

"Mind you, I've attended church for as long as I was able. I read my Bible and abide by God's word as much as anyone can. I was a good wife and I loved my husband very much. But . . . Jenny's father wasn't Lord Fennimore. I loved another man, too, while I was married."

He hoped she wouldn't feel the sudden tension in his hand.

Because as sins went, it was an impressive one.

Everything he knew and assumed to be true about Lady Fennimore jostled and shifted in a struggle to accommodate it. He yanked back a rearing reflexive sense of judgment ("Good God, Lady Fennimore!") they both knew what she'd done was wrong. He did her the favor of assuming she hadn't done it lightly. All he truly needed to know was what she needed from him now.

And once again, he would need to feel his way through.

Still, it took a moment to recover his equilibrium.

"And you regret this?" he began, carefully.

"Oh dear me, no. I most certainly do not," she said with relish. "And therein lies the trouble."

"But you wish to be absolved of the sin."

She sighed. "I wish I'd the courage to say no, I do not care whether or not I sinned, and take that risk when I get up to Heaven for the final judgment. But I'm about to meet my Maker, and if God saw fit to appoint you my heavenly escort, as it were, then I would like to know how to . . . ensure a place. I shouldn't like to debate St. Peter when I arrive or meet with any nasty surprises. I haven't the wardrobe for Hell."

"Were you married to Lord Fennimore when you met Jenny's father?"

"Yes."

So if she was looking for the name of the sin, it was "adultery," but they both knew that.

"You see, Reverend, you may never know this, but love, real love, the kind that you *fall in*, isn't like Corinthians. The "suffereth long" and "is kind" nonsense. It's like the Song of Solomon. It's jealousy and fire and floods. It's everything that consumes. I defy even *you* to resist it should it visit you in this lifetime, no matter the circumstances, and I don't know whether I would wish it upon you. It's a . . . beautiful suffering. We have our God and our laws and so forth to tell us how to live, but God made us flesh, didn't he? And your handsome flesh, my dear boy, seems rather an amusing test of a vicar. Good luck controlling those urges, I say, should the right temptation present itself."

Heat started up at the back of his neck and the tops of his hands, and he prayed he wouldn't flush like a bloody schoolboy because Lady Fennimore of a certainty would notice and enjoy it. He wasn't about to say to her, "For God's sake, I'm hardly an innocent, Lady Fennimore." Because he wasn't. Nor was he about to say, "I have every faith I can control *my* urges when I'm married," to a woman who had just confessed abandoning herself to her own.

He just hadn't lost himself to the pleasures of a woman's body in . . . so long. He'd been stripped down nearly to mind and spirit only; his parish owned his body. He worked so ceaselessly the dawn seemed to arrive mere seconds after he fell into bed at night. Desire came in sudden, fleeting, sweet jolts these days—the curve of a woman's hip as she walked away from him, or the laugh of a woman who reminded him of a certain lusty widow at Oxford who could do extraordinary things with her mouth. Things of that sort.

His thoughts worried over that splinter again. Freckles. Green eyes. A soft, full blur of a mouth.

Lingering with these kinds of impressions was an indulgence he couldn't afford.

Beautiful suffering. Indeed.

"Temptation assails all of us at some point," he decided to say, entirely innocuously.

Lady Fennimore studied him. Then smiled at what she recognized as his skillful dodge.

"You'll forgive me if I torment you a little, Reverend. You see, it assuages a little of my own guilt. Do you think God will forgive me? I cannot regret it, you see. I can only think God is responsible for passion, for God gives us bodies with which to express it and hearts in which to hold it. And he gave me Jenny to remember him by, and surely babies are blessings. My husband never knew, and he loved Jenny."

She looked up at him hopefully.

Vicars, he often thought, are essentially God's lawyers on the earth. Interpreters of the law, the finders of nuance, sifters through rationalizations to get at the truth or the need of the moment.

Guessers, in other words.

And once again, he would need to fight his way through the darkness. For he could talk of God's love, and brotherly love, but the love of the sort she described . . . it occurred to him suddenly that he'd never had time to mull what it meant to *him*. The women in the village thought it meant embroidery and jam. He thought of how his cousin Colin, perhaps the most infamous sower of wild oats in all of England, who'd once plummeted from a trellis leading up to a married countess's balcony, had settled down with his wife Madeline, and how everything he felt about her was in the way he said her name. Or about his cousin Olivia . . .

He suspected whatever had happened between Olivia Eversea and Lyon Redmond, who had infamously disappeared after she allegedly broke his heart, was a fire and flame and flood kind of love.

Olivia was hardly an advertisement for it.

Still, love of the kind Lady Fennimore described,

the kind that *owned* you, gave you no choice but to surrender, surely wasn't so common that it should be renounced. No matter the course it ran.

For he'd never known it.

One of the Deadly Sins paid him a fleeting visit: Envy. He was susceptible because a beautiful woman had just embedded herself like a splinter in his consciousness. Suddenly, he wanted to *feel* again.

"I think there is no question of the sin, Lady Fennimore," he told her gently. "But you can repent the sin and not the love."

He hoped she wouldn't decide it was a heretical notion.

Lady Fennimore blinked. Her head tipped in birdlike consideration; her eyes fastened on him fiercely. He hadn't been lying; her eyes were lovely, a pale, crystalline blue, enormous and vivid in her sunken face. He imagined her suddenly as a lush young woman in the arms of a lover, at the mercy of a passion stronger than everything she'd grown up believing to be right.

"Why, if that isn't a clever solution, Mr. Sylvaine," she allowed almost reluctantly, eyes narrowed now. "I shall do just that." She sounded pleased, as though he'd given her an alternate route to London, one in which the roads were less rutted, and the coaching inns served fresher beef. She settled back into her pillows with satisfaction.

He was tempted to pantomime mopping his brow. Instead, he said:

"Would you like me to pray with you?"

"If you would. I do like the sound of your voice," she conceded drowsily. As though everything else about him was wanting. "Something from Common Prayer. You choose it."

He bit back a smile and slid his fingers into the old, familiar pages. Reflecting that there was nothing common at all about any of the people he knew.

SHE MIGHT HAVE been born in a dirt-floor cottage warmed by peat, with cattle poking their heads in the windows and noisy siblings heaped up in the bed like so many kittens, but she hadn't lived in the country since she was a small child.

And Mother of *God*, it was quiet.

Damask Manor the house was called. It only just escaped being a cottage by virtue of two or three rooms (there were ten of them) and the outbuildings, but it possessed a measure of charm: An arbored walkway led up to the house; three gabled windows looked out over Pennyroyal Green; it was made of sandstone and glowed in the afternoon sun, and all the rooms a family would live in faced south and were filled with light. A wide staircase led up from a foyer marbled in squares of black and white. The gardens were simple and small and meticulously groomed (by a gardener, yet another person who needed to be paid) and would be awash with roses, she'd been assured, come June. A small bit of farmland was attached to it and could be worked. It was an eternity away from Grosvenor and St. James's Square and all the estates the earl had owned, all of which were entailed and in the hands of his heir, a petulant, chinless young man by the name of Percival.

But Damask Manor was hers to keep. Because the earl had won it in a card game.

Much like her.

It was fate, one might say.

At the moment, it felt much too large for her, her glowering maid, and the small staff she could just barely afford to keep. She suspected she could shout, and it would echo the way her voice had today when she'd shrieked like a fishwife at the vicar.

She swiped her hands down her face again at the memory. The *shame* of it. So few people knew of her origins. She really must go up to bed early tonight and hope the shreds of her composure magically knit themselves back together whilst she slept.

A maid of all work had gone to collect the mail from a shop called Postlethwaite's in town while she was at church, and while Henny saw to the preparation of lunch, she inspected her letters. No invitations, no flowers, no gifts had arrived. She ought to be accustomed to that now, but more than a decade's worth of being showered with all of those things didn't fade from memory overnight.

The letter from her brother Seamus first. His handwriting was swashbuckling, with great fat loops and spiky heights. The fact that he'd managed to send a letter at all meant that he'd at least enough money for a stamp, and this filled her both with hope and dread, for Seamus's jobs tended to be uncertain, often not entirely legal, affairs. He was charming enough, and handsome enough, to cajole his way into a new one with regularity. Some of his other tendencies—a yearning for variety, a fondness for women—tended to interfere with the keeping of the jobs.

*You will be surprised. dear sister of mine. to know I
have a Job! You will not be surprised to hear I've need
of a new suit of clothes and lodging or I shall not be able
to keep it. and I haven't any blunt for that. I feel
certain you will pay the cost to avoid having me live with
you permanently. But we'd have such fun! Ha ha!
I vow to repay you one day. VOW.*

With much love (and you know I do love you).
   Seamus

She knew that he did, damn his worthless eyes.
She would send him money because she loved
him, too, and was fresh out of lectures. And God
knows she didn't want him living with her though
she missed him.

There was one from her sister Cora, in Killarney.
When she broke the seal, something spilled into
her palm. Silky and fragile as a cobweb, it was a lock
of red-gold hair from the newest—the sixth—baby.

She was momentarily breathless with longing.
Slammed by thoughts of what could have been. By
what she'd dared to hope for. All of which she'd
lost much too soon.

Evie took a steadying breath before she read.

*Her name is Aoife. She is very pretty but
has the colic. Timothy is testier than usual. We
walk gently around him. All the other children
are alive and send their love.*

Dry, brief, affectionate: She heard Cora's voice
plain as day. It was a miracle she wrote at all, with
six children.

And clever Cora had named the newest baby for *her*! No English employer of opera dancers would allow her to keep a name featuring a lot of unpronounceable vowels all crammed together, so she became Eve instead of *Eefa*. Cora never *asked* for money; Evie sent it as a matter of course. She would find a gift for baby Aoife that would be shared among six children and likely destroyed within minutes or at least dismantled by the boys for other uses. Ah, but it taught survival, she supposed, and flexibility. Certainly Evie had grown up strong, but she was the oldest, and she hadn't a choice in the matter.

At least Cora's husband, Timothy, drank less than their own father had, and hadn't yet run off like their father did though it was possible he was only a baby or two away from doing so. Eve knew how to read between the lines of her sister's brief letters.

"Testier." She suppressed a little clutch of fear and crossed her fingers. A colicky baby could make anyone testier. Hopefully, not testy enough to flee just yet.

She'd saved the third letter for last because she wasn't entirely certain she wanted to open it. She'd recognized the arrogant script, the heavily inked pen, waxed close with the vehement press of a signet.

A seal that might have been her own but for the turn of a card one night.

Finally, she slid her fingers beneath the wax to break it, and in so doing released a Pandora's box, the London version: Just the script alone conjured the chink of champagne glasses, chandelier light bouncing off jewels and silk and crystal, clever, brittle conversation, endless laughter. Endless wanting of *her*.

She took a bolstering breath.

My dearest Evie Green-Eyes,

London is a drear place without you. Even the nectar of gossip fails to sustain me, but this could be because it isn't nearly as interesting when you aren't the center of it, if you'll forgive me, given that the last bit that went round naturally wasn't much fun for you. I am bored to distraction and hungry for the sound of your laughter, and I am unfashionable enough not to cut you should you deign to return to London. Unless you forbid it, I will visit you in Sussex—you! In the country! How quaint!—a fortnight hence. Send me a letter to tell me I'm welcome. I still enjoy lamb and all of the other things we've discussed at length in our acquaintance. I harbor the fondest hope you'll make me the happiest man alive and indulge me in them one day.

Yrs,
Frederick,
Lord Lisle

It was so alive, his letter, so very *Frederick*, in all his elegant, wry, self-important glory. Something flickered in her, possibly hope or familiarity. Or perhaps it was simply hunger—oughtn't Henny ring for supper soon? It was undeniably pleasant to know she was wanted and remembered. By a staggeringly wealthy viscount, who was invited to dine with the King, no less.

Take *that*, Reverend Sylvaine.

Although the impenetrable Reverend Sylvaine, he of the blue eyes and towering cheekbones, would likely be unimpressed, as he seemed impervious to everything else: insults, flirtation, her very best unblinking gaze. And then she recalled again the casual gift of the cravat and felt another wash of shame at her gracelessness. *Not* her finest hour. If only she could undo it.

If only she could undo *him*.

Because something about the man—the stillness, his calm confidence, the see-through-her blue beam of his gaze?—made her itch to unravel his control. Though to what purpose, she didn't know. To prove that she could? To prove she could gain the upper hand over someone who was *better*, as Henny had put it, and who had so effortlessly, through doing almost nothing at all, reduced her to breathlessness today? More likely it was to see why he was wrapped so very tightly. Because once she uncovered *that* secret, undoubtedly he'd lose the power to unnerve her, the way a revealed magician's trick lost the power to awe. She couldn't recall a man ever scrambling her wits with just a few words.

She'd vowed long ago to never allow herself to be at the mercy of a man. She had made certain she was in control of whom she chose and whom she left, that the choices were all hers to make.

For look how surrendering to a man had turned out for Mama.

She absently rubbed the foolscap of Frederick's

letter between two fingers. Perhaps she should write to Frederick and tell him that she had sworn off men, that no man on the face of the earth could ever again possibly inspire desire in her. That she'd decided she'd never again be a *commodity* for men.

Knowing Frederick, he'd consider it an aphrodisiac and come running straightaway.

At least then she wouldn't be alone.

She placed his letter carefully aside. She would perhaps write to him later. But her thoughts shied away from London; her memories of it were edged all around with razors, now. They had all turned on her so thoroughly, so relentlessly, and with such vicious glee, all while she struggled with loss.

The silence of the place enclosed her again. She tapped the feathered end of her quill pen against her chin and gazed out the window. The view offered nothing to distract her, just more of those rolling Sussex hills and small, bushy, green trees, which likely meant everything to a boy like Paulie, for instance, who would grow up knowing all of them by heart.

And it was *this* she wanted, she realized suddenly. An opportunity to create her own history. To begin again. To decide what she wanted rather than allowing the needs of survival to dictate her life. But damned if she would be bored in the process.

She refused to languish here, like the Queen of Scots in exile (things certainly hadn't ended well for *her*, regardless). Enough wobbling about directionless, like a spun top. There was no undoing what was done: The people of Pennyroyal Green seemed to know about her. Or at least some of them knew *something* about her, which meant that in all likelihood *all* of them would soon enough. So remaining incognito was out of the question.

Then again, perhaps this was all for the good. Because now she had an opportunity to do what she seemed to do best, at least whether it was on the stage at the Green Apple Theater, or Covent Garden, or captivating just the right man: win people over.

But she would need an ally. Someone who could be a liaison between her and the women of the village.

Perhaps even someone who had their rapt attention every Sunday morning.

Perhaps someone who was likely duty-bound by his role in life to be compassionate and diplomatic toward his parishioners, regardless of whether they shrieked incomplete insults at him in a long-dormant Irish accent.

Someone, in other words, who was missing a cravat.

She hesitated only a moment before reaching for a sheet of foolscap. But he would need winning, too.

She dipped the quill and set out to do just that.

Chapter 5

"OH, REVEREND. YOU'VE RETURNED FROM LADY Fennimore's house." His housekeeper, Mrs. Dalrymple, all long face and tremulous mouth and enormous woebegone eyes, hovered in the doorway. He heard the warning in his housekeeper's voice even before she said her next words. "You've . . . a visitor . . . waiting in the parlor."

Wave upon wave of meaning and portent rippled out from the way she said "visitor."

"Does my . . . visitor . . . perhaps have a name?" he coaxed.

"She did not give it." A slight meaningful emphasis was given to "she."

Mrs. Dalrymple knew better than to allow female interlopers in to trouble the vicar. She was the soul of discretion and discernment, a deceptively powerful impediment to female attempts to infiltrate his haven. She could stop an army with her passivity.

He sighed. "Thank you. I shall be in directly. You've made—"

"Tea. Yes, sir. The *silver* service, sir."

So it was the sort of visitor Mrs. Dalrymple considered worthy of tea in the silver service.

Despite his weariness, he began to feel curious.
"You are a wonder, Mrs. Dalrymple."
"I do me best, sir," she said placidly.

HE STOPPED BY the mirror, smoothed his hair, gave
his armpit a sniff since he'd been walking hard
all day, decided he wasn't terribly offensive, and
was momentarily startled again by the absence
of his cravat, and when he remembered how this
came to be, his thoughts tugged at their tether—
they wanted to surround the countess again. He
frowned the thought away.

He would do well enough for a visitor, whoever
she might be.

It proved to be very nearly the last person he expected to find. He stopped in the doorway, saw a
beautiful young woman dressed in heavy blue silk,
the veil she'd likely worn as a disguise pushed up
to rest on the top of her head

"Lady Ardmay. To what do I owe the pleasure of
your visit?"

Until very recently, Lady Redmond had been
known as Miss Violet Redmond. Otherwise, that
Redmond chit, as Lady Fennimore called her.
Speak of the devil.

"Good afternoon, Reverend Sylvaine. I am not
here, you understand. You've never seen me at the
vicarage."

He understood. "I do not engage in gossip, nor do
I ever reveal a confidence, if that's your concern."

She gave him a slightly conciliatory smile. "Forgive me. I did not mean to imply that you ever
would. It's just . . . no one knows I am here. I took
certain pains to ensure I wasn't seen entering the

vicarage. It may not surprise you to learn that I've never consulted with a member of the clergy. I've come on a matter of some sensitivity."

This was rather implied, given the drama of the veil and the refusal to give her name to the house-keeper. As if the housekeeper wouldn't recognize Violet Redmond by voice or stature or sheer sense of entitlement.

"Perhaps you'd do the honor of pouring for the both of us?" He gestured to the tea.

She did, and they sipped a moment, and sugar was stirred into cups with little clinking sounds, before she spoke.

"I am with child, Reverend."

He composed his face into neutral planes and braced himself for a confession that would shave years off the life of an ordinary man. Given that this was Violet (nee) Redmond, he would not be surprised to learn the father of the child was the Archbishop of Canterbury, but he pitied the Archbishop if the Earl of Ardmay ever learned the news.

"Congratulations. Babies are wonderful," he offered carefully.

She nodded her thanks. "It's because of the baby that I'm here. Indirectly. Something . . . has come into my possession. I might have been inclined to hurl it into the Ouse a year or so ago, as I am hardly impartial in the matter. But I've since learned a thing or two about . . . love." She glanced up at him almost defiantly, as if love was blasphemy or too indelicate a subject for a vicar. If only she knew the conversation he'd had today. "And I believe this is about love. I . . . I want to do the right thing. I would like to have it off my conscience before the baby is

born, and I wish to bequeath it to someone who,
shall we say, is required by duty to exercise his
conscience and judgment about what to do with it."

Trust the former Miss Redmond to arrive at *that*
interesting definition of a vicar's duties.

She extended her hand and uncurled her fingers;
he leaned forward and looked down into her palm.

It was a moment before recognition settled in.
The woman in the miniature was younger, more
radiant, softer, more innocent. And hopeful.

"It's my cous—it's Miss Olivia Eversea, isn't it?"

"Yes."

He stared down at it, puzzled: Why would Violet
possess a miniature of Olivia?

And then all at once he thought he understood,
and the little hairs rose on the back of his neck.

"May I . . ." He took it from her palm, turned the
miniature over, and saw the girlish script there.

"Yours forever. O."

He thought of the Olivia he knew now—still
lovely, but brittle, too thin, too glib, deflecting suitors so skillfully they scarcely knew they were being
rejected. There was only one person in the world to
whom Olivia would give a miniature signed *Yours
forever.*

He risked a question that was likely unfair, but
Violet had come of her own accord, and in truth he
didn't care whether it was fair. He thought only of
Olivia.

"Did your brother Lyon give this to you?"

He watched her closely. It amused him distantly
to think that Violet was struggling both with the
fact that he was related to the Everseas and that it
would likely never do to lie to a vicar.

"Yes." A hush, that word.

The silence in the room beat like a heart.

He knew his next question wasn't necessary, or even fair. He didn't care. He asked it anyway, for Olivia's sake. His voice was steady, almost disinterested, even as his heart slammed in his chest, steady and hard, like a soldier's boots coming down.

"Recently?"

He watched Violet almost like a predator. She breathed in and out. In and out. In and out. Any moment, she could answer the question that haunted Pennyroyal Green. All of English Society. And the Everseas and Redmonds in particular.

She reached for her teacup. The surface of the tea ruffled; her hands were trembling.

"I think he meant her to have it. I hoped you would decide whether to return it to her."

He knew then, definitively, that she'd seen him. If she hadn't seen him, she knew where he was.

The knowledge slammed into him. He drew in a breath, held it. No one had seen Lyon Redmond in years. He'd disappeared. No one knew where he'd gone. Only that the golden child, the eldest Redmond, had allegedly disappeared when Olivia Eversea broke his heart, breaking the hearts of his family, stirring old wounds and animosities between the Everseas and Redmonds that always festered beneath surface politeness.

But not one person knew the whole truth of what had happened before he disappeared, either.

Unless it was Olivia, and she never said a word about it.

"Is he alive? Is he in Sussex? Where is he?"

His voice was still steady. But the questions were quick, and they were demands, and when Adam demanded something, he invariably got it.

He fixed her with an unblinking stare, neither sympathetic nor judgmental. It willed the answer from her even as it drove her nervously to her feet.

His manners reflexive, he stood, too.

"I can tell you truthfully: I don't know," she said. She was in a hurry to be gone, he could see.

They watched each other warily.

"Please keep it, Reverend. I leave you to decide whether she ought to have it. She doesn't seem happy, does she? And she'll only get older and older. Then again, who can say whether she doesn't deserve whatever penance she's now paying?"

A faint hint of bitterness. Whatever had happened had cost her a brother.

"Thank you for entrusting me with it," was all he said.

AFTER THE DAY he'd had, Adam thought he could be forgiven for thinking the door of the Pig & Thistle looked like the entrance to Heaven. His cousin Colin hailed him—he was sharing one of the sturdy, battered wooden tables with his brother Ian—Adam sank into a chair across from them. They were watching Jonathan Redmond *thunk* darts into the board with exquisite precision.

"Which Eversea do you think he pictures when he hits it?" Colin asked idly.

Ian snorted.

Adam said nothing at all by way of greeting. He stretched out his legs, leaned back, and closed his eyes, and for a blissful minute felt only the warmth of the fire and pub, heard only the buzz of conversation, felt the wood of the chair beneath him, all of it allegedly carved from Ashdown forest trees. He allowed himself the luxury of experiencing only his senses. Every conversation he'd had today, everything he'd experienced, had reminded them they'd been too long denied.

When he opened them, Polly Hawthorne, Ned's daughter, was standing next to him.

He smiled at her.

She flushed scarlet to her scalp. "I enjoyed your sermon about loving thy neighbor, Reverend Sylvaine."

"I'm so happy to hear it, Polly."

"I do, you know. Love my neighbor." Her big dark eyes drank him in worshipfully.

"Ah. Well. Very good," he said cautiously.

His cousins were fighting smiles. Polly, who might be all of sixteen or seventeen, had long nurtured a *tendre* for Colin (indulged but not returned) and still hadn't forgiven him for marrying Madeline, and had been as darkly unbending as a de Medici about it. Out of habit, she refused to acknowledge his existence. Ian always needed to give the ale orders. But Adam seemed to have supplanted him in her passions.

"Bring Adam a pint of the dark, won't you, Polly?" Ian intervened in Polly's reverie, when it seemed Polly would never speak again. She gave a start and flashed a brilliant smile and slipped through the pub crowd with the grace of a selkie.

"I enjoyed your sermon today, too, Reverend," Colin said solemnly. "I positively felt stains lifting from my soul as I listened."

Adam yawned. "Splendid. At that rate, your entrance to Heaven will be assured a few thousand sermons from now."

Ian laughed. "Sooo, Vicar . . . why so weary? Thinking about your notorious new parishioner and all the excitement she's bound to cause?"

More surprises. "I've a notorious new parishioner?"

"I thought you met today. She was in church today, so I heard. I didn't see her. She's taken Damask Manor. Inherited, that is, I believe, from her late husband. A servant knows a servant who told . . . somebody. You know how it is. Seems the whole of Pennyroyal Green knew by noon today."

"Oh. Of course. The Countess of Wareham. I did meet her." In his weakened state, the thought of her rushed to his head like the Pig & Thistle's dark: complex and bitter and silky.

"What did you think of her?" Colin took a sip of his ale.

"Mmm." He tipped his head back. "Funny, but she reminded me a bit of . . . oh, a wild bird that needs soothing."

Colin choked on his ale and spluttered.

Ian's hand had frozen on its way to lifting his ale to his mouth.

"What's the dev—what is the *matter* with you two? It was just an observation."

"Bloody *lyrical* observation." Ian was wildly amused. "Don't you know who your . . . what did you call her? Turtledove? . . . is?"

"Wild bir . . . who is she?"

Polly plunked a dark ale in front of him on the

table. And walked away heartbroken when he absently slid over his coins and hefted it to his mouth without looking at her.

"She's the Black Widow," Ian said simply. "Haven't heard of her? Then you don't read the London broadsheets."

"No. I spend my days erasing stains from souls, but you know that. What on earth is a Black Widow?"

"Colin, why don't you tell the story since you know it best?"

Colin stretched and cracked his knuckles and cleared his throat.

"Well, in the beginning, Reverend Sylvaine," he intoned, "there was the Green Apple Theater. The Countess of Wareham was known as Evie Duggan then. She was an opera dancer. Sang a bit, danced a bit, acted a bit, showed her ankles, wore gossamer clothing. There was a song-and-dance bit about pirates I liked a good deal. She became *quite* the attraction. We *all* vied for her attention. Spent my allowance on flowers for her more than once. She would have naught to do with me, of course, because she knew what she wanted, and I wasn't it. Not enough money. No title. Mind you, she was frank about it and never unkind. Such were the charms of Miss Evie Duggan that she rapidly moved up in the world—started appearing in plays at Covent Garden. And then she—"

"Who was it that fell over the theater balcony trying to get a look at her bosom, Colin?" Ian interjected, drumming the sides of his ale thoughtfully. "The night of *Le Mistral*, when she was there with the earl? Rumor, never substantiated, had it one could see her nipples that night if you were close enough."

"Carriger," Colin supplied. "He's never been quite right in the head since."

"I hope he at least got a look at her bosom on the way down. It's marvelous. From . . . what I can tell, that is."

"—and then a man wealthy enough came along," Colin continued, "or something along those lines, for she gave up the theater and became what we'll call a professional courtesan. And then *another* man came along who had more money and power, and she gave up the first man. And then she married the earl. In other words, the Countess of Wareham, your 'wild bird,' was a . . . courtesan, Adam."

The word seemed to stretch languidly out on the table in front of them like a nude on a chaise.

It was a voluptuous shock.

Adam's lungs ceased moving for an instant. Spiraling out from the word was a world of moral chaos, a demimonde that encircled God-fearing people like wolves outside a paddock of sheep. At least that's how many of his parishioners viewed it. And what most of the mothers of Pennyroyal Green likely taught their daughters.

Interestingly, it was his obligation—his vocation—to abjure that sort of moral chaos. And he largely did. He didn't mind *hearing* about it. Which was all well and good, given his relatives.

"I know what a courtesan is, for God's sake," he finally said irritably. "You needn't deliver the word like a pantomime villain."

It took a moment for the words to struggle out.

His *sense* knew he ought to shove it away reflexively. His senses weren't quite ready to relinquish the word.

"That's right. He's a vicar, not a saint, Colin," Ian added helpfully. "And you were relieved of your virginity *ages* ago, Adam, am I right? Some lucky housemaid?"

Adam shot him a filthy look.

Though Ian was quite right.

Colin continued his tale. "Well, the *uproar* Evie caused in her day—she once caused a duel by winking at the wrong man. One heir lost an entire estate in a wager over whether he could bed her. I could go on and on. Politicians, even Prinny, yearned after her. She was showered with jewels; they all competed for her attention. And for her grand finale, she married the Earl of Wareham when he won the right to do it in a card game."

Adam received all of this information like little blows.

"Of course. Of course she did."

Then he lifted his ale and drank half of it in a few gulps.

"Played another man for the honor of marrying her, the earl did," Colin continued blithely. "And I wish I could say she lived happily ever after, but then the Earl of Wareham died just a short while after they were married. Rumor has it she killed him, which was absurd, because nearly everything he owned was entailed. And then Mr. Miles Redmond—you know the Redmond famous for exploring exotic lands and who crawls about studying insects and whatnot? He gave a lecture in London on poisonous spiders. There's one in the

Americas called the black widow—apparently the females kill and eat the male after they mate. The ton *loved* it. They took to it instantly. That's what they called her. Ceaselessly."

There was a beat of silence while Adam mulled this.

And then he raked his hair back in his hands. "Oh, God."

Too late he realized he'd said it aloud. He hadn't meant to.

"I imagine she's heard rather a lot of *those* two words in her day," Ian said idly.

"No. It's just . . . something I said to her today . . ."

"Iniquity" was what he'd said to her. *One must be stealthy to stop iniquity in its tracks*, to be specific. He'd said it in jest. And her head had jerked toward him as though he'd struck her.

His lungs tightened in shame. It wasn't as though he could apologize for it. What on earth could he say? "If I'd known you were a renowned tart, I'd have chosen my words more carefully?"

"Did you introduce Mary Magdalene into the conversation?" Ian wondered.

Adam just shook his head slowly.

"Whatever it was, old man . . . don't berate yourself. I sincerely doubt your 'wild bird' has an innocent or fragile bone in her body." Colin said this with marked admiration. "She's always known precisely what she wanted, how to get it, and she got it, too, when she married Wareham. And *that's* the thing the ton never could forgive her for. I admire her for dozens of reasons, from those green eyes of hers to the ambition, and she's a good egg when it comes right down to it, but the woman is silk-encased cast iron and quite formidable. Her sort does nothing without a reason."

Her sort. And now he remembered what Maggie Lanford said. *She's not our sort.*

He saw again the countess's hand flattening against her rib cage, the stunned hot spots of pink in her cheeks.

And just then he realized he'd just flattened his own hand over his ribs. As if her pain were his own.

He surreptitiously moved it and closed his hand safely around his ale. Tightly.

Fragments of what he knew about her orbited his mind. A petite woman with innocent freckles and a soft, carnal blur of a mouth and blazing green eyes and a glacially aristocratic accent that apparently caved like rusty armor when she was good and startled to reveal . . . what he suspected was her true self. Or part of it, anyhow. That feisty temper and Irish accent and the quickness with a retort.

He sensed she'd *learned* the rest of it: the imperious demeanor, the accent, the boldness, the innuendo-soaked flirtation. From a protector, no doubt. Or from having protectors.

For actresses must be skillful mimics, of course.

Why would a woman become a courtesan? What led her to the decision to live forever on the outskirts of polite society? That was, until one fateful card game.

He stifled a stunned, slightly hysterical laugh. It occurred to him that he hadn't said any of those words—"courtesan," "actress," "protector"—aloud in possibly *years*, if ever, so alien were they from his daily life. And from the life of nearly everyone who lived in Pennyroyal Green. With the notable exception of his cousins, of course.

"Do either of you know her origins?"

The Irish accent was the missing piece of the puzzle.

"Seems to be a bit of a mystery surrounding that," Ian told him, catching Polly's eye and gesturing with his chin for more ale for all of them. Which she brought straightaway, gifting Adam with a glorious smile which, in his distraction, he failed to notice, breaking her heart for the thousandth time. "Never gave it much thought."

"Mmm," was all Adam said.

He had no trouble believing that the countess was scandal incarnate.

A wayward little surge of protectiveness—toward her, and toward himself—made him keep this notion, and their encounter on the downs, and the Irish accent, to himself. "What do you suppose she was doing in church this morning?"

Colin shrugged. "Belated concern for her immortal soul? Craving a new experience? I daresay when another man she deems worthy of her favors comes along, she'll be gone. Until then, I doubt anyone will receive her should she deign to call. Nor will anyone call on her. Unless it's the town vicar, of course. Out of, oh, say . . . parish duty."

A fraught little silence followed. It contained both challenge and warning.

For unlike his cousins, Adam had never had the option of flinging himself into gleeful debauchery. He'd *hardly* led a joyless existence, but to do debauchery properly—gaming hells, horse races, bawdy theater, the very *idea* of courtesans—one must have plenty of money and time.

Whereas God willing, neither of his cousins would ever administer last rites to a baby as it drew its last breath, then comfort the sobbing mother.

In other words, though it hardly mattered much of the time, there was a gulf of experience and privilege and obligation between them. Adam was both more and less innocent than the two of them.

Not to mention the countess.

And now, ironically, his entire way of life depended on behaving faultlessly and standing before his parishioners and reminding them of the perils of behaving, in essence, like the Everseas.

Or like the widowed Countess of Wareham.

Adam would be ruined if his name became linked to the countess in any way. Whereas if Ian, for instance, wanted to pursue her, there was very little stopping him. One would almost expect it of him.

All three of them knew it.

Courtesan. His imagination sank deeper and deeper into the word as if it were comprised of dense furs. He couldn't seem to extricate himself. For the very word conjured exotic realms of pleasure.

He was far too long overdue for pleasure. That was the trouble.

And once again, his fingers tightened around his ale.

"I suppose I *could* pay her a visit. Perhaps crawl up the trellis to her balcony. Isn't that how one normally pays visits to countesses? Or should I go in through a window?"

Colin had once plummeted from a trellis leading up to the balcony of a married countess. Ian had once been ignominiously sent stark naked out the window of a duke's erstwhile fiancée and forced to walk home in one boot.

Both of them *hated* to be reminded of those two little episodes.

"Get married, Adam," Ian suggested, not unsympathetically. "It solved the problem of . . . Colin." As if Colin's oat-sowing was a contagion stemmed by matrimony. "And virginity grows back if you go too long between."

Adam rolled his eyes.

A raggedly tipsy cheer went up then; Jonathan Redmond had apparently just won another game of darts. They turned toward the sound just as a man sitting across from them looked up. His eyes were dark; his nose was bold, his chin square. Not an elegant face, but a face with character. He raised a glass and nodded politely. Adam and Ian and Colin returned the greeting with similar nods.

Colin lowered his voice. "Lord Landsdowne. Every day for the past fortnight he's sent flowers to Olivia. A subtly different bouquet every time, just different enough to intrigue her. It's actually begun to drive her just a little mad. I think she might even be anticipating the next one with something like eagerness. Devilishly clever, if you ask me. And every day he sends the same message: He would very much like to call on her."

Adam remembered why he recognized the name. "He's the one who entered the wager in White's betting books, isn't he? About Olivia?"

This was noteworthy. Not one of Olivia's myriad

suitors had dared go so far as to enter a wager regarding Olivia since Lyon Redmond had disappeared. Olivia had made clear in ways both subtle and overt that it was a bet no one could ever win.

Fire and flood and jealousy. What was it about Olivia that Landsdowne thought he *must* have? The fact that she could *not* be had? Was it purely the challenge of it? Or was Olivia Landsdowne's equivalent of an embedded glass splinter? An inappropriate woman who'd managed to fascinate him into a bombardment of bouquets?

The Song of Solomon said nothing about foolishness. Perhaps *he* would be the one to immortalize foolishness in verse.

"But he won't win that wager," Colin said with grim certainty. "Because he doesn't know Olivia. And that's my point: There's nothing heroic about futility. And Ian's right. Getting married is the best thing I've ever done. Do you *really* want to discover whether virginity grows back?"

Adam sighed gustily, pushed himself away from the table, and stood. "Good night, cousins. It's been edifying, as usual. And just for that, you can pay for my second ale."

"It makes you testy if you go long between, too," Colin called after him. "So I hear."

"Chirp chirp," Ian added.

It was purely an accident he trod on Ian's outstretched foot as he departed.

Chapter 6

ADAM ARRIVED HOME AFTER TEN O'CLOCK TO DIS-
cover that Mrs. Dalrymple had collected all the
wadded foolscap and dumped it on the fire. Where
it belonged, as far as he was concerned. Saturday
was for wadding; Sunday was for burning.

"They do make excellent kindling, Reverend,
and I like to think of all your words floating up to
God in the smoke," she'd told him.

"I'm certain God would be relieved that I burned
them, rather than inflicted them upon my parishioners," he'd told her dryly.

Often he welcomed the blessed silence after
days filled with goat-related disputes and Lady
Fennimore and the like. But tonight, after the
warmth and hum of the Pig & Thistle, the quiet
of the vicarage rang like a blow to the head.
There were days when he felt the isolation of his
job keenly; he belonged to everyone and yet to no
one.

Tonight, he sat down at the table in the spotless
kitchen and stared down and thought dryly: If I
were married, at least I'd have someone to help me
get my boots off.

He tried to imagine it. For instance, Jenny kneeling there to give a tug on his boot, her soft, fair head shining in the . . .

He couldn't do it. His thoughts felt permanently dislocated in the shape of a petite brunette. God willing, it was nothing a good night's sleep wouldn't cure.

He opened his eyes and lifted his head when he heard Mrs. Dalrymple's solid tread in the hall.

"Oh, Reverend Sylvaine, I did hear you come in. Something arrived for you while you were out."

As usual, he looked first at her face for clues to what it might be and found it carefully stoic, ever-so-slightly disapproving.

Then he looked at her hands. The missive might have been edged in flame or dipped in something foul, so gingerly did Mrs. Dalrymple hold it. He could see it was sealed in wax. In her other arm was tucked a soft-looking package bound in brown paper and string.

"I thought you might like to see this straightaway. It was brought to the house by a footman. Powdered hair and all dressed in scarlet and yellow like a bird, he was, and this package for you along with it."

He stared at her. A scarlet-and-yellow footman?

"Reverend?" she said, a bit uneasily, after a moment.

He realized he'd stopped breathing. He exhaled carefully.

"Of course. Thank you, Mrs. Dalrymple. I'll just see what it might be, shall I?"

She extended her arms, and he took the package and the message from her. She waited. Presumably she could cast it into the fire with great haste.

"Thank you, Mrs. Dalrymple," he said, gently but firmly.

She backed away, apparently loath to leave him alone with it.

He *wanted* to be alone with it.

He examined the handwriting, as if it would provide clues to her. He in fact wanted to postpone the moment of opening it, the moment when he learned more about who she was. To prolong the unexpectedly pleasurable shock of its arrival. For what he read might undo all of it.

He finally broke the seal.

Dear Reverend Sylvaine,

While I'm assured your cravat is beyond salvaging, I'm certain our horse would thank you for the gift of it if he could. I hope you will accept the enclosed by way of thanks for your kindness. It belonged to my husband, but since he is no longer alive and since he possessed forty-seven of them if he posessed one (I am never certain of the number of s's that ought to be in that word, I hope you will forgive me that and my spelling in general), I cannot think it's an inapropriate gift, though mind you I am no expert on what is apropriate. I hope we may begin our aquaintance again over tea on Tuesday next at Damask Manor, where I will attempt to demonstrate that I do have manners, contrary to what you likely currently believe. I understand it is the custom of Pennyroyal Green natives to feed the vicar as often as possible, and when in Rome! I shall endeavor not to bore you.

Your neighbor,
Countess of Wareham

He was charmed motionless by the poor spelling and the apology.

He read it again. His thoughts ricocheted between suspicion and sympathy. She was a professional enchantress, after all.

He'd read it three times before he realized he'd been smiling nearly the entire time he'd read it.

He slowly unfurled the cravat and ran it through his fingers. Silk, it was, and spotless as the soul of a saint.

It had once belonged to a man who'd won the right to marry her in a card game.

No, not at all an appropriate gift for a vicar. And this was part of its charm, too, and part of its danger.

He had a duty to all parishioners; he'd dined with nearly all of them. And if she intended to become one of them, he could hardly decline the invitation.

She never does anything without a reason, Colin had said.

A strategist, his cousins had described her. Who knew how to get what she wanted and had always gotten it. Clearly, she wanted something from him.

God help him, he couldn't wait to find out what it was.

"No jewelry," Henny had advised adamantly. "He's a vicar. He'll likely already know you've been a kept woman, and you needn't remind 'im of it by decorating yerself overmuch."

In the intervening days, Henny had discovered that Reverend Sylvaine was related to the Everseas— a cousin on their mother's side. And that the sister

of Mrs. Wilberforce, their housekeeper, kept house
for Pennyroyal Green's doctor. Which likely solved
the mystery of how the entire town had learned exactly who had taken Damask Manor.

So Evie wore no jewelry, apart, that was, from
the St. Christopher's medal she always wore. It
hung warmly between her breasts, and her hand
went up to touch its reassuring shape as she stood
in the drawing room and craned her head to see
Reverend Sylvaine hand off his hat and coat to her
footman. Who seemed puzzled, as if he'd never
before seen a coat that hadn't been brushed and
groomed within an inch of its life by a valet.

And then the vicar turned and took a few steps
into the room. He halted when he saw her standing
against the hearth, right below a gigantic portrait
of a glowering, bearded, ruffed fellow, likely one of
the earl's ancestors.

How had she forgotten how tall he was?

Or how tall he *felt*, more accurately.

The very air in the room seemed to rearrange
to accommodate him. She felt him as surely as if
he'd disturbed a wave of it and it had rushed forward to splash her. She folded her hands against
her thighs; her fingers laced together like creatures
clinging to each other for comfort. She didn't move
to greet him; she couldn't seem to speak. All of her
faculties seemed preoccupied with just *seeing* him.

They in fact eyed each other as if the carpet were
a sea dividing two enemy territories.

It was then she noticed he was holding a small
bouquet of bright, mismatched flowers in one fist. It
ought to have made him look beseeching. It didn't.
On him it might as well have been a scepter.

From the distance of a few days, she realized she'd made a number of miscalculations when she'd anticipated winning him over. A few things had paled dangerously in her memory: the impact of his eyes, even from across the room. That long, elegant swoop of a bottom lip. That palpable confidence, as if he were a man who had nothing to prove because he'd already proved it.

She wondered at the source of that. He was just a *vicar.* He wrote homilies about goats and read them to country people on Sundays. Likely a sheltered man, whose entire world was comprised of Sussex. While *she* had made the unimaginable ascent from peat bogs to Carleton House to countess. She knew what Prinny's breath *smelled* like, for heaven's sake, because he'd leaned over her more than once in an attempt to look down her bodice. If a way could be found past Adam Sylvaine's reserve, she was the one who could forge it

She glanced down at his boots, and the creased toes of them seemed to reassure her of this.

Just as the reverend glanced down at her hands. And he looked up again, with the wry, challenging tilt of the corner of his mouth. Because there was no way the man didn't understand his physical impact. He'd watched her hands lace, and she sensed he knew she was trying not to fidget.

"Thank you for inviting me to your home, Lady Wareham."

And then there was his voice.

Her heart was beating absurdly quickly.

"Thank you for coming, Reverend Sylvaine." Very elegantly, graciously said, she congratulated herself.

And with that, it appeared they'd exhausted conversation.

She cleared her throat. "Are vicars allowed to imbibe? May I offer you a sherry? Will that do for a demonstration of manners?" she said lightly.

He smiled. The dimple made a brief appearance. She eyed it, as fascinated as if the moon had risen in the room. "I'll allow it's a start. But I'll take port if you have it."

It was a contest to see who would speak most noncommittally, it seemed.

He seemed to realize the absurdity of remaining rooted to the spot and moved into the room with a few long, graceful steps. She watched his eyes touch on things: the cognac-colored velvet-tufted settee, the spindly, satin-covered chairs, the portrait of God-only-knew-who above the hearth.

What did he know about her? Did he imagine she ravished lovers on the settee? Was he smiling politely while the word "HARLOT" blazed in his mind like something fresh off a blacksmith's forge?

"Of course I have port. And, oh, look! You came bearing gifts. How . . . very kind of you."

She held out her arms, and he duly filled them with the flowers; and then, to her surprise, he fished a small jar from his coat pocket.

"Since you're new to Sussex—native wildflowers. And the honey is . . . made by the bees that drink from the flowers."

She eyed him cautiously. Flowers and what bees did to them—supped, flitted—were popular metaphors in the poems fevered young bloods had written to her. She wondered if this was an innuendo of some sort.

Or perhaps everything would sound like an innuendo until she knew precisely what the vicar knew about her past.

Once again, the footman appeared. Relieved, she deposited the gifts in his arms and told him to bring port and tea.

She turned to her guest again.

"Flowers and bees," she mused brightly. "It sounds a bit like the beginning of a sermon. Perhaps something about the lilies of the field and how they don't toil?"

"Perhaps. I'll be certain to tell you if I use the idea, so you can come to church to catch up on sleep."

She laughed.

And when she did, his face swiftly suffused with light, as if he'd heard celestial music.

And then it was there and gone, as if it had never been. And he was politely inscrutable then.

"Please do sit down, Vicar. You're by way of towering over me."

He perused the selection of spindly-legged chairs, likely deciding which chair he would be less likely to crush; he chose one with a tall, fanned back and four bandy, gilded legs.

She settled in the settee next to him and turned. She freed her hands from each other and deliberately laid them loosely on her lap.

They confronted each other like diplomats from two nations about to negotiate a treaty. She amused herself by imagining they ought to have hired an interpreter who could speak both vicar and countess.

He didn't look comfortable in the chair. His back was aggressively straight, as if he was trying to avoid the embrace of its fanlike shape. It occurred to her then that perhaps his posture wasn't so much rigid as tense.

"You have the distinction of being the first to fall asleep during one of my sermons, Lady Wareham."

An interesting opening salvo. What would she do with it?

"Oh, I don't doubt it, Reverend. I expect none of the women would want to miss a moment of gazing upon you."

His silence was so instant and palpable, she nearly blinked. It was like a door slamming in a tinker's face.

For heaven's sake. It was *baffling*. She was, by all accounts, a beautiful woman. He ought to have been flattered, or at least intrigued. Surely, he possessed *some* measure of vanity? Despite its being a deadly sin? No man who filled a room the way he did, or possessed those cheekbones, could escape it.

She waited.

He seemed more comfortable saying nothing at all than anyone she'd met in her life.

"I do apologize for sleeping," she found herself saying, haltingly. Though she meant it. His silence pulled the words from her. "It was impolite, to say the least. It's just that it was very warm where I sat, and I fear I was very fatigued, and your voice is so—" She stopped abruptly. Alarmed at what she was about to confess.

"What of my voice?"

Oh. The way he asked the question . . . so gently, so conversationally, so confidingly, in that voice of his . . . she *wanted* to give an answer to him, like an offering, to please him.

An excellent skill for a vicar.

Or a seducer.

"I like your voice." She said it faintly. It wasn't frilled with flirtation. It was simply true.

She felt a bit raw saying it. And a trifle resentful. As though a confession had been extracted from her under duress.

He took that in without a word.

And then one of those smiles of his appeared, so slowly it bordered on the sultry, which gave her time to experience it fully. And to lose her breath before she could brace herself.

It hovered there on his face, the sun peeking out from storm clouds. And she felt that smile at the base of her spine, like a shock of heat.

And for the space of a heartbeat, she suspected she was entirely at his mercy, and if he smiled longer than that, she would be in grave trouble.

For a man of God, he certainly savored his triumphs like the very devil.

Fortunately, the smile faded naturally, just like a sunrise.

She set out to retrieve her composure. By seizing his.

"And while I'm apologizing, perhaps I ought to apologize for saying "bloody" straight to your face. I fear I was startled."

"I liked the 'bloody.' " He wasn't the least nonplussed. "And the rest of it. And you see, I just said 'bloody,' too. When in Rome, as you said."

"But . . . are vicars *allowed* to say 'bloody'?" She was momentarily diverted from her goal.

"Oh, I'm certain the Almighty forgives a few slips now and again. If I go about saying it all the time with wild abandon, it might be another matter."

"Wild abandon" was quite the evocative turn of phrase for a vicar, she thought.

"Perhaps there's a secret quota, and if you exceed it, you'll be smote."

His grin was gorgeous. She leaned toward it helplessly. Like a child, she wanted to urge, "Again!"

He eased back just a little more into the chair.

"I invite you to test it," he said. "I suppose it's a matter of how daring one is prepared to be."

And then there was silence. For alas, two double entendres in a row—the word "daring" on the heels of "wild abandon"—clogged their halting, fitful conversation. She could see they'd both had the same thought at once: Evie Duggan, who inspired duels, balcony topples, and wagers in which she was the prize, was the very personification of daring and wild abandon.

And all at once her past filled the room as surely as if her former lovers lolled about the furniture.

How to extricate them from the little conversational ditch they'd toppled into?

Or better yet, how to exploit it?

"There were two before I was married, Reverend Sylvaine."

"I beg your pardon?"

"Two. Men," she said slowly. "Only two. If you didn't know before, I'm certain by now you've been briefed about my past, and I thought it might be best to acknowledge it straightaway; otherwise, it will hover always on the periphery of our conversation."

She held her breath as he fixed her in the beam of those blue, blue eyes. Counting her eyelashes, no doubt. Or peering into her soul in order to catalog her sins.

"Why did you stop at two? Why not six? Or seventeen? Or is Greed the one deadly sin you shy away from?"

He said it so conversationally it took a moment for the shock to settle in.

She went rigid. Her mouth parted. She fought to keep her jaw from swinging.

"I . . ." It emerged a cracked squeak.

Seeing right *through* her is what he'd been doing.

"Disconcerting me is much more difficult than you might think, my lady. In other words," he said mildly.

And then gifted her with another wicked smile.

She was impressed, despite herself. "Only two," she managed hoarsely, somewhat inanely.

"I'm not in the business of judging, Lady Wareham, despite what you might think. I suppose I'm in the business of guidance, if you understand the distinction. And as it so happens, I've been, shall we say, *briefed* on your history—"

"Ah, have you, then? Do give Colin my regards," she said with sweet irony.

He nodded. "—and while it's undeniably vivid, you're one of many, shall we say, colorful people in Pennyroyal Green."

"Oh, what a shame. If nothing else, I could always take comfort in my singularity."

"I'm reasonably certain you can still take comfort in that, my lady," he said dryly.

"I've been *waiting* for you to begin flirting with me, Reverend. May I count that?"

"Absolutely not. I haven't the faintest notion how to flirt."

"But surely the opportunities for *you* are rife. Perhaps if you—"

"You misunderstand me. I don't want a lesson." Blunt as a hammerblow. Bordering on rude, in fact.

An indignant flush rushed her cheeks. It was a moment before she could speak.

"I thought vicars would need to at least have some mastery of diplomacy," she said tartly after a moment. Her voice a bit frayed.

"I do. I assure you. It's just I suspect you don't require diplomacy, Lady Wareham, as I don't think you're delicate, and it takes so much more time. Life is short enough as it is."

Well. She wondered whether she was offended or flattered.

She was definitely speechless.

He gave the arm of his chair a brief drum with his fingers. "Do you know why I liked it when you said 'bloody'?" He sounded at least vaguely conciliatory.

Instead of answering, she sneaked a glance skyward, as if waiting for him to be smote.

"Because it seemed sincere."

"I'm sorry to hear it. It was me at my worst."

He made an impatient noise. "It was you being *truthful*. I prefer you to be who you are. And you should know that I very much dislike being *steered*, Lady Wareham."

He never raised his voice. But the quiet vehemence of command was in every implacable syllable of that last sentence.

And thus the bloody man neatly flipped the sword from her hand.

She wasn't about to try, "Why, whatever do you mean by *steered*, Reverend Sylvaine?" Because he wasn't padded with vanity or pride or pomposity or any of the other things that conveniently obscured a man's vision; he'd recognized her flirtation for precisely what it was: an attempt to maneuver him into doing what she wanted.

It had always worked so beautifully *before*.

But flirtation had also always been her version of fairy dust. She could fling it into a man's eyes and dazzle him and yet never be fully known. And then never be fully hurt.

Their gazes locked.

Inwardly, she flailed, and hoped it didn't show.

She could at least take some comfort in the fact that she was as good as *staring* as he was.

Be who you are. For so long she'd been who she'd needed to be in order to survive, whether it was on the stage or in a man's bed. Absently, she sought reassurance; her hand went to touch her St. Christopher's medal hidden between her breasts.

His eyes idly followed her hand there. She saw the moment when he tried to look away, the infinitesimal jerk of his chin. But he couldn't.

His eyes lingered, darkened. He was trapped as surely as if he'd waded into honey.

And it stopped her breath.

In that moment, she experienced her own skin as he might: cool, silken, made expressly to be savored by fingertips. Feverish heat rushed over the backs of her arms. Her eyes nearly closed.

It lasted only seconds, all told. Her hand fell gracefully to her lap again. His gaze freed itself and returned to her face. But his eyes were abstracted; the echo of some emotion darkened, tensed his features, flexed his hands on the arms of the chair. She saw him *will* his body to ease.

It shook her. Instead of being an immovable edifice, he was *far* from impervious to her as a woman. The knowledge should have thrilled her. She supposed it did. But the thrill was the unnerving sort. For she now knew that part of whatever she felt when he was near was the sheer strength of his will. Which held something powerful in check when she was near.

And she'd seen what happened to the things in the paths of breaking dams.

This was not a man who would do anything lightly. Or by halves.

Still, she'd been handed back her sword, in a sense. And though she knew it was a risky game, she couldn't resist a feint.

"What is *your* number, Reverend Sylvaine?" she asked softly. "Six? Seventeen? Two? Or is an unmarried vicar *allowed* to have a number?"

He knew exactly what she meant.

And for a moment she felt almost sorry she'd said it. His stillness was different. Almost as though he'd been hurt. The tension in his jaw might have been anger. Did he feel mocked? Surely, he wasn't an innocent in the matter of women. She doubted this; he was too self-possessed. Was he appalled, did he judge her, despite what he'd said?

All she knew was that his eyes burned into her. And she thought how easily a woman of lesser strength might be consumed in that flame.

It was so silent the tick of the clock echoed like a third heartbeat.

And then the Reverend gave a slow, faint smile that she felt everywhere in her body. And shook his head slightly to and fro.

Good try, Lady Balmain.

She smiled, too, despite herself.

He glanced at the clock. "I fear I've other duties to see to, Lady Balmain. Why don't you tell me why you invited me here today. Because I suspect there's a reason."

"Very little eludes you, does it, Reverend Sylvaine?"

"How quickly you learn, Lady Balmain."

She gave a small smile. Suddenly, she felt nervous and foolish. The man allowed for no circumspection; she couldn't lead him into what she wanted.

She would have to baldly tell him, and it opened yet another window into her. It seemed unfair to be the only one in the room sporting windows.

She straightened her spine. She cleared her throat. She was not a ninny.

"Very well. I should like to confess something."

He nodded. "I assure you that anything you tell me will be held in the strictest confidence."

"You needn't brace yourself for anything disconcerting. Or hope for anything shocking," she couldn't resist adding, with a glance up through her eyelashes.

A small ironic smile. "I wouldn't need to regardless, but thank you for the preparation."

She inhaled. Her fingers twined nervously again. And then, to Adam's astonishment, the faintest of pink slowly moved into her cheeks.

"I should like to have friends."

Chapter 7

SHE LOOKED UP AT HIM HOPEFULLY, CLEARLY, AU-
thentically abashed.

"And you . . ." He hesitated to complete the sentence. ". . . Haven't any" seemed a cruelty.

"Of the fair-weather variety, I'm certain I have
many. Or I did once." Her hands were still knotted. She noticed him noticing and loosened them
immediately. Suddenly, she burst out, "And a pity
it is that Mr. Miles Redmond's ship didn't sink
before he could return to tell the whole of the ton
about the poisonous black spider that eats her mate
after making love! What kind of man spends his
time crawling about after insects, I ask you? Black
Widow, indeed!"

He tried not to smile. Perversely, he liked her
temper.

And the tilt of her chin, and the short straight
blade of her nose, and how her cheek curved just
so, taking the light like porcelain.

"Mr. Redmond probably didn't anticipate that
the ton, collectively, can be more poisonous than
the spider in question."

She looked into his face, studying him. She reminded him of himself, in fact, the way she read

features. He saw her shoulders relax when she decided he was sincere.

"I'm sorry Monty died, you know. More than anyone knows. It was a terrible moment. Breakfast, servants milling in and out, but just the two of us at table. One moment he was smiling at me and saying, 'Evie, love, will you pass the marma—' and the next moment there was a terrible thud and he was facedown in his eggs and kippers. The housekeeper shrieked and shrieked. She'd eggs in her hair and all over the front of her, you see. They'd quite sprayed her. I'll never forget the sound." She shuddered.

Adam silently congratulated himself on bringing honey, not marmalade.

"How awful," he said softly. "Were you frightened?"

She looked faintly surprised by the question. "I suppose. But what good does shrieking ever do, unless a brigand has leaped upon you, and you need help, and even then I'd simply elbow him hard or take a knee to his baubles. I went to feel for his heartbeat in his throat, you know. He hadn't one. And then I . . ."

She cast her eyes down suddenly. And he realized at once she was overcome by a sudden cascade of emotion and memories. It was a moment so swift and subtle, anyone might have missed it.

She exhaled and looked up again. ". . . and then I lifted his face up out of his eggs and cleaned his face with his napkin. He hated to be untidy, you see."

He admired it fiercely. For a moment his voice was lost.

For he recognized strength when he saw it.

Quite formidable, Colin had called her. Adam didn't doubt this.

But she wasn't indestructible.

And again a wayward little flame of fury licked at him at the ton for what it had done to her, despite how she may have conducted her life. And even at Colin, for blithely dismissing her as hard.

He loathed injustice.

"I'm so sorry for your loss, Lady Balmain."

She studied him again, as if deciding whether he truly meant it.

And then, at last, she quirked the corner of her mouth. And sighed.

"He was kind and funny, and I don't care what anyone says, I cared for him, and I meant to be a good wife, because Lord knows he shocked even me by going through with the wedding, bless him. But he wasn't young, mind you. The doctor said too much . . . marital activity . . . was a strain on his heart. If I had known! But I take some comfort in one thing: I do believe he died happy."

"I've no doubt at all that he did."

She froze. Her eyes flared in surprise.

He was nearly as surprised as she was that he'd said it.

And then a smile began at one corner of her mouth and spread slowly to the other, and her eyes warmed with it.

"Now that," she said softly, "*was* flirting, Vicar."

For a moment he lived only in that smile, and the world was peculiarly weightless. "Was it? You're the authority."

He held her eyes fast with his. For he was no coward.

It was a dangerous, ill-considered little moment, and he ought to stop it.

She surprised him. She ducked her head again. He knew, with a peculiar satisfaction and disappointment, that he'd disconcerted *her.*

Which perhaps was all to the good.

She sipped at her tea. She glanced up at him, and for a moment his view was of her big green eyes staring at him with something akin to wariness over the rim of the porcelain cup. He knew that throughout his visit, he'd been measured and remeasured by those eyes, and it amused him. Despite what he'd said, she would probably continue to *try* to maneuver him with flirtation like a dog with a sheep, until she realized it just couldn't be done.

Until she gave up and was entirely herself.

But that . . . that might be even more dangerous if her laugh was any indication. For if light had a sound, it was that laugh. Her face went brilliant with it, her eyes disappeared with mirth, and he'd immediately felt it was his mission in life to make her do it again.

He began to understand how she had managed to capture the imaginations of so many men. He had a suspicion he'd in fact only scratched the surface of it.

He was glad of the moment of silence. He used it to impose detachment.

The tea seemed to reanimate her.

"I was alone again, when Monty died. I never liked to be alone, you see. I grew up with so many brothers and sisters in a tiny cottage in Killarney—"

"Which is where the Irish accent came from."

A swift smile. "Yes. I'm Irish. And I don't know how much time you've spent in London, but it's positively teeming, and I never did live alone even there, even in Seven Dials—there was always at least Henny for company; though why I tolerate her, I ask you. I was surrounded by friends and gaiety until Monty died. And listen!" She leaned forward. "Do you hear that?"

Seven Dials? She'd dropped *those* provocative words into conversation casually. He absorbed this in stillness for just a moment.

Another clue into how her character had become tempered. Like a blade.

The clock on the mantel wheezed as it prepared to chime out another hour. That was all he heard.

"I'm sorry. What do you hear?"

"Absolutely nothing! That's the trouble! Silent as a tomb, this countryside is! But if you listen very, very carefully—very carefully, mind you—I believe you can hear mice snoring in the rafters."

He laughed; he couldn't help it.

She smiled as though he'd just awarded her a prize. "I should like to enlist your assistance, Reverend Sylvaine. Because I have reason to believe that the women here know of my past and are hardly likely to welcome me with open arms. And I confess I overheard you speaking to a woman outside of the church on Sunday about a winter festival. And about a Pennyroyal Green Lady's Society? Well, I should like to play a part," she concluded brightly.

He froze. His mind went utterly blank for an instant.

He was tempted to say, "Good God, *anything*

but that. You can sing a bawdy song in front of the church on Sunday if you wish, but not that."

He tried to imagine bringing this news to Mrs. Sneath. He couldn't quite manage it.

"You'd like to become a member of the Lady's Society?"

She nodded.

He drummed his fingers thoughtfully again.

"Tell me, Lady Balmain . . ." he began pleasantly. "And by all means, please do correct me if I'm wrong . . ."

"Very well," she said cautiously.

"Did you once wink at a man and cause a duel?"

"Well, yes. You see, there was something in my eye. It was all a great misunderstand—"

"Or inspire a young man to fall out of a balcony to get a look into your bodice?"

"He'd been misinformed," she said hurriedly. "There was nothing out of the ordinary to see, just a—"

"Show your ankles on stage at the theater?"

"And . . . sometimes my calves," she allowed weakly.

". . . and enter matrimony as a result of a wager?"

"Can you blame the man? I'm an irresistible prize."

She tried a winsome smile.

He sighed. And let his head tip back against the velvet embrace of the spindly chair. And eyed her with something just shy of balefulness.

Just when he thought there might be a limit to the types of surprises he might encounter.

The longer he was quiet, the pinker she grew in the cheeks. Temper or mortification? If he'd been a wagering man, he'd wager it was more of the first than the second.

"So you're judging whether I'm worthy of the women here." Her voice was low and quietly angry. "Despite what you said about judging."

"I'm questioning your choices."

"How would *you* know what sort of life I've lived, or why I've made the choices I've made?"

"That's precisely it, Lady Balmain. I don't know."

"How *dare*—"

He held up a hand. "Allow me to attempt to explain." He took a breath. "Many of my parishioners will live and die in Pennyoyal Green; many may never set foot in London. And they live and die by a set of rules they feel hasn't yet failed them. Those rules include attending church regularly, making an effort to avoid appearing in the scandal sheets or cause riots at the opera as a result of wearing gowns that may or may not expose nipples, and not accepting an allowance and fine lodgings in exchange for having sex with a member of parliament. They find such things, in fact, alarming and threatening to everything they hold dear."

The words rang very damningly in the room.

She was breathing more quickly now. "Those were not the only reasons. The . . . fine lodging and allowance."

He had the sense he was tormenting her. He loathed making a strong woman stammer. He could feel his own stomach knotting in sympathy.

"It's just . . . please try to understand. These are *my* people, Lady Balmain. I care very much about them. I would do anything for them. Their trust is *precious* to me. You've asked me to help you ingratiate yourself with them. And I can only do my best by them as long as my character is sound. They *rely* upon my character and discretion and good judgment. I've yet to hear a reason why I should trust yours. Do you care to convince me that I should?"

Her shoulders rose in a deep breath. She exhaled at length and smoothed her hands along her thighs as if she could erase her past.

And then she jerked her chin up high. Like a soldier carrying a flag into battle.

And again he was suffused with admiration.

"Very well, then. I know it all *sounds* very damning, Reverend. But it's easy to draw conclusions from things you *hear*. It may surprise you to hear that I've never had the opportunity to be reckless. That the choices I made were not a product of *whimsy* or weak moral fiber. That the events you cited—balcony plummets and duels and the like—were choices made by other people, not something I caused, as though I were a mesmerist and I waved my hand and they all did my bidding."

Tell me more, he wanted to urge her. But there was an air of finality about what she'd just said. As though she felt she'd told him quite enough.

"Choices *they* made in response to you. You sound rather like Chaos's Muse."

She struggled with, but lost the battle to, a crooked, wicked smile here, and he couldn't resist meeting it with one of his own.

"*Why* do you want friends? Why should I believe it's not yet another whim of a woman who's so jaded and sophisticated she's simply in search of new ways to amuse herself? These people are not playthings."

He heard the harshness of his own words; he admired her again immensely for not flinching.

She did go still. But he liked the notion he was up against a will as strong as his own. It became clearer by the moment how she'd managed to rise so far in life.

"*Surely* you believe everyone deserves a chance, Reverend Sylvaine? Pennyroyal Green is my home now. I didn't choose it, but I don't intend to leave. And I don't intend to languish. Entertain the possibility that I'd hoped I was beginning another life entirely when I married the Earl of Wareham. All of those things you described are *behind* me, Reverend Sylvaine. Theater. Duels. Gambling. Scandal sheets." She paused strategically. "Men."

The word rang in the room. Almost like a challenge.

Ah, the strategic pause. He admired it. He couldn't help it—he was amused. It was the work of someone who knew a bit about timing and the stage. She would never be able to leave *all* of it behind, he would wager on it.

"So you don't still crave an audience, Lady Balmain?"

"Said the man who holds one captive every Sunday morning."

"And you won't feel the need to foment . . . excitement?"

"I just . . . I just want an opportunity to be a friend. To begin again. To be . . . who I am," she tried coaxingly. Another attempt at flattering him.

This one was a bit more effective. She seemed entirely, humbly sincere. She was still flushed and awkward, and he suspected she was very unused to asking for anything outright. Her hands were still knotted against her thighs.

And God, she was lovely like this, too. Still all contrasts, all softness and angles, pride and prickly vulnerability.

He blew out a breath. Distantly he was amused by his dilemma.

He'd be urging into the midst of a band of worthy women a creature as exotic and dangerous as any fox appeared to any hens, and he wasn't certain figurative carnage wouldn't ensue. Title or no, the countess's beautiful manners weren't innate; they were layered over her like gilt and subject to slippage. And he knew of a certainty she was unpredictable, and his parishioners, with the notable exception of his cousins, thrived on predictability and repetition: seasons, crops, the birth of calves, the christening of babies, mischief from the Everseas.

But he was always on the side of courage. And hope.

Then again, he was also in favor of self-preservation. He imagined Colin's expression when he heard that Adam had been an emissary for the countess.

But what was he put on the earth for if not to help? Surely, this was his primary motive.

Once he said the words, he couldn't unsay them. So he said them.

"Very well," he said softly. "I'll help."

With the strange sensation he was sealing his fate.

Her face was luminous. "*Thank* you, Reverend Sylvaine. You won't regret it."

And in that instant, he felt as though the entire reason he'd been put on earth was to put that smile on her face.

THE AUCTION WAS to take place in the ballroom of Sir John Fesker's manor house. He'd graciously agreed to it, saying magnanimously, "Anything for charity, Vicar." He'd also been promised the role of auctioneer and the use of an enormous gavel, which was the real reason he'd agreed.

Adam arrived at half past the hour to discover all of the women clustered at the far corner of the ballroom, as surely as if the house had been tipped on its edge and they'd all rolled there, like billiard balls.

The reason for this—a petite dark-haired woman holding a basket—was standing on the opposite side of the room, nearest the door. One would have thought the basket she held contained a cobra. Her spine was straight and her chin was high and her expression was serene but not haughty. Quite as though she owned the room and had requested all of the women to stand in the corner so she could admire them from a distance.

Evie had consulted with Henny, who was gifted when it came to costume and invested in Evie's plan to make friends, for this very important choice.

"Ye'll want to seem like one of them, m'lady, but no fancier than the fanciest lady there, soooo . . . I think your blue pelisse over the striped muslin with the long sleeves, and a fichu tucked into the top, mind, as you dinna want them thinking overmuch about yer bubbies."

It was a very good reminder, as in the past it had been to Evie's benefit if her company did think

about her bubbies, and she in general found fichus
rather hypocritical.

She *felt* him arrive before she saw him. Those
broad shoulders nearly cast a shadow at her feet.
There was a swift and peculiar clutch of the heart,
as though she were being engulfed or sheltered.
She turned around swiftly, looked up, and, yes,
found him faintly smiling.

"Good afternoon, Reverend Sylvaine."

"Welcome, Lady Balmain. I've reviewed the
premises for pitchforks and boiling oil. I think
you're safe enough. Although there may be some
danger from daggerlike stares."

They both noted the cluster of women at the
front of the ballroom. Baskets were lined, ready for
bidding on tables near them. Another table held
ratafia, and when he glanced over there, it solved
the mystery of what had become of the husbands
and men of the town.

"I wore armor. Note my modest fichu." Eve gestured toward it.

She suspected he sorely longed to note it, but
noting it would require looking directly at her
breasts, which he wasn't about to do in front of an
assembly of his parishioners.

His eyes remained steadfastly on hers. The man
was a fortress.

"I should have thought your maid would have
been armor enough," he said easily.

"Oh, Henny would frighten them far worse
than I, so I thought it wisest not to bring her. She's
unable to tolerate anyone's treating me like other
than a queen. Unless it's her, of course. The abuse
I *endure* from her, I ask you! And if you think my

vocabulary is startling when *I've* had a shock, you should hear hers."

He smiled, and all around the room women watching him shifted restlessly, livid with envy that the smile wasn't directed at them, and craned to bask in its stray rays.

"It's a good quality in a friend."

"I suppose it is."

It was then Adam noticed how tightly she was gripping the edges of the basket.

He was tempted to touch her arm and wish her peace and luck. He refrained, of course.

They would know soon enough whether this was folly.

He *was* curious about something. "Did *you* actually bake a cake?"

"You needn't sound so skeptical, Reverend. I do know how to bake. Though . . . it *has* been some time since I attempted it . . ." Her forehead was faintly troubled. She added almost hopefully, "It's a ginger cake." As though she wasn't entirely sure that it was but was optimistic it would taste like one.

Her hand absently touched her throat. He'd watched her do that any number of times when they'd first spoken over tea. A fine chain looped about her neck and disappeared into her bodice. He suspected a charm of some kind dangled from it, and again he wondered who had ever been strong for her, if she sought comfort in a talisman.

"Will you bring it up to the table now, then?" he asked her.

"I suppose I will." She didn't move. She did square her shoulders.

"Godspeed, Lady Wareham."

She did smile at this, albeit wryly, and bore her cake off into the lion's den.

He watched her walk, as regally as someone about to be presented to the queen, right up to Mrs. Sneath. They exchanged a few words; Mrs. Sneath relieved her of the basket rapidly, as though it did indeed contain a snake, and gestured, almost shooed her, in the direction of the rows of chairs, while behind them the cluster of women in the corner shifted and buzzed with low conversation, like a cloud of disturbed bees.

Mrs. Sneath had been silent for a long, long time when he'd broached the topic of the countess.

"She's a very striking woman," she began carefully. "The sort your cousin Mr. Colin Eversea might have known some years back, I suspect. I've heard she can captivate even the most stalwart of men like a veritable Circe."

She was clever, Mrs. Sneath. But not direct. Perhaps she was concerned Adam was exhibiting latent rake tendencies.

"Pennyroyal Green is blessed with more than our fair share of striking women, wouldn't you say, Mrs. Sneath? I imagine that's why I noticed nothing unusual about the countess."

Surely this was the sort of lie that could be forgiven.

"Oh, Reverend." She laughed and blushed, and would convey his words to all the women in the town, thus fanning into a bonfire the hopes of many of them.

"You are a good man, Reverend Sylvaine," she said carefully, though it had the faintest, faintest ring of a reminder. "I understand that your compassionate nature compels you to convey her request to me. But what you suggest might be difficult, indeed. If Napoleon had confronted a mass of women determined to protect their morals and the morals of their families, he might have turned around and gone straight back to France."

"Don't you think, Mrs. Sneath, that if one's morals are solid, then one woman with a basketful of cake is hardly likely to corrupt them? Wouldn't the sheer volume of moral certainty you ladies possess be more likely to influence *her*?"

He thought this very unlikely in the present circumstances. If any influencing was about to take place, he suspected quite the inverse.

"Excellent point!" Mrs. Sneath seemed pleased with this. "It's why you are the vicar."

"Wouldn't it be an interesting challenge to welcome her graciously into the society and see whether one's morals can withstand the strain of her?"

He told himself it didn't matter whether she noticed how heavily laced with irony the sentence was as long as she embraced the intent.

She seemed captivated by the notion. "Perhaps if we consider her a prodigal daughter? Or . . ." and this seemed to animate her. ". . . a soiled dove?"

"I expect she could be . . . wait. A what?" He was a bit uneasy now.

But Mrs. Sneath's reformist zeal was stirred. "A lost sheep returning to the fold!"

She was delighted at the prospect, and so he let it be.

Mrs. Sneath was hurrying over to him now. "I've taken the countess's basket, Reverend," she

said with the briskness of a subaltern reporting
to a commanding officer. "But I shan't hope for a
miracle. As I said, acceptance might be more difficult than you think. My niece was quite taken with
you, by the by. She left a gift with me for you. I'll
send it over to the vicarage. I think you'll be very
pleased. Very pleased *indeed*."

He mentally made room for another jar of preserves in his pantry and wended his way to the
back of the room, which was gratifyingly full. The
poor were with them always in Sussex, and he
sincerely hoped the audience would reach deeply
into their pockets. It did simplify his job to some
extent, when there were funds to feed and clothe
the hungry and repair their roofs.

Though his life in general seemed to resist simplicity.

Mrs. Sneath hurried away, and Adam made
his way to the back of the room and stood, hands
behind his back.

There was a pleasing sort of pianoforte-key sym-
metry to the assembly, the men in their best dark
coats arrayed alongside women in brighter finery,
all in the several dozen rows of seats provided by
Sir John.

And in the final row sat the countess, in blue, all
straight-backed dignity, entirely alone.

A narrow strip of pale nape between the collar
of her pelisse and bonnet, with dark curls escaping. It seemed all at once absurdly vulnerable, that
pale skin. Proof again she was human and could
be hurt.

She didn't fit into the pianoforte-key arrangement.

He couldn't help but think she was an entire Hallelujah chorus of a woman.

Yet another thought he wouldn't be sharing with his cousins. Or with anyone.

Chapter 8

Once the bidding had gotten under way, the sidelong glances and the yawns and stretches that were really excuses for the men to peer over their shoulders at her finally ceased, and she sat alone in the row, she hoped, forgotten. But as basket after basket was claimed with good-natured bidding, Evie was half-amused, half-appalled to realize her palms were clammy inside her gloves because every bid brought her closer to the moment her basket would be offered.

She didn't see the vicar in the audience. Likely he was off bestowing goodwill and partaking of confidences, she thought. Basking in the rays of admiration. Deflecting flirtations.

She did think she caught a glimpse of a profile that had years ago been familiar, a man's. The very shape of loathing itself. But then he'd turned his head to face the auctioneer. Surely, she was simply seeing him through a filter of trepidation? When one has a past, one has a tendency to see it out of the corners of one's eye under times of great strain. She knew this through experience. She still, on occasion, dreamed of the rooms in St. Giles and woke thrashing.

The auctioneer was thumping his great gavel with abandon.

". . . Next we have Mrs. Bainbridge's *legendary* lemon seedcakes. Who among us would risk offending Mrs. Bainbridge's excellent cook by bidding less than three shillings? Your future invitations to dinner depend on it!"

Much genial laughter was followed by escalating bids ricocheting about the room.

"One pound for the seedcakes if I get an invitation to dinner!"

"Two pounds for the seedcakes. But I'll give ten for her cook!"

Roars of laughter greeted this. Thanks to the fever of bonhomie and the warm glow of charitable giving blended with the ratafia and flasks slipped from the pockets of men and sipped liberally, the seedcakes went for the exorbitant figure of two pounds fifty. Mrs. Bainbridge was compelled by shouts to stand and curtsy, to much applause.

The auctioneer moved to the second-to-the-last basket on the table. Hers.

Eve's heart pounded as though it were opening night in Covent Garden.

"Now this basket contains a ginger cake donated by none other than . . ." He paused, at great length and stared at the sheet of paper, as if he hoped if he stared at the words long enough, they'd transform into different ones. At last, with a strained heartiness, he completed: "the Countess of Wareham!"

Well, that effectively dammed the bonhomie spigot. All was suddenly creaking chairs and cleared throats and uneasy rustling. She felt they were all acutely aware of her. And yet no one, not a soul, turned around to look at her. Not one word was muttered.

The auctioneer rallied. "Do I hear one shilling for the ginger cake!"

He heard nothing at all is what he heard.

Just more rustling.

He seemed momentarily daunted by the glacial silence. Evie could only imagine his view: accusing, righteous eyes, row upon row of them. She'd stood on the stage before a bored silent audience before. It was enough to make even the most stalwart of souls perspire a river.

"Who will bid one shilling for the ginger cake? A favorite after any Sunday dinner!"

"Ginger cake. Is that the Black Widow's new nickname?" came a man's whisper. It unfortunately carried brilliantly in the silence.

"She wouldn't do it for less than five shillings, I heard."

A few filthy little chuckles were stopped by an appalled feminine *shhhhhhhh*.

"It's excellent for digestion, ginger!" the auctioneer coaxed desperately. "Ooooone shilling! For the poor of Sussex, ladies and gentlemen, who deserve and need your charity, for there but for the Grace of God . . ."

Mouths remained steadfastly, punishingly clamped shut. After all, opportunities to shun a genuine harlot, the Black Widow herself, were few and far between, and they were all taking full delicious advantage.

The moment stretched torturously, dreamlike. Her stomach tightened until she couldn't breathe, then tossed like a skiff on a stormy sea. Evie thought, perhaps if I walk out now, just drift right out of here, one day I'll eventually believe it was a dream.

She knew she couldn't. Not just for her own sake.

But the sake of Reverend Sylvaine, who had risked his reputation for her.

"Perhaps we haven't any lovers of ginger cake present today," John Fisker tried. "Perhaps we should—"

"Five pounds for the ginger cake."

The voice was almost bored.

In unison, all the heads turned, mouths dropped open into "O's." Gasps fluttered up ribbons on bonnets.

The vicar was used to being stared at, so he didn't even blink. He stood in the back of the room, hands clasped behind his back, one knee slightly, casually bent. He didn't smile. He didn't look at her. His face was inscrutable.

She did note a distinct ironlike tension about his jaw.

It was then she wondered what a man like Adam Sylvaine looked like when he was truly furious.

She wondered if she was the only one present who suspected he was.

The eyes continued beaming in his direction. Stunned silence prevailed.

"I like ginger cake," he said, finally. As if in answer to a collective silent question.

He would, of course, be inundated with ginger cakes by the end of the week.

"Do I hear SIX pounds for the ginger cake?" The auctioneer sounded a trifle dizzy. He had the gavel upraised, poised for a tremendous blow.

The audience was dumbstruck. Confusion clearly had a grip. Gazes flitted between her and the vicar and back to her. Hissed conversations took place. But like the vicar, Evie was used to stares, both the worshipful and censuring kind, and like the vicar, she had a special smile she used for audiences. Small, serene, noncommittal, impenetrable, with just a soupçon of warmth. She donned it now, and all the stares could find no purchase or satisfaction, so they turned around to face the auctioneer again.

"Going once . . . twice . . . three times! Reverend Sylvaine is now the proud owner of a ginger cake! And thank you to the Lady Wareham, and the poor of Sussex thank you for the generous, *serendipitous* donation today."

Evie gave one regal nod. As if she'd planned this beneficence all along.

She didn't look back at the Reverend Sylvaine.

She wasn't certain whether she was relieved or humiliated. But she realized he'd just, before nearly the whole of the town, cast his lot in with hers, to some degree.

She would need to do him proud.

And what must five pounds mean to a *vicar*?

She glanced over her shoulder then, to find Adam nodding just at the auctioneer, apparently a signal. Sir John Fisker hastened over the silence with a clear of his throat.

"Right. Yes. Next we have . . . well, if it isn't our final basket of the day! Inside we have . . . it looks like . . . tea cakes with currants contributed by Mrs. Margaret Lanford!"

The audience bestirred themselves to clap

for Mrs. Lanford, and when the heads swiveled toward her, Evie recognized her as Paulie's mother, she of the frosty stare and righteous silence and easy condemnation. She was wearing her best clothing today, from the looks of the bonnet almost flattened beneath the weight of a cluster of dusty grapes.

"Do I hear one shilling for the tea cakes?" Sir John Fisker urged. "They've currants in them! A favorite of children everywhere!"

"Why, one shilling is a *bargain* for a box o' rocks!" the man next to Mrs. Lanford called. His thick neck rose up out of a tight collar, and his stiff black hair was very short, rather like bristles on a boar. "Right useful, rocks are!"

A rustle of chuckles from the men.

"Can I skip 'em across the pond, Lanford?"

Then the man was Margaret Lanford's husband. An argument against marriage, that, Evie thought.

"Better than that. You throw 'em at foxes when they get near the henhouse!"

More laughter.

"Aye, but you can build a wall with 'em to keep the foxes *out*. They'll withstand the winter, those tea cakes," came another voice.

"Use 'em to keep the door propped open on warm days!"

The men, the hateful beasts, were having a *wonderful* time. She loathed how some of them behaved when they were full of drink.

She watched as the women alternately exchanged dark looks, shifted uncomfortably, or stared stonily ahead. Emotions twitched over their faces, from anger to fear.

And from where she sat, Evie had a perfect view of the vivid red color that had washed up the back of Margaret Lanford's neck. Her face was likely a painful scarlet. She saw her throat move in a swallow.

And then her shoulders twitched and squared, in the way one does when attempting to accommodate a humiliation with dignity.

Evie ought to know.

"Two pounds," Evie said then. In a drawl so regal it could have cut diamonds.

It silenced the room again. The stillness was followed by an uneasy, yet decidedly fascinated rustle of murmurs. A few dared to peek over their shoulders.

And then, all at once, it welled in her, the deliciousness of a calculated risk, the thrill of a bit of theater. She might never see these people again. What had she to lose?

"Although . . ." she mused, raising her voice, "who can put a price on the loving labor the women of this fine town put in day after day after day? All in an attempt to feed their families, to keep them healthy and happy. *Three* pounds," she said firmly, as if she'd reconsidered the value.

It was a startling figure. In the silence that followed, tension gathered almost palpably, roiling like storm clouds, hovering portentously. All around her, she saw the spines of women stiffening like coiled springs; everywhere, jaws clenched, bottoms shifted restlessly.

Sir John Fisker bestirred himself. "Do I hear three pounds one shil—"

A woman sprang up. "Three pounds *five* shillings!"

And then she sent a scornful glare down at the man next to her, likely her husband, who had been one of the chucklers. He recoiled in shock.

Mr. Lanford, he of the bristly hair, shifted in his seat. "Now . . . just a moment, here . . . surely you're jesting if you think anyone will pay three—"

"I wonder, Sir John," Evie mused, loudly, glacially. "Is there a basket of *appreciation* Mr. Lanford can bid on? Perhaps a basket of *manners*?"

Another risk that paid off in laughter. Some of it nervous, granted, some of it from the men, and some of it bitter, that from the women. But laughter, nevertheless.

"Do I hear four pounds, one shilling?" the auctioneer wondered, with something like glee.

Evie wasn't done. "It's priceless, in fact, labor and commitment these women ceaselessly give to their families. Day after day. The worry, the planning, the skill, I ask you! Who are we to put a value on it? How fortunate we are to have this rare opportunity to bid on it! These tea cakes are nothing less than a beautiful miracle. They represent all that's best of womanhood, all that our great country *is*."

Mrs. Sneath could bear it no longer. She leaped upward, the flowers on her bonnet swaying.

"Four pounds for the glorious tea cakes!" she boomed rapturously.

Olivia Eversea, from the opposite side of the room, sprang up. "Six pounds!"

This elicited a gasp. Olivia basked in the shock for a moment. She was never more radiant than

when she had a cause, and she glowed like an
avenging angel.

And then, to the horror of their husbands,
women all over the audience began bouncing up
like voles from holes.

"Six pounds one shilling!"

"Six pounds TWO!" came a shout from one of
the women who'd glared at Evie in church.

"Six pounds three!"

Up and up and up the bidding went, shilling
by shilling, while everywhere in the audience
husbands cringed, murmured pleas, or issued
futile commands, reached up placating hands and
tugged at skirts, only to be swatted away.

Six pounds was a good deal of money for most
of these people, in all likelihood.

Evie turned around, craned her head.

The vicar was grinning from ear to ear.

She flashed him a smile of wicked triumph, brief
and surreptitious, swiveled back to face the auctioneer, and decided to avert disaster.

"TEN pounds," she said definitively. Taking
pains to sound bored.

The hush that followed was almost spiritual in
nature. It settled over the crowd like a blanket of
new-fallen snow.

And then, one by one, triumphant smiles lit the
faces of all the women, like stars winking on in a
dark sky.

When at last Sir John Fisker found his voice, it
was gravelly with emotion. "Do I hear ten pounds,
one shilling?"

Eyes slid toward her. Evie gave her head an infinitesimal shake, discouraging further bidding.

"Going once . . . going twice . . . *sold* to Lady Balmain for ten pounds, Mrs. Margaret Lanford's miraculous tea cakes!"

He gave a little jubilant hop and brought the gavel down with a hearty *THWACK!*

Cheers erupted.

Chapter 9

"Congratulations, Lady Wareham. It seems you bought friends for ten pounds. A bargain really, all told. Quite an impressive bit of theater."

"Theater! The man was an oaf. I ask you! To speak that way about your wife in front of an audience. He *begged* to be put in his place. It was entirely sincere."

The vicar hiked a brow.

She sighed. "Very well. I grant you, a bit of it might have been theater. It's all in the timing, you see, and one learns timing from the stage. Nearly everything I've ever learned has proved useful again, Vicar. And I've learned a *very* good deal in my day."

She liked to imagine he was blushing on the inside though he appeared entirely unmoved. Apart from the faint smile. Given the man was the enemy of the innuendo, this was an improvement.

There was a silence.

"Thank you for bidding on the ginger cake," she added.

His face suddenly went stony. "Well . . ."

And that was all he said.

"I sincerely hope it's edible," she added.

"For five pounds, I plan to have it gilded and ensconced as a memorial to charity in the vicarage. Perhaps I'll have it engraved. Perhaps I'll be buried under it."

"Erect it in the town square. You can call it 'the Vicar's Folly.'"

He laughed. She felt like it was raining guineas when he laughed. It was abandoned as he was restrained. She basked in it.

She didn't ask him whether he had five pounds. The answer worried her. In truth, her ten pounds was a bit of a risk, given her new need for economy.

"I'm not certain I've entirely won the day yet," she said worriedly, "ten pounds or no."

The women were arrayed in a phalanx on one side of the ballroom, eyeing her with varying degrees of wariness and shy curiosity while they supervised the dispersal of the baskets to the winning bidders. Some, especially those who had sprung up and shouted, looked abashed. She suspected they all felt a bit the way one does the morning after a particularly debauched evening, where one suddenly remembers just how a silk stocking ended up dangling from the chandelier.

And then Mrs. Sneath approached the ladies, looking like a soldier in Turkey red wool. They clustered round her like metal filings to a magnet. Much muttered conversation took place, a bit of gesturing, then at last Mrs. Sneath burst from their ranks as if she'd been launched.

She'd been sent as the emissary, it appeared.

"Prepare to be *properly* introduced, Lady Balmain," Adam said calmly. "This may be your defining moment."

Eve smiled brightly and straightened her spine.

"Lady Balmain, I'd like to introduce you to the inestimable Mrs. Sneath, without whom this event would not have been possible. She's an indispensable part of our community here, and we owe her a great deal."

Mrs. Sneath nodded approvingly at this introduction, as if it was only what she deserved.

When they exchanged curtsies, Adam was uncomfortably reminded of a bullfighter confronting a bull. Something about Mrs. Sneath's red hat and cape.

"Lady Balmain," Mrs. Sneath began briskly, officiously, "the spirit you displayed today is precisely what we, the members of the Committee to Protect the Poor of Sussex, appreciate. I can only assume that a poor soiled dove like yourself has perhaps suffered a bit at the hands of men, and now would like to serve as a cautionary tale and perhaps help others less fortunate as a way to redeem yourself in the eyes of society. Your speech today was brave, very brave indeed."

She beamed her approval.

Out of the corner of her eye Evie saw the vicar straighten alertly, as if something delightful had just occurred. He said nothing at all. He simply turned his head toward Evie, his expression benign and expectant.

But the bloody man's eyes were glinting.

"Let me think now . . . have I suffered at the hands of *men* . . ." Eve tapped her chin thoughtfully. "Well, I suppose I did suffer a bit when Lord Englenton sent a string of pearls to me after my first performance at Covent Garden rather than the sapphires I wanted. It was *very* disappointing."

And then she smiled, slowly. It increased in width and brightness, until it was, when full grown, decidedly wolfish.

Mrs. Sneath's smile congealed. Her mouth was clearly unwilling to relinquish it, but the light in her eyes went out, and they darted wildly from the vicar to Evie and back again.

"I did return the pearls, however," Evie confided sadly. "It wouldn't have been right to keep them."

Mrs. Sneath's body nearly deflated with relief. "Of course you did, my dear. Because keeping them would have been sinful." She said this firmly, as if her conviction alone was enough to make it true, enough to purify Evie's soul.

"It certainly *would* have been sinful! Because I preferred the necklace sent to me by Lord Eskith, and it wouldn't have been fair to play the two against each other, now, would it have been? Duels are a nasty business."

Mrs. Sneath's smile wavered again. "Quite," Mrs. Sneath decided to say, finally. Albeit somewhat hoarsely.

She sent an imploring, almost conspiratorial glance at the vicar, one that said: *She certainly doesn't know the definition of sin, does she? Perhaps she can be taught.*

Mrs. Sneath was certainly indomitable, and not stupid. She had a sense of Evie now. She just hadn't decided how to manage her.

The vicar nodded once, encouraging Mrs. Sneath to continue. His hands were folded behind his back now. For all the world as if he'd settled in to enjoy a cricket match.

Mrs. Sneath rallied. "Well, it's heartening any-

time a still-young woman like yourself decides to
repent her ways," she tried. Her eyes were glittering determinedly now. Her words had the stentorian ring of a woman accustomed to getting her
way.

Evie took a breath. She tipped her head in ap-
parent thought. And then she leaned toward Mrs.
Sneath and lowered her voice.

"Mrs. Sneath, may I confide in you? I feel I must
be truthful in all things."

She leaned toward Evie, and righteous hope and
dawning triumph circulated with hopeless, prurient curiosity on her face.

When their heads were very close together Evie
said in a conspiratorial hush: "What would you say
if I told you I repent nothing at all?"

Mrs. Sneath's face blanked. And then she reared
back and blinked rapidly, as if she'd just sustained
a slap to the side of her head. "I'm afraid . . . I suppose I don't . . ."

"Oh, don't be afraid," Evie interjected soothingly. "I'm quite harmless. But I do know a thing
or two about getting what I want, and it strikes me
that you might find this skill useful when it comes
to helping the poor of Sussex. And I should like
you to tell the women of your committee that they
should never allow men to treat them like anything other than queens. If they'd like to know how
to accomplish this, I'd be delighted to share what I
know about men."

And then Mrs. Sneath and Evie stood apart.

Mrs. Sneath appeared stunned motionless. And
then the gears of her mind began almost visibly,
furiously working. Her eyes twitched.

At last, something like a faint delight settled across her face.

"I'll convey this to the ladies," she said finally.

"Thank you, Mrs. Sneath." Evie gave her a small, regal smile, which Mrs. Sneath, little did she know, imitated, before she curtsied and ferried her information about the countess away to the ladies.

"Why is it," Adam said conversationally, after a moment, "that I suspect everywhere you go, Lady Wareham, uproar ensues."

"A wise man once told me to be who I am."

"Ah. But what I neglected to tell you is that I haven't any wisdom at all. I simply do a lot of guessing, and it somehow comes right much of the time."

"We'll just have to see if this is one of the times, won't we, Reverend Sylvaine? At least I'm never dull."

"There are days when I *long* for the opportunity to feel boredom," he said, half to himself.

"Oh, look, she's returning and she's bringing re-inforcements."

Mrs. Sneath was indeed returning. She was flanked by Mrs. Margaret Lanford, she of the glorious Tea Cakes with Currants, as well as two young women: one with blond curls whose gaze was so fixed to the vicar he might as well have been the North Star, and who tripped over her feet once on the way there and was seized by the elbow and righted by Mrs. Sneath. The other young lady had dark hair and powerful dark slashes of eyebrows and a direct, intelligent, albeit slightly imperious gaze. It was the sort of face doomed to be called handsome the whole of her life, never "pretty." Her posture was arrogant, and her dress was a bold yellow, in the first stare of fashion. She was a rich man's daughter, Evie knew almost instantly.

"Lady Wareham, I'd like to introduce Mrs. Margaret Lanford, Miss Amy Pitney, and Miss Josephine Charing."

They all exchanged nods and curtsies when Mrs. Sneath made the introductions. Josephine was the blond young lady, it turned out; Amy was the imperious one.

Their eyes were bright and fascinated. The younger women were flushed and a bit fidgety, perhaps with the excitement of viewing what Mrs. Sneath likely characterized as a fallen woman at such close range. Evie was tempted to hold out her hand for them to sniff.

She wasn't much older than the two youngest, but the gulf in experience was as wide as the Atlantic Ocean. Appalling and fascinating them would have been child's play—and *might* be very entertaining—but that would only keep them at a distance. She told herself firmly: You wanted friends, Evie. *Be* a friend.

After a moment of staring, Mrs. Lanford handed over her basket. Evie took it as graciously as a queen being handed a scepter.

"I'm very much looking forward to tasting the tea cakes, Mrs. Lanford."

"I hope they're to your liking," Mrs. Lanford said stiffly.

"I'm certain they will be."

What if they were indeed like rocks? Perhaps she could invite Paulie Lanford over and they could skip them like stones across the pond behind the manor.

Mrs. Lanford nervously craned her head over her shoulder. Looking for her husband, Evie thought, who seemed to have made himself scarce. "I must away," she muttered, and ducked a shallow curtsy and hastened off.

Mrs. Sneath cleared her throat, which seemed very much the equivalent of sounding reveille.

"We've discussed it, and we thought one of the best ways for you to decide whether you'd like to join our Lady's Society, Lady Wareham, is to experience a little of the work we do. We are very much concerned with the children, with the poor, the elderly. The weak and defenseless."

The three pairs of eyes across from her were shining, and not entirely benignly.

Ah. So some sort of test was imminent, it seemed. So be it. Evie gave them a regal, neutral smile. "A sound plan."

"We should like you to join us at the O'Flaherty house tomorrow."

"I'd love to," she said immediately, even though she hadn't the faintest idea what that meant and even as she thought she heard the vicar suck in a breath.

"I'll bring my carriage round to Damask Manor at eight o'clock in the morning. Until then, Lady Balmain."

They all curtsied their farewells. Josephine trailing a look and a smile at the vicar.

She turned to Adam, a question on her face. "The O'Flahertys?"

"That would be Mr. and Mrs. O'Flaherty," he

said slowly. "They're a poor family. I've rallied some men to help with repairs there. We'll begin tomorrow."

"Is there anything in particular I ought to know about the O'Flahertys?"

He paused. "Let me put it like this, Lady Wareham. I think you've just been given the equivalent of the task of cleaning the Augean stables. Figuratively speaking."

"What are the Augean stables?" She wasn't the least bit sensitive about the gaps in her education. There was no point in apologizing for it. She simply acquired information as she could from whom she could, and she quite liked knowing things. As she'd told him, it was remarkable what could be useful.

"Do you know who Hercules was? Strong chap, Greek, was given a lot of tasks to perform to prove his worth?"

"Mmmm. A friend may have mentioned him to me once or twice," she said vaguely. "My education in the classics is a trifle patchy, Reverend, and I admit I wasn't trained in the traditional feminine arts, so to speak. Though I do know how to sing, play a little pianoforte, sew passably, and I do know quite a number of useful French phrases. *Je voudrais fumer ton cigare,*" for instance."

She thought she might succeed in disconcerting him through stealth. She'd just said, in the most conversational tone achievable, very nearly the most prurient thing possible.

It was a French euphemism: "I would like to smoke your cigar," which of course meant something else entirely.

She *did* like how still he went. How the blue

of his eyes intensified. How he didn't blink for a good, oh, three seconds or so.

But then he just shook his head ever-so-slightly, to and fro.

And in the end, *she* was the one who felt the flush beginning.

How did he *do* that?

"The Augean stables were filled with endless horse muck, Lady Balmain," he told her. "Piles and piles of it."

"Oh, Reverend Sylvaine. You're such an *incorrigible* flirt."

He grinned and touched his hat. "Good day, Lady Wareham. I'm off to retrieve my ginger cake. Good luck tomorrow."

Chapter 10

WHEN HE RETURNED TO THE VICARAGE AN HOUR
or so later, he discovered Colin sitting comfortably
at the kitchen table, eating an apple.

Adam reflexively, guiltily, thrust the basket
holding the ginger cake behind his back.

"Oh, there you are, cousin," Colin said pleasantly. "And a good day to you. Mrs. Dalrymple let
me in." He finished his apple with a final bite and
balanced the core delicately on the table.

Then he shifted in his chair, fished about in his
coat pocket, and one at a time, counted pound
notes out onto the table while Adam watched. One.
Two. Three. Four. Five.

"Because I heard you lost your mind and bought
a ginger cake for five pounds. And I know you
can't spare the blunt."

Olivia must have tattled.

Adam scowled at him. And then he heaved the
basket up onto on the table.

Colin peered in. "Looks like a ginger cake, all
right."

"All of those people supposedly gathered self-
righteously to help the poor, then shunning something that could have been had for a shilling. The

pleasure people take in mass condemnation . . . people I know and generally like were savoring the torture of her. I would have done it for anyone."

"Now, here's a philosophical dilemma for a vicar . . . is it a *lie* if you don't know you're lying? Is it a lie if you're lying to *yourself*?"

"Is it a *sin* if I tell my cousin to bugger off?"

Colin laughed. "Very well. You might *well* have done it for anyone else. And it's a rare day ginger cakes baked by countesses who used to be courtesans come on the market. One must snap them up when one can. For the bargain price of five pounds. Nothing quixotic about that at *all*."

"Very well." Adam shook himself out of his coat. "For the sake of discussion, let's assume *you'd* baked a ginger cake and donated to the auction. Here you sit now, a churchgoing, cow-raising, cousin-tormenting ordinary sort of bloke besotted by his wife. But all of those things are recent developments. *You* weren't even given a proper shunning when you were in *Newgate*. Instead, you were immortalized in song. A broadsheet with your signature on it fetched a good *hundred pounds*, from what I understand, for a pub owner in London. In other words, when you were at what many would consider your most incorrigible, the townspeople would have been rioting for the opportunity to buy your ginger cake. Not sitting in cold silence and savoring your discomfort over something that could have been had for a shilling. Now that I think of it . . . fetch me my quill! I feel a sermon about hypocrisy coming on."

Colin listened to all of this with equanimity, nodding along. "Oh, I wager if we dig about some, we can find a few pockets of resentment toward me. I assure you I wasn't, and I'm still not, beloved by everyone. But it's not Evie I'm worried about. I know I'm hardly in a position to judge her, am I? I'm worried about *you*."

Adam was silent. And then:

"What," he ground out, with infinite, infinite patience, "precisely are you worried about?"

Colin opened his mouth to speak. Then shut it again. Considered what he was about to say. "Will you . . . sit for a moment?"

Adam sat. Heavily. Whipped off his hat, flung it across the table so that it skittered like a dealt card, loosened his new cravat. Glared balefully at Colin.

Colin seemed to be considering where to begin. He toyed with the apple core somewhat diffidently.

"Have you ever been in love?"

"Colin. For the love of *God*."

"I have," he said bluntly. "And when you lose love, it tears a hole out of you. The pain can be gruesome. I thought I lost Madeline once, and I swear for a few days I thought I might never be whole again."

"Perhaps you should write a poem about it. Add another verse to your song."

Colin blithely ignored the sarcasm. "But you see, I had a lot of practice with women even before she appeared. A lot of *it*. And Evie Duggan . . . how shall I put this? It's as though . . . you're fencing with a foil, and she's fencing with a saber. You're in two very different classes, my friend."

"Oh, please. Certainly you can manage more originality than a *sword* metaphor?"

"Listen to me, Adam. Men have made fools

of themselves over her since she first showed an ankle at the Green Apple Theater. For most of her life it has practically been her professional responsibility to break hearts. She plays them like a hand of cards, keeping, discarding, coming up trumps. She's not cruel, she's just practical. I suppose we all do what we need to get by. Her past is likely to crop up at unlikely moments, and not in pretty ways. Me, I've made a fool of myself countless times in so many ways over many women. But you're . . . just not the sort. You're like Chase, or Marcus: You've an innate . . . dignity. An authority, which I suspect you were born with. Useful in a vicar, that. And as I rather like you, it would pain me to see her make a fool of you. And I should hate to see you hurt."

"I see. So my new directive is to spare you pain."

"I know you will because you've an altruistic nature."

Adam barked a laugh, and it tapered into a long-suffering sigh. "If you've such a high opinion of my *gravitas*, consider the possibility that my judgment is just as solid."

It was interesting to be compared to Captain Chase Eversea, Colin and Ian's brother, who was *born* with an air of command and had proved it in the war. Colin, as the youngest of his family, ought to know how Adam had come by his gravity. How watchful and careful he'd learned to be, and why.

"Ah, see. You've just demonstrated your dangerous naïveté. Some women are simply like shooting stars; you *have* to look. You have to reach for them. You have to try to catch them. Judgment doesn't figure, Adam. Other . . . *things* . . . figure."

"Sabers," Adam suggested sardonically. After a moment. Figuratively speaking, of course.

"Sabers," Colin agreed. "Sabers *always* figure. And from what I understand, the lady truly knows how to handle a sword."

Adam curled his fingers into a fist, and the knuckles whitened. *Je voudrais fume ton cigare.*

He disliked hearing her discussed this way.

Which really rather proved Colin's point.

"I expect the town will view your ginger-cake heroics as charity. I'll finance your folly this time, but if you lose your head *again*, I can't promise anything ..."

"Thank you for your concern. But I didn't lose my head this time," Adam said with infinite, infinite patience, "and I don't intend to lose it. My dignity, you see, makes this impossible."

Colin grinned at this.

All of the things Colin said about her were likely true. And it was true she attempted to steer him with flirtation. And it was probably true she'd given her body to men in exchange for money. But these things warred with the other things he knew about her: Her expression when she spoke about her husband and how he died. How her hands knotted when she talked about wanting friends. Her leap to the defense of Margaret Lanford and her tea cakes, even after what the audience had done to her. And then there was her beauty, and he seemed to find something new in it every time he saw her. All of this had wound tighter and tighter and tighter. Until the auction ...

Watching what the audience had done to her had been unbearable.

Colin was right, of course:

He *had* lost his head today.

Possibly the first time in history Adam Sylvaine had ever done such a thing. It had been as reflexive as defending himself against a blow.

It wasn't as though he had five pounds to spare.

"My mother is proud of you, you know, Adam. Genuinely. She thinks you might just be the dawn of a new age of respectability for the Everseas, never mind that Genevieve managed to marry a duke. 'Imagine—my nephew, a vicar, and an excellent one, too.' 'We're glad we gave the living to him, when there were so many other choices.' She goes on like that, she really does."

"I'm grateful," Adam said shortly. Abstractedly.

He was. He always would be.

But never had the yoke of his own respectability chafed so completely.

They sat in thoughtful silence a moment. And then Adam looked up.

"Do you want to know the worst of it, Colin? I did lie."

Colin looked at him sharply.

"I *don't* like ginger cake."

There was a beat of silence.

"Splendid," Colin said mildly. "I'll just take this off your hands then, won't I?" He scooped the basket toward him with one arm.

Adam was irrationally tempted to forbid it. But he pocketed the five pounds. He would donate it to the church fund.

"Tell me if it's edible, so I can compliment the countess."

"I will. And oh—I almost forgot. This arrived

for you. He gestured to a package tied up in string on the sideboard. "Sent over by Mrs. Sneath. A gift from her niece, apparently."

Adam slipped off the paper and string.

He beheld a pristine new cushion. Surrounded by exquisitely embroidered cornflowers were the words:

Love Thy Neighbor.

MRS. SNEATH KEPT an elderly barouche, and it was in this that she, Evie, Miss Amy Pitney, and Miss Josephine Charing were carried to the outskirts of Pennyroyal Green the following morning, past Miss Marietta Endicott's Academy for Young Ladies, past the remains of the gypsy encampment, down a road that grew increasingly rutted, until they took a turn into a little valley.

The three women sat opposite Evie, who sat alone alongside the basket of tea cakes she'd purchased for ten pounds. She hadn't yet sampled them. She suspected the O'Flahertys would have a greater use for them, anyhow.

They now stood outside what an optimist might call a cottage; though if not for the smoke spiraling from the chimney, it could almost as easily pass for a haystack. She suspected it had been built shortly after The Conqueror had landed on English shores though a few modern conveniences, like the chimney and a few windows, had been added since. The thatched roof appeared to have contracted mange. The fence skirting the tamped-earth yard was fashioned partly of weathered boards, but primarily of what looked like the sort of long branches shaken from trees in storms. It was splintering in some places and collapsing in others. A sorry, weathered barn sagged behind the house, as did a sorry, weathered mule. Another building, which was likely meant to hold crops, was picturesquely deteriorating in the distance behind it. Enormous, leafless, oak trees ringed all of it.

A scattering of feral-looking chickens alternately stabbed at the ground with their beaks and eyed the visitors menacingly from the corners of their tiny eyes.

"Do you hear that?" whispered Josephine.

They all held very still.

Faintly, Eve heard a high-pitched sound, almost like a chorus of mosquitoes.

"And *that's* from a distance," Amy Pitney said. "Just wait until you get closer. It's screaming. *That* is what Joshua should have brought to the walls of Jericho. A few days of this, and the soldiers would have turned tail and run."

"There are *six* of them," Josephine confided on a whisper. Though why they were whispering when they were easily fifty feet away from the cottage door baffled Evie. "Possibly seven. Or there could be eighteen. They never hold still, so it's difficult to count, and their mother is so tired she can barely finish a sentence, so I've never been able to get a clear answer. They're all running about like dervishes. They *climb* things. And leap about. And scream. Oh, how they scream. And it's *everywhere* sticky. With jam and . . . things I don't want to think about."

"*She* won't even go in the house," Amy said contemptuously, looking at Josephine. "Not after what happened that first time."

"I don't see *you* diving in, either, Miss Nose-in-the-Air."

"At least I never wept like a baby."

"You'd weep, too, if one of the little beasts yanked the combs straight from your hair! I've such fine hair and a tender scalp. Then again, you wouldn't know about that sort of thing. All of your hair went to your *eyebrows*."

Immediately, the two of them were bristling like a pair of cats, scarlet with rage and stiff-legged.

Evie remained poised to intervene in case more hair-pulling ensued.

"You're only here because you want to impress the *vicar*," Amy finally said with low venom.

Josephine gasped. "As if he'd look at you! Do you think he wants a slew of beetle-browed children?"

"At least *I've* an actual suitor."

"Because your papa bought him for you!" Her voice was truly raised now.

"Enough," Mrs. Sneath barked. "You will not discuss the vicar in those terms. He is a good man of unshakable morals whose head cannot be turned by such frivolous matters."

She was speaking to the girls, but she aimed the comment at Evie.

Evie interjected coolly, "Do you want to know a secret about handsome men, ladies? Not just the ordinary handsome men, but the ones that stop the very heart?"

They froze in place, swiveled, arrested by the poetry, and by the momentous notion that she was about to lift the lid on her Pandora's box of knowledge.

"Yes or no, please."

They nodded eagerly.

Mrs. Sneath was instantly nervous. "Perhaps you ought to tell *me* first, Lady Ware—"

"Shhhh," Josephine said abruptly. Riveted.

It was Mrs. Sneath's turn to bristle.

"Most of them, the truly magnificent-looking ones, find it irresistible when you pretend you aren't interested in them at *all*. They're accustomed, you see, to the attention. They expect it. I've a word you should clutch to your bosoms: 'aloof.' This sort of man finds it fascinating. And heaven knows you oughtn't *fight* over a man. For shame! You deserve to win him on your own merits."

That was fundamentally true. Though she suspected if the vicar knew she'd just told them to be aloof, he'd be abjectly grateful.

"Really, Lady Wareham, is *now* the time for such a lesson?" Mrs. Sneath objected.

"It's just, Mrs. Sneath, that it's distressing to see your excellent cause undermined by such division between these worthy young ladies, when men are often the cause of problems in the world. Managing them, I do believe, is the key to peace on earth."

A number of conflicting emotions rippled over Mrs. Sneath's features as she contemplated the ways in which Evie had likely managed men.

"You . . . do have a way with words, my dear," Mrs. Sneath approved conditionally. She seemed poised to spring and clap a hand over Evie's mouth should something too notorious seem about to slip from it.

"Where is their father? Mr. O'Flaherty?" Eve asked. "Is he home?"

The chickens appeared to be coming closer.

Nonchalantly studying them out of the corners of
their tiny, evil eyes.

They all took a shuffling step backward.

"John O'Flaherty? If he's not at the pub he's flat
on his back somewhere snoring off inebriation beneath a tree. He's often simply missing for weeks at
a time. No one knows where he gets to. He's an unpleasant man, to be certain. I think Mrs. O'Flaherty
and the children are afraid of him."

Evie would have wagered her life on it. She knew
all too well that kind of fear.

"Well, he must come home now and again if
there are this many children inside. Are they all
his?"

The girls flushed slowly pink again and looked
in a variety of different directions. At their feet, up
to the sky, at the tree in the yard.

Mrs. Sneath interjected hurriedly, "Really, Lady
Wareham. Is it appropriate to speculate to unmarried young ladies—"

Evie rolled her eyes. "Oh, for heaven's sake.
Where do you think children *come from*?"

"They're all the spit of him. Ginger hair and
voices that could pierce the eardrums of the dead.
Even the baby. Perhaps especially the baby."

Evie's estimation of Miss Amy Pitney rose with
this report. But *did* this young lady with the stern
brows yearn for the vicar?

"She's a good girl," added Mrs. Sneath pointedly. "Mary O'Flaherty is. Only the one man for
her." Deciding perhaps that Evie needed to be reminded of her place.

"Of course she is," Eve said. "And everyone
knows that good girls are always justly rewarded."

Everyone missed her irony.

Miss Amy Pitney cleared her throat. "Lady Wareham . . . since we've all done our best to help the O'Flahertys and haven't succeeded in the way that we'd hoped, we thought you might have a go."

Six eyes regarded her, glittery with challenge again.

Evie studied their faces for clues as to what *sort* of challenge might await her but saw none.

Honestly, given all the other things she'd experienced in a lifetime, surely the O'Flahertys and their multitudes of children would scarcely rank. It could hardly be dangerous? Surely these women wouldn't allow her to walk into a lion's den?

"I'll give it a go," she said brightly. "I'll consider it a *privilege*."

"Wonderful!" Mrs. Sneath boomed. "As we've forgotten the food and clothing we intended to bring for the children, we'll return for you in a few hours."

"You'll . . ." She froze.

The three women were wearing expressions of studied innocence.

"I see. Very well. I'll just get started, shall I?"

Eve took a few cautious steps forward into the yard, through the gate.

She paused. She took three more.

Looked over her shoulder.

The three women waved gaily at her.

So she squared her shoulders, took a deep breath, and marched confidently, if not speedily, forward, flicking her skirts at the menacing chickens, who stalked her toes like footpads in a St. Giles alley.

She slowed as she approached the door, however.

The windows were all but obscured with the smut of cooking smoke, as though no one had scrubbed them for years, or as though whoever was inside didn't want anyone on the outside to peer in.

And the high-pitched sound was . . . definitely louder. Definitely discernible now as voices.

When she was about the length of her own body away from the door, Josephine called:

"And—oh! They've a dog!"

Just as a huge, yellow dog burst from the house.

Evie stared into the gaping, slavering maw punctuated with white teeth and emitting ear-shattering bays and knew these were the bowels of Hell.

"Christ Almighty!" she shrieked.

She tried to run from her doom, but the dog lunged and reared and planted its huge paws on her shoulders, holding her fast. Its breath was like the devil's own privy.

It painted her face from her chin to her forehead with a big wet pink tongue. Twice.

It wasn't about to get a chance to do it again.

"Take liberties with *me*, will you, you great . . . fetid . . . beast?" she growled, and gave it a hearty push. It fell from her shoulders, issuing deafening woofs and slapping a huge, fernlike tail like a club against her calves, body wiggling with the sheer ecstasy of having a new person to sniff. Which it tried to do, both from the front of Evie and from the back. She found herself rotating in circles like a dog chasing its tail to avoid the nose.

She heard giggling from out near the fence. And then the jingle of tack and the crunch of the sound of hooves and carriage wheels pulling away.

Finally, she was able to plunge a hand into her basket of tea cakes. She hurled one across the yard.

"Fetch!" she implored the dog.

The tea cake ricocheted off one of the oak trees and slammed into the dog's great head.

It yelped in surprise and retreated, then sat down and regarded her with soulful betrayal.

Well. That rather answered questions about Mrs. Lanford's tea cakes.

Chapter 11

"FINE WATCHDOG YOU ARE," SHE SAID WITH DIS-gust. She got hold of its ruff and led it up to the door, while it wiggled and thumped its tail all the way there. It was thin, she saw now, and she wondered that it hadn't helped itself to a meal of chickens. Or maybe it had, and that's why the chickens were so resentful.

"She has a big voice and a big body, so not many learn she's a rank coward and a bit of a slut, aren't you, Molly?"

The dog grinned up at Mary O'Flaherty, who stood at the door. She was wearing a faint smile and an apron splashed with what appeared to be an infinite variety of effluvia over a faded-muslin morning dress, clearly washed, ironed, picked out, and resewn any number of times. A baby was in the crook of one arm and a small child clung to her hip. Both were sniffling, teetering on the brink of sobs.

And now that the dog had ceased its woofing, Evie heard it now: the screaming.

It wasn't so much screaming as simultaneous laughter, bellows, shouts, kicks, singing, and sobbing. Punctuated by thumps and thwacking sounds.

Evie smiled slightly. And tightly. She knew the sound well. Her own childhood had sounded very like it.

She released the dog, and it bounded in to join the melee.

One peer around the shoulder of Mrs. O'Flaherty told her the house was chaos itself.

Her heart raced; every cell in her body hummed a warning. She knew it wasn't rational, and yet the feeling was a bit like swimming back toward a wrecked ship after one has at last safely reached the shore. She'd tried never to look back at her past since she and her brothers and sisters had escaped from Killarney to London in a tinker's cart so many years ago. And here it was, so familiar, it was as though she'd never left.

"I never seem to catch up once a new baby arrives," Mary said wearily. "I would apologize, but it speaks for itself, doesn't it?"

Evie didn't deny it. "From where do you hail, Mary? I'm a Killarney girl, myself. My name is Evie Duggan."

"Ah, a Duggan from Killarney? Did ye perhaps know the Duncans?"

"Doesn't everybody? I assume you mean the John Duncans."

Mary smiled. "Oh, aye. But they said ye was a countess. The ladies from the committee."

"I am. And who says a girl from Killarney can't do well for herself?"

Mary O'Flaherty smiled wearily. Her hair, a faded red and curly, was raked back into a knot, but bits of it straggled down and clung to her cheeks, and she'd deep purple crescents beneath her eyes, and her skin had the drawn, grayish cast of someone who'd likely not had a decent night's sleep in many a year. Everything about her face was narrow: her mouth, the bridge of her nose, her blue eyes. "Well, *I've* come up in the world, as ye can see."

Evie decided she liked Mary.

But stepping all the way into the cottage took a good quotient of her courage. It exerted such a potent association, part of her was certain she'd never escape it once she did. The smell and noise became one and crashed over her senses in a wave: that unmistakable *boy* smell, of feet and sweat and dirt, old food and dog and sour milk all mingled with the high-pitched, excited cacophony of children.

She plunged in, took a deep breath, and immediately employed one of the several useful things her brother Seamus had taught her:

She put two fingers in her mouth and gave a melee-shattering whistle.

The children froze, astonished, and stared at the interloper.

Long enough for her to count them, and to get a good look at the tableau. Including the baby and the toddler clinging to Mrs. O'Flaherty, there were seven of them. Three identical little boys and two girls, none older than eight years, all thin and pale and sharp-featured and topped with dazzling red hair. They were dressed presentably enough, or at least they were covered in clothing, but there didn't seem to be a single pair of shoes between them, and not one of them could be described as clean. This was abundantly clear even in the dim, smoky light of the room, which featured two beds, a hearth, a smoky stove, a quantity of mismatched wooden chairs that seemed to have all been tumbled to create a fort of some kind, dishes scattered across a scarred table and tipped over a frayed carpet, and a cat, who slept up on a high shelf. *Everything* wore a coat of dust and smoke—the curtains, the furniture, the counterpane, the hearth, the cat.

And then she noticed that all of the children were wearing what appeared to be crude, blunt, wooden swords—fashioned from oak sticks, no doubt—strapped to their hips. Two of the boys, about six years old if she were to guess, were wearing admiral's hats folded from old sections of broadsheet. They'd wound up a third smaller brother in twine from shoulders to hip, and he writhed like a caterpillar on a sagging settee. They'd been hovering over him and prodding him with their swords when she walked in.

"Halp!" he squeaked.

"Silence!" one of the boys hissed, and gave him a poke with a sword.

The littlest girl appeared to be cheering them on. The tallest girl was standing near the stove and stirring something in a kettle. She wore a sword on her hip, too.

Eve was reminded of a production she'd once participated in at the Green Apple Theater, which involved bawdy pirates. Inspiration struck—as it will occasionally in circumstances of dire need.

"I'll have your attention!" Evie snapped out sharply. "Right this instant!"

They whirled on her, surprised, and froze. Before they could rebel or stir or squeak, she demanded, in the frostiest, most stentorian, most intimidat-

ingly aristocratic voice she could muster, the kind
that carried to the backs of theaters:

"I'd like to speak to the captain of you children
at *once*."

This was met with wide-eyed, drop-jawed, per-
plexed silence.

"But . . . we've no captain," said one of the boys.
Sounding worried.

"Halp," whispered the tied-up boy.

"No *captain*?" She advanced into the room and
took a dark, frowning look around. "No *captain*?
We must remedy that at *once*. Quickly: Which one
of you is the oldest? Tell me now!"

All the heads swiveled toward the hearth.

"That be me." The little redheaded girl, her blue
eyes narrowed, hands on her hips.

"Your name?" Evie barked.

"Katharine."

With a pang, with a sense of vertigo that came
from looking back more than a dozen years, she
saw herself in that pinched white face. All the
bravado and fear and distrust, eyes that had seen
far too much for her age. She likely went to sleep
hungry, woke up afraid, did her best to help her
mother and avoid her father. But she still had a ca-
pacity for awe and hope, which flickered over her
face as she looked up at Evie and saw her face and
her fine clothes. But she drew a shutter down over
it quickly. Awe and hope made one vulnerable.
Katharine had already learned that, clearly.

It nearly broke Evie's heart.

She drew herself up, and announced, "I am the
Countess of Wareham, and word has reached me
that this particular crew needs a leader. And how

old are you, Katharine?" she kept her voice crisp. Though she yearned to reach out a hand, touch her bony shoulder.

"I am eight years old."

"Splendid. Just the right age for a captain. It's a good deal of responsibility, mind you. One must be very clever and brave and very much enjoy giving orders."

"I am," she declared, drawing herself up. "I do!" This was delivered with relish.

Very good. Pride and arrogance had their dangers, but were often so much better than diffidence when it came to surviving in the long run.

"As I am a countess, you will show me your curtsy, Katharine, and you young men—bow to me now!"

To her amazement, the ones who weren't tied up hopped down from the settee and bowed. And the girls curtsied. It was all a game to them now, and she needed to continue to make it feel that way.

"That will do for now," she said haughtily. "Though you all need practice. Remain standing, please."

"Listen, Captain Katharine." She knelt next to her. "This"— she lifted the St. Christopher's medal up from her bodice and pulled it over her head—"is the captain's medal." She looped it around Katharine's neck. "It will give you luck and help keep you safe if you hold it and pray, and it's a mark of authority. Don't allow it *ever* to leave you. Do you promise me? Do I have your solemn vow?"

Captain Katharine nodded, enthralled by the beautiful clean lady and the sudden gift of jewelry.

Evie stood again. "Now, the captain's job is to

rally the troops to make sure the ship is fit for sail
and protected against pirates and marauders at all
times, as well as to protect the babies in your care.
The HMS *O'Flaherty* must be *spotless*, mind you.
From floor to ceiling. And so must the proud mates
who sail her. How else will you properly serve your
liege mother? For she is your commander, and you
sail at her pleasure."

She gestured to Mary O'Flaherty, who had
taken a seat in a rocking chair, clutching the baby,
watching all of this with dazed wonder. She shot a
wry glance at Evie when she learned of her promo-
tion to queen. But even the baby and toddler had
gone silent, marveling at the brightly colored mad-
woman who'd burst into their house and begun
bellowing and gesturing.

"Now I shall appoint the ship's officers and
assign duties. But it will be up to you and your
queen to make sure they're done well and done
often. First: Untie your brother at once! You are a
crew now, and you will look after each other and
protect each other, not tie each other up. And for
your first command as a crew: Fetch me pails of
water, boys!"

WHEN ADAM ARRIVED at the O'Flaherty house an
hour later with a wagon of lumber and a few volunteers, he saw Miss Pitney, Miss Charing, and
Mrs. Sneath arrayed outside the fence, staring with
trepidation at the house.

He stuffed the jar of honey he'd brought into
his coat pocket and swung down from the wagon.
When he landed, the toe of his boot sent something
rolling, and he paused to look down.

It appeared to be a tea cake.

A second look told him that there were, in fact, three tea cakes on the ground.

"Good afternoon, ladies. What are we all looking at today?"

"Good afternoon, Reverend. She hasn't yet come out."

He wondered why the two young ladies, both of whom usually tripped over themselves to greet him, refused to meet his eyes. They seemed unusually aloof.

"You sent Lady Wareham in on her *own*? Did you leave her alone here?"

They didn't answer this though there was a good deal of foot shifting and hand-wringing and eye darting. So: Yes, they had. He stifled a surge of anger.

Miss Amy Pitney said, "It's just that the screaming seems to have stopped, and it's gotten very quiet. It's unnerving."

"Has anyone at *all* come out? And how did these"— he prodded a tea cake with his toe—"get here?"

"Well, two little boys *did* come out of the house carrying a pail. But they screamed "Pirates!" when they saw us and fired the tea cakes at us. One of them struck Amy in the side of the head."

"The largest target," whispered Josephine.

Amy rounded on her.

Mrs. Sneath. "We decided a tactical retreat might be best, and we were reassessing how we might approach safely."

But Adam had stopped listening. He scrambled for the house at a run, scattering the chickens and exciting the dog, who woke up from her nap beneath the tree and ran alongside him happily.

He paused outside the ajar door and listened, and heard . . . nothing at all.

For a moment, a vision of horror visited him: He imagined the room littered with unconscious bodies, a result of a tea-cake battle.

He nudged it cautiously open a foot more.

And blinked in shock.

The windows were flung open; the room was filled with light, and air circulated friskily. The faded rug had clearly been taken out, beaten within an inch of its life, and straightened nicely, the dishes had been collected and scrubbed and stacked, the hearth had been swept, the furniture righted, and the youngest girl was wielding a broom in the other part of the room, sending up luxurious clouds of dust.

One of the boys was scrubbing at the walls with a rag, making inroads into the gray layers of smoke, another was hard at work on a window, and the oldest girl, Katharine, was wearing an apron and stirring something that smelled almost appetizing simmering on a woodstove.

Every last one of them appeared to be tiptoeing as they went about it, and not one of them so much as hummed. And yet the humming sound persisted. Mrs. O'Flaherty was also asleep in her chair, mouth wide open, snoring softly, but that wasn't it; the toddler was asleep in his mother's lap, thumb inserted into his mouth.

It wasn't until he was deeper into the room that he saw Eve: she was standing near the window wearing a paper admiral's hat. She appeared to have a rag of some sort pinned around her dress, a makeshift apron, and she was holding the baby in the crook of one arm.

She was rocking and crooning softly,

> *"Oh, if you thought you'd never see*
> *The end of Colin Eversea*
> *Well, come along with me, lads,*
>   *come along with me . . ."*

A versatile song, that one, he had to admit.

She looked as though she'd been hard at work all morning, too: flushed and shiny-faced, and her hair was coming out of its pins. She sported what appeared to be two enormous muddy paw prints on each shoulder, like epaulets.

He froze. And drank in the sight.

Something about his motionlessness in a room humming with quiet activity alerted her. She glanced up and saw him. Something flared swift and hot in her eyes—a reaction, he suspected, to what she might have seen in his.

She ducked her head abruptly and seemed to lose her place in the song, and the rhythm of the baby rocking stalled. The baby stirred and fussed a bit, and she cooed and began again.

Then she glanced up again and smiled and held a finger to her lips and winked.

And resumed the "Lullaby of Colin Eversea."

> *The pretty lad was mighty bad . . .*

The baby yawned and waved a fist about, like a cheer.

Adam could have, in fact, stood there all day watching her, listening to the wildly inappropriate lullaby.

He liked *her* voice, too.

Alas, one of the little boys spotted him. He froze midscrub. And then bellowed:

"A marauder, Captain Kate!" He lunged for the tea cakes, levering his arm back. "We must protect the HMS *O'Flaherty*!"

"Put that down, Cedric," Eve said sternly, still on a hush. "He's the vicar, and you know it, and you will show him the same respect you show me."

"Which means you should bow to him," the oldest girl said, and glanced to Evie, enjoying her authority.

"Very good, Captain Kate. That's exactly what it means. Show him how beautifully you bow."

Cedric bowed, and Katharine curtsied, and all the other children bobbed and bent, too.

Adam was agog. He approached Evie gingerly, hating to disturb the harmony she'd achieved. He peered down into her arms with something like trepidation.

"It's a baby, Vicar. They're not *too* frightening once you get accustomed to them."

He looked up at her. "I know about babies," he said evenly.

She tipped her head curiously at his tone, narrowing her eyes a bit. Then returned them to the baby.

"Lady Wareham . . . How did you . . . ?" He gestured widely. He meant everything that had happened in the O'Flaherty house today.

She half smiled. Her eyes remained on the baby. "Well, in Killarney, there were eight of us in one room. One needed to compete for *everything*, you see, from food to a word from our da to a place in the bed where your brother's foot wouldn't go up your nose, because Seamus did like to sleep backward. I was the oldest, you see. I learned how to get what I needed when I needed it. And then I needed to mind the rest of them later on when . . ."

"Mind them?" He kept the question soft. Noncommittal. But his heart was beating strangely faster. As if he were reaching the end of the route drawn by a treasure map.

"Someone needed to, didn't they, when my parents were gone?" Almost absently, driftingly said. She kept her voice lulling, singsong, for the baby.

He asked a question he was almost certain he knew the answer to.

"Do you look after them still?"

It might have been one question too many. For a time, he thought she wouldn't answer. Her face had darkened a little.

But then she slowly lifted her head. And fixed him with an unreadable gaze. A hint of defiance in it. He noted that what looked like a child's smudged fingerprint now mingled with her freckles.

"Of course," she said softly. "Will I let them go hungry now?"

Their gazes fused.

And now he understood the source of the vulnerability that peeked through the gloss of her exterior: It was her family. For when one loved, one was vulnerable.

"Of course not," he agreed softly.

She returned her eyes to the baby, and her face softened with something like yearning, an ache, and he stood and drank in that expression the way flowers take in sun. He wanted to ask more questions, and more, and more. But everything about her posture now, her closed face, forbade it.

He risked a look at the baby then. It was terrifyingly miniature, the baby, such a fragile thing to be surrounded by the chaos of this room. He knew all too well what a dangerous place the world could be for a new human. It gazed up at him in dazed wonderment, then furrowed its tiny brow, an expression he'd seen more than once on the faces of parishioners come a Sunday morning.

It was then they realized that Mrs. O'Flaherty had stirred from her chair and come to join them, smiling down at the baby.

"Go on and hold him, Reverend Sylvaine," she said gently.

Adam froze.

Evie looked up at Mrs. O'Flaherty, surprised.

"Go on," Mary insisted gently.

Adam exhaled and nodded shortly, like a man bracing himself for a surgeon's stitches.

So the countess gently transferred a warm, squirmy bundle into his arms.

Adam slowed his breath, as if he could slow time for the little one. He looked down fiercely into the tiny face. As if the weight of his solemnity, of his sheer desire to keep him safe would shelter and protect him. Just to be certain, he silent prayed for precisely that as he stood there, with the baby fitted warmly in his arms.

He was aware of Eve watching him. Clearly bemused. The faint, puzzled frown not unlike the baby's.

He inhaled deeply and exhaled a long breath, then gingerly gave the baby back to Mrs. O'Flaherty.

"He's wonderful, Mrs. O'Flaherty. Thank you. Congratulations," he said gently. "I'll see him for the christening?"

Adam turned around and walked out of the door, past all the preternaturally industrious O'Flaherty children.

Eve stared after him and frowned a little.

"Men can be so funny," she laughed softly. "Frightened of such a tiny thing."

"Oh, I don't think that's it, Lady Wareham." Mary shifted the baby to fit more comfortably in her arms as the toddler wobbled over to tug on Eve's skirts. "I don't think much frightens that man. It's just that I lost a baby last year at his age. He was very frail, the little one, and I knew he wouldn't be long for the world. He died right in our reverend's arms, took his last wee breath, as the reverend gave him the last rites."

Eve's breath snagged. That fierce expression on his face as he looked down at the baby . . . as though he was *daring* Harm to ever reach out its evil bony fingers for that child. For it would need to answer to him.

Shame heated her face. *They're* my *people, Lady Balmain.* Fiercely possessive, protective, unyielding. A man who would likely do nearly anything for those he loved.

So . . . strangely like her.

Just a vicar. And with those words she'd tried to reduce him to something manageable, maneuverable, understandable. She'd given no thought as to what the word truly meant. Or why his control was so necessary: It was in proportion to how much he felt and how much he needed to give day after day.

And once again, she felt like a flailing child, humbled and abashed.

How temptingly easy it was to imagine him as a father to a baby.

"Oh, Mary." Her voice cracked a little, faltered. "I'm so sorry. I do know what it's like . . . when I was young, you see, I've lost brothers and sisters . . ."

It was a perilous world for babies, especially when they grew up in cottages like this one. It was an inescapable fact of life.

Mrs. O'Flaherty nodded stoic acknowledgment. "I was so glad of him, Reverend Sylvaine. He was just lately come here to Pennyroyal Green, and new as a vicar, but never did I see any man so gentle. And so kind to me and mine in my suffering; somehow he made everything easier. But no one is untouched by the death of a little one. I wanted him to hold the new baby. To feel the new life after such a sad loss. There's always hope, aye?"

Such wisdom and generosity in the midst of chaos and fear. Eve couldn't speak through a tide of emotion.

"Aye," she agreed, finally, softly.

"Aye, we're lucky to have the vicar," Mary said, smiling softly down at the baby.

ONCE OUTSIDE, ADAM stalked past the chickens, over to the two ninnies and Mrs. Sneath, standing by their barouche.

"I think it's safe to go inside," he said mildly. "And there's plenty of work for everyone. There will be for some time."

"Did she survive, Vicar?" Mrs. Sneath sounded as somber as if he'd come to administer extreme unction.

He paused in thought for dramatic effect. Perhaps Lady Balmain's influence was rubbing off on him, as well. "Mrs. Sneath, I've provided a lost soul for you to reform. Now, do you recall how you'd once hoped to witness a miracle?"

"Before I die, it's my fondest hope, Vicar."

"Go inside. I think you'll find your prayers have been answered."

Chapter 12

"Ye look like ye've been tossed out of a carriage," Henny greeted Eve. "And then you rolled down a hill and came to a stop in a ditch. Did those women take you out into the woods and steal your reticule? I didna like the looks of the big one."

The big one being Mrs. Sneath. Henny was only partially joking. She and Mrs. Sneath had recognized something very similar in each other and had instantly treated each other with wary respect, the sort two master criminals might have for each other.

"Will you help me out of this dress, Henny? Do you think we can salvage it?"

Henny scrutinized her with an eye honed by long experience with all manner of clothes, from filmy, bawdy pirate costumes worn on the stage to the most glorious of evening gowns, including the one that had caused a balcony plummet. A triumph, that one, as far as Henny was concerned.

"And what is . . . did ye dance with a *dog*? Now that's one thing ye never did get up to at the Green Apple Theater stage. I wager there's money in it."

"There was indeed a dog!" Evie reminisced.

"I'll sponge the worst of the stains now and

really have a go at it on laundry day. But it may be fit for a day dress only from now on."

Henny was one of the few people she'd ever met who enjoyed doing laundry. She ruthlessly stirred and soaked and scrubbed and slapped and squeezed and tenderly coaxed her clothing into lasting for years.

And then she studied Evie shrewdly.

"Weeellll . . . ye're certainly cheerful for all that you look like the very devil, pawprints and all."

"You should have seen it, Henny. All was chaos. Seven little children and those women sent me in on my own and the place rivaled the worst tip you've ever seen, and I managed to rally them. I did! Do you remember the bit with the pirates at the Green Apple Theater? Well, I had an inspiration, and it worked. We cleaned it from top to bottom, but there's more work to do yet. We all had a *wonderful* time. I think I may have friends!"

Henny was watching her closely. "Mmm."

"And the vicar brought a crew of men, and they took down the fence and built a new one!"

Made thoughtful and subdued by her new knowledge of him, Eve had watched surreptitiously through the O'Flahertys' freshly cleaned windows as Reverend Sylvaine shed his coat and unbuttoned the top two buttons of his shirt and rolled his sleeves and gone at the fence with the three other men, all sinewy strength and shouting orders and sweat soaking through his shirt. She'd never known physical labor could be so thoroughly engrossing. She'd never known a man so unpretentious. So wholly who he was.

Maddeningly uncompromising, of course. But unpretentious.

"Do tell," Henny said knowingly.

Evie stopped her recitation.

"*What?*" she said irritably to Henny.

"You've a glow about you," Henny declared suspiciously. "That's what."

"It's likely sweat."

"Looks a wee bit like love."

Evie rolled her eyes. "You really ought not to touch the liquor during the day. And besides, what do you know about love?"

"More than you, as you willna let them get near yer heart. Ye nivver fall in love, ye fall in commerce."

Eve froze and glared terrifyingly at Henny. Sorely wounded.

Though it was entirely true.

Henny was unperturbed.

Eve stepped out of her dress and scooped it up and thrust it at her.

"And lucky for you *that* is; otherwise, I couldn't pay your wages, as if you've ever been of any real use."

"Ye *might* allow yerself to give it a try. Just fer the variety, m'lady. Everyone should feel it at least once. You'll know then what makes life worth living."

Evie was so surprised, she found she had no reply. Henny knew her better than anyone, but she so seldom played that hand. And she was in one of her maddening, inscrutable self-righteous moods.

And she went still, breath hitched again when

she recalled the expression on the reverend's face when she'd glanced up from the baby. Yearning shot through a ferocity bordering on possessiveness. There and gone, as if it had been a product of shifting light.

This was a man who did nothing by halves. He felt things, or he did not.

And she closed her eyes and allowed the memory of that moment to possess her: It was all light and exhilarating fear and newness. She felt, for God's sake, like a baby bird perched on the edge of a nest. She'd never even known she had wings.

"And there is more mail for you," Henny added pointedly. For she believed Evie's siblings were barnacles. Charming barnacles, particularly in the case of Seamus, but barnacles nevertheless. "I fetched it from the shop. I think Mr. Postlethwaite might be sweet on me." She said this with considerable smug satisfaction.

It wasn't impossible. Henny exerted a certain fascination for many men—her presence was undeniably unforgettable. She'd boasted more than one unlikely conquest over the years, including a coalmonger, a butler, and the earl's man of affairs.

Eve examined the post.

An icy little fingertip of fear touched the back of her neck.

Two more letters, from Seamus and Cora. This was worrisome. Clearly, they'd been sent very soon after the others since Evie had only just replied to their first letters. Seamus had promised he'd cause no more incidents requiring political intervention. And so far he'd kept it.

It was Cora and the children she worried about most.

My Dearest Sister,

Having a job is a wondrous thing. I've met a woman. She is an angel fallen to earth, and she thinks I have more money than I do. This could be because I told her that I did. I'd hoped you would make her fondest wish come true.

I jest! But she is wonderful, and I feel quite strange around her. I wonder if this might be love. Is it uncomfortable, love? Do you know? Does it itch?

Once again, I jest. I do humbly look forward to anything you wish to donate, however. Long to see you, too. Love to you and to Henny

P.S. they're still talking about you in London. Not at all flatteringly.

Seamus was forever meeting angels fallen to earth. The fact, however, that he'd written about it straightaway was a trifle suspicious. She wondered if she ought to worry whether the next letter would announce a wife. And then a child. And then another mouth to feed.

From Cora:

Timothy hasn't been home for two nights. Elspeth is teething. The baby looks like you. Miss you. Much love.

Oh, Christ.

It was just the two nights, she told herself. Her sister's husband could still come home.

And yet fear spread its ice into her belly.

She made "he could still come home" a prayer as she stared unseeingly out the window.

EVE'S FIRST OFFICIAL caller in Sussex arrived two days after her conditional triumph at the HMS *O'Flaherty.* Her footman brought the news to her.

"A Miss Josephine Charing is here to see you, Lady Wareham."

She instantly and gratefully abandoned the embroidery she was attempting to come to terms with, sucked on a bead of blood she'd managed to pinprick into her forefinger, and leaped to her feet.

"How do I look, Henny? Presentable?"

Henny dropped the mending she'd been attending, did a swift study of Eve, then whipped a fichu from her apron pocket and thrust it at her. Eve hurriedly tucked it into the bodice of her day dress.

"I'll go be a maid now, shall I?" Henny said, pleased for her. She hurried off.

Eve gave her shoulders a shake, straightened her spine, and turned to the footman.

"Send her in, please."

It was some time before Miss Charing appeared, for she was placing one foot carefully in front of the other, as if the floor itself was lava, or as if she didn't want to slip and possibly get *iniquity* on the hem of her dress. Her head was swiveled slowly to and fro, taking in tile and fixtures and staircase with nervous, wide-eyed wonder.

"Good morning, Miss Charing. I keep all of my

paramours on the third floor, so you needn't fear you'll see any here."

Miss Charing gave a start. "Oh, do you? Do they mind?"

"Oh, for heaven's sake. No. I do not. The house is resoundingly empty, and I'm happy for the company." She smiled invitingly. "Who has *time* for paramours when the poor of Sussex need our help?"

"Of . . . of course," Miss Charing agreed weakly, after an uncertain moment. "I imagine paramours can be . . . demanding." She said this almost hopefully.

"Sometimes. The wise woman knows how to manage them, however."

She smiled warmly to make sure Miss Charing knew she was jesting.

Miss Charing had eyes the color of cornflowers and knew it, as the ribbon on her bonnet matched them exactly. She had soft, blunt features in a pleasingly round face, a face as comfortable as a pillow. Loose blond curls fringed her forehead.

"Would you like tea? Perhaps a scone? I believe they're fresh."

"Thank you, Lady Wareham, you are too kind."

Evie nodded the request to the waiting footman.

"My mother doesn't know I'm here. She's not certain she entirely approves of you." This was said as though Miss Charing herself wasn't entirely certain whether she approved of Eve.

"Now, that is a pity. I wonder what will tip the scales in the favor of approval?"

Miss Charing missed the irony entirely.

"Perhaps when she meets you. I'm certain she will like you. There will be an Assembly in a fortnight, you see, with music and dancing, and there's talk of inviting you."

"*Is* there talk? How delightful." More irony. Despite herself, she was charmed by Miss Charing's faith in her appeal.

That was when they both became aware of a faint thudding sound, accompanied by a clattering and jingling sound, which grew louder and came inexorably closer.

Miss Charing went still. And then surreptitiously craned her head to look about.

"Lady Balmain . . . do you hear . . ."

Moments later, Henny thudded into the room, bearing a pot of tea and cups and a plate stacked with divine-smelling scones, and Miss Charing shrank wide-eyed into her chair and froze, the way a hedgehog might when confronted with an unfamiliar predator.

Henny settled the tray down with a rattle, beamed approvingly at the two of them, then marched out again.

Miss Charing stared after her long after she was completely out of sight. Perhaps making sure she was truly gone and didn't intend to return.

"That's Henny," Eve said sweetly by way of explanation. "Will you pour?"

"I'd be pleased to," Miss Charing said weakly, politely.

They sipped in silence for a moment.

"I must confess, Lady Balmain, that there is a reason for my call today. You told Mrs. Sneath that you knew a thing or two about getting what you want. And that if we needed advice about men, you might be willing to share what you know."

"I did indeed say that."

"The thing is . . . I should . . . like to captivate a man."

"An admirable goal," Eve approved crisply. Probably somewhat heretically, she thought belatedly. Miss Charing's mother likely had good reason not to entirely approve of her.

"I have never before captivated one, to my knowledge. How does one *know*?"

Eve was tempted to say, *Gifts of jewelry are an excellent sign.* "Well," she began carefully, "it often depends on the man in question."

Miss Charing inhaled at length, seeming to suck courage from the room. And then she exhaled, wringing her hands.

"It's the . . . Reverend Sylvaine, you see."

She said his name with a sort of restrained, exquisite torment. Eve suspected his name was frequently said in just the same tone all over Pennyroyal Green.

Miss Charing rushed on. "And I do think his sermon the other morning . . . Love thy neighbor? . . . Well, I suspect *I* may have been the inspiration. Because he always smiles when he greets me. Have you seen his smile? It's lovely, don't you think?"

Eve hesitated. His smiles, the varieties she'd seen so far, were very good, indeed.

"I can see how one might think so," she allowed carefully.

"And there's his face, of course," Miss Charing said matter-of-factly. "One never tires of looking at it. I imagine you've seen your share of handsome faces in London, so perhaps you haven't noticed."

This was true. She'd scarcely noticed much about the vicar's looks.

Apart, perhaps, from the dimple. And the blue eyes.

The shape of his mouth, the myriad subtle colors in his hair, the shoulders.

The forearms.

"I expect he might be considered handsome," she agreed noncommittally.

And the thighs, she remembered vividly, suddenly. And with that she stopped breathing a moment.

"And he never fails to thank me for the work I do with Mrs. Sneath. So *polite*!" She said this the way another woman might say, 'And he's so rich!' "But I'm not entirely certain, you see. I thought you might be able to help me know for sure."

A number of conflicting impulses competed for her attention, none of them charitable, all of them mischievous and unworthy and really quite surprising, given that she had allegedly entirely given up on the notion of men. A habit of supremacy, she supposed: She was used to winning them.

She forced her sense, not her *senses,* to make the ruling on how to proceed. It was so counter to what she wanted to do that she felt nearly virtuous.

"Well . . . let's have a think about this. Does the Reverend Sylvaine behave differently from other young men when he's near you?"

"It's very difficult to notice other young men when he's about, so I fear I'm not certain," Miss Charing said apologetically.

"Allow me to try to explain. Do any young men seem to . . . lose their ability to speak around you?"

She considered this. "Mr. Simon Covington, perhaps. Goes silent as the tomb when I'm near. But Miss Amy Pitney says it's because I don't allow anyone else to get a word in. She thinks she's *so clever.* A pity for her that 'clever' is her best quality. She thinks she can fascinate the vicar with talk of *botany.*" She wrinkled her nose.

"I ask, because if a man doesn't immediately commence with flattery, another way to know if you've captivated him if he seems to be a bit overwhelmed by your presence. At a loss for words. Intoxicated by your beauty. That sort of thing."

Miss Charing slowly mouthed the words *Intoxicated by your beauty* to herself, as if they were a delicious new delicacy.

She mulled this. "The vicar once seemed to all but run from me at an Assembly earlier this year. I was talking and talking—I told him about the preserves my mother and I were putting up, you see—and suddenly he moved away very quickly, for he said he had pressing business. Could that perhaps be construed as overwhelmed?"

"After a fashion," Eve allowed cautiously.

"Most of the time, I rather lose *my* ability to speak around him," she said glumly.

Something for which he might just be grateful, Eve suspected.

"And then when I do recover it, I cannot seem to stop speaking."

She thought of the flare in his eyes as she stood in the O'Flahertys' house. Yes, in her way, Miss Charing had described the vicar in a nutshell: He had the potent ability to make even her speechless. And she could imagine his frozen panic in the face of a babbler. He hadn't the patience for babbling; he was a man of economy.

"*Do* you think my beauty is intoxicating?" Miss Charing asked artlessly.

"The right man is bound to think so," Evie said diplomatically.

"Well, that sounds true," Josephine sounded heartened. "I'm certainly pretty *enough*. Compared to some girls. Who have rich fathers. Who needn't be at *all* charming in order to attract a suitor." She said this darkly. Then she confessed despairingly. "It's just . . . I've no hope of leaving Pennyroyal Green, you see, Lady Balmain; I will never have a London season. I've no fortune. I cannot travel far, and my mother fears for my prospects. I cannot get a rich man to look at me with any seriousness, but the vicar isn't rich, now, is he? And I should like to marry for love."

Marry for love. A luxury for a girl like Miss Charing, whose very life depended on marrying, period. Evie half wanted to shake some sense into her. Her sister Cora had married for love, and she had six babies and a husband who seemed to be teetering on the brink of leaving her if he hadn't left already. Her mother had married for love, and Evie had lived the consequences of her mother's decision her whole entire life. Love, in fact, was for Evie a bit like London was for Miss Charing: a land she couldn't afford to visit.

And yet.

"Ye ought to try it. Just for the variety," Henny had said.

As if it wasn't as perilous as walking a St. Giles alley at night.

"I should like to captivate the vicar," Josephine concluded. "Do you suppose you can help?"

Evie smiled brightly, all the while thinking, *Imagine* the folly of trying to make that man do something he doesn't want to do.

"I will tell you a secret, Miss Charing."

Miss Charing leaned forward breathlessly.

"Be *yourself*. And if you focus on finding something to appreciate in every man, and make certain they know it, they will all find you fascinating. They'll compete for your attention. You might find yourself spoiled for choice. You might find yourself seeing them in a different light, and might fall in love with a quality you didn't notice before."

Miss Charing sat back hard in her chair, quite struck dumb by the profundity of this. Her eyes were wide as she silently took this in.

"Do you think so? Really? Even the vicar?"

Evie stifled a sigh.

"I just gave you one of my closely guarded secrets," Evie said, which didn't answer Miss Charing's question.

"Thank you, Lady Wareham," she all but gushed. "Do you know, Mama said the women of the town were worried about their husbands and the single men of Pennyroyal Green when such a notorious countess took Damask Manor. But I told them you'd married an earl, for heaven's sake, and you were a widow now—what use would you have for their husbands? Or a vicar, for that matter?"

"Oh, I've quite given up on men *entirely* in favor of giving advice about them," Evie assured her. "I've no use at all for them. And thank you for coming to my defense."

"Mrs. Sneath will be happy to hear it!" Miss Charing said delightedly. "And you're welcome. I hope to see you at the Assembly after all. Perhaps you can tell me whether I'm following your advice correctly."

Chapter 13

E<small>VE HAD ONLY JUST SEEN</small> J<small>OSEPHINE OUT AND WAS</small> ready to take up her embroidery again when the footman reappeared.

"You've another visitor, my lady. A Miss Amy Pitney."

"Well." Eve wasn't entirely surprised. "Do send her in."

Beaming, Henny leaped up, whisked away Miss Charing's teacup and replaced it with a clean one, then made herself scarce.

Miss Amy Pitney appeared rather more briskly than Miss Charing had, her slippers clacking confidently along the marble. She likely lived in a house as fine if not finer.

"Good day, Lady Balmain. I hope you don't mind my calling upon you."

She said it as though there was never any doubt she'd be gratefully received.

"I'm delighted to see you, Miss Pitney. Would you like some tea? It's fresh."

"I would, thank you."

Eve poured for the two of them.

She did rather have her nose in the air, Eve thought, amused. But she suspected the demeanor was compensation for the fact that she knew she wasn't pretty, and she'd decided hauteur would give her presence. But she wasn't *unattractive.* Her face was long, her chin square, her eyes dark and clever and darting beneath those severe, abundant brows. Her green walking dress exquisitely suited her coloring and was painstakingly fashionable, from the number of flounces at the hem to the color of the trim.

She looked about curiously. Her eyes settled on the portrait over the mantel.

"I haven't the faintest idea who that is," Evie admitted. "I was considering giving him a name."

Miss Pitney smiled at that. But she was tense, and the corners of her mouth couldn't seem to reach very high.

"I was very impressed with your work with the O'Flaherty children, Lady Wareham," she began coolly. She sounded as though she were interviewing a governess.

Evie slowly hiked a brow.

And said nothing. Deciding Miss Pitney could benefit from a little humbling. And she'd recently learned the effectiveness of a little strategic silence from a man who used it like a weapon.

Miss Pitney had the grace to flush.

"You see, I've a reason for calling today. You did say to Mrs. Sneath that you had some experience getting what you want, and that you'd be delighted to share what you know about men."

"I certainly did say that."

She inhaled. Clearly she was tormented by what she was about to say next. She exhaled.

"I'm not pretty," she said matter-of-factly, on a

rush. She raised her chain arrogantly. "Not like some people who shall remain nameless. I have long since come to terms with the fact that I must rely on my wit and intelligence—unlike other featherheads, who shall remain nameless—and my fortune for suitors. I think perhaps I might appreciate them more as a result. Unlike others, who shall remain nameless, who have been careless with the *affections of others.*"

Her voice escalated toward the end of the sentence. She clapped her mouth shut and flushed, surprised by her own outburst.

So Miss Pitney was a girl of hidden passions.

She wondered if Simon Covington, the young man rendered speechless by Miss Josephine Charing, was the subject of them. Or whether she was about to be subjected to more conversation about the vicar's appeal.

"I've a suitor who seems very sincere in his affections. But he's handsome, you see. Very handsome. And I should like to—"

"Miss Pitney, may I make a suggestion?"

She hiked that obstinate chin, peeved at the interruption. "If you must."

"Some of the most famous courtesans have been, shall we say, not traditionally attractive. Charm is an essence, not a façade."

Miss Pitney went motionless. Then mouthed, "Charm is an essence, not façade," to herself, fascinated.

"Believe in your own appeal, and it will radiate. Men will be as moths to flames."

This might have been a bit of an exaggeration.

But Miss Pitney took this in for a good while.

And her face radiated hope, and she was lovely in that moment, the way that hope can make one lovely.

"Even the . . . vicar?"

She'd evidently decided to aim high with her new knowledge.

She rushed on. "He is a clever man, and I feel certain he can see beneath surfaces. I always like to have a topic ready to discuss, you see, when it comes to men. He comes to our house for dinner at least once a month—my father is the doctor here in town, Lady Wareham—and we've chatted about botany. A lovely chat, for there's just a small parcel of land behind the vicarage, part of the living, he's working, and . . . well, then he gave the sermon about loving thy neighbor, the other morning, and his voice is so very *confiding*. And I felt as though . . ." She stopped and gave a rueful smile. "Then again, I'm certain every woman in the church thought he was speaking directly to them."

Thus demonstrating that she was indeed clever.

"An optimistic interpretation of the sermon, perhaps, on the part of the women of Pennyroyal Green," Eve suggested diplomatically. "It's lovely to hear a man speak kindly, when husbands tend to take their wives for granted."

"When one is overlooked with great consistency, one becomes observant, Lady Wareham, and I suppose I am. Perhaps *you* didn't make that mistake about the sermon as you've known so . . . many men . . . and he might not seem exceptional to you."

She paused, perhaps hoping to be treated to a discussion of the many men.

Eve hadn't made that mistake about the vicar because she'd been *sleeping*. But Miss Pitney again had a point. "Since my husband the earl died, I find I don't think very much about men one way or the other," she decided to say. With a wistful smile.

She could have sworn Amy Pitney stifled a sigh of relief. Eve was certain Miss Pitney would ensure every woman in Pennyroyal Green heard about it by telling, for instance, Mrs. Sneath.

"Your suitor, Miss Pitney . . . do you care for him?"

Amy fidgeted in thought, her nails tapping, *chink chink chink*, against the side of her teacup. "I do," she said softly, almost wonderingly, with a little laugh. "At least I think I do. He's very charming and persuasive . . . he has such lovely manners. I hardly dare hope he genuinely finds *me* appealing. It's nothing he says or does in particular, mind you, that makes me uncertain, just something I fear. I ought to be grateful for the attentions, but . . . shouldn't one wish to marry for love?"

Eve knew more than a little something about being desired for something other than her engaging personality.

"How do you know when a man is sincere, Lady Wareham? I'd hoped you'd be able to meet him and tell me what you think of him. I've been disappointed before, you see . . ."

How did one know if a man was sincere? This was an excellent question. Eve mulled it in silence, allowed images to drift into her mind. One answer was, "when they win you in a card game and marry you, to the shock of everyone." Myriad men had sincerely wanted to get her into bed; myriad men had sincerely wanted her simply because other men did. But the truest answer, she realized was: when he plays no games at all. When he doesn't know how to flirt, and merely says what he's thinking, and doesn't judge. When flattery makes him squirm, and epithets make him laugh, and you want to tell him things, and he's too busy building fences and comforting people and the like to treat romance as a toy.

Then you know a man is altogether sincere.

"Sincere men are very rare, indeed," she said softly. "If I'm fortunate enough to be invited to the Assembly, I will of a certainty tell you what I think of him, Miss Pitney. But please do believe in your own appeal."

"Thank you, Lady Wareham."

This girl, thought Eve, might very well become a genuine friend.

Eve walked Miss Pitney to the door, then walked with her as far as the arbor to wave her off.

She watched her go.

And then paused and inhaled deeply and sighed contentedly, not at all dissatisfied with the morning as it had progressed so far. She tipped her head back. Enormous clouds tented her overhead, and the sun pushed its way through them, turning them a luxurious nacre color. A long spade leaned against a bench, left by the gardener, who was no doubt filling in vole holes or whatever it was gardeners did. Perhaps I'll become one of those women who become passionate about roses, she mulled. Since I clearly will never become passionate about embroidery.

She thrust her arms up in a stretch and was

about to turn for the house when a rustling sound froze her. She turned cautiously.

All at once, one of her shrubberies began shaking violently.

She scrambled, stumbling backward with a stifled shriek. And then froze in helpless horror, hand to her throat, as it swayed to and fro, very much as though it was attempting to tear up its roots and charge at her.

She lunged for the spade and swung it up over her shoulder, poised to beat the devil out of it.

The shrubbery gave one final heave and out popped the vicar.

He brushed himself off nonchalantly.

The spade slipped out of her hands and clattered to the ground. "The *devil* . . ."

She glared at him. Her entire body vibrated with her thudding heart.

"No, not the devil," he said mildly. "Are you disappointed?" He grinned at her. "I am. You didn't shriek at me in Irish. Or say 'bloody.'"

She was sorely tempted to say it *now*. The bloody man ought to have looked ridiculous emerging from a shrubbery. He contrived instead to look like a satyr, a forest God, tiny green leaves in his gold hair and scattered over his coat.

"Perhaps I'm getting accustomed to you leaping out of nowhere. I feel, however, I should ask why you were lurking in my shrubbery."

"I wasn't lurking. I dropped something, and it rolled in, and I had to go in to fetch it."

"Are you certain it wasn't just because you saw Miss Amy Pitney departing my house and decided to plunge in before she saw you?"

"It was serendipity, I'm sure, that I dropped something which rolled into your shrubbery just as Miss Amy Pitney was departing."

"God was on your side."

He offered her a crooked smile here. "Ah, but I have proof." He held out a jar. "It's plum jam. The women of Pennyroyal Green are generous with their . . . what did you call it at the auction? 'All that's best of womanhood, all that our great country is.' My larder overfloweth."

Evie took it graciously. "So delighted you can foist one of them off on me."

He laughed, and it was just what the day needed, that laugh, to make it completely beautiful. Her heart squeezed helplessly, and she went silent, blank and abashed.

"She's a clever girl," she said carefully, after a moment. "Amy."

"She is," he agreed neutrally.

"She likes *you*," she added slyly. Irrationally, she wanted to watch his face when she said it.

He sighed at length. "She does try much harder than she needs to. She doesn't need *botany* to fascinate. She's a lovely person in her own right."

"I'm beginning to suspect as much." She detected no yearning in his face and was ridiculously relieved.

"I have, in fact, had two callers today. And I've you to thank for it." She presented this with a certain triumph.

He paused. "I'm pleased to hear it." The softness in his voice threatened to make her blush. His face reflected her own pleasure.

"In fact, it may not surprise you to know, Reverend Sylvaine, that the young women of Penny-royal Green have been coming to me for advice on men."

He froze in the brushing of leaves from his coat.

"Have they now?" he said slowly, with great trepidation.

"I'm not at liberty to tell you who the other one was, and you hid in the shrubbery from one of them. I've told each of them that they merely need to be themselves to be admired. It's the most versatile advice I've ever received.

"And possibly the most dangerous I've ever given."

She smiled.

"I'm here because I've brought something else for you." He reached into his coat pocket and fished out a book. She heretically hoped it wasn't a Bible.

"*Greek Myths,*" she read when he handed it to her. "What a pity. I thought it might be conversational French."

She tested the results of this little statement with a flick up through her eyelashes.

He just shook his head slightly, with a faint smile. "I thought you might be particularly interested in the trials of Hercules."

She studied his face and found it inscrutable. Her heart sank just a very little. "Why do I have the suspicion that you're trying to tell me something, Vicar?"

"Nothing much eludes *you*, Lady Balmain. Mrs. Sneath confides that while you just may have purged your wicked impulses through hard labor and sacrifice—"

"Are you disappointed?"

"—but I've just come from a meeting with her regarding the Winter Ball. And I'm informed that the ladies have another project in mind for you. This afternoon, in fact. If you're available."

"Before I'm construed as 'acceptable.'" She tried to disguise the faintest little hint of aspersion in her voice.

"I've no doubt you'll make it look like child's play."

"Do you know what it is?"

"I do. I'd call it . . . the Nemean lion. If we're comparing this Herculean labors, that is. The Nemean lion posed as a beautiful woman to lure warriors into a cave, whereupon she turned into a lion, devoured them, then gave their bones to Hades."

There was a silence.

"How very thoughtful of the lion to share her spoils with Hades," Eve said faintly.

"She likes *me*," Adam had added mildly. "Lady Fennimore does."

This was the name of the lion, apparently.

His eyes glinted wickedly. And then his hand went up to brush a few more little leaves clinging to his hair, and she saw a flash of brilliant red.

Her heart stuttered.

Blood. Trailing into the cuff of his shirt.

"Rev . . . are you aware that you're bleeding?"

His face blanked. He pulled his hand away from his forehead and stared at it, surprised. "I suppose the hawthorn fought back when—"

She was next to him in an instant. "Show me," she demanded.

Surprised, he obeyed immediately, pushing

up the sleeve of his coat, unfastening the cuffs of his shirt, peeling it back a little. "It's my arm. I scratched it through my shirt, I suppose."

"Excellent. Then we won't need to amputate." She flashed a smile up at him. "Hold it up just so, try not to do any more bleeding on your shirt, for I doubt you've a dozen spare ones, and come with me."

She turned and had no doubts he would follow, for when she used that voice, people obeyed, even the vicar.

And he did. Silently.

She led him past a small garden patch planted with winter vegetables and through a kitchen door.

The kitchen was empty, but the ghost of Mrs. Wilberforce's scones hovered in the air. Cloud-filtered sunlight pushed through the window, muting and blending the colors of the cupboards, the great stove, the table and chairs, into shades of mauve and gray and pearl and charcoal. It was as though they'd entered one of the clouds outside.

"You'll need to take off your coat," she ordered softly.

He hesitated. And then never took his eyes from her as he slowly shook out of his caped greatcoat, and folded it over a chair. And then he shrugged out of his coat.

It seemed absurdly intimate, standing in the homely kitchen, watching the vicar divest himself of his clothes. And she stared at him, flustered as a girl for a moment.

She swiftly turned her back and rifled through a row of labeled tins on the shelf and found the one called St. John's wort.

She brought a basin of water with her to the table.

Without a word, he settled his long body into a sturdy wooden chair pushed up against the old oak-board table.

"Let's have the sleeve of your shirt rolled up, shall we?"

She settled in across from him with a basin of water.

He rolled up the sleeve, unveiling his arm a little at a time, and she waited, as breathless as if this were the unveiling of a public monument. And she was held still. Why hadn't she been prepared for how it would feel to be this close to his bare skin? Because he was so guarded, his arm, bare and vulnerable, seemed unduly significant. It was toasted a pale gold by the sun; he would never brown. The broad, strong wrists, the long elegant fingers, callused palms of a man who labored, the pale blue road of veins in which flowed that stubborn blood of his, the crisp gold hair—it all seemed unduly fascinating.

In large part because she could instantly imagine him unveiling the rest of his body.

At least he revealed a gash across the pale underside of his arm.

She cleared her throat.

"Have you a handkerchief? Or do you give them away to parishioners, the way you do cravats?"

"I haven't a handkerchief." His voice was subdued, too, amused.

And like a magician, she slowly slipped the fichu from out of her bodice and dipped it into the water.

This silenced him.

And as she leaned forward, she knew his view was into her cleavage.

"Your cravat sacrifice was an inspiration," she told him. Casting a glance up at him through her lashes.

He said nothing. His senses had likely been clubbed senseless by an eyeful of bosom.

Gently she cleaned the blood from his scratch, while he submitted, humble as a boy.

"'Tis a mere flesh wound," she told him. "No stitches necessary."

Knowing this formidable man, even her own admittedly fine bosom wouldn't conquer his faculties. He'd find a way to rally his senses soon enough. And yet his pulse gratifyingly thudded beneath the surface of his untenably silky skin covering the shockingly hard muscle of his arm. There seemed no give in that muscle. So like the man, those contrasts. She felt a wayward surge of protectiveness. Of gratitude, that she could do this much for him.

"You've done this before, have you?" His voice was a little frayed. Faintly amused.

"Oh, countless times, Reverend."

"For you . . . needed to mind your siblings."

"Yes."

A hesitation. "Was it difficult, minding them all on your own, without your parents?"

She paused her fichu on his arm. She knew at once this wasn't an interrogation, but there was a thrum of urgency in it.

He wanted to know her. And that little sunburst of joyous fear pierced her breathless.

"I suppose I didn't view it as difficult or easy or . . . it was simply my life, and I did what needed to be done. They're all I have, my family. And I would lay down my life for them."

He simply nodded.

She knew he was watching her. She kept her eyes on his arm, but she felt warmth over the back of her neck, her arms.

She looked up at him. "Mary O'Flaherty told me about her baby, Reverend Sylvaine. The one who died. She was very grateful to you."

His face went abruptly closed. "Ah, well."

It was the thing he said when he was moved, she realized. When he didn't want to accept thanks for an immeasurable kindness. What he'd said to her when he'd bought the ginger cake.

Perhaps all in a day's work, for him.

"Is it difficult, being a vicar?" she asked softly.

He gave a short rueful laugh, surprised.

Then breathed in at length as if to fuel the answer. And exhaled.

She realized her own breath was held, and her heart thumped in anticipation. She was ravenous in a way she'd never been before to know anything about this man.

"I suppose I don't think of it as difficult. It's my life." They both glanced up, exchanged small smiles acknowledging he'd echoed what she'd just said.

"There's the blood gone. This next bit may sting a bit." She laid her ruined fichu aside and took up the St. John's wort. Dipped her finger in and laid it gently on the scratch. His skin was warm, and she slowed. *I'm touching his bare skin.*

He didn't flinch.

"Lady Balmain?"

"Mmm?"

"Why two?"

She froze as if he'd yanked the floor from beneath her. She felt herself plummeting in surprise. And then she caught herself abruptly.

Why two men, was what he was asking.

He wanted to know.

She wanted him to know.

"I needed the money to take care of my family. And the theater isn't the road to wealth, Reverend Sylvaine."

"Why?" There was an urgency in his voice again. A demand. It wasn't quite desperation. More like a need bordering on impatience.

She felt pressure welling inside her. In her way she was as contained as he was, unaccustomed to laying her burdens down or sharing her thoughts with anyone. Reflection, regrets—those had always been a luxury for someone whose every action had been considered, a contribution toward survival. And they were so guarded, so much a part of her, the confidences were like shy beasts. Reluctant to be coaxed forward.

"Why those two men, or *why* wasn't I a respectable seamstress or housemaid—or a flower girl instead?" she heard the edge in her own voice.

"Both." Clipped.

She exhaled. "I hadn't the skills for the first, and we would have starved if I were the second."

"And the men?" he pressed. Still the suppressed urgency. But his voice that was like a path she wanted to walk down, simply to see where it led.

She understood then in that moment that *she* was safe with him.

To a degree, that was.

She composed herself. "Well, you see . . . Seamus was in trouble you see—not his fault, of course; it never seems to be." She said this dryly. "He's a charmer, has a good heart, my Seamus, but he can be a bit . . . impulsive. He was jailed briefly. And the MP promised to get him out if I retired from the theater and became his mistress. He made good on his promise, for Seamus roams the earth free to plague me yet. And the *second* man . . . I suppose you can say he wooed me with more wealth, better connections."

She glanced up to see if the vicar's thoughts on any of this were reflected on his face. Of course they weren't.

But he appeared rapt.

"The first released me from our agreement very amiably; he was getting older, you see, and wanted to retire permanently to the country. And after that, I was able to send more money to Cora. I worry about Cora, you see. She's my sister, and she has so many children, and . . . Well, the second man introduced me to the Earl of Wareham, whom I married."

They were both utterly still. Utterly silent.

His expression was unreadable.

A flush heated her cheeks.

"I know it's the sort of thing that would horrify nearly everyone you're acquainted with. It isn't so different, Reverend Sylvaine, from how many young women begin marriage. I could have fared so much worse. Think of Mary O'Flaherty. They were decent enough men. And I preferred survival, my own and my family's, to near-certain death on the streets."

And she supposed, in the silence that followed, with her finger slowly, delicately stroking the balm over his wound, she awaited a verdict. A judgment, though he claimed not to judge.

He gave nothing away of his thoughts. There was no tension in his arm. The muted light of the room seemed to pillow them in a peculiar safety.

And the silence went on long enough for her to realize that his presence, the warmth of his skin beneath hers, worked on her senses like laudanum. And again she felt that perilous urge toward surrender, of wanting to melt, vanish into him.

"Sometimes the only choices we have, even the ones made out of love, isolate us." He said this quietly.

She looked slowly up at him.

His eyes met hers.

He understood. And she understood: Who asked *him* about himself? Who truly saw him? Who took care of him? The people here saw in him their own desires and needs; they saw him as a set of qualities, as beautiful and kind and trustworthy. He was what they needed him to be.

Not unlike her.

"You're . . . lonely." It emerged inflected with revelation. She didn't add "too." She knew that was understood.

How had she ever thought his blue eyes placid as a lake? But there was untold power in any water: to buoy, to drown, to toss, to carry one to the safety of shore.

"Two," he said softly. Deliberately as laying down a chess piece.

Her mouth began to part in a question.

"Two is my number as well, Lady Balmain."

Their eyes locked.

She was so close she could see the tiny scar next to his ear. See that his lashes were tipped in darker gold. All of it seemed desperately valuable and precious. The shape of his face was an ache inside her. Outside, a light rain began to fall, spattering the window.

And suddenly it was as if the very air was a silken web that wound round them both.

Only two. Practically an innocent. So unlike all the men she'd known, and he must have known it. And yet the thoughts swelled and crashed and swelled again, a torrent of unprecedented jealousy, raw and unfamiliar: *Who? Who knows how it feels to be covered by your body? Who knows the taste of your mouth, the feel of you inside her? Who has tangled her bare legs with yours, seen your eyelashes against your cheek while you sleep, your hair smashed across the pillow, knows the scrape of your morning beard against her cheek?*

What are you like when you lose control, Reverend Sylvaine?

"How long has it been?" she whispered.

Time suspended. There was only the duet of their breathing, and their own reflections in each other's eyes, and her fingertip motionless on his skin. His pulse raced, thumping. An echo of her own. She could feel his breath, swift, soft, warm, on her face.

And then his chest moved as he filled his lungs with air, struggling for his will.

Slowly, slowly, he withdrew his arm from her.

He sat back in her chair and turned his head toward the window. His hands lay against the table, the knuckles white and tense. His throat moved in a swallow.

He didn't look at her. As though he didn't trust himself to do it.

"I've a parishioner to visit." His voice was quiet. He'd saved both of them, and she knew it.

He stood slowly, like a man drugged or wounded. He reached for his coat and pushed his arms into it.

She simply nodded. Both relieved and strangely destroyed. For if he had touched her, she would have been undone.

And if she had touched him . . . likewise.

She stood, too. Feeling stripped bare. She couldn't speak.

"Thank you for patching me up again," he said with a faint, rueful smile.

Thank you *for undoing me,* she thought ironically. Still dazed.

"Oh, I've any number of useful skills."

Lud. On the heels of everything, it sounded like the worst of innuendos.

A hint of a smile. "I believe it," he said simply. "I'll perhaps see you again at the O'Flaherty house?"

"I expect so. And I understand I may be rewarded with an invitation to the Assembly almost a fortnight from now. With music and dancing. Should I be deemed *acceptable,* of course."

He took a good deal of time to settle his hat on his head, as if it contained all of his good sense and control, and he wanted to make sure he restored it.

And studied her somberly for a long moment, a look in his eyes that made the breath hitch in her lungs again.

"I'm an *excellent* dancer, Lady Balmain," he said softly.

It sounded like both a promise and a warning.

He touched the brim of his hat and let himself out of the kitchen.

"ISN'T THAT . . . THE vicar? Walking in our direction up on the green, there?" Josephine said this.

Mrs. Sneath and Miss Josephine Pitney and Miss Charing all craned their heads out of the window of the carriage as they rolled up the road on the way to fetch Lady Balmain.

He was indeed unmistakable. They waved through the windows. But even as they approached, he didn't look up at the sound of their carriage wheels. As if he were utterly deaf.

"Just look at his expression," Mrs. Sneath said. "So absorbed. Like he's had a miraculous visitation."

"It does look that way, rather," Miss Pitney said thoughtfully.

"Such a good man," Mrs. Sneath maintained stoutly.

"Where do you suppose he's going?" Josephine yearned after him with her eyes as he passed.

"To Heaven, of a certainty," Mrs. Sneath said to her admonishingly.

"Where do you suppose he's *been*?" Miss Pitney said this.

They all turned their heads in the direction from which he'd come.

The road that led to Damask Manor.

"Important parish duty," Mrs. Sneath said definitively, of course. As if the force of her conviction could make it true.

Chapter 14

Two hours later, Mrs. Sneath, Miss Josephine Charing, and Miss Pitney delivered Eve to Lady Fennimore's house.

"Lady Fennimore is a very elderly dowager. She enjoys the company since she cannot leave the house any longer. Perhaps you can read to her," Mrs. Sneath suggested. "Something edifying to both of you." She'd thrust a Bible into Eve's hands. A passage was marked.

"She's terrifying," Miss Charing had confided to her, out of earshot of Mrs. Sneath. "She's a horrible old lady. If you haven't cried in years, even if you've never wept at all in your entire life, I wager she will find a way to make you do it. Even Miss Pitney— and her heart is as cold and hard as an olive stone, I assure you—wept."

"I got a bit of camphor in my eye, and it stung," Miss Pitney insisted huffily. "Her room is filled with the stuff."

"Her daughter Jenny holds up well, I think, beneath all of that. She says her mother wasn't always like that, but I've never known her to be anything else. And she likes the vicar, Lady Fennimore does." Her tone said, *But who doesn't?*

They abandoned Eve at Lady Fennimore's, with the promise to fetch her in two hours.

Eve was then ushered by a diffident young woman named Jenny, Lady Fennimore's daughter, into a manor house scarcely more impressive than her own. She didn't see any bones strewn about, which she supposed was promising.

And then she'd been led up to a stiflingly hot room, fire roaring, curtains flung open, sun pouring in. The center of the room was occupied by an ancient, bedridden woman.

"Ah. So you're the whore everyone's been nattering about."

She had enormous blue eyes. One of the consolations of old age for her, clearly, was the opportunity to shock. Which she'd embraced with unfettered glee.

"*Have* they been nattering on about me, Lady Fennimore?" Eve asked pleasantly. "Although one can't be a whore unless one is paid for favors. And I haven't been paid for favors in simply *ages*. So I'm not certain I qualify any longer."

Lady Fennimore narrowed her eyes. "Doing it simply for the pleasure of it now, are you?"

"Can you think of a better reason?"

This gave Lady Fennimore pause.

But only for a moment.

"To bring children in to the world," she said huffily. "I've brought several of my own into the world, you know."

"Of course. The making of children is a splendid excuse to make love. I've a riddle for you, Lady Fennimore. What do you suppose is the primary difference between a whore and a wife, all told?"

Lady Fennimore appeared to give this some genuine thought.

"Skill," Evie told her.

And damned if Lady Fennimore didn't smile at this, albeit slowly, with an evil little gleam in her eye. "We all of us do it for the money, don't we, when it comes right down to it? Sell ourselves into marriages. Perhaps your way is best after all. Why did they send you in? Are they trying to shock me into an early grave so they won't need to decide which milksop to send in next?"

"From the looks of you, Lady Fennimore, your grave is hardly early."

Lady Fennimore glared at and raised her head slowly, slowly, quiveringly slowly, a few inches off the pillow. It hovered there, as if she were trying desperately to pop it off her neck and launch it like a cannonball at Eve.

Then she dropped to her pillow again.

A moment later, she smiled to herself.

"I imagine your life has been interesting," she said to the elderly woman.

"Not as interesting as yours, my dear. When one lacks a moral compass, one can stray every which way, I suppose, which allows for a variety of experiences unavailable to most of us."

"To milksops, you mean to say?"

Lady Fennimore smiled again, this time looking delighted. "You're not one of them, are you? A milksop?"

"Never quite had the luxury of being a milksop, I confess."

"My dear, why *are* you here? Why should you want anything at all to do with the tedious ladies of the committee and their good deeds for the poor and the poor, helpless infirm such as myself?" She grinned wickedly at this.

"I'm new to Pennyroyal Green, Lady Fennimore, and I wanted friends. And helping the poor seemed an excellent way to go about it while staving off boredom."

"Casting you in with *me* is hardly a friendly act, now, is it? I'd say they were trying to drive you off since you've had the unmitigated gall to want to befriend those righteous prigs. Still, it's unutterably too easy to make them cry. So dull. And I can't move from this bed, I need to poke and prod them in order to derive some sort of entertainment."

"Well, one discounts the powers of endurance a whore can acquire. I can assure you I won't be weeping. Prod away."

Lady Fennimore cackled delightedly, and it devolved into a cough, and wracked her until she collapsed against the pillow, her eyes fluttering closed.

"Here now," Evie said, her voice both soothing and practical. She handed her a handkerchief.

They sat quietly together for a time. Evie glanced about the room, looking for clues to the woman's history.

"You married an earl, I'm told."

"I did. And then he passed away, and I was terribly sorry."

"My condolences, dear." It sounded sincere. "They say you killed him."

That sounded sincere, too.

"His heart gave out. Too much marital activity."

"Ah, the pleasures of the marriage bed."

"I'll wager you were wicked enough in your day, Lady Fennimore."

She looked momentarily startled. "Have you been speaking with the vicar?"

"Ah, have you shared your secrets with him, then? Everyone seems to. One gets the feeling he'd never share a single confidence, however."

"He's a good man," Lady Fennimore said. She fell quiet. "But for the love of God, don't tell him that. It would be just the thing to make a handsome man insufferable. The 'good' is in the trying, you see, and I shouldn't want him to stop trying."

And Eve was thrown by her comparison to a man who was "better." *The good is in the trying.*

"You see, I have never in my life met a—I suppose the polite word is 'courtesan'—before. Have you ever been in love, dear? Or is that forbidden in your profession?"

"Nothing is forbidden," Eve said tantalizingly. "They've given me a Bible to read to you. Shall we?"

Lady Fennimore waved her hand dismissively. "I've read that thing a million times if I've read it once. Did you love your husband . . . your name again?"

"Eve, you can call me. I cared for him."

"Ah. So you didn't *love* him. I would see it in your face, you see."

"Did you love yours?"

"Yes."

"But you weren't in love with him. For I would see it in your face."

"Touché, my dear."

"Who *were* you in love with?"

"Aren't you a cheeky thing!" Lady Fennimore raised her hand and slapped it down delightedly.

"I thought you loathed being bored."

"Mmm. Do you know, you remind me of the vicar. And not just because the two of you can tolerate me. It's more a sort of . . . purity."

Evie almost choked. "No one has ever before accused me of purity, Lady Fennimore."

"Perhaps it's because you've been bad, and he's been good. But there's a fearlessness to both traits, I think. Both require a certain strength."

"Just as there's a fearlessness to having one foot in the grave."

Lady Fennimore cackled again.

"I do believe you're considered some sort of trial for me, Lady Fennimore. What will you tell them?"

"And you want these people as friends."

"I do. I think I like them."

Lady Fennimore tilted her head dubiously. "Very well. I'll tell them you dutifully read the Bible to me. And I'll ask them to send the whore as often as possible before I die."

"I've never been more deeply touched, Lady Fennimore."

"You'd think touching is all one does in your previous profession . . ." she said drowsily. "Go ahead and read that Bible now, will you? I've need of a nap. Choose something truly dull. My guess is that Mrs. Sneath marked it for you."

"Pssst. The ratafia is against the back wall," Colin said, correctly reading Adam's expression. He'd arrived alone at the Assembly to find an already giddy throng of Pennyroyal Green and greater Sussex denizens.

"I was hoping for something a bit stronger. I'm feeling the need for fortification tonight."

Adam wasn't adverse to gaiety, but he was facing a gauntlet of empty dance cards and hopeful, dreamy female eyes.

"Join me in the library, then, in ten minutes, and don't let Father see you on the way there. He hates it when I drain his decanters without telling him."

Mr. and Mrs. Jacob Eversea had graciously loaned their smaller ballroom for the purposes of the Assembly, the sort of largesse occasionally expected of them as pillars—along with the Redmonds, of course—of Pennyroyal Green.

"Brandy sounds perfect. I'll be with you in . . ."

Her impact was total. As if he'd bolted an entire decanter of Jacob Eversea's best brandy.

Her hair was twisted low on her nape. Cream kid gloves covered her arms up to her elbows; her shoulders were very nearly bare, so negligible were the sleeves. He saw no jewelry. But these were mere details. The lines and colors and contrasts of her— black and pearl and cream, the arc of her throat, her bosom, the delicate shoulders, the narrow waist falling into the flare of her hips—were the Song of Solomon made flesh. She was more real than anyone in the room. The North Star in a firmament of stars.

She was standing with Miss Josephine Charing, and together they were perusing what appeared to be dance cards. She hadn't yet seen him. Though the force of his gaze really ought to have spun her around like a weather vane.

Colin followed the direction of his eyes. "Miss Amy Pitney is looking very well tonight," he said wickedly.

Adam didn't hear him.

"I fear you're about to make straight for her, Adam. See, there you go, one step, two steps . . . one more step, and I officially accuse you of losing your head . . . *Adam!*"

Adam halted. He *had* been heading in her direction. As though she were gravity and he'd been given no option but to obey her laws.

He exhaled. And turned to look at Colin. Who was staring at him. And for once Colin looked somber. "Old man . . ."

Adam made an impatient sound. Shook his head once sharply.

Colin seemed at a loss. "Just . . . realize that everyone here watches everything. They'll watch you, Adam."

As a warning, it didn't penetrate.

"I've changed my mind about the brandy," Adam told him shortly.

Colin gave him one last, long look.

Adam didn't notice when Colin abandoned him for the brandy, shaking his head.

"I THINK YOU should look simple," Henny had advised her. "*Blend,*" she'd added with less confidence, for it was of a certainty Eve never would be anything other than conspicuous. And so her dress was plainly cut, her hair was done up in a simple knot; she didn't look as though she were *trying*. To be seen, or to lure, or to ensnare, or to corrupt. No nun would ever behave so faultlessly tonight, Evie decided.

She knew the eyes were on her anyway, in the form of darting glances. She was accustomed to eyes. She was accustomed to acting the way she *needed* to act. She would contrive to be so excruciatingly uneventful they would soon seek relief in their own private dramas and hopes, for every ballroom inevitably magnified them, this she knew from experience.

Over the past fortnight, she'd won them—very nearly—and they her, though they still treated her somewhat gingerly. Several ladies had called upon her. She'd visited the O'Flahertys several more times. She made appearances in church, and didn't fall asleep. And for perhaps the first time in the history of Pennyroyal Green, Lady Fennimore had heartily, vocally approved of someone, which they ought to have seen as a warning rather than an endorsement, Evie thought.

"He hasn't yet arrived." Amy Pitney was avidly watching the entrance to the ballroom. "He's staying with friends nearby, and I know they're all coming. Oh, he's difficult to miss, I assure you. He's handsome the way the Everseas are handsome—you know, the sort of handsome that makes your head swim a bit the first time you see it? It's alarming, really, sometimes. But . . . do you know, I think he intends to speak to Papa tomorrow night."

She was talking about her suitor, but her eyes kept drifting toward a young man standing amidst a group of other young men surrounding Miss Josephine Charing. Who seemed to be chatting gaily—her mouth moved and moved and moved. But she stopped now and again, and listened with flattering attention to one of them.

The young men were drinking it in like nectar.

Something tensed in Miss Pitney's face. With an effort, she fought it back. Evie suspected it was her heart giving a yearning lunge toward its beloved and being yanked firmly back.

"Are you acquainted with that young man?" Eve asked casually.

"That's Mr. Simon Covington. We grew up together as neighbors. I've known him . . . my entire life." She said it flatly.

In that sentence, Evie sensed a world of things.

"He really cares for that featherhead. God knows why," Amy added tersely.

"And *you* care for him," Eve said easily.

Miss Pitney's eyes widened. She pressed her lips together hard. And then she surrendered with a sigh. "How did you know?"

"I've powers of observation of my own, Miss Pitney."

Amy's smile was bittersweet. "I always have, you know. Cared for him. I've watched him moon after Josephine since she acquired . . . what now fills her bodice. About the age of fourteen."

"Do you suppose she has admirable qualities, too?" Evie said dryly. "You see, Miss Charing, I believe you're clever enough to understand me when I say that I know a bit about the *pleasures* of being reduced to the sum of my parts. Of being as much desired as despised for it. It's as unfair as being overlooked because you don't believe you're pretty."

Miss Pitney blinked. Eve had the sense that no one had ever spoken so bluntly to her before.

She had the grace to flush. She sighed. "Very well. Josephine *is* generally quite kind. She's a good daughter, she genuinely cares about her work for the Sussex poor, she's loyal to her friends, and she was a friend to me for so long that I *miss* her . . . but she doesn't even *see* him, and I find that unforgivable. He's quiet and clever and thoughtful and . . . so much more. And I know that he suffers when he watches her eyes follow the vicar everywhere, or when the other boys natter on. He doesn't *tell* me, of course. But I know that he does."

"I've quite come to terms with the fact that he doesn't care for me the way I care for him. And likely never will. I'm not a ninny, you know. I'm not like Josephine, who despite her circumstances— that's her *only* ball gown, you know, and you can *see* where she picked out the hem and resewed it— still wants to marry for love. One must be practical about such things."

She hiked her stubborn chin. As if she could imperiously order her feelings into alignment.

Evie knew that clever girls often tried to talk themselves out of heartbreak. But she'd never before heard her own philosophy reiterated—one must be *practical* about such things—and it shocked her to discover how distasteful she found it. She wouldn't wish it upon someone she cared for, and yet she'd lived her entire life in precisely that way.

Of *necessity*, she'd told herself. Perhaps it once had been. She wondered if necessity had evolved into habit, then into cowardice, somewhere along the way.

"Ye *might* allow yerself to give it a try," Henny had said to her.

At the very thought, Evie suddenly felt adrift, exposed and nervous and overwhelmed, like a

child who'd escaped into a crowded ballroom out
of sight of its parents. So little was new to her, and
this was. And it wasn't something she could learn
by imitation.

Her eyes restlessly searched the crowd again, as
they'd done from the moment she'd arrived.

At last.

Adam Sylvaine stood across the room, watching
her with an expression that ignited her heart like a
firework. It seemed to leap and burst, all glory and
disaster.

Don't look at me like that, she desperately wanted
to say to him. He was illuminating her with that
gaze as surely as if he'd aimed a lantern at her.

Surely, it would draw all eyes.

She turned her head away with extraordinary
effort, a motion that felt almost unnatural. And for
a moment she was a captive of her racing heart.

To find Miss Pitney watching her steadily. Eve
was nonplussed to realize she was unaware of
whether seconds or an eternity had passed while
she was locked in a gaze with the vicar. And Miss
Pitney gave her no clue.

She took a steadying breath. At least now she
knew what to say to Miss Pitney.

"The way you feel about *Simon*, Miss Pitney . . .
is the way your suitor should feel about you. It
seems it want the best for him no matter what,
and if what's best for him means Miss Charing returns his regard . . . so be it. It's up to you to decide
whether he does, and what to do with the information when you have it, of course."

She seemed to like this information.

"I shall introduce you when he arrives." She

smiled. It was the smile that made Amy Pitney genuinely pretty, and Eve found herself hoping that her suitor would make her do it often.

EVE DECIDED TO visit the punch bowl. She found Miss Charing standing near it, eyeing a row of sandwiches with a certain wistful longing. She turned and brightened when she saw Eve.

"Oh, good evening, Lady Wareham! I'm so delighted you could come. I've done it, you know. I've gone about finding things to appreciate in gentlemen this evening. I even found something to appreciate in Mr. Henry Grundy. Which wasn't easy to do, mind you. And I do believe he wears stays, in order to button his shirt over that belly of his."

Eve laughed. "Truly? That's heartening news, Miss Charing. What did you find to like?"

"I admire his doggedness in attending every entertainment now that he's a widower. It's rather touching, isn't it? So I told him I quite admired his stamina."

"You didn't! And what did he do?"

"Well, do you know . . ." She leaned forward and confided. "He *blushed.* And he requested a dance, so very sweetly. I would give it to him, but my card is entirely filled. So I apologized. Perhaps you'd like to dance with him? Since you are not interested in acquiring another husband or in any men at all, it would be a kindness to dance with all the men who don't need wives or who otherwise might find partners other than willing. And you are so kind."

You are so kind. She was nonplussed and quite pleased to be seen this way.

"How novel to be a consolation prize! What a

pleasure it would be to be so useful. I've always wanted to dance with a man who wore a girdle."

Josephine smiled uncertainly, clearly undecided whether Evie was joking. *God bless the literal-minded*, Evie thought.

"And do you know . . . I've found something to appreciate in Mr. Simon Covington. I stopped to pay attention, you see."

Evie followed Josephine's gaze across the ballroom. Simon Covington, lean as a sapling, was watching her with soulful, dark eyes, the most appealing feature in his long, sensitive face.

"He listens very well. Which is thoughtful, don't you think? And his eyes are . . ." Josephine drifted. "They're *brown*," she said dreamily.

"They certainly *are*," Evie agreed.

"And he laughs when I say something funny. And he asked after the health of my mother."

"All very admirable qualities in a man. Did you find a compliment for him?"

"Do you know . . . I tried. But it's the oddest thing, Lady Balmain . . . when he looked at me a minute ago . . . I just couldn't quite find my voice."

Evie smiled at her, genuinely delighted by this turn of events. And then Eve stood on her toes and peeked at Miss Charing's dance card.

"Hold there, Miss Charing. I thought you said you'd given away all your dances. I see you've a waltz remaining."

"Oh," she said. She was flustered.

Then she leaned toward her and confided once more.

"I used to always keep a waltz open, you see, in case the vicar wished to dance with me. I did dance with him, just the one time. The top of my head reached his collar." She reflected upon this. "I used to imagine I was the one who had the privilege of sewing his buttons on."

The privilege. And Eve thought of patching him up again, tending to his wounds. It was precisely how she'd felt.

"You used to keep a waltz open?" she coaxed.

"It's just . . . one wants to look at Reverend Sylvaine. And listen to him. But as for Simon . . . I do believe he wants to look at me. And listen to *me*. And it makes me feel . . . it makes me feel. . . ." She went misty-eyed again.

"It's a very good sign if you can't finish your sentences when you think of a man."

"Mmmm?" Josephine said. Watching Simon.

"I wonder if the Reverend Sylvaine will be disappointed if you give your waltz away to Simon," Evie teased. Knowing that Josephine wouldn't hear her.

Because Mr. Simon Covington had detached himself from the wall he was leaning against and was approaching them, wearing a smile as gleaming as the toes of his boots.

And Evie, who was used to being as central to an occasion as a brilliant chandelier, might as well have been the wallpaper, for he didn't seem to notice her at all.

And even as she was pleased that Josephine seemed to be giving Simon the sort of attention he was due, she spared a thought for Miss Pitney.

Who was another person who knew that love was an indulgence, and a rarity, and had decided to be hopeful rather than disappointed, which took great courage.

SHE'D WATCHED ADAM dance with the young
women of the village. Watched their radiant faces
as he steered them around, gazing down atten-
tively, saying in all likelihood exactly the right
thing. Reels, quadrilles, two waltzes. She'd tucked
herself into a snug, inconspicuous location near the
ratafia. And watched.

Purely out of curiosity and a soul-purifying act
of charity, and because no one had yet asked her to
dance and it was assumed she was still somewhat
grieving and wouldn't want to do anything quite
so merry, she did dance with the gentleman who
wore stays. Even over the music, she could hear
them creak like a saddle. But there *was* something
gallant about him—Josephine was right.

She found that she didn't miss the adulation, the
swarms of men vying for her attention, the envi-
ous glances, the schemes and flirtations, the constant awareness of herself. She felt lighter, almost
gossamer, without them. She made for the punch
bowl as surreptitiously as possible after that, then
leaned herself against the wall, near, ironically, a
bust of Hercules, to watch the festivities.

And overheard three young ladies giggling
over whether they'd be the ones blessed enough to
dance a waltz with the vicar tonight. Apparently
his waltzes were rare and coveted.

"Why Lady Wareham!" came a familiar voice
behind her. "What a pleasure it is to see you in
Pennyroyal Green."

She turned to see Colin Eversea.

A gorgeous rascal as ever. He had the same
vivid, dancing light in his sea-colored eyes. He

was indolently, gracefully tall and still lean. A little harder now with age, but then, weren't they all.

Both Colin's bow and Evie's curtsy were playfully ironic.

"*You're* looking well, Colin."

"You're looking as dazzling as ever, too, Evie. When last I saw you, you were . . . singing a lusty song about pirates? Or was it the night of *Le Mistral*, with Signora Licari in the lead role and you and your dress were the talk of the ton?"

"When last I saw you, you'd disappeared from the gallows in a puff of smoke."

He nodded at the lobbed return. They both had a certain amount to rue about their pasts.

"My sincere condolences on your loss, Lady Balmain. He was a good egg, Wareham."

An unfortunate choice of words, but she knew Colin meant them. "Thank you," was all she said.

"If it's any consolation, the ton may yet write a song for you."

She rolled her eyes. "It's no consolation at all, but it's given me something yet again to worry about, thank you, Colin. I'm aware of the multitudes of words that rhyme with 'widow.'"

"I don't find my song a consolation, either. And it grows and grows, that song."

"I sang it as a lullaby to the O'Flahertys' baby. It's never too soon to learn about the Everseas if you live in Pennyroyal Green."

He laughed. And lightly tapped her glass of ratafia with his.

"I believe congratulations on your marriage are in order, Mr. Eversea," she added.

"Thank you. I needed to do *something* to ease my heart after you broke it."

Eve rolled her eyes. "I broke nothing but your streak of effortless conquests."

He grinned at that. "Speaking of the O'Flahertys and lullabies, I hear you've been engaged in good works with our worthy Mrs. Sneath and her regiment of women?"

"I have, indeed."

"You've been spending a good deal of time with my cousin Reverend Sylvaine in the process."

She went still.

She slowly turned to look at him.

Met his eyes evenly.

And then anger did a slow flare. "Out with it, Colin."

"He's not like us, Eve. He possesses a sense of humor, but he's not a *light* sort. If he's just a diversion, and if you've a heart, play with someone else. Because of a certainty someone will be hurt."

The anger and hurt spread through her, bitter and scalding as raw gin.

If she had a *heart.*

Her eyes burned. Her breath went ragged in a struggle to be polite. Her words emerged, measured as evenly as bricks.

"How would you know what I'm *like,* Colin?"

He stared at her. Then gave a short nod, acknowledging that he'd been gravely insulting.

But he didn't apologize. And he didn't relent.

"He's just . . ." And he quirked his mouth humorlessly. "He's just one of the few genuinely good people I know, Evie. That's all."

She stared at him.

He met her gaze steadily.

And I'm not good? I'm not worthy? I'll ruin him? How dare you?

She turned abruptly away from him. A million retorts crowded and closed her throat.

What must it be like for someone to worry whether *she* was hurt?

But she knew Colin was genuinely concerned. And despite it all, she couldn't fault him for it. She would defend her family, too.

It still didn't mean she owed him any explanations or promises.

She coldly gave him her profile and silence.

"Enjoy your evening, Lady Balmain," he finally said quietly. He bowed and took his leave of her.

She fell back hard against the wall, and closed her eyes. Her entire body the battleground for dozens of warring emotions. She stayed that way, next to Hercules, as a quadrille reached its natural end. And she hoped she remained hidden.

But when she opened them again, her view was of a wall of a chest, and what she instinctively knew had once been her dead husband's cravat. Because he would, of course, find her, no matter where she might be.

Adam Sylvaine stood before her.

And the strains of the third and final waltz beginning.

Chapter 15

HIS PRESENCE ROBBED HER OF HER VOICE. SHE could only stare up at him. Heart too full and too afraid to speak.

"Is aught amiss?" he asked immediately. In a voice that suggested he would immediately remedy anything that troubled her.

Her face and eyes must still be burning from Colin's little visit. He'd seen the high color.

"Naught is amiss. I'm recovering from a vigorous dance with a gentleman who wore stays."

"That was quite a few dances ago. And then you rather disappeared."

So he'd been watching her much the way she'd been watching him. How she admired him for not pretending otherwise, for never employing stratagems.

"I haven't danced in some time. Perhaps I'm a bit rusty," she suggested.

"I'm an excellent dancer. If you dance with me, you'll scarcely need to make an effort at all."

She smiled at that, she couldn't help it.

There was a hesitation, touching and thrilling. "I'd hoped you would honor me with this waltz, Lady Wareham."

And suddenly the moment was fraught.

He gazed down at her with those endless eyes.

Oh, Reverend Sylvaine. You shouldn't have asked.

I cannot. We cannot. But saying it would acknowledge what there was between them. It was a conversation she didn't want to have in the ballroom, or perhaps ever. It would be such a simple thing to beg a headache, or an ankle twist. Her acceptance here among the ladies was so tenuous. They would watch her. They *always* watched him.

Surely he knew it.

And all around them were young girls, never married, who yearned for a waltz with the vicar, who'd spent the entire evening in anticipation of it. A rogue surge of envy swept her. Oh, to be an innocent, for just a few minutes. To fall stupidly, freely, hopelessly in love, without reservation, without thought of the consequences. To fit into the circle of his arms and sail about the room, everything she felt aglow on her face.

His eyes held her fast.

He held out his arm.

She watched her hand go up, rest lightly on it. Like a bloody bee lighting on a flower, it seemed necessary, part of the natural order of things. She'd really had no choice in the matter.

And despite it all, the ballroom floor might as well have been a cloud when she took her first few steps touching him.

ADAM LED HER out to the floor as though he'd captured something wild and rare and precious.

He was stunned and wondering at his good fortune. He savored everything. The flush his gaze put

in her cheeks and throat and how she'd dropped
her eyes quickly, then raised them again, gathering
composure. The fit of his hand against her waist,
and the swift rise and fall of her breath beneath
it, the warmth of her body against his hand that
made him want to pull her closer and closer, to feel
the sway of her breath against his body. How small
her hand felt in his, fragile as a bird, though this
was a woman who'd conquered the O'Flahertys
and wooed Lady Fennimore, and London, and sur-
vived St. Giles.

It all filled him too full to speak.

She said nothing at all. And neither did her eyes
leave his face.

But a carousel of gazes on the perimeter of the
ballroom watched the vicar and the countess move
effortlessly, beautifully together, unsmiling, apparently not speaking. On first glance, one might not
even think they were enjoying themselves.

And yet they never, never took their eyes from
each other.

"How is your arm?" she finally asked.

"Better."

He didn't want to speak. He simply wanted to
feel.

She smiled at this. "Your conversation never
fails to dazzle."

"Neither do you."

He said this so seriously, so abruptly, it silenced
her again.

Beneath his hand, he felt her take in a deep shuddering breath.

"Thank you," she remembered to say.

Which made him laugh, for some reason.

She looked up at him as if everything about his face was a miracle. As if she was remembering him.

He smiled slightly.

She smiled slightly, gave her head a marveling shake.

"You *are* an excellent dancer."

"I never lie," he said easily.

"What else do you do well, Vicar?" she tried.

But in the moment, with their bodies touching in some places but not enough places, it emerged less as flirtation than a serious question. Almost an invitation.

She'd unnerved herself.

His hand flexed over hers, pressed against her waist. His eyes went nearly black.

"Everything," he said softly. "And I never lie."

And that put an end to the conversation.

And round and round the room they went, unraveling each other step by step by dangerous step.

THE MUSIC EVENTUALLY ended, and with it the world they'd created of a waltz.

Adam was loath to surface from it, but once the music ended, the ballroom intruded inexorably—people, colors, and sounds that had nothing to do with the countess. And he bowed and she curtsied as if they were ordinary people enjoying an ordinary waltz in an ordinary town, and not as though a number of women scattered about the room wore expressions ranging from incredulity to heartbreak to thunder.

He brought her to where Amy Pitney and Miss Josephine Charing stood—together, and apparently voluntarily. They seemed to have reached a sort of accord. Each wore similarly abstracted, rosy, hopeful expressions. Which Adam suspected were related to the men who stood next to them.

Mr. Simon Covington Adam knew well; he was a parishioner who often volunteered to help with the projects for the poor. Bookish and wiry and deceptively strong, he was a son of a country squire and had been raised much like Adam, amid dogs and horses and guns and books. An excellent young man.

The man standing with Amy was altogether different. 'London' was stamped upon him, from the cut of his clothing and the shine of his boots to the flawless line of his profile and the Byronic tousle of his hair. His posture was languidly confident; hands folded behind his back, one knee casually bent. He gave Adam a polite white smile. It was courteous, entitled, assured, as though he was humoring the countryfolk of Sussex with his presence.

But his gray eyes pierced. He was, in fact, alarmingly good-looking—not a weak chin, nor bulbous nose or protruding ear or petulant lip or scar in sight. An artist's interpretation of handsome, in fact.

Eve had gone rigid. She dropped her hand from Adam's arm.

She was staring at him.

The man was staring at *her* in a way that made Adam want to reach out and, in a very un-Christian way, close his hands around his throat.

Amy breathlessly made the introduction. "Lady Balmain and Reverend Sylvaine, I'd like you to meet Lord Haynesworth."

And much to Adam's enormous displeasure,

Haynesworth promptly said, "A pleasure to see you again, Lady Wareham. And to meet you, Reverend Sylvaine."

It didn't prevent Adam from politely making his bow.

A casual observer might not have noticed how rigid Evie's spine had gone, or how immobile her face was. Her smile was bright, and her eyes continued to shine.

The clever eyes of Miss Pitney, upon whose face mingled hope and pride and that vulnerable hauteur, sensed something. Her smile faltered as she looked between the two of them.

"How do you do, Lord Haynesworth?" Eve said, as though she was disinclined to admit pleasure had anything at all to do with their acquaintance.

Or at least this was Adam's hope.

"Oh! Are you . . . already acquainted, then?" Miss Pitney's smile and her eyes officially became disengaged.

Josephine and Simon looked on, only half listening.

"I was a friend of the late Earl of Wareham's, and my path did cross with the countess's now and again in London. My condolences again on your loss," Haynesworth said smoothly. "He will be greatly missed.

"Very kind of you." The words were entirely uninflected. "He *is* missed."

She wasn't blinking, Adam noticed. As though she didn't trust herself for a moment to close her eyes in front of this man.

Haynesworth wasn't blinking, either.

The music began again. And suddenly, his manners as smooth as expensive cognac. Haynesworth said, "My late arrival here tonight means I was unable to find dancing partners, and Amy—that is, Miss Pitney—has committed this dance. Would you be so kind, Lady Balmain, as to humor me? If at all possible? For the sake of the affection we shared for Wareham."

It would be the height of impoliteness to refuse him. Everyone standing there knew it.

And her hesitation was brief. "I would be so kind," Eve said. And smiled.

The kind of smile every skilled actress could produce.

"Would you like to see my scar, Eve? It's healed nicely. I understand some women find that sort of thing exciting."

She nearly shivered with revulsion.

She didn't want to touch the Haynesworth. She hadn't wanted to touch him when he'd offered to pay for the privilege of touching *her* years ago when she'd first seen him at the Green Apple Theater, and she certainly hadn't wanted to touch him now, with a smile pasted to her face, his hand resting where Adam Sylvaine's hand had rested moments earlier, because any place Adam Sylvaine had touched her felt sacred now.

Lord Haynesworth would never forgive her for being a better judge of character than she was a singer.

"No one *made* you duel, Lord Haynesworth. That was your own foolish decision."

"Oh, Evie," he drawled, so condescendingly she was tempted to knee him in the cods then and there. "Just one night, Evie. That's all I ever asked of you. The *blunt* I offered! And then I risked my life over you."

She rolled her eyes. "Two bored aristocrats shooting each other for sport is not 'risking your life' for *me*. That was you posturing for other men."

"You have to admit, Eve, you weren't unmoved when first we met."

"That was before I realized you were attractive on the outside only."

He gave a short laugh. "I'm a changed man, Eve. I'm in *love*."

She stared at him stonily to show him she knew precisely how ridiculous this statement was.

Eyes locked in enmity, they circled the ballroom.

"Why Amy Pitney? She's a decent, lovely person. And you are neither of those things."

He was unruffled. "I like her. That decent girl has a decent fortune and a father who fancies himself related to a viscount and his daughter with a title, even one who's been nearly drained of his fortune by his multiple impressive properties."

"And by mounds of gambling debt. And his expensive, unusual habits when it comes to women."

His eyes shone unpleasantly. "She likely has few prospects in this village. She's had a London season or two and came up empty-handed. I'm rescuing her from spinsterhood. I'll thrill her in bed a few times, then return to London, and we'll live our separate lives the way every married couple does. I'm capable of being decent—after all, she's a well-bred girl. *She* wasn't an opera dancer or a prostitute. What she doesn't know certainly won't hurt her."

"It will eventually hurt her, I can assure you. She's not a stupid girl, Amy."

"She wants my title. She's excited by my looks—do you see how she blushes when I'm about? She wants to be seen on my arm. What harm is there in wanting her money? She has a good deal of it. Surely *you* of all people would understand that."

She ignored this. "Has your reputation *really* run you aground into Pennyroyal Green? Have you really exhausted your options for heiresses? I know your financial straits are likely dire by now, but no woman should be consigned to a lifetime of *you*. But I won't see Amy Pitney hurt."

His handsome face went rigid with a suffusion of fury. He quickly mastered his features, but it lingered in how hard he squeezed her hand.

"Don't you believe people can change, Evie? Haven't *you*?"

She was genuinely surprised by this. "I haven't changed at all, Haynesworth. I was a courtesan. Which isn't a character flaw. Whereas raping opera dancers could be construed as one."

Again, eyes locked in cold antipathy, they circled the room.

"Did she tell you it was rape?" he sounded bored. "Typical melodrama. Annie O'Hara was always the hysterical sort."

Evie didn't dare look at Adam Sylvaine as she circled the room. She felt tainted by the touch of Haynesworth in the moment, and she was sure he'd be able to read it in her face. And yet he was safety and goodness and protection, and she couldn't resist the flick of a glance.

"Well, well. What does the large vicar in the bad clothing mean to you, Eve? You ought to have seen your expression when he delivered you at the end of the waltz."

She said nothing. She didn't want to hear Adam's name in this man's mouth.

"Like that, is it?" He gave a nasty little laugh. "Imagine how easy it would be for me to change his impression of you. I still want you, Eve. I know you can pleasure me in any way I please. And I know how to give pleasure to even the most jaded of women. It comes with a goodly amount of experience."

"So does the pox," she said briskly.

His face went lividly dark then.

"Don't ruin this engagement for me, Eve. Or I'll ruin you."

"You can't ruin a woman who's already allegedly been ruined, Haynesworth. And they know all about me. There's an adage about lightning striking, and so forth."

"I never *dreamed* you'd say something so naïve. Ask yourself this: Do you really think Miss Pitney will forgive you for shattering her dreams about me? Do you really think she'll thank you for confirming that all I want her for is her fortune, not her womanly charms? Do you really think a plain woman will want to hear a beautiful woman confirm for her how worthless she is apart from her fortune?"

Oh, God. And Eve knew he was likely right about all of those things.

She waited a bit too long to reply. So Haynesworth likely knew she was realizing he was right.

"She's a sensible woman," she tried.

He gave a short, confident laugh that tempted her to trod on in his instep. Damn his flawlessly made boots.

"Now that's a contradiction in terms, Lady Balmain. My offer stands."

WHAT HAD COLIN said? *Her past is likely to crop up at unlikely moments, and not in pretty ways.*

In the form of smug, flawlessly handsome London aristocrats who smiled enigmatically and put fixed, false smiles on Evie's face, for instance.

The morning after the Assembly, Adam sat at his desk, dragging the feathered end of his quill beneath his nose in thought. He could hear Mrs. Dalrymple moving about in the kitchen; the inviting sound of a rolling pin smacking down on dough. Some of his endless supplies of preserves would become a tart, it seemed.

He was supposed to be going over the vicarage's accounts. Thinking about ways to use the small plot of land that came with the living in order to bring in more income.

Instead, he was going over and over his waltz with Eve.

And thinking about Haynesworth.

And suffering.

Never let it be said he couldn't do several things at once.

What and who was Haynesworth to Eve? For it was clear he was *something*. Adam had watched Amy Pitney being led away by her dance partner for that waltz, and she'd craned her head over her shoulder at Evie and Haynesworth, her face worried.

She was a clever girl; she'd sensed it, too.

And after that, Eve had vanished without, to his knowledge, bidding anyone farewell. Like Cinderella racing against the clock. Though Haynesworth seemed to be everywhere out of the corners of his eyes for the rest of the evening. Smoothly smiling, calmly attentive to Amy Pitney. And more than once aiming what appeared to be a knowing smile in Adam's direction.

The evening was over when Evie vanished, as far as Adam was concerned, but he was obliged to stay, and he did.

And why shouldn't Eve's past follow her to Sussex? She was the sort who inspired powerful, wealthy men to reckless competition for her affections, to shooting each other and falling from balconies. And who was to say she wouldn't ultimately choose a future with one of those men?

It was a serrated thought. He couldn't move or breathe for it.

Who was to say she wouldn't, in fact, see Haynesworth while he was here? Why shouldn't she? There were freedoms in being a widow, after all. Haynesworth was everything to which she was accustomed; he was her old way of life. And perhaps a reminder of what she missed, despite the broadsheets. Gossip was fickle; ultimately, it would tire of sucking the marrow from the Black Widow nonsense and perhaps the ton would welcome the return of Eve.

But Adam knew he would see her today at the O'Flahertys.

It was this thought he lingered over. Anticipation made him breathless.

Somehow . . . somehow he would know the truth by looking into her face.

Or at least he told himself that much.

"Is the vicar in? Mrs. Dalrymple made free to let me, given that I'm a relative."

Ian stood in the doorway of his office.

"The vicar's in to you. Did you bring me any jam or embroidered pillows?"

"I need to bring offerings to get an audience with you these days? Very well, how about this: I did bring a bit of news that might interest you. John O'Flaherty was seen in the Pig & Thistle last night."

Adam leaned back in his chair. And then sighed at length.

"I prefer jam," he said.

"Sorry, old man. But I knew you'd been doing some work on their home, and I thought you'd like to know what you may need to contend with."

"Was he drinking?"

"Oh, yes."

"Ned Hawthorne *served* him?"

"It seems he'd brought in his own flask."

Adam dropped his quill and stood immediately. A reflex, an instinct. He wasn't due to round up his volunteers to go out to the O'Flahertys' for a few hours yet, but something told him he should go now. He kept a horse at the vicarage.

He reached for the coat he'd draped over the back of his chair and shoved his arms in.

And then paused. He hated to ask it. But he couldn't help it.

"Ian . . . by the way, do you know anything about Lord Haynesworth?"

"Haynesworth . . . well, he's land rich and cash poor. Describes a lot of aristocrats, doesn't it? Likes to gamble. I don't know him very well but don't care for what I do know. Seems a bit too polished, if you know what I mean, and when you're that polished, all that reflection is usually for the purposes of hiding something."

Which is what Ian was doing at the moment: hiding something. Adam sensed it.

"What *aren't* you telling me?"

Ian stared at him, hesitating. And then he sighed. "I do believe he fought a duel over Evie—sorry, Lady Wareham—some years ago. But then fighting duels over Evie was all the rage at one time."

Adam's expression must have been eloquent.

"Sorry, old man," Ian said gruffly.

"For what?" Adam's voice had gone taut.

"For whatever it is you're feeling right now. Because judging from your expression, you're not enjoying it."

Adam gave a short, humorless laugh. "Have you been talking to Colin?"

"I always talk to Colin," Ian said innocently. "And the most advice I'm qualified to give is keep your head down. You're a grown man. If you want to know more about Haynesworth, there's a bloke called Mr. Bartholomew who lives a few miles outside town who had some business dealings with him, if you'd like to know more. He's a barrister, and I think there was a good deal of trouble there. And now I'm off to see a man about a horse, and I'm late. Au revoir, cousin. Good luck with O'Flaherty and . . . everything else."

Chapter 16

"Henny, you've had that sniffle a good long time now."

Evie was in the kitchen packing a basket with a few things for the O'Flahertys before she departed—some seedcakes freshly baked by Mrs. Wilberforce, a few old London broadsheets for fresh admiral hats, a quarter of a wheel of cheese—while together with Mrs. Wilberforce they planned a shopping list of things to purchase in town.

Henny was busy grinding her nose into a large handkerchief, so it was a moment before she could speak.

"'Tis all this greenery here in Sussex. Me lungs are fit only to inhale coal smut."

"Speaking of filth and unpleasant things . . . you'll never believe who appeared at the Assembly last night. Lord Haynesworth."

Henny froze and stared at her over the wads of her handkerchief. And then revulsion shimmied over her face.

"Shall I snap his neck like a chicken for you?" Henny said idly. "Rotten git."

"He has his eye on Miss Pitney."

Henny was alarmed. "That poor girl with the

fortune and the eyebrows? You'll tell her about
him, aye?"

"I'll have to, won't I?"

"Can ye see that on your conscience? I think ye
may have enough trouble getting past St. Peter at
the gates as it is. Ye must tell her."

Eve sighed. She knew she did. She didn't look
forward to it in the least. But if Haynesworth intended to speak to Miss Pitney's father this week,
there could be no postponing it.

"And speaking of things that are lovely . . . did
ye dance wi' the vicar?"

She *had* danced with the vicar. All night in fact.
In her dreams. As if she was a green girl after a
first dance, who'd never once awakened next to a
nude, snoring, portly MP.

Evie noticed Mrs. Wilberforce freeze alertly in her
writing. And she remembered that her sister worked
for the Pitneys, and though she was likely trustworthy enough, why feed grist into the gossip mill?

Instead of answering, she asked Henny, "Have
we any mail?"

"Aye. You've another letter, too."

Eve eyed it, her heart sinking. Yet another.

And Cora typically only wrote if the news was
very good, very new, or very bad.

She hesitated, then took a deep breath and broke
the seal.

He's been gone a week now. Little Tommy is teething.
The baby looks a bit like you Aoife!

Much love,
Cora

Evie lay that letter down and stared at it.

An anvil seemed to take up residence on her chest.

"Not beef this week, Mrs. Wilberforce," she said suddenly, just as Mrs. Wilberforce wrote "beef" on her list of items to buy in town.

It was just too costly, when there was only herself and the servants to feed.

Cora, all of her nieces and nephews . . . how on earth would they all survive if their father never returned? For Eve could only just pay for her household as it was. There was the bit of land that could be worked outside the manor, but she hadn't the staff to do it, and wouldn't know to whom to rent it.

Mrs. Wilberforce looked up from her list.

"Very well, m'lady," she said kindly. "No beef this week."

SINCE MRS. WILBERFORCE was going into town anyway, Eve rode with her atop their wagon. She would walk the rest of the way to the O'Flahertys' from outside the cheese shop; they'd agreed that Mrs. Wilberforce would come to fetch her home in an hour or two.

"And Mrs. Wilberforce . . . will you stop in at the doctor's surgery and see about some herbs for Henny's cough? Unless you have a tisane or a posset or some such for it?"

"I do have a tisane for it. But I'll see to it, m'lady. It never hurts to have a number of options, now, does it?"

A philosophy to live by, to be certain.

Evie embarked on the short remainder of the walk to the O'Flaherty household, singing softly to herself, swinging the basket, enjoying the weather, cold as it was. It was nearly clear, with enough breeze to carry a hint of the sea across the downs.

But she slowed as she approached the O'Flaherty land.

Something was amiss.

There was an air of hush about it. As if the house itself was a frightened, crouching creature. No Molly the dog roared out the door to greet her. Even the chickens looked more subdued, but then they'd been fed more often lately. They eyed her basket with more idle curiosity than anything else. They left her toes alone as she approached the door.

She walked slowly, her senses so heightened the very sound of her own footsteps against the earth made her feel pursued.

Halfway across the yard a voice reached her through the ajar door. A man's voice, raised and slurred with drink. Trampling over the conciliatory, desperately placating murmur of a woman's voice.

She didn't hear the children at all.

Eve stopped. Held herself perfectly still, like a cornered animal. The slurred cadences were too familiar. Her heart hurling itself against the walls of her chest, she forced herself forward through air that suddenly seemed thick and threatening as lava.

"And I want to know who ye've been letting into this house in me absence!"

Eve pushed the door farther open, gently, gently, so quietly. Just a few inches.

Straightaway, she saw the children, cowering in a corner. Molly the dog was crouched before them, shivering. The baby was behind them in its cradle, making soft, fussing noises.

No one noticed her.

And a man, stocky, his face the color of brick, his hair likely once dazzling and now faded to an anemic shade of rust, stood in the center of the room.

He'd lowered his face until it was inches from Mary Flaherty's, and snarling and swaying. Likely Mary's face was hardly in focus for him. For Eve could smell John O'Flaherty—alcohol and layers of unwashed sweat—from where she stood.

"What did I tell ye, Mary, about accepting charity? This—" He plucked a hunk of bread and flung it down on the table, where it bounced onto the floor. Molly the dog eyed it wistfully. "Charity bread! And you and everyone in town saying I canna provide for ye! Is that what you tell them? Ye *like* makin' a mockery of me, now, don't ye? *Don't* ye?"

"No, John," Mary said dully, soothingly. "Not at all. I promise you. It's just that with the new baby—"

And time slowed then, as John O'Flaherty stepped back and raised a hand good and high.

The better to swing it across his wife's face.

And Eve shrieked like a banshee and flew through the door at him.

And Adam, just a few feet behind her, saw her do it. In two long strides, he was inside. He lunged for her and seized her about the waist. She thrashed and kicked to be free, so he tucked her under her arm and hurled her toward the door.

And it was he who stepped between John O'Flaherty and his wife, and took the fist to the jaw.

Evie gasped when his head snapped back, and he went down on one knee.

But when O'Flaherty reflexively tried again—like a windmill that had no choice but to keep going around—Adam's hand shot up and seized his wrist in midair. For a moment, their two arms locked, straining against each other. And then in one swift deft motion Adam twisted O'Flaherty's arm around his back and yanked it up good and high.

O'Flaherty yelped; his face bunched in pain and darkened to the color of brick.

The roar of breathing, his and Adam's, was all anyone heard in the room. Not one sound came from the children huddling in the corner.

"Now, John." Adam's voice was calm. Conversational. "You and I both know if you move at all, this will hurt worse for you. And like as no you've gauged my size and yours and, well, let's be reasonable, I'm sober and you're not and the odds are against you. Very against you."

John O'Flaherty seemed to take this in. He nodded, almost reasonably, though the cords of his neck were still taut with fury. He gave a token struggle. Apparently confirming precisely what Adam had just said, because he gasped.

"I'm not going to let you hit your wife. And I'm not going to let go of you until you're out of this house. We're going to walk like this to the door, then I'm going to walk you *through* the door, then you're going to keep walking down the hill, through the town, *past* the pub, out of the town, and you won't turn around, and you won't come back. If you turn around," he said almost apologetically, "I'll flatten you. I will take you down very quickly. What I do to you, in fact, will hurt considerably worse than a hangover, and last considerably longer. I invite you to test me."

Again, very reasonably.

John O'Flaherty mulled this. "Sounds fair," he conceded. Wisely.

"Shall we now?"

In a peculiarly mutated form of waltz, they shuffled, Adam maintaining his hold so tightly his knuckles were white, the muscles of his forearms bulging. John O'Flaherty cooperating, as though he knew he'd done something wrong.

A few feet outside the door, Adam released him abruptly. John staggered, then righted himself. He gave his head a shake and looked back at the house.

"Keep walking, John."

Adam watched as John O'Flaherty trudged up the road.

And then he touched his face. It had been a glancing blow only, just enough to knock him off balance. He'd likely have a bruise. But, then, he'd had bruises before. He could accommodate them better than Mrs. O'Flaherty could.

Mary O'Flaherty was scarlet with shame. "I'm so sorry, Reverend Sylvaine. He seldom . . . that is . . . only with the drink. Almost never . . . almost never in front of the children. I . . ."

She turned and hurried to her children. And they were so accustomed to it that not even the little one cried.

Captain Katharine was in the corner, one protective arm looped about her huddled brothers and her sister. Molly the dog, nearly as tall as the youngest girl, sat among them. The baby was waking, fussing softly in her crib. With her other hand, Katharine held on for dear life to her St. Christopher's medal.

"It worked, Mama," she said. "Lady Wareham's captain's medal worked. Da is gone!"

Eve made a small sound of pain. As though something had snapped inside her.

She turned on her heel and walked out of the house.

Mary O'Flaherty had ceased noticing him, busy with the children, and she was safe for now. So he followed Eve.

She'd walked as far as the big oak tree and stopped. She flung her body back against it and stared up through the stripped branches.

He leaned against the tree alongside her; there was room enough for the two of them, even a third person, to lean. The tree had been there for centuries and had likely seen worse than the O'Flahertys. And better.

" 'Almost never,' " she quoted bitterly.

He had nothing to say to that. They leaned in silence for a time.

"Why are they like that?" she asked finally. Listlessly.

"They?"

"Men. Some men," she corrected.

He moved just an inch or so, until his shoulder just barely brushed hers, and he could feel her ease just slightly into the comfort. He remained as still as if a butterfly had lighted on his hand.

"Sometimes it's poverty," he began softly. "A man gets to feeling helpless, so tortured by the fact that he can't support his family. There's nothing most men like less than to feel helpless."

"You're not rich."

"Oh, how I love to be reminded of it."

She half smiled. She reached up to touch her throat, but dropped her hand again. Remembering again that her St. Christopher's medal was now hanging around the neck of Captain Katharine.

"I wish I had a cheroot," she admitted. "I smoked now and again, when I was in London. Very calming, cheroots."

"And here I was thinking there was a vice you'd somehow missed."

Another small smile. "*You* arrived just in time. My cousin Ian warned me John O'Flaherty had been seen. Instinct made me come ahead of the volunteers." He gestured to where his horse was tethered.

She was lost in thought. In memories, no doubt.

"Do you ever feel helpless, Reverend Sylvaine? Utterly at the mercy of circumstances?"

He wasn't about to admit to that particular word: "helpless." Neither that, nor to being at the mercy of circumstances, because his current circumstances involved the complicated, glorious ways he felt about Evie Duggan.

"I meant it when I said my work involved a lot of guessing."

"Well, then. I'd say you've a knack," she said dryly.

He blew out a breath. "Your father drank?" He asked this question as if they were continuing a conversation.

She turned her face slowly up to him. At first incredulous, then indignant, then pinched with pain.

"Evidence of your knack." She said it ironically,

almost bitterly amused. "There was naught I could do to stop it, you know, when I was young. Da drank, and he hit Mum when he did. I did try to stop it."

He could feel every muscle in his body tightening, bracing himself for the next question.

"Did he hit you?"

But he was certain he already knew the answer. He imagined a man raining blows on a little girl, and fury was acrid in the back of his throat. His head went light from it. And he thought: I will turn back time. In that moment, he felt he really could do it, such was the force of his fury. I will undo whatever harm came to her.

She must have felt his tension in the arm that just barely brushed hers. She stirred a little.

"Only a few times," she said distantly. "It was Mum who stepped in, like you stepped in today. She wouldn't let him get near us. It was always Mum who bore the brunt. And then he left and never came back; and then she died."

Such a succinct, brutal way to summarize a childhood, he thought.

"And do you know . . . I swore then that I would never be at the mercy of any man. Ever. I would always choose when to begin and when to end with a man."

He heard this as a confession and a warning.

And thus more and more of the mosaic of her life shifted into place. Being born into chaos was why she'd planned her life so carefully. And why she remained so desperate to protect her family—because she'd never been able to protect her mother as a child.

And her family was all she had. But some of her puzzle was still missing.

"How did you come to be in London?"

"A tinker passing through our village told me I was so pretty I could make my living on the stage." She slid him an ironically flirtatious look. "I managed to persuade him to take all of us there in his wagon. All the little Duggans."

"Ah, the advantages of being pretty. And persuasive."

She gave a short laugh. "Mind you, all he got was a kiss for his trouble. My brothers and sisters were small, but we would have torn him to pieces if he'd tried anything else, but the tinker was decent, for all of that. He gave me my St. Christopher's medal. Bit of tin, but he said it was for luck. And I might have been pretty, but I was a peasant, and there are only a few choices for a girl like me who needed to make a good deal of money in order to keep her family from the workhouse or the hulks. Fortunately, I was directed to the Green Apple Theater. You see, I've a bit of a knack, too," she added with a quirk of her mouth. "Or so I discovered. I could entertain. Or entertain *sufficiently*."

"And so you were able to take care of your family."

"Mind you, it wasn't glamorous at first—I wouldn't recommend a room over a Seven Dials whorehouse as your next residence, for instance, Reverend Sylvaine."

"And here I was sorely tempted."

"It's just . . . seeing the O'Flahertys . . . Adam, I'm worried sick about Cora," she confided. Her voice nearly a whisper. She half laughed, half moaned and swiped her hands down her face. "For history repeats, doesn't it? And in the last letter I had, her husband had gone missing. Will you pray for her?"

She turned hunted eyes up to him.

"I'll pray." It was a vow. Anything he could make right for her, anything he could do, he would.

A rogue breeze sent a few dead leaves tumbling and scraping after each other over the ground. It looked like pursuit.

"Such a kind thing to do, Eve," he said, his voice soft, fierce. "To give your medal to little Katharine. Such a good thing."

She shrugged with one shoulder. "I used to think it helped when I held on to it. It was so much better than nothing. It's a horrible feeling, helplessness. God, how I hate to be at the mercy of anything."

For a moment they watched the road together, as if it were the source of all surprises, for good or ill.

"How do you do it? How could you talk to him as though he was . . . human?"

It wasn't an accusation. It sounded as though she truly wanted to know.

He drew in a breath. "Well, my father was . . . is . . . a bit of a tyrant. Unpredictable. Subject to rages, free with his fists. I learned to read him the way you can read the weather, in order to stay clear of him, and I think it's how I became observant. And . . . I had to try to understand him in order to outthink him. And when I understood him . . . it wasn't a far leap from there to compassion. I didn't like him, mind you," he said distantly. "And I don't like John O'Flaherty, either. I think he's despicable. But I pity him."

He'd never said these things aloud to another

soul. He wasn't certain he'd drawn these conclusions quite this clearly before this moment.

But he wanted to give something of himself to her. Even as he knew these exchanges of confidence bound them ever closer together, like a cat's cradle, even as he knew they simultaneously unraveled each other.

"And there are days . . . nearly every day . . . when I hope O'Flaherty never returns to his family, like your da. And when the O'Flaherty boys are old enough to work their scrap of land and raise stock, I think somehow, with luck, with my help and the worthy Mrs. Sneath's battalion, they'll all survive the better for it with their father gone. But sometimes a man's family is all he has, the only thing that keeps him going from day to day. He may not deserve them, but it's not an easy thing to deny him whatever comfort that might bring. And everyone, like you say, deserves a chance."

When he turned, he found her eyes on him with an expression he couldn't decipher. Something open and aching, something like pain that could just as easily have been joy.

It smoothed into inscrutability so swiftly it might have been a trick of the light.

"I would have liked to rip his throat out," she said almost absently. "O'Flaherty."

"I know."

She half smiled. "Such *calm* in the face of my violent confession."

The decision made itself. It was a pure extension of the moment. He slipped his hands in the pockets of his coat and closed it around the box Lady

Fennimore had given him, nudged it open with his thumb, felt the fine chain beneath his fingers.

He closed the little gold cross in his hands and lifted it out.

He hesitated only a moment before he spoke. "I'd like you to have this. Lady Fennimore gave it to me. Said it brought her luck and protection. She said I'd know to whom I should give it."

He opened his hand and showed her what it was.

She peered down at the tiny cross. Her breath went out of her, softly, in surprise.

A faint flush washed over her cheeks. For a good long while she didn't look up at him. Perhaps she didn't want him to see her expression. Perhaps she was considering what it meant to him, and what he wanted from her, and the consequences of accepting a thing.

"Oh, but I'm grown now." She strove for lightness. "I shouldn't have need of protection. I couldn't possibly acc—"

"Eve."

She stopped abruptly. Her face lifted, her eyes widened at the quiet vehemence he'd given her name.

"It's all right to need help on occasion. It's all right to let someone else look after you for a change. And, sometimes, *accepting* a gift is a gift you give to someone else. And that's all it is."

She hesitated. Her lips pressed together in indecision. And then she blew out another breath.

"Will you . . . will you put it on for me?"

And slowly, slowly, she turned around and cupped a hand to the knot in her hair and lifted it.

Revealing that fine trace of dark hair at her nape, the pale soft skin.

A motion so sensual, so intimate, it felt nearly as though she'd lifted her gown over her head and let it drop to the ground.

She angled her head, sending an oblique glance over her shoulder through lowered lashes.

Then turned away from him again.

She never could resist a challenge, and she flirted like breathing.

And oh, God, she knew. She knew what it did to him.

Just as he knew what he did to her.

In some remote place in his mind, the word "Haynesworth" stirred. Distantly, he wondered how many men she might have looked at in just the same way.

But Haynesworth seemed infinitely far away from them now.

Once again, the world was comprised of the two of them.

Suddenly, his fingers, usually quite reliable, were so clumsy it was though he'd just been given the use of hands for the very first time.

He fumbled what felt like endlessly with the clasp to open it. He brought the necklace around the front of her; he lowered it slowly, slowly, until the cross gently bumped the swell of her breasts.

And deliberately he dragged it up, up, up, the fine chain a slow caress over her skin, until he felt the weight of the little cross settle against her collarbone. And he watched, enthralled, as gooseflesh rained over the back of her neck.

Her shoulders were swaying now with her quickening breath.

He could hear his own breath, too.

His head seemed to float above his body. Latching it was another exercise in eternity. His trembling fingers brushed against her unconscionably satiny skin as he did, against the silky dark hair at her nape.

And then it was done.

His fingers hovered there, just above the latch. Loath to leave her.

She never wants to be at the mercy of any man, he thought.

He suddenly felt like the oak tree, planted there forever, doomed to remain motionless a mere hairsbreadth away from a woman he didn't dare touch with more than his fingertips.

He closed his eyes against an onslaught of *want* so total it could just as easily be called anguish. Dear God. Just to lay a kiss there, just there, beneath her ear where her heart beat, and know he had caused the swift slam of it. To slide his arms around her, to follow the eloquent line of hip to narrow waist, to bring his hands up over her breasts, to gently crush the weight and give of them in his palms, to hear her moan. To drag his fingers over her nipples to make her jerk with the pleasure of it. To slowly furl up her dress and slip his hands between her thighs, sliding up to find the hot, silky skin above her garters. To search higher, and higher, to delve into the wetness between her legs. To feel her legs falling helplessly open for him, asking for more, for deeper, for the release he could give her.

To free his stiffening cock, then to turn her, and bend her, and plunge into her as she braced herself against the tree and took his thrusts . . .

His breath was a low roar in his ears. He was shaking now.

And in vain he struggled to breathe through it, the way he would any pain.

It was useless. He'd tipped to the other side of desire, and he fell completely.

To hell with bloody Lady Fennimore and her *beautiful suffering*.

He watched, as if in a dream, as his mouth lowered. And first just his breath stirred the fine dark hair. And then his lips, at last, were against her skin. He pressed, slowly, lightly, a kiss there.

Her breath hitched. Half sigh, half moan, the most wholly erotic sound he'd ever in his life heard.

His lips lingered softly, so softly. His breath, his mouth, savoring her.

Her head fell back heavily, languidly, inviting his lips to glide along the silky contour of her throat, to the pulse thumping beneath her ear. He circled it with his tongue. Covered it with his half-open mouth. Her body swayed hard with her breathing.

Molly the dog began barking.

It cost him every bit of control he possessed, he lifted his head again. In that moment, it felt like the hardest thing he'd ever done.

"There," he finally whispered, into that eternal silence.

She said nothing.

The tattered sound of her breathing said everything.

And they stood like that, frozen in a moment, a hairsbreadth away from touching each other, Adam's erection straining against his trousers. In an agony of want and indecision.

As Miss Amy Pitney's coach turned the bend.

And as she looked out the window she saw the vicar standing behind the countess. So close it was entirely possible he was touching her.

The countess's eyes were closed. Her face seemed to be suffused with some enormous emotion.

And then, when they heard the wheels of her carriage, they moved apart as abruptly as scattered ninepins.

The countess moving for the house, the vicar for the back of the house.

In a half hour or so, the voices of Mrs. Sneath, Amy, Josephine, and Jenny, Lady Fennimore's daughter, helped Eve restore the O'Flaherty household to a cheerful uproar.

The reverend stayed with them inside the house until his other volunteers arrived, then all the men descended upon the outbuildings, hammering and shouting and laughing over the work, while inside the house, Eve bumped into things. And started sentences and forgot to end them. Or ended them by staring into space.

She let the soup boil over, and competent Captain Katharine dashed for the stove and rescued it. She began to sweep the floor, then paused, her hands on the broom, until one of the boys pulled it from her hand.

"Fine deckhand you are, Lady Wareham!" he declared. "Thirty days in the hold!"

"An excessive punishment, surely," Evie said mildly.

She sat down to take the baby momentarily from Mrs. O'Flaherty, and one of the other boys sat next to her. He'd nearly succeeded in nicking a comb from her hair before she noticed.

What she didn't notice was that while Amy and Jenny were tutoring the youngest girl and the boys, and playing and laughing with the children, they hadn't said a word to her.

Because the kiss reverberated through Eve. It had taken her over; it flowed in her veins instead of blood. She could scarcely see anything; she only felt. All she needed to do to experience it again was to imagine it, and the place beneath her ear sang. A simple press of the lips against her throat had undone her.

Fear and joy moved through her body, two terrible, glorious partners in a reel.

She wanted him she wanted him she wanted him.

She didn't notice when Amy Pitney paused in a moment of helping one of the boys with his reading and stared at her from across the room, her face closed, hard and speculative.

"Lady Wareham, the medal worked. It really worked," Captain Katharine whispered to her, leaning companionably on her shoulder, in that carelessly affectionate way children do, as Evie did her best to help mend one of the endless piles of rent pinafores and short pants. "He left again. Da did."

"I'll tell you a secret, Captain Katie. The medal only works if the person wearing it is strong and clever. And you are."

"I *know*," Captain Katharine confided on a whisper.

Eve bit back a smile. How she loved that child's confidence.

"And sometimes very strong, clever people are tested a bit more than other people, but that's because they're meant for great things, Captain Katharine. So sometimes what seems like the end of a trial is really just a part of what will be a long, exciting, wonderful story, with lots and lots of interesting parts in it. Have you heard the story of Hercules?"

Captain Katharine shook her head.

"We'll have to read it together then, won't we?"

The thought of stories involving trials and lots of interesting parts and the need for bravery made Eve remember Amy. If Haynesworth intended to speak to her father this week, then she would need to have a difficult conversation with her straightaway.

One of the more difficult conversations she would ever have, she suspected. But the kiss in her veins was an opiate. And somehow, she thought this might make it all easier.

And if Haynesworth hadn't been part of her past, she might never be warned she was about to make a terrible mistake. And for this, at least, Eve supposed she ought to be grateful.

She looked up at Amy. Only to find Amy watching her with a peculiar, cold, speculative expression.

"Amy," she said to her, "would you join me for a walk? I've need of some air."

Chapter 17

OUTSIDE, THE SHOUTS AND LAUGHTER OF THE MEN working on the outbuildings filled the air. Interspersed with barks from Molly the dog.

Amy was silent as they walked a few feet into the center of the yard. Eve stopped. "I've something to say to you, Amy."

Amy crossed her arms and levered up her stern brows. "By all means, speak, Lady Wareham."

"You're aware I've known quite a number of men in my day. I am, perhaps, in a position to assess the character of men. Do you believe me?"

Amy gave a short laugh. "I believe you've known a lot of men in your day. And I believe you're very good at assessing character."

Eve couldn't quite gauge Amy's mood. Or her tone. She'd seemed to learn irony overnight. There was high color in her cheeks, and she hadn't blinked, and her arrogant jaw was righteously set. Her eyes were hard. It wasn't difficult to see how Josephine had arrived at an olive-stone comparison.

"Well, then," Eve continued. "Since you know of my past, you may know that I was employed for a time as an Opera Dancer at the Green Apple Theater. I knew Lord Haynesworth then."

She waited, gauging Amy's response.

No gasp of surprise, no widened eyes, no twitch. Just a hard, cold stare. "Go on." More of that irony.

"Very well . . . well, I'll be very succinct. He fought a duel for my attentions. I fear I didn't welcome his attentions even then, and the duel was unnecessary, unpleasant, and illegal. I fear he is in fact altogether . . . disrespectful to women. He was rather forceful with me, and he behaved dishonorably when I knew him."

It was a horrible litany of crimes for an innocent, hopeful young girl to have to hear. How she wished she wasn't afraid to say *precisely* what Haynesworth had done.

Amy crossed her arms around herself, as if to ward off her influence. She gave another of those short, unpleasant laughs.

"He told me you would say that." She said it almost to herself. Her face was closed, resentful, as though she possessed some sort of secret.

A chilly little breeze of unease blew through Evie.

"Amy," Eve said gently, "I fear it's true. I don't repent my past. It was what enabled me to care for my family. But I did meet many people as part of my career. And one of the ways I managed to survive in a world rougher than you can imagine, and rougher than I hope you ever know, is that I became a very good judge of character. Haynesworth is handsome and charming, but he's ruthless and selfish and childish about getting what he wants and thinks he deserves, and he's very much in want of a fortune. I hated so to tell you, but I think you deserve so much better than a husband like him, and can and *will* have so much better. And I thought you trusted me to tell you."

With every word, Amy's face went increasingly scarlet, until she was blotched and contorted with furious hurt.

"In truth, it's the other way *around*, isn't it, Lady Wareham?" she said bitterly. "He refused *your* attentions because he wanted nothing to do with an *opera dancer*. And now you're trying to punish him for it by interfering with our chance at happiness. Because that's the way you are. 'Aloof,'" she quoted, and barked a caustic laugh. "And all the while you wanted us to remain *aloof* so you could have the vicar's attentions for yourself! How *difficult* it must have been for you to be forced to leave London and all the constant adulation you're so accustomed to, that you think you deserve. And I thought you were my friend."

It was Eve who flinched, shocked. "Amy, please listen—"

"And—" Amy delivered her coup de grace with furious triumph. "Jenny knows her mother gave that cross to Reverend Sylvaine. And he gave it to *you*."

She aimed an accusing finger at the necklace around Evie's throat.

It took every bit of Eve's control to keep her hand from flying up to touch it.

Bloody hell. Gifts of jewelry always seemed to carry a consequence.

"You really are a Black Widow, aren't you? You're dastardly clever, I'll grant you that. The vicar is a *good* man, Lady Wareham. And he's a man, so he isn't to blame if his head is turned by you and your ways. But *he* won't fall into your . . . your . . . *web*."

Even through her temper, Evie almost laughed. Amy was clearly suffering in the throes of her very first, real, righteous torment. But Eve had worked with actresses and befriended opera singers, and histrionics were practically the language they all spoke. To her it was nearly humdrum. She was torn between giving Amy a good hard shake and patting her soothingly.

She knew neither would be welcome.

"Well done, Amy! Perhaps *you* ought to take the stage. But I *am* your friend. And I swear on the life of everyone I hold dear that I'm telling you the truth about Haynesworth. You're hurt and angry now, but I want you to remember this: The vicar *is* a good man. Please think about why you believe this is so. And you're so very sharp-eyed and clever: Ask yourself whether Haynesworth measures up to him, or to Simon Covington—what makes these men *good*? It's true not many of us are spoiled for choice in life, and many women are forced into decisions we'd prefer not to make. And you're right. You *may* never know a grand passion." Eve said this baldly, and Amy's chin hiked defensively up. "You may eventually *settle* for someone. But you are a good person, an attractive person, and you *don't* need to marry yourself to misery. And I promise you Haynesworth is exactly that."

Amy was huffing out angry breaths now. Her eyes were narrow and hot.

She clenched her fists and turned away from Eve and looked out over the yard, at the chickens, all of whom were growing plumper and less angry, and were now prone to laying eggs in hidden places in the yard. The henhouse was being repaired.

"You don't have to believe me, Amy," she said more gently. "Go ahead and hate me. But if you've a shred of logic remaining in your head, ask your father to look more closely at Haynesworth's finances, or into his connections. A good man will withstand a little scrutiny any day. And I couldn't live with myself if I didn't at least *try* to talk some sense into you."

They turned their heads toward the barn when they heard shouts and laughter. Reverend Sylvaine was standing atop it, shirt open two modest buttons-worth, sleeves rolled up, hands on his hips, gesturing to Simon Covington to hand him up something.

He saw Amy and Eve and waved.

Reflexively, Eve and Amy waved back.

They were silent for a time. Soft sounds, the quiet *bock bock bocking* of the chickens and laughter bursting through the windows of the house, in stark contrast to the furious emotion.

Amy said almost casually, "You do know that the entire town will shun the vicar if he takes up with you, Lady Balmain. And it will be the ruination of him."

The words landed on Eve like a slap.

She stared at the girl, who defiantly tried to meet her gaze. But Amy hadn't as much practice as Evie with burning a hole into someone with her eyes.

She shifted her eyes back to the barn.

Eve's voice shook with the effort to control her temper. "Consider that he gave the cross to me because he thought I might have need of the comfort,

Miss Pitney. And consider that a good man recognizes the good in others. Consider that he views me as a friend, and only that. "

Consider that you're a hypocrite, Evie.

Amy turned back to her, and said with weary incredulity, "Oh, for heaven's sake. At least do me the honor of assuming I'm not stupid. I may be plain, Lady Balmain. But I'm not blind. And neither is anyone else in this town."

ADAM BOLTED THREE cups of coffee and wolfed a slab of buttered bread in the Sunday predawn darkness. Sunday service loomed. The foolscap remained nude of words, as intimidating as a bloody abyss, mimicking his empty mind. He held his quill over a sheet of foolscap, praying for inspiration to pour down through it and magically produce the sermon he hadn't managed to finish yesterday since he'd been hammering boards into the O'Flahertys' roof.

Yes . . . yes! He felt a twinge of something! It was coming now!

He scrawled:

I kissed her I kissed her I kissed her

Well.

As a sermon, it was a failure, but his parishioners would doubtless find it edifying.

Light seemed to pour from the words, soak into him, fill him with a rising tide that threatened to burst from him in a roar of emotion that would terrify Mrs. Dalrymple right out of her slumbers. He held himself very still, as if he contained something volatile, explosive. He allowed the joy to pulse in him for a moment. Surely, he deserved that much. Surely, there was no *harm* in just that much. And yet he knew this was how the rationale for every sin began: "Surely there's no harm in stealing one ha'pence from the collection plate—no one will miss it." "Surely one kiss does not adultery make." That sort of thing.

If he lived in the memory—considered nothing that came before or nothing that would come after—he felt weightless. But the escalating momentum—a waltz, a cross, a kiss—of whatever lay between them had the power to carry him inexorably, dangerously down, down, down, like an anchor thrown overboard.

He now understood with piercing clarity why scripture was so unequivocally unforgiving about lust. Because he believed quite sincerely he would die if he didn't make love to Eve. This in fact felt truer than anything he'd known or been taught before. And if he allowed *this* thought to elbow aside his will and good sense, he would soon be useless to the people who needed him and trusted him most. A fraud of a vicar.

He drew a breath, exhaled in a rush so scouring it was nearly punishing.

And then he carefully, deliberately, shredded the words into strips—*I* and *kissed* and *her*—and fed them to the fire. Which seemed absurdly symbolic in dozens of ways.

And just as little Liam Plum set the church bells to ringing, calling the town to service, he managed to dot the last 'i' in a sermon about helping one another.

AND MINUTES LATER, groggy, but relieved not to be *completely* ashamed of the quality of his eleventh-hour sermon, Adam stepped up to the altar, notes rustling in his hands.

He lifted his head to smile at the congregation.

And shock did a slow, jagged plummet through him.

A cluster of his relatives sat near the front. One of them was wearing an expression of sympathy that bordered on "I told you so" (that would be Colin). The only other people in church were Mr. Brownwell, Mr. Eldred, and a scattering of other parishioners who, he instantly surmised, abjured gossip more than the others.

In the back row next to Henny sat Eve. Wearing a serene, impenetrable, neutral smile. She was straight-backed and utterly still, as if no one would see her if she didn't move.

Not one of the women who belonged to the Society for the Protection of the Sussex Poor were present.

Except, that was, Mrs. Sneath. Who sat dead center, alone, like a pin inserted in a battle map. Her head tilted, her expression peculiarly sympathetic, a trifle mournful, faintly obdurate. The expression his mother used to wear when she'd fed him cod-liver oil: *It's for your own good, Adam. This will hurt me more than it will hurt you, Adam.*

And behind these people the empty pews, glossy, shined by centuries of shifting Pennyroyal Green bums, seemed to unfurl dizzyingly in his vision. An illusion: The church was small. He expected it had seen emptier services throughout its history.

Still, the point seemed made.

Mr. Eldred, he of the goat dispute, sat in the front row and turned his head to and fro, mildly puzzled. Then he crossed his legs and spread his arms out like wings across the backs of his pew, looking quite pleased to have it to himself.

Adam realized now he'd found safety and reassurance in the number of eyes aimed up at him on Sunday mornings. How ironic it was that he'd forgotten how dangerous eyes could be, too. Belatedly, impressions penetrated now: The sound of Amy Pitney's carriage wheels when he'd stood outside the O'Flahertys' with Eve, the two of them frozen in an anguish of desire. The expressions of stunned amazement on her face as he'd led the countess onto the ballroom floor.

And yesterday he'd stood on the O'Flahertys' roof and watched as Eve and Amy Pitney appeared to have a heated discussion, complete with arms waving and then defensively crossed. He'd thought then that it might have something to do with the decorating committee.

It occurred to him that he might as well have read *I kissed her I kissed her I kissed her* aloud to everyone present in the church, for he suspected it was what they would hear in his every word anyway.

"Thank you for coming." His voice was steady and resonant. "Lately, I've had the pleasure of witnessing the miracles that can be wrought when we help one another. I believe . . ."

He paused. His voice seemed to echo mockingly in the nearly empty church.

"Go right ahead, Reverend. Tell us about helping one another," Mr. Eldred urged happily, in a near whisper, from the first pew.

And so Adam did. He got through the words, every single one of them. He even managed to inflect them with a certain amount of feeling. But he heard them only distantly, as if he were speaking underwater.

As though an anchor had carried him down, down, down.

"WHATEVER CAUSED IT, Adam," his uncle Jacob Eversea had said pleasantly as he left the nearly empty service this morning, his voice low. "Put it to rights, eh?"

He'd given him an affectionate back pat, which could just as easily have been a warning. For what Jacob Eversea giveth he could just as easily taketh away.

And now Adam sat in Mrs. Sneath's parlor, in the regular scheduled meeting of the Committee to Protect the Sussex Poor, encircled by all the women who'd punished him with their absence this morning.

Confronted with the reality of his presence, however, they all looked vaguely abashed and diffident.

Adam thought it best to seize the rudder of conversation immediately.

"How are the plans for the Winter Ball progressing, Mrs. Sneath? Do you need my approvals for any expenditures?"

"Oh, it's all going very well, you'll be happy to hear, Reverend Sylvaine. Decorations are proceeding apace. Lady Fennimore has agreed to donate flowers from her hothouse, and I think we'll be able to persuade the orches—"

"Do you believe the countess will be able to lend some of her expertise with regards to decorations?"

The hush was almost comically instant. Eyes looked everywhere but at him, then at him and away again. Cheeks were almost universally pink. Hands plucked fitfully at skirts. Many of them seemed to find the contents of their teacups fascinating.

Mrs. Sneath cleared her throat. All eyes swiveled in relief to her.

"With regards to the countess, Reverend Sylvaine. We've some business to discuss with you. And I fear you may find it a bit disappointing—I in fact find it terribly disappointing—as it involves a matter in which you've taken a special interest."

"I'm all ears, Mrs. Sneath."

"Now, I know we've viewed the Countess of Wareham as a special project . . ."

"Parishioner, Mrs. Sneath, I view her as a parishioner. And entitled to all rights of a parishioner. Not a project."

"Very well. And *as* such," Mrs. Sneath continued bravely, "you've been valiant in your efforts, as have I, to be accepting of her past and to offer her the benefit of the doubt when she expressed a sincere interest in a new beginning. I have admired her efforts toward that end immensely. She is a *very* charming person. I know you have tried your best to counsel her and to steer her in the proper direction. Which, naturally, could be the only reason you gave to her a cross once belonging to Lady Fennimore."

The women in the room became as statues, petrified in the act of fidgeting or sipping.

Adam's jaw clenched, and he slowly turned his head to stare at Jenny Fennimore.

Who dropped her eyes and took a noisy sip of her tea.

"You are a very good man, Reverend Sylvaine, but sometimes merely setting an example of goodness is not enough. And while the Countess of Wareham has undeniably been remarkably helpful with the O'Flahertys, based on some new information we have obtained, we nevertheless believe we have cause to curtail her association with the committee."

He despised the waiting expressions on their faces. They were dying to hear what he had to say about this.

"I see. Since we are in agreement that everyone deserves a *chance*, Mrs. Sneath, pray tell, what led to this decision?"

Mrs. Sneath exchanged a glance with Miss Pitney, who, with an air of martyred womanhood, nodded some sort of assent.

"Lord Haynesworth, who as you may know resides in London much of the year, was pained to inform Miss Pitney that when the countess . . ." she lowered her voice to a delicate whisper . . . "was an opera dancer, she eagerly sought his attentions and he rejected her advances. The countess has since made an attempt to greatly disparage his good name with Miss Pitney."

Haynesworth.

The word slithered through his gut, dark and synonymous with an insidious doubt.

"I'm certain Christian duty was behind his compulsion to share this story. That his own character is unbesmirched, and he has no other motive for claiming such a thing."

He directed this to Miss Pitney, who was trying out a new bold stare, which wavered beneath his ironic delivery.

She swallowed and turned away.

If Miss Pitney didn't know about the alleged duel Haynesworth had fought over her, it would be churlish to mention it before everyone. And it would hardly do Eve any favors.

He fought to keep his voice level and dispassionate, even as a pressure welled in his chest.

"The countess has been a friend to all of you, is this not true? She has worked hard on behalf of the committee. She has welcomed you into your home, and you have welcomed her into yours. You enjoy her company."

"This is true. We have undeniably enjoyed her company. Yet so much is known about her and yet unknown. And there is no denying the story is unsavory, Reverend."

"No."

"And that there is no denying her history."

"No."

"Which lends credence to his story."

"Perhaps."

"And if the viscount were to take up residence in Sussex . . ." And here Miss Pitney ducked her head demurely and blushed fetchingly, and affectionate looks were aimed in her direction. "Well, you see the difficulty, Reverend."

"I do."

The slightest of pauses here before Mrs. Sneath spoke again.

"We have reason to believe the countess has engaged in a pattern of such behavior."

Ah. Very delicately put. She'd saved this for last. He understood now. *He* was to be assumed the innocent victim of her wiles. A good man, but *just* a man, susceptible as any to a beautiful face and the skillful advances of a born temptress. And once the temptation was removed, well, he'd align with his senses once more, and once more be the object upon which they could impose their hopes and fantasies.

And yet . . . he breathed in sharply as he saw again the artful angling of Eve's head, the glance through her lashes, as he'd lowered his gift of the cross around her neck. Her allure was legendary, devastating, proved. It had driven Haynesworth to challenge another man over her.

Could it merely be a coincidence Haynesworth was in Pennyroyal Green now?

What really lay between the two of them?

Adam wished, in that moment, that he'd been cowardly, or less able to see clearly. Because it took all of his courage to confront the fact that something of truth must lie within all of this.

His knuckles whitened around the brim of his hat.

"Thank you for sharing your thoughts with me, Mrs. Sneath. Have you discussed your concerns with the countess?"

"I think our concerns will make themselves known to her soon enough."

Very oblique, that. He sensed an onslaught of shunning was imminent.

Distantly, he marveled. He'd been neatly trapped. By a group of determinedly self-righteous embroidering women. His lungs tightened, as surely as if the walls of his life were closing in.

If he defended her overtly, it would merely feed their suspicions and gossip.

And God help him, he wasn't certain she warranted the defending. And quite briefly, he loathed all of these women in the moment for hurling kindling on his own doubts. For tainting a memory.

"Since I know you're the kindest and most charitable of women, I do hope you consider your decision carefully."

Mrs. Sneath merely smiled brightly at him and refrained from answering.

"We've a gift for you, Reverend, before you go."

She handed to him a uselessly tiny pillow exquisitely embroidered with ivy and roses.

Ornately stitched in the center were the words "Proverbs 6:25."

The text of which read: *Lust not after her beauty in thine heart; neither let her take thee with her eyes.*

Proverbs 6 was in fact filled to *brimming* with admonitions about lust.

He slowly levered his head up.

And suddenly all the room twitched like ants beneath a magnifying glass at whatever burned from his eyes.

The. Bloody. Gall.

He'd held their babies, cried their bans, ushered their loved ones into peaceful deaths, absolved. He'd seen their faces every Sunday, eaten at their tables, counseled them in their griefs and woes. He knew they harbored fantasies and hopes about him, and there was no denying this had likely made his job both easier and harder.

And they held his future in their hands.

He felt as if their hands were around his throat.

And yet . . . perhaps they truly thought they were trying to save him from her.

Perhaps he needed saving.

Perhaps he was the only one who couldn't see it.

The thought tasted like cold metal in the back of his throat. He was tempted to rend the pillow in two, watch the shreds rain down on all of them.

He lowered it away from him instead.

"Thank you." A more ironic expression of gratitude was never uttered. "How I do appreciate your gifts. Next to the Bible, I've always found pillows to be the most reliable form of moral guidance. Perhaps one of you talented ladies would be so kind as to complete my collection? It seems to be missing one of my favorites. John 8, verse 7."

Let he who is without sin cast the first stone.

More fidgeting.

"Or perhaps you think Mathew 19:12 offers more appropriate words for me to live by?"

There are eunuchs who have made themselves eunuchs for the sake of the kingdom of heaven.

He could see which ones were true biblical scholars by the dropped jaws.

"Mrs. Sneath's niece was kind enough to give me one that says "Love thy Neighbor." *And look what happened*, he left unspoken.

Mrs. Sneath's eyes flew wide in alarm.

He'd better leave before he said something he *truly* regretted.

"I'll give the Mathew a try, Reverend!" Miss Charing piped. Somehow not quite grasping the point.

He leveled a look at her. Parted his mouth to say something. Thought better of it.

"Thank you, ladies, for your good work on behalf of the poor, and for your tireless efforts at keeping the stain of sin from the souls of Sussex." Irony was his permanent dialect now, it seemed.

"You're quite welcome, Reverend," Mrs. Sneath said sincerely.

"I shall see all of you at the ball?"

Much mutedly enthusiastic nodding.

"And Miss Pitney." He said it so curtly everyone flinched.

She was instantly all righteous, erect posture and arrogant, hiked jaw. Her color was defensively high.

The color of guilt, he suspected.

"Ask Lord Haynesworth if he knows a gentleman by the name of Mr. Bartholomew Tolliver."

He touched his hat to them and saw himself out so briskly it fluttered up the ribbons on their bonnets.

Chapter 18

Two hours later, Lord Haynesworth offered his arm with a look so warmly appreciative, Amy felt herself blush scarlet to her scalp.

She looped her arm less and less tentatively through his each time he did this. He felt so much like a man; the muscle beneath his coat was sturdy and thrillingly hard, a little frightening, a little alien, beneath her hand. They walked across the carriage drive of her home, past the fountain, toward the small wooded walk she'd known since she was a child.

"I can scarcely believe the Winter Ball is just two days away," she told him.

She wondered if she would be an engaged woman by then. The thought made her so breathless that, for an instant, the green expanse blurred before her vision.

She wondered when a man felt sufficiently confident of a woman's regard to ask for her hand in marriage. She felt as though she was participating in a ritual with defined steps, each of them steering her closer to a conclusion. It was considerably less romantic than she'd thought it might be. Rather more like a game of backgammon.

Perhaps it had to do with years of relying on being clever instead of pretty. She couldn't break herself of the habit of *thinking*. Thinking and stifling torment had been her chief pastimes when it came to men, it seemed.

And yet . . . she'd seen how Josephine now stared at Simon.

How the vicar looked at the countess when they'd danced the waltz.

It didn't appear as if any of them had even been *capable* of thinking.

Her stomach knotted. It was so desperately unfair. And yet her prize would seem to be the greatest of all of them.

But now thanks to the vicar's blue, relentless eyes and his disciplinary little tone as he'd bade them all farewell an hour ago, all she could do was think. His words had inserted themselves into her haze of hope like a burr.

The vicar is a good man. Please think about why you believe this is so.

No matter what she believed of the countess, she knew this was true. Reverend Sylvaine was a good man. He would never lose his mind over *her*, of course, for she hadn't green eyes and an effortless charm, but he'd never been anything but kind and truthful.

"I can hardly believe the Winter Ball is just days away," she said to Haynesworth. Who likely had no idea how rapidly the wheels of her mind were spinning. A *normal* girl would have been besotted.

"Too far away. What a pleasure it will be to dance with you again, Amy."

He did always seem to know precisely what to

say. Years of practice in London, no doubt. Deflecting advances. Saving himself just for her.

How did she become sardonic in her thoughts?

Perhaps it was a matter of simply stopping the *run* of them.

"Tell me, Walter." How strange, how mature, it felt to use his given name. Walter. Walter. Walter. The more she thought it, the stranger it felt, and it occurred to her *he* still felt something like a stranger. This prize of a man whom she thought of in terms of a string of qualities that really had nothing to do with his character: handsome, rich, attentive, mine. She was ferociously proud of him. She was desperately hopeful.

She was freshly furious at the countess for making her *think*.

"Do you know of a gentleman named Mr. Bartholomew Tolliver?"

The arm she was so proud of holding tensed.

Please please please answer straightway. And once again, her nerves blurred her vision.

The hesitation was infinitesimal. And yet. And yet. She feared that little silence was the sound of a man deciding what to say. When really the answer was simple.

"I know of an attorney by that name. Why do you ask?"

"An acquaintance of mine mentioned you might know him since you both have so many business dealings in London," she expounded.

"A pleasant man," he decided upon.

And smiled at her. At least she couldn't think when he smiled; it was like looking into the sun. *This* much he had in common with the Reverend

Sylvaine. And she suspected this was why he'd done it.

"Is your father at home, Amy?" His voice was urgent, soft. He sounded like a swain who could scarcely wait to claim her.

And yet he'd never tried to kiss her. He'd been all that was proper.

She was haunted again by an image she'd seen so swiftly, it might as well have been a dream: the twin expressions on the faces of the countess and the vicar. They'd each felt something so powerful it could just as easily have been anguish or ecstasy. She'd been dumbstruck by it through the carriage window as she'd rolled up to the O'Flahertys'.

She knew she hadn't imagined it.

Even a good man can withstand a little scrutiny, the countess had said.

And even as she hated the countess just a little right now, she half wished she was here.

"Father's away visiting a neighbor," she told Haynesworth.

"What a pity," Haynesworth said softly, with great feeling.

And even as Amy surged toward the words, hope flickering in her chest, she pictured her father sitting upstairs even now. And when Lord Haynesworth took his leave, she would go upstairs and give the name Mr. Bartholomew Tolliver to him.

THE FINAL EVENT of the Winter Festival was a ball to be held at the Redmonds', who, like the Everseas, did like to take their turn in offering largesse and didn't seem to particularly hold the fact that Adam was related to the Everseas against him. Blue, white, and green streamers, the color of Sussex sky, sea, and clouds, fanned from the ceiling, tenting the dancers.

Flowers of the hothouse variety in every color imaginable had been donated to the cause of the Winter Ball and were now stuffed into urns picturesquely positioned about the ballroom. Creating excellent nooks for couples to flirt or for wallflowers to hide their misery.

Or for countesses to hide from murmurs.

"You've done naught wrong." Henny was incensed on Eve's behalf when the ladies had stopped calling upon her, and when she'd been informed the decorating committee wouldn't need her services after all, since they had it all well in hand.

Nothing *outright* had been said to her, of course, apart from Amy Pitney's outburst. And she supposed it could all be coincidence that the ladies had been busy for a week, too busy to call. And perhaps they truly hadn't needed her help with the decorations. And perhaps it had been pure whim they'd all, en masse, decided not to go to church, the day after Amy Pitney had pointed an accusing finger at the cross around Eve's neck.

Perhaps. Then again, Eve might be scandalous, but she wasn't stupid, to paraphrase Amy Pitney.

She also wasn't a coward.

She'd dressed in garnet silk, and she'd gone to the ball.

Because she wanted to see Adam. For she hadn't seen him since his voice had echoed in that nearly

empty church, and she wanted to look into his eyes
to see what all of this meant to him.

THE NOOKS WERE also convenient, discreet places
for the breaking of hearts and shattering of dreams
and the ripping off of blinders.

Miss Amy Pitney stood motionless behind one.
Stricken and furious.

Lord Haynesworth stood before her, equally
motionless.

"At least now you know the worst about me," he
finally said, quietly. "It wasn't a proud moment in
my life, and it's why I hesitated to tell you anything
more about Tolliver."

"Mr. Tolliver told Papa that you nearly ruined
him." Amy felt raw and foolish. "That you owe him
thousands of pounds in gambling debts."

"I intend to repay him."

How strange it was that he felt more real to her
now, exposed for the fortune hunter he in all likelihood was.

"With my fortune?" she said grimly.

"Amy . . ." His handsome face was pleading;
his voice soothed. "Surely you care a little for me.
Haven't we come to mean something to each other?
My heart . . . please don't break my heart."

She studied him. And it did look like *something*
was breaking. Given how white he was about the
mouth and the sweat beginning to bead his brow.

He made so bold as to drag a finger along her
arm. She shivered.

"I swear to you those days are all behind me. I
only want a quiet life. And a confession about the
owing of debts is hardly the way to win the woman

you admire more than any other in the world, is it? I've never met another soul so knowledgeable about botany."

She almost smiled. She was *almost* convinced. She willed her formidable mind to accept his explanation. For the alternative was not only unpalatable but unthinkable: The countess had been right. Amy herself had been unfair. And this man could very well be her last chance at matrimony.

Surely, she could do better. And that heretical thought was courtesy of the countess, too.

He read her mind. "*Please* don't allow a woman like that to poison your thoughts, Amy."

"A woman like . . ."

He nudged his chin in the direction of the countess, similarly ensconced in a nook. "I hated so to tell you, but she recently offered herself to me in exchange for money. Her fiscal circumstances not being what they once were, you understand. I told her my affections were powerfully engaged elsewhere, and it was out of the question."

"Off-offered herself . . . ?" Amy choked, and her face went up in flame. "What do you . . ."

"It means what you think it means."

"Why . . . why would you *tell* me such a thing?"

"To prove my affection for *you.* She's utterly ruthless, Amy, and has no morals, despite what appearances may be."

She stared at him. "Said the pot about the *kettle.*"

"I beg your . . ."

"Leave me. Leave me *now.*" Amy covered her face in her hands, shoulders heaving in outrage. "When I uncover my face, I want you to be out of my sight. I'm counting. One . . . two . . . three . . ."

"I'll give you a little time alone, shall I?" Haynes-worth said agreeably.

As if this were just another female mood that would pass like a breeze.

"Go!"

WHEN ADAM STEPPED into the Winter Wonderland the Lady's Society had created from the Redmonds' ballroom, the first person he saw was Mrs. Sneath, presiding like a commander at the helm of the room.

The next person he saw was Miss Amy Pitney. She stood clothed in icy righteousness, enjoying the protective hovering of a bevy of indignant, cooing, silk-clad females. Her face was stunned. He thought he could see the tracks of tears down one cheek.

It appeared the Winter Ball was off to a roaring start.

"So . . . how goes the festivities?" he asked Mrs. Sneath with cheery irony.

"Do you like the decorations, Reverend?" Mrs. Sneath dodged answering his question specifically.

"They're quite handsome. I fear the . . . atmosphere . . . leaves a bit to be desired. Is there aught amiss?" He said it mildly.

"Oh, I hesitate to tell you, Reverend, but I fear I must. Miss Pitney is terribly upset. I suppose we should be grateful to Lord Haynesworth for making such a confession, but, honestly, such things were never part of our discourse before the countess came to Sussex, and you can't expect a young girl to hear them without distress. Miss Pitney had begun questioning him on some of his other proclivities, and it all came out."

"*What* came out, Mrs. Sneath?" So Miss Pitney *had* been questioning. Good for Miss Pitney.

"I fear it has been said that the countess . . ." Mrs. Sneath cleared her throat discreetly. "*Recently* offered a certain type of companionship to Lord Haynesworth in exchange for money."

Adam suddenly couldn't feel his limbs.

"Isn't that how it is with courtesans?" Mrs. Sneath sounded genuinely curious, if saddened. Gazing up at the silent vicar.

A haze of red swept before his eyes.

"I honestly don't know, Mrs. Sneath. Why? Are you considering a new way to raise funds for the church?"

Mrs. Sneath reared back. "I hope this doesn't distress you unduly, Reverend," she stammered.

"Don't worry about me, Mrs. Sneath. I've a number of pillows I can turn to for moral support."

It was his tone as much as his words that froze her in shock.

"Let me ask you this, Mrs. Sneath. I know you to be a sensible woman. A fair woman. A genuinely good woman. Why do you suppose Haynesworth would claim such a thing when Miss Pitney began to question his past? Do you really believe such a thing of the woman you've seen hold the O'Flahertys' baby and read to their children? Who has welcomed you into her home and leaped all your hurdles? Or perhaps 'Love thy Neighbor' is just a pillow to you."

He abandoned her to ponder this in open-mouthed astonishment while he went in search of Haynesworth.

The way a bullet seeks a target.

HAYNESWORTH HAD REMOVED himself to stand near the punch bowl.

He was watching Eve.

Who was an island unto herself in the room, standing against the wall, alongside an urn bursting with flowers. The other ladies eddied about her as if she were an iceberg, and they were ships that could be dashed upon it if they came too close.

She wore a small, faint, regal smile that neither welcomed nor rejected, and a dress of garnet silk that made her look like a flame.

Against it, her face was unnaturally white.

She looked up and saw Adam. His heart lunged toward her with the abandon of Molly, the O'Flahertys' fetid dog.

And feeling idiotic, he firmly called it to heel.

And with an effort, turned his head away. He stood casually near Haynesworth.

Who didn't turn to look at him when he began to speak in that bored London drawl.

"She's quite something, isn't she, Reverend Sylvaine? The countess? You can't afford her, I should warn you. Best spend your time pursuing that yon sweet thing, whose dowry is likely two cows. The one with the roses in her cheeks and bosom out to *here*." He illustrated with extended arms and fanned hands. "Miss Charing."

"Why did you do it, Haynesworth?" Haynesworth didn't realize it, but Adam's words—low, even, abstracted—were the equivalent of the soft *snick* of a sword drawn from its sheath.

His fury, quiet as it was, rare as it was, disturbed the air around them.

For heads, one by one, began to turn, as if alerted by a distant battle cry.

They were being watched.

"Do what? Plow the countess?" An ironic smile flattened Haynesworth's mouth.

"Lie to Miss Pitney about her."

Haynesworth made a sound, somewhere between a laugh and a yawn. "What on earth makes you think I lied?"

"Because the countess enlightened Miss Pitney as to the true color of your character. Thus threatening your search for a fortune."

Haynesworth was quiet for a time. And then:

"The *things* courtesans learn. If ever you come into money, Reverend, allow me to recommend that as a way to spend it. Though I've seen the way she looks at you. She might let you have a go for no charge at all, for the novelty of saying she'd taken a man of God to Heaven."

Rage splintered everything into crystalline detail. Adam's world narrowed to Haynesworth's moving mouth and, across the room, Eve's white face and her eyes, unnaturally brilliant eyes, fixed on the two of them.

"Oh! How about this, Reverend?" Haynesworth turned to him in a hideously, falsely jovial hush. "I'm sure you can afford the tuppence I'd charge to describe to you how it was when I *did* have her. And she was worth every pound I paid for the privilege. Shall I tell you about her tits, how high and firm they are, and about how I flung her legs around my shoulders when I fu—"

Haynesworth's head snapped back, and he went

down like a ninepin, with an impressive *smack* on the marble.

Adam stood over him now, holding the fist he'd launched into the man's perfect, square jaw. "Apologize to Lady Wareham, and tell everyone it was a lie."

"Lady!" Haynesworth managed to gasp contemptuously.

"Apologize to her now, or I'll lower the heel of my boot into your larynx until you do—you do know what a larynx is, don't you, Haynesworth? My boot is hovering over it right now—and I walked through a pasture full of unhealthy, incontinent cows to get here."

Never had a man spoken so quickly. "I apologize to Lady Balmain."

"And everything you said about her was a lie."

He took his time with this one.

And Adam was certain he did it to allow the crowd to swell and gather about them.

"It was a *lie*, Haynesworth."

"I lied about it all," the lord ground out resentfully

"And apologize to Miss Pitney for lying to her."

"I apologize to Miss Pitney."

Adam lifted his boot.

He doubted anyone would believe a statement extracted under duress.

And he felt the emptiness of the gesture heavily. He stood over the man, his eyes burning down into him.

"Get up." He didn't extend a hand.

Haynesworth lay flat another moment longer. Then, turning on his side, gracelessly pushed himself to his hands and knees.

Adam didn't offer to help and didn't wait. He didn't look up at the astonished faces of the crowd.

He just sought the exit like a trapped wild thing.

EVE TRIED TO push through the crowd to catch up to him, but his long legs made it nearly impossible; he vanished within seconds. And so she hiked her skirts in her hands and ran. It wasn't as though she wasn't already conspicuous.

She heard him before she saw him, breathing in, breathing out, the sound of a man wrestling with his temper. He'd stopped to lean against the house.

He didn't turn. He didn't even lift his head.

For a long time, neither of them said a word. He didn't even acknowledge her presence. His mood seemed as dark and impenetrable as the night.

"Thank you," she tried.

He didn't turn toward his voice. His eyes were fixed on the horizon, as if he wished himself over the sea. "For what?" His voice was flat and distant.

"For . . . defending my dubious honor."

"Of course. Then again, it's probably only the sort of excitement you're accustomed to from men."

More flatness, this time shot through with irony. Her sense of unease grew. She cleared her throat.

"Your hand. Are you hurt? Is it—"

"No." A guillotine chop of a word.

And now the unease began to churn in earnest.

"Adam . . ." she tried softly. "Please tell me what's troubling you."

Another of those silences. Not a man for superfluous words, Adam Sylvaine.

"Is it true, Eve?" The words were quiet, but edged with something like pain.

"Is what true?"

And that's when he finally turned to look at her. Each ugly word measured out slowly, punishingly.

"Did Haynesworth pay you for sex?"

Shock momentarily destroyed all thought. And when she could speak, her words were broken, awkward.

"I . . . please tell me . . . you can't *possibly* think . . ."

"Did. He."

"No." She whispered it hoarsely.

He simply stared at her in the dark.

"Adam . . . Please tell me you *believe* me. He's lying, if that's what he said. He pursued me once, and I rejected him. He's punishing me for it."

He took this in. "He fought a duel over you?"

"Yes," she admitted on a near-anguished whisper.

"Chaos's muse," he muttered bitterly amused, half to himself. "How many other Haynesworths are in your past?"

Shock gave way to a low, simmering anger. She bit out the words.

"You've no *right* to these questions."

"How well I know."

And now fury sizzled between them.

"Do you really believe him, Adam? Or are you just jealous of someone who isn't afraid to touch me?"

The barb found its mark. She heard him hiss in a breath.

"Eve . . . I do not think we should see each other

again. Not unless I'm standing at the altar, and you're in the pews. Ever."

Everything stopped. Time. Her breath. Her heart.

"You can't mean it," she almost whispered. "Adam. We're . . . *why*?"

He turned to her and said it slowly and coldly, as if he was explaining it to an unintelligent child. "I'm their *vicar*, and I just struck a man in the face. Because of you."

"It was . . . glorious. He deserved it."

"It was *shameful*. And I realized standing there that I would have *enjoyed* hurting him even more. The ass. It solved nothing, and I feel like hell. I should apologize to every person in that room. That's not who I am. I don't know *who* I am anymore."

"I would wager everything they've already forgiven you. They'll likely erect a monument to the event in the square."

"They might forgive me *once*."

The implication being that since she was controversy incarnate, it was bound to happen again.

"And you . . . I doubt they'll ever forgive you. I did your reputation no service, believe me. I merely compounded it. Although perhaps this pleases you."

She could find no way in to this man. He was a cold and furious and implacable stranger.

Tentatively, she stretched out a hand. "Adam, surely we can talk about—"

"Please don't touch me."

Her hand dropped as though he'd shot it out of the sky. And she fell along with it, in an endless, sickening plummet. She couldn't speak through the vertigo.

"The church was nearly empty on Sunday, Eve. Can you guess why?"

She *knew* why. She answered this with silence.

Which stretched like a prisoner on the rack.

"Are you sorry you did it?" Her words had the ring of accusation.

She meant the necklace. She meant knocking Haynesworth to the ground. She meant the kiss. She meant everything.

"No." His voice was weary and dull.

And final.

All at once, a caustic loathing burned her throat. She hated him then for his inability to speak anything but the truth. She hated him because she knew he was right, and she hated herself for being selfish and wanting him to stand by her anyway. She hated him because everything she was and the life she'd lived jeopardized everything he was and the life he wanted.

She hated him for that nearly chaste kiss that had seared her soul. For nothing that followed after could possibly compare.

And she could never, never change any of it.

She wrapped her arms around her body to keep herself from doubling over from pain. To keep herself from screaming from the injustice of it.

"It's cold. Go inside, Eve, before you catch your death."

"Ah, but if I did catch my death, *then* you'd come and sit beside me and hold my hand and murmur prayers, wouldn't you, Adam?" she said bitterly. "Because that's what you do. You're not afraid to do *that*. You could bear to see me *then*. For I'll no longer be a risk, and you'll no longer be afraid to touch me."

He jerked as though she'd struck him. For a moment, he stared at her, as rigid as a crouched wolf, his blue eyes blazing. She could feel the intensity of his gaze even in the dark.

She flinched when he advanced upon her. He stopped when he was so close his thighs nearly brushed hers; the wounded hand he cradled was a scant inch from her breast. Distantly, she heard the revelry inside, a low hum of voices and laughter, a universe away, naught to do with either of them; and then she only heard breathing, his and hers.

And with just his nearness, her entire body— her lips, her throat, her breasts—sang like a note touched, until her body hummed with need, bittersweet, frightening, total, irrevocable.

She understood then how much it had always cost him not to touch her. How much he'd wanted to.

She suspected that they would both likely incinerate if he did.

He whispered, each word slow and flat and measured and bitterly amused:

"Do you *really* think I'm that bloodless, Eve?"

He didn't wait for an answer. He backed away two steps, three steps, taking what felt very like his last look at her.

And then he turned and walked up the road to the vicarage.

And she watched him go. Of course, a man who knew himself, who was only himself, wouldn't doubt and wouldn't look back.

He didn't.

Chapter 19

ADAM FLEXED HIS HAND AS HE REACHED FOR HIS quill. Every word he wrote punished him a little for hitting Haynesworth because his knuckles had been split. A nice little form of penance, that. But the swelling in his hand had eased quite a bit, and now he could use it for *usefully* violent things, like chopping wood. Which he quite looked forward to these days.

He flung his quill down.

He stripped off his shirt and flung it aside and went outside to attack the woodpile with an axe, turning big logs into manageable logs into kindling into splinters. He'd done this at the same time every afternoon for a week now, and word had gotten out. He'd drawn in the process a surreptitious audience of women who took up the hobby of gravestone rubbings for the first time in their lives. Crouched behind ancient buried Everseas, Redmonds, Hawthornes, and the like in the churchyard, they rubbed the stones and watched. They didn't know why the vicar needed so much wood but were prayerfully full of thanks that he did.

Mr. Eldred stopped by the vicarage full of glee. "I was right there when ye done it, Reverend! Smack!

Nivver heard a sound quite like it. Down he went! That'll put the fear of God into a fellow, eh? Forget about the sermons. Just go about hitting a bloke when 'e get up to no good and the like! Haha!"

Everyone somehow assumed he'd primarily been defending Miss Pitney's honor when he'd knocked Haynesworth to the ground. He'd been forgiven promptly, as Eve had predicted.

The countess hadn't fared quite as well, naturally. There might be some confusion regarding the nature of her transgressions, but it had been tacitly decided she wasn't worth the trouble she was bound to cause. She had been officially cut.

If only she wasn't so determined, he thought. It would have been so much easier. If only she wasn't so *herself*.

"I'm sorry," the first message she sent over with a footman said. "Perhaps if Mrs. Sneath prayed harder for my salvation?"

He crushed it and threw it on the fire.

She sent a jar of honey to him. Which was meant to be funny. In another circumstance, it might have been.

He gave it to Mrs. Sneath, who gave it to the poor, who would never know it was from the countess.

At last she sent over a tiny package. Wrapped in paper and tied in string. He unfolded it, holding himself very still, willing emotion to stay at bay, willing anticipation to quiet. And still his fingers trembled.

In it he found a silk handkerchief.

Embroidered at one corner were an awkward but completely recognizable collection of Sussex wildflowers. And his initials, A.S.

Do you see what you've driven me to? I've taken up a
hobby in earnest. You can see that things are desparate
indeed. And I know you likely gave yours away.

It was the "desparate" that nearly destroyed him.
There was something so very *her* about the word:
unapologetic and open, sophisticated yet innocent.
So . . . dear.

The Eve she showed only to him.

It tears a hole out of you, Colin had said. When
he'd thought he'd lost Madeline.

Adam tipped his head into his hand and crushed
the handkerchief in the other. For a long time he sat
that way, breathed in, breathed out.

He wanted to believe her.

He had no right to his feelings of betrayal. Or
even of doubt.

Knowing this didn't help.

And then he smoothed the handkerchief flat.
With a deep breath, he folded it neatly and tucked
it into his pocket.

That was the day he asked Lady Wareham's
footman to wait for him in the parlor under the
watchful eyes of Mrs. Dalrymple.

He returned to his desk and scrawled two words
on a sheet of foolscap, flung sand over it, folded it.
And for a moment he simply couldn't move because his heart felt as leaden as one of Mrs. Lanford's tea cakes.

He abandoned thought. He abandoned feeling. He pretended he was made only of reflex and
handed it to the footman.

Who, he swore, looked him full in the face with
something like entreaty before he took it away.

But after that, the messages stopped.

Ah. But at least attendance at church was restored.

PLEASE STOP.

She read the words over and over, searching out some softness, some give, some chink through which she could insinuate charm and persuasion. But he was a bloody fortress, the man was, and he'd known what he was about when he'd written just those two words. He knew *her*. He'd given her no way through them.

He hadn't even signed the message, as if he was so exhausted, so thoroughly exasperated with her, he couldn't be bothered.

She understood why he was doing it, and she had the grace to feel ashamed.

She was torn between hurling the scrap of foolscap across the room and salvaging it tenderly. She opted for the latter. She laid it aside as gently as if it were his injured hand.

And sat motionless, feeling as hollow as a bell without a clapper.

She hadn't slept well in nearly a fortnight. She'd had no callers in that time, either. She visited the O'Flahertys twice; she'd once watched through their windows as Mrs. Sneath's barouche stopped in the drive and turned around and departed at the sight of her own carriage.

She held her breath for a moment so she wouldn't feel the hurt of it all over again.

She exhaled.

How she hated the silence. She wasn't meant for it.

And though it felt a bit like admitting defeat, she finally sat down to reply to a letter.

Dear Freddy—

I should be happy for a visit from you. Come as soon as—

A mighty sneeze behind made her jump, sending her quill smearing across the foolscap. It was followed by a cough so violent and wracking, the porcelain vase on the table rocked to and fro. She thrust out a hand to still it.

"Lud, Henny, I hope you have a handkerchief the size of an apron, the way you've been going about."

Henny gave a mighty valedictory sniff when the fit of coughing ended and did indeed produce a handkerchief roughly the size of a bedsheet from her apron pocket. " 'Tis but a cold in the head. The man who delivers the coal . . . well, he had a bit of a sniffle, ye see . . ."

Evie narrowed her eyes at Henny. She suspected she'd made yet another odd romantic conquest.

Henny's eyes were nonchalantly wandering the room.

"You sound horrible. I'm a bit concerned you might jar your organs loose with a cough like that. Perhaps Mrs. Wilberforce can prepare another tisane for you?"

"Ack, I willna be choking down one of her poisons made of leaves and twigs and whatnot. Tea and a rub of goose fat on me chest, and I'll be right again. And maybe a spot of rest."

Eve wrinkled her nose at the notion of goose fat.

But then she looked at Henny. Really looked at her for the first time since Adam Sylvaine had stomped away from her in the dark.

Her heart gave a lurch. Her eyes were too bright in a face gone frighteningly pale.

Apart, that was, from a faint green cast about her mouth and two pink spots on her cheeks.

Icy little tendrils of dread crept over her limbs.

She forced herself to ask lightly, "Don't you think we ought to send for the doctor, Henny? Just for an opinion? I've seen you looking more in the pink of health."

Henny spent the next minute or so coughing before glowering fiercely. "He'll only bleed me. I needs all me blood. Just look at the size of me."

"Well, perhaps we can visit the gypsies on the outskirts of town and have our fortunes told. They have potions, too."

It was the kind of enticement Henny normally couldn't resist. She was superstitious as the day was long and thought gypsies were easily as wise as vicars or doctors any day.

She hesitated. "I think a spot of rest in my bed will do me right." She sounded nearly conciliatory.

And this, more than anything else, frightened Evie.

"You rest *straightaway*. Go up to your room, and I'll have some soup sent up to you, and Mrs. Wilberforce will see to the goose fat. And a . . . and willow-bark tea! For fever."

And not even a token resistance. "Verra well, yer majesty."

Not even a "I always knew you wanted to poison me."

"YOU'VE GONE AND done it, haven't you?"

Adam gave a bit of a start; the room was so warm and close, he'd begun to doze. Lady Fennimore was growing weaker by the day; he spent as much time sitting with her in silence as he did speaking now, but neither of them minded.

"What have I gone and done, Lady Fennimore?"

"You've a bit of a hunted look. You're thinner, which makes you look a bit like one of those martyrs, which isn't a terrible look for a vicar, mind you. It's persuasive. Your eyes are a bit too bright. And you move slower up the stairs now, as though you carry a great weight, or you haven't been sleeping. Either you're constipated, or you're in love, the hopeless variety. They're often indiscernible. Ask Jenny for a tisane if it's the first—an old family recipe works a treat. I fear there's no cure for the second except for what you might expect."

He was speechless. He stared down at her, and her eyes snapped open suddenly. A trap! She took a good long look at his expression. Satisfied, she closed them again and smiled.

"Fire and flood and jealousy, Reverend," she murmured. "Set me as a seal upon thine heart, as a seal upon thine arm: for love is strong as death; jealousy is cruel as the grave: the coals thereof are coals of fire, which hath a most vehement flame."

The Song of Solomon. It sounded like a prayer, but for what? He wanted deliverance from all of those things.

He hadn't seen Eve in three weeks now. She'd stopped going to church. He'd seen Henny once, from a distance, as she shopped in town. But then

Henny was as visible as the cliffs of Dover from a distance.

Lady Fennimore was quiet for so long, her breathing so even, he thought for a moment she'd drifted off. But then she smiled slightly again. "D'ye know, Reverend Sylvaine . . . he died twenty years ago, Jenny's father did. But I think about him still. I still see him as he was. And I'm looking forward to seeing him again soon. My heart always had two chambers, one for him, one for my husband, and for most moments of my life, well, my heart was in two places with two different men. No one knows this except you. I think you may understand a bit of this now. Indulge a dying woman and nod yes or no, there's a good lad."

"Now, Lady Fennimore, it's unfair to bargain that way."

"What's fair about life?" she asked reasonably.

And for the first time he said aloud what amounted to a confession. "Would you be satisfied with an "I don't know?"

"As good as a confession." She confirmed and opened her eyes and smiled at him, with a hint of the old wickedness. "Sometimes, the only way out of the fire is through the fire, m'boy."

He drew in a long breath, exhaled. And then he indulged in a moment of closing his eyes, since hers were closed, too. When he did, he felt weariness sink straight through his bones. He thought about what it might be like to live every moment of a life divided. About sharing his life with someone who could never know him fully, or own all of his heart, but who would mean peace, who *fit* his life. Someone like Jenny.

And then he thought about Eve and . . .

He couldn't think about Eve.

And he thought about Olivia, and Lord Landsdowne's quiet determination, that daily bouquet of flowers, and wondered whether Olivia still had a chance for happiness.

Or if her heart was now a husk.

He decided then and there what he would do about the miniature of Olivia given to him by Violet Redmond. There was little he could do about his own circumstance, but he might be able to affect hers.

"Of course, it's possible it's only lust," Lady Fennimore mulled. "And if it's only lust, mind you," Lady Fennimore added practically, "well, there's only one way to find out, isn't there? And then again, lust has a way of passing. It's the love bit that tortures you. Can you pass the laudanum to me, young man? Works a treat, the laudanum does. I sleep and have wonderful dreams. It's almost as good as listening to one of your sermons."

He sighed. Her hand simply lay in his now; she didn't grip it. She was relinquishing a little more of life each day, and she didn't feel the need to hold on to him or to secrets, to any of the petty concerns that keep humans so tethered, so entangled.

"You choose the prayer, Reverend."

He remembered St. Francis then.

He prayed as much for himself as for her, for Olivia, for Eve, for everyone in Pennyroyal Green.

Lord, make me an instrument of Thy peace;
where there is hatred, let me sow love;
where there is injury, pardon;

where there is doubt, faith;
where there is despair, hope;
where there is darkness, light;
and where there is sadness, joy. O Divine Master,
grant that I may not so much seek to be
      consoled as to console;
to be understood, as to understand;
to be loved, as to love;
for it is in giving that we receive,
it is in pardoning that we are pardoned,
and it is in dying that we are born to eternal life.
Amen.

"You'll be lucky if you ever write anything near as good, m'boy," Lady Fennimore commented drowsily. "Read that one at my funeral."

Chapter 20

HE RODE OUT TO EVERSEA HOUSE THAT AFTER-
noon. A light rain had settled the dust on the roads,
and his horse's hooves thudded softly. He liked the
sound of it; he'd missed it. He decided to run for
it, to let the wind lash his face and hair, to scour
from him everything consuming him, if only for
a moment.

He arrived invigorated, perspiring, and mud-
splashed. He waited in the foyer while the footman
went to fetch Olivia and watched as two other foot-
men carried in an exquisite arrangement of hothouse flowers, all vivid reds and purples mingling
with a profusion of spiky greenery.

"Adam!"

Olivia's slippers clattered across the marble; she
put her cheek up for a kiss.

"For you, Miss Olivia," the footman told her.
Halting in the delivery of the bouquet to inform
her.

She was given a card to inspect.

"From Landsdowne," she reflected, idly. Her
mouth quirked as she cast her eye over the blooms.

"What else does the message say?"

"It says he wants to call on me. But then he says

the very same thing every day. Some people never *do* know when to give up."

"A quality he shares with you."

Olivia looked up at Adam sharply.

She pinned him with a fierce gaze, eyes narrowed, suspecting quite rightly he meant that in more than one way.

It would take more than Olivia to unnerve him, however. He was so weary he thought every emotion would skate neatly over him without sinking in.

"Is this a social call, Adam? You work so hard, I'm honored to merit a little of your leisure time."

He wasn't certain what kind of call it was. "As you *should* be," he teased. "Would you care for a walk outside? It's just that I've spent an hour inside with Lady Fennimore, and her rooms are heated to tropical temperatures, and I fear I may begin growing moss on my left side."

"I'll fetch my shawl!"

She ran upstairs to get it, then they burst out into the filtered sunlight again.

They walked across the vast circular drive, past the fountain, where a few little islands of ice floated, rapidly melting. It was the quiet season; she and Ian were the only Everseas who lived at home anymore, and Ian was often away in London.

They talked of family, of the people in the town, of the work at the O'Flaherty house. He didn't mention the countess. She, perhaps knowing him well, didn't mention the fact that he'd just knocked a man to the floor with his fist in defense of a woman no one in Pennyroyal Green would receive in their homes. Which, for all he knew, she considered mundane, given the kinds of things that normally happened in the Eversea family ranks.

When they'd reached a row of benches tucked among a series of rosebushes, he stopped abruptly.

"Olivia, I did come here for a reason today."

Her eyes widened. "You should see your expression, Adam." She sounded so calm, so wryly amused. As though the worst she could experience had already taken place, and nothing else would ever cause more than a ripple in her composure. "So very, very somber."

"Something that once belonged to you has been entrusted to me. I should like to return it."

He could see that she was prepared with a bright quip. So before she could say anything, he slipped his hand into his pocket and retrieved the miniature. "Olivia. Open your hand."

With a sardonic lift of her brows, she extended her palm.

And he settled the miniature into it.

Her hand jerked as though the miniature had come freshly off a blacksmith's forge.

He watched the color vanish from her face so quickly, he thought she might faint. Her face rippled in shock or revulsion, like she wanted to drop it.

He reached out a hand to steady her, and she shook her head roughly. She didn't want to be touched.

And then she swallowed hard. She took a long, unsteady breath, staring at the thing, her own young face, turning it over to read her own handwriting.

She hadn't yet looked up at him.

He put his hand gently on her arm anyway. Because he knew he could at least give a measure of peace.

She didn't shake it off.

Her voice was scraped raw when she spoke. "Where did you get this? Did you get it from . . ."

It occurred to Adam that no one had heard Olivia say the word "Lyon" in a very long time. She wasn't sure anyone had said the word to her, either.

But he would say it. He would make it real. He would make her think about it and decide. Because if he had any influence at all, he wanted her to have a chance to be happy. He didn't know whether he would ever be, but he would be damned if he would be surrounded by martyrs if he could help it.

He spoke quickly, succinctly, impartially.

"No. Lyon didn't give it to me. I suspect he gave it to someone else—recently—who then gave it to me. I don't know why. I cannot tell you who gave it to me. It was given to me in confidence, and I protect all confidences entrusted to me in my role as vicar. I've told you all I know. I suspect you gave it to him. I don't know where he is, or whether he's alive. But I wanted you to have this."

She breathed in and out raggedly for a moment. And then:

"*Why?*" The word was furious. Anguished.

Her eyes glittered with tears, and her jaw was white with tension. She hated to cry, he knew—she never liked to be thought of as a baby—so the tears were likely making her furious, too. No one could recall seeing Olivia weep since Lyon had left. Not even on the day they'd almost hung Colin.

"Forgive me if I'm blunt, Olivia, but I think I need to be. We all skirt around the subject of Lyon, as though you're fragile or a looby who needs to be coddled or a martyr. I don't think you're any of those things. I think when the wound was fresh, it was kindest to skirt around all of it. But I think you've now come to *count* on everyone's avoiding it, and you're so very *excellent* at being angry, so very clever and cutting, so deft about dodging the subject, that everyone has given up, exhausted. Because if you avoid it, then you don't have to think about what kind of life you want, or the time you might have wasted pining for him. I rather wonder if it's all become habit to you, and you're afraid to give it up out of stubborn pride. Should I duck? Are you about to throw that at me?"

It took a brave man to say this to Olivia Eversea when she was white-hot with fury.

Her eyes were shards of ice, narrowed.

"You've a bloody nerve, Adam Sylvaine." She drew every single word out, for full intimidating effect. She made his name sound like an epithet.

But he was braver than she was angry. It would take a good deal more than Olivia to unnerve him.

"Am I wrong?" he simply asked.

She glared for a good while long. And when he didn't flinch or apologize or placate, just waited with that immovable infinite patience he could demonstrate whenever he wanted something, she sat down hard on the bench and closed her eyes.

He sat next to her.

They sat in companionable silence for quite some time, absolutely silent, a sympathetic breeze playing over them. Cooling the fever out of her face.

She turned tear-brilliant eyes up to him. Her mouth crooked at the corner.

"I loved him." Her voice was hoarse.

And no one, no one, had ever heard her say those words aloud, either.

He just nodded.

She covered her eyes with her hand and breathed a shuddering breath. And then another.

"*Love.*" What a wilderness of pain, of yearning, of loss could be contained in that word. Patient and kind nonsense, is how Lady Fennimore had put it. Love wasn't for cowards; he wondered if it was for the wise. He supposed love itself made you stupid at first, or no one, no one would ever fall in love at all.

Olivia lifted her head up, and her eyes clouded over, perhaps with memories, as she stared toward the house.

And then her face darkened; her jaw tensed. "He wasn't perfect." A hint of ice in her voice now.

"You don't say."

The corners of her mouth lifted at that.

"I learned of another dalliance of his recently."

He made a sympathetic noise.

She was calmer now. Her voice was slow and soft. Not that crisp brittleness that characterized so much of her speech these days, like a fine coat of ice laid over emotion.

"What do you think it means, Adam? Why should he return the miniature now?"

And herein lay the risk. But if Olivia wanted an excuse to live again, she could decide it meant he was done with her.

"I think you should take it to mean whatever you wish it to mean."

She looked hard at him, trying to read his face

like an oracle. For a breathtaking instant, he saw it flicker over her features: She was daring to envision laying the burden of loving Lyon down. But then the pain settled in again, warring with the yearning that had shaped her for so long. So difficult to relinquish for someone as steadfast and as stubborn as she.

She said nothing at all for quite some time.

But he was prepared to sit with Olivia for as long as she needed him to.

The longer he was still, the more he felt his own weariness; the more his muscles, the ones he'd been abusing with wood cutting and fence building and roofing and the like, announced their grievances, reminded him that he was trying to drive love out, or at least desire out, like a demon possessing him. If he allowed it to take hold, he imagined his fate would be very like Olivia's, for they weren't very different: He was as steadfast, as immovable. He knew himself well.

Once he loved, the condition, he suspected, would be permanent.

A beautiful suffering, Lady Fennimore had called it. He was hard-pressed to see what was beautiful about it at the moment, unless it was, for instance, Eve's face as she held the O'Flahertys' baby. He closed his eyes and allowed that image to fill his mind's eye.

Finally, Olivia straightened and tugged her shawl about her tightly. "I'm glad you gave it to me," she said finally. She turned and gave him a genuine smile. A small, determinedly brave one. But a smile nevertheless. "Thank you, Adam."

"Will I go now?"

"If you wish. I think I'll sit here for just a little while longer, if that's all right with you."

It was.

He left her. He did glance once more behind him as he walked for the house.

Olivia was staring down at the miniature, frowning faintly. Perhaps searching for something she recognized in the face of that girl.

SHE VISITED HENNY'S rooms one last time before she went up to bed. An enormous fire roared in her sitting room; the gust of heat as she walked toward the bedroom was enough to nearly send her staggering backward.

Henny was so heaped in blankets she seemed twice the height she normally was. Her face was sheened with sweat. She muttered fitfully; Eve thought she heard the word "Postlethwaite"; the word "rats." She murmured something about "Eve" and "rag-mannered baggage."

Worry churned her stomach into nausea. She placed a hand gingerly on Henny's forehead. She pulled it away terrifyingly hot.

And then Henny made a moaning sound. Ghastly and inhuman and so unlike any sound she'd ever made, it iced Evie's bones.

She retrieved blankets Henny thrashed from her, shook them out, tried tucking them in around her again with arms gone useless, clumsy with fear.

Henny thrashed them off again.

The weight of Eve's life, such as it had been, settled on her, and she felt flattened, trapped, the breath squeezed from her. There was no one, no one besides Henny to whom she could reach out.

If Henny died . . .

She felt the abyss whistling behind her.

She'd been wrong when she told Adam she didn't need protection.

It's all right to let someone else look after you for a change, he'd said.

And even though he'd pushed her away, even though she was hardly lucky for *him,* it was all she had in the moment.

So she covered the little gold cross with her hand. And prayed. She would pray without stopping if she needed to.

But she would be damned if she'd weep.

ADAM HAD ANTICIPATED that his monthly dinner engagement at the Pitney family's sprawling home might be a little awkward, given that it was hardly a secret he'd flattened the doctor's daughter's suitor with his fist a few weeks earlier. He prodded at his minted peas, wondering whether any of the sprigs he saw might be hemlock. He sampled them anyway; they were delicious, as usual; the doctor kept an excellent cook.

Amy's hopeful mother had situated her directly across from him at the table. He anticipated spending the evening pinned beneath her accusing eyebrows. Instead, he saw much more of the narrow white part of her hair, as she bent her head and poked at her dinner, subdued.

As it so happened, the topic of Lord Haynesworth never arose. The doctor cheerfully chatted with Adam about the Cambridge Horse Faire. "Haven't been in years, Reverend! I hope to go down this—"

A thump on the door interrupted him. There

was a murmured exchange of words as the door was opened.

And then a footman appeared at the table, holding the doctor's coat and hat and bag.

"The Grundys' baby is coming, Doctor, and Mrs. Grundy is having a terrible time of it. She sent for you. The midwife thinks it might be breech."

"Bloody—" The doctor stopped. "You'll excuse me, Reverend? I know you understand. Babies do want to be born. Please stay and enjoy your dinner."

And then he was gone.

"Oh! I must go and see about the cake!" Mrs. Pitney decided shortly, and quite transparently, thereafter, and disappeared into the kitchen.

Leaving Amy and Adam quite uncomfortably alone.

Amy spent some time dragging her fork along the sauce in her plate.

She finally spoke. "I sent Lord Haynesworth away."

"Good," he said shortly.

A silence ensued. Finally Amy settled her fork down.

"May I ask you a question, Reverend Sylvaine?"

"Certainly."

He wasn't in the mood to expend charm on a young woman who'd helped make his life a torment. Despite his responsibility to her soul.

"Do you think Haynesworth was lying about the countess?"

"Did he strike you as an honest person, Miss Pitney?" He said this mildly.

But the stare he fixed her with made her duck her head.

And despite himself, he knew compassion for her. Her pride had been singed, her hopes dashed.

"I fear I will never appeal to anyone." The words were low and choked.

And he knew the admission cost her. For he knew how much she admired *him*.

Which was how he knew she sincerely wanted his help, for her pride was formidable.

"Miss Pitney, why do you suppose Envy is one of the Deadly sins?"

Her head jerked up again, eyes narrowed.

"It's a sin against yourself. It harms you and blinds you to many things, including good intentions. God saw fit to make you perfect the way you are. Not more or less perfect than *someone else*— perfect as you *are*. You need to believe it for the right person to see it. And the feeling when you are truly seen for who you are . . . it simply cannot be mistaken."

She looked out at him with her clever, dark eyes. And he saw something of mute apology in them.

"Perhaps I need to sew 'Thou shalt not Envy' on a pillow."

He almost smiled. "Perhaps you do."

Mrs. Pitney returned to the table just as another urgent thump sounded at the door.

Voices raised in urgent argument reached them.

"But she's *very* ill, sir. The countess fears she might not live through the night. Can you please tell him?"

"There's a baby being born the wrong way 'round at the Grundy house, so that's where he is. I swear to you, sir, he's *not here*."

And Adam pushed out his chair, craned his head, and caught a glimpse of a footman.

Liveried in scarlet and gold.

He was being ushered away from the door, trailing the words: "Can you please tell the doctor to come straightaway when he returns? *Please?*"

Adam managed the words calmly enough, though the pounding of his heart sent his blood ringing through in his ears.

"Can you tell me what the trouble is?" he asked the footman, when the servant returned to the room.

"That maid employed by the Countess of Wareham. Henrietta? She's been ill, and she's taken a turn for the worse, I understand. The countess fears for Henrietta's life. I was terribly sorry to send him away. Sir?"

Adam had slowly risen from the table as the footman spoke.

"Will you get my coat, please? And have my horse brought around? At once."

He didn't wait for an answer.

He didn't look at his hosts.

He strode the hallway, a roaring in his ears, aiming for the door, and intercepted the footman with his hat and coat and seized it.

And then galloped for Damask Manor as if the Nemean lion itself pursued him.

Chapter 21

A HARD GALLOP LATER, HE THREW HIMSELF DOWN from his horse at the arbored entrance of Damask Manor and left the reins tangled in the hawthorn. Then bolted for the door.

He thumped it with his fist.

It was flung open so swiftly, he stepped back.

Evie stood there in bare feet and a night rail, her hair a wild tumble around her white face. The taut fear he saw in it snaked around his heart.

"The doctor couldn't come, Eve. He was called away."

Her knees buckled.

His hand whipped out, and he seized her elbow before she crumpled. He gently took the lamp from her grasp. And when he lifted it, he saw that her eyes were swollen and red and shadowed beneath, as though she hadn't slept in weeks.

It made him desperate.

"She won't die," he said firmly. It wasn't a promise he could make, but if it killed *him* to do it, he wouldn't let Henny die. "Take me to her."

HE FOLLOWED HER up to Henny's room, silently, swiftly. Rapt, he watched her bare feet touch down on the wooden stairs. The candlelight found hidden colors in the spirals of her long hair, flickering shadows showed him tantalizing glimpses of her slim legs through the muslin of her night rail. He hungered after her with his eyes.

Neither said a word.

And then they were in the dense heat of Henny's sitting room, where an enormous fire leaped and thrashed in the hearth as fitfully as Henny did in her bed.

"I'll sit with her, Eve. Rest. Leave us. Please lie down and rest in the sitting room."

She turned toward his voice as if it were a raft in a stormy sea. Fear had stolen hers; it seemed in the moment there was naught left to say, anyway. Henny was sick. Henny might be dying. Adam had come. There it all was.

It was clear he wouldn't go in to Henny until she obeyed him.

And so she did.

She was too weary to do anything other than surrender to his certainty. He'd come. It was a miracle. Or perhaps it was her answered prayer, which amounted to the same thing, she supposed.

And all at once the weight crushing her shifted, lightened. Which is when she understood she'd *always* felt lighter near him. As though, she thought drowsily, she'd been given the use of wings. Or more likely he *had*, which is why he was so suited to help others bear their burdens.

Thoughts like these were how she knew how very, very tired she was.

She curled up on the sitting-room settee next to the fire, drew her knees up, and rested her cheek on them. She'd done all she could for Henny; she'd brought in the best person she knew to pray for her. Surely, Adam Sylvaine of all people had some influence with God.

And she wanted to stay awake, she did. But his will was stronger than hers, and it seemed she had no say in the matter. For the first time since she'd last seen him, she slept.

THE ROOM WAS dark and stifling as a coffin; it smelled of the goose fat and the astringents of possets and tisanes, all of which had allegedly failed Henny. Of sweat and illness.

Adam dropped into a kneel next to the bed. He placed his hand on her forehead, jerked it back briefly; the heat of her was like a forge. He replaced his hand, left it there.

Then he captured one of Henny's thrashing hands in his other hand and gripped it hard.

And prayed.

She moaned and muttered in her sleep, each little mutter a clue to her life. He heard "McBride." She snarled something like "snap his neck." Her great legs kicked out and nearly knocked him over, sent her blankets tumbling onto him.

And still he prayed.

He breathed with her, willing her breath to match the steadiness of his own. He willed her temperature to match his. Willed her health to match his robust health.

In the dark of the room, it was easy to feel as though he'd slipped into eternity, a place where time no longer moved or mattered.

And so he didn't know for certain when it happened, only that it did; he could feel it when the fever's grip began to loosen its hold on her, almost as if she'd been aboard a runaway cart, and it had at last lost momentum.

And still he prayed.

And he might have dozed. It was impossible to know in the twilight depths of that room, to know sleep from wakefulness from prayer.

But something roused him to full alertness. And he realized a new sound had entered the room. Or rather, an old sound had transformed.

Her breathing was no longer labored.

It was steadier. And steadier still.

And at last . . . steady. The normal deep in-out sway of a person peacefully asleep.

And all of her wayward limbs ceased flinging about.

Her fever had broken.

He dropped Henny's hand and folded his own together, dropped his head hard to touch them. And dragged in an enormous, shaking breath.

Thank God.

He realized then that he was shaking, too.

She smiled a little, in her sleep. She murmured something. He thought it sounded like "Postlethwaite."

Which was nearly as startling as the sudden break of a fever.

EVE AWOKE WITH a jerk, her heart pounding in panic. She swiveled her head about. And froze when she saw Adam sitting on the settee a foot or so away from her, watching over her.

Adam!

Was she dreaming? Had *she* died?

"Henny's fever broke," he said immediately. His voice was a weary rasp. "She's on the mend."

Eve sat bolt upright, hand to her throat, still not convinced she wasn't dreaming. And listened.

She heard it for herself, the reassuring rise and fall, rise and fall of a deep, restful sleep.

And then she sighed, flinging her body backward against the settee, her entire body deflating with the relief of it.

He gave her a small smile.

She struggled with tears of relief. "How . . . what did you . . ." She gave her hair a shove out of her eyes.

She saw him avidly follow the black waterfall drop of her hair with his eyes.

"I prayed. I sat with her. I held her hand. Perhaps the fever just needed to reach a point where it was prepared to break. I don't know for certain. I could feel it when it began to ease from her. All I know is that . . . she's with us still. Will likely live to plague you for a good while longer."

He sank back against the settee then, pressed his back against the giving softness, and just watched her. The firelight cast Eve in amber and cream and pink—the pink was her nose and the feverish blotches on her cheeks.

He watched her toes disappear beneath the hem of her night rail like forest creatures retreating into a burrow. She tucked her knees up and pulled her night rail taut over them, pulled her hands into her sleeves, laid her cheek on her knee for an instant. She would have looked as innocent as a girl if the firelight hadn't obligingly limned her body in shadow, showing him for a swift instant that reverberated through him like a lightning strike the elegant arc of her spine, the round contours of her buttocks, the upthrust of her breasts.

And sensation traveled his spine like a lit fuse.

And then her hair was spilling down over her arm and knees in anarchic black ringlets, disguising all of it.

"I don't know that I could have borne it if she'd died," she said softly. With a rueful laugh at her own expense. As if she hadn't the right to be anything other than strong.

"I don't think there is anything you cannot survive and somehow turn into a strength."

She turned abruptly to him. "Do you . . . do you think I'm hard, Adam?"

"No. No. God no. Tempered, like a sword?"

"Not like a blossom?"

He laughed softly. And as though they'd been crowding the exits of his mind, longing for escape, he freed them. They emerged one at a time, slowly, like dancers in a procession.

"No. You're difficult . . . Unique . . . Courageous . . . Funny . . . Strong . . . Smart . . . Loyal . . . Loving." They seemed to exit in the order in which he'd experienced her. Other words queued behind these. *Magical. Beautiful. Dangerous. Remarkable. Mine.* He wouldn't say them. They hummed as an undertone in every single one of the other words, anyway.

She drank each word in as though he were building her, word by word, right before her eyes. She dropped her eyes to the settee.

"I'm so glad you came." Her voice was broken.

Nothing could have kept me from you. He knew the

truth of it. He'd had no choice in the matter. His heart and soul had driven him to her.

He just nodded, too weary, too full of the enormity of the truth, to speak.

She dropped her eyes to where his hand lay flattened between them on the settee. And her breath hitched as she noticed his healing barked knuckles, the ones he'd split on Haynesworth's hateful jaw.

"Oh, Adam."

And gently she scooped it, lifted it with hers, and held it.

His breathing stopped. And time slowed to a silken river.

"I never again want to be the reason you're hurt. I . . ." Her voice cracked wonderingly. "I can't bear the idea of you being hurt at all."

She looked up at him. She looked rueful, almost frightened by her admission. Her skin taut over her features now.

"Eve," he said hoarsely. "Evie."

He took his hand from her and slid it up through the silken chaos of her hair, capturing her, winding himself deeper and deeper into a snare. And he melted toward her, softly urged her head back.

There was no preamble, no finesse. Just a slow, incinerating unleashed hunger, when he kissed her.

Eve sighed from the crushing relief of it, trembled from it. A lifetime, it seemed, she'd waited for this. And he took her mouth with a shocking confidence, urging her head back and back, cradling it in his big hands as though she were made of porcelain, mercilessly setting fire to her nerve endings with lips and tongue and the velvet heat of his mouth, so thoroughly, so nearly savagely, her bones went molten. She was comprised now only of need: hers and his. And herein lay the danger of this man. But it was too late; she was on the other side of desire now, and there was no thinking, no return. She was his.

She'd never dreamed a kiss could be a beautiful drug. She spiraled in the throes of it, amazed, and terrified, then desperate for more, until their mouths met with a sensual near violence, tongues tangling, lips colliding and parting in order to meet again.

He groaned low in his throat and shifted to accommodate the hard swell of his cock. Quaking from desire, awkward-limbed and frantic, she slid into his lap, straddling him, her body jerking from the pleasure of his straining cock against her. She hooked her arms around his head. He released her hair from his fist, let it tumble over both of them. His eyes burning into hers, he skimmed his fingers along her jaw, along her lips, down her throat, snagged them in the collar of her night rail, dragged it lower, lower, until her shoulders were bare. He kissed the place her heart clanged, in the soft, hidden well beneath her jaw. He was trembling, too, and she wondered how long it had been since he'd taken a woman and whether he thought he had the right to take her now.

She took the decision from him. She reached for the buttons of his trousers. He wrapped his arms around her as she did, his hands hot against her shoulder blades even through the muslin of the night rail. And he didn't stop her, didn't say a word, as she, with trembling, graceless fingers, loosed them, one by one. He just kissed her softly—her mouth, her eyelids, her throat.

She lifted out the miles of linen shirt from his trousers, and his cock, thick and hot, sprang into her fist.

He hissed in a breath as she dragged her hand down hard over it. When she brought it up again, caressing the silky taut head of it, slick now, she ducked his forehead against her throat. His breath gusted against her skin. Her touch was expert; she knew from the tension in his body, from the rhythm of his breathing, just how hard, how fast, how to make him mad with want for her—but never before had giving pleasure been indistinguishable from her own. Her own desire was a thing with teeth now; the more she touched him, the more she needed to take him, or she might die. She stroked him again, and watched his head tip backward. The cords in his neck were drawn tight, his eyes squeezed closed. And then, suddenly, his hand closed over hers, stopping her.

For a fleeting moment, she was terrified he meant to stop.

But then he seized her night rail in both hands and eased it off over her head; it floated to the floor.

She could feel it when he stopped breathing. Unprepared for the impact of her body on his senses.

Like a man who scarcely knew where to begin to feast, his hands remained still, spanning her waist. But his eyes burned into her. She was shy, suddenly, when she saw herself through his eyes: as a gift, as a miracle visited upon him, as wholly herself.

It was a relief when his arms went around her, clothing her in his heat, for she'd never felt so *seen*. He was entirely dressed, and she was nude, and she liked it; the vulnerability whetted her desire.

When his hands began to move, she closed her eyes, isolating herself with the pleasure, lost to the wonder of being touched by him for the very first time. His hands coursed the slope of her hip to the nip of her waist, across the curve of her belly, slipped between to find the vulnerable skin hidden inside her thighs. He delved deeper, to find her folds wet with wanting him. All of this was swift, thorough, a claiming; he was impatient now. And with that confidence that assumed rightly she was in his power now and that his will was hers, he slipped his hands beneath her hips and raised her, and eased her down over his cock.

He groaned softly as he filled her. "God, Eve. My God."

They were motionless for a time, savoring that moment of joining. The sway of their breathing, as her breasts rose and fell against him. His breath fell hot against her throat as he ducked his head. And then she moved over him, rising, sliding down again as he cupped her face for an invasive, soul-seeking kiss, then slid his hands down and filled them with her breasts, his thumbs dragging with exquisite roughness over her ruched nipples.

She jerked from the shock of the pleasure. "Please. God. Like that. Yes."

His hips arched up, his hands guided her up, then down again. The friction inside her was exquisite; every thrust ramped her pleasure; she was frantic with it. She moaned low in her throat, begged him with his name.

He ducked his head to circle her nipple with his tongue, to take it lightly in his teeth, and she arched backward in his arms.

Lightning coursed everywhere through her. *"Adam."*

She'd had lovers who had approached her body as though they'd a compass and map; she'd known where they would touch her and how and when. There was no strategy here. The totality, the purity, the instinct of Adam's hunger and demand was more erotic than anything she'd known before. All was frenzy now, and carnal rhythm, and the roar of breath, his hands urging her to ride him hard, their bodies colliding, rocking, greedy for deeper, more, harder. *So. Good.*

She saw it in his eyes when he was lost to only the pursuit of his own bliss. Distant and hot. His jaw tightened. His breath ragged. "Eve . . . I'm . . ."

He was rigid now, so close to his release. But her own pleasure consumed her steadily, like flame to tinder, until she was more pleasure than human, then only pleasure. Every cell of her skin lit with it until the bliss was unbearable; and then he thrust a final time.

She tucked her head against his throat to muffle a scream as she shattered into glittering shards of bliss.

They held each other until breathing settled. She became aware of the room again as a series of sensations: her hands against the breadth of his back beneath his shirt, the lift and fall of his breath as it settled. Perspiration cooling on her skin. The silkiness of his hair against her forehead. He'd rested his own forehead there. His fingers glided over her back, along her spine.

She had a suspicion they were both postponing the moment when they needed to look each other in the eye. The thought set her in motion; she gently slipped from his arms, slid away from him, and stood.

She felt him watch her as she moved, her limbs still feeling like rags, humming with satiety. Her head floated. She retrieved her crumpled night rail. She lifted it over her head, thrust her arms in, let it drop over her body, like a curtain on an act.

And then she drew the ribbons of it closed as if she could rein all desire in with just one tug.

She watched him reassemble himself somewhat awkwardly; standing to button up his trousers, stuffing his shirt back into them.

And then they stood to look at each other, quietly. His face was sheened with sweat. He'd pushed his hair back.

And Henny breathed evenly in the other room. Evie glanced at the clock.

Only fifteen minutes had passed since last she looked.

Someone would need to say something.

"Thank you for coming tonight," she said almost formally.

Oh, God. They both heard it precisely the same way at the same time.

And for the very first time, she saw the vicar blush.

And then, so did she.

He didn't reply. He was studying her almost somberly, disguising awkwardness and uncertainty with his usual self-containment. The two of them knew the language of tension and longing very well, they'd done the dance of desire and banter, but now that they'd come apart in each other's arms, tasted each other's sweat, been inside each other as deeply as two people ever could, neither of them had the language for what happened next. Everything she considered saying seemed too inadequate or too fraught.

At last he stepped toward her. And then gently hooked a finger about a strand of hair clinging to her lips. Drew its silkiness out, that look of faint wonder visiting his face again.

And then he almost whimsically tucked it behind her ear.

A tenderness that was in some ways more intimate than the lovemaking itself.

Everything in her being rushed toward him then; she was suffused with light.

And then, like a wave, it swelled into a terrible panic.

She suddenly wanted him to leave immediately.

Her mind was too full and her body too sated, and fear throbbed at the edges of her very soul. When she'd been a mistress, a man might bid her farewell with a slap on the bottom or an affectionate buss. Never had she given herself to a man simply because she wanted him: never had she felt the need to be joined with him or perish. Her entire survival had depended upon her ability to plan. Not on her ability to feel.

And never, never could she afford to allow herself to be at the mercy of any man. Particularly a man with whom she could never have any sort of future.

The nameless enormity of what she felt, the beauty and totality of it, was in direct proportion to the pain it could bring.

"I'll just go in to see Henny now," she said quietly.

And turned for the room, knelt next to Henny's bed. Crouched down behind it as if it were a fortification.

Resting her head against the bed, in an attitude of prayer, though she didn't know what she'd pray for.

She'd left him standing next to the fire. She looked up from her place of protection and saw him looking in at her, the expression on his face as though he'd at last seen something truly holy.

It was the last thing she remembered before she fell asleep.

Chapter 22

Evie woke with a jerk and a stifled shriek when she realized her pillow was undulating beneath her cheek.

A rat! The damned rats are at it again! She heaved her body backward and prepared to give the bed a good pounding.

A blinking, disoriented moment later she realized she'd nodded off not in her old rooms above a St. Giles whorehouse but kneeling on the floor next to Henny's bed, her head resting against Henny's great round blanket-covered calf, which was rotating as Henny turned in her sleep. Rats were of her *past.*

She supposed it was useful to know her reflexes were still alert, however.

She squinted in the pallid light squeezing between a gap in the curtains and shoved the weight of her hair from her eyes. It was then she smelled him: on her hands, in her hair. She froze. Male, musky, overwhelmingly erotic and unnerving, so *him* her heart contracted. Desire spiked through her again, fresh and shocking, as her body awakened to a new craving; now that she'd given it a taste, it wanted more. Now. She indulged the craving for a dangerous second, allowed in memories: his hands threaded in her hair, then reverent and demanding and so confident on her body. His eyes burning into her, his face buried in her throat, the fierce pleasure of possession and searing pleasure in his blue eyes, how it felt when he moved in her.

Joy and panic rushed at her again. She batted the joy back sternly.

Mother of God, what had she *done*?

She became aware of a weight about her shoulders; she reached up and she touched wool, not lawn. She brought his coat down into her arms.

He'd covered her and gone home in the cold dawn without it. She cradled it, eyes blurring.

"I didn't die, then?" came a croak from the bed.

Evie instantly whipped the coat behind her and propped her elbows up on the bed to get a look at Henny. She was pale as kneaded dough and none too fresh-smelling, but her eyes were bright and shrewd.

"Do I look like an angel to you, Henny?"

Henny scrutinized her. "Well, I'm not certain at all ye'll be goin' to Heaven," she said quite sincerely, if apologetically. "And I would have thought the same was true fer meself. But an angel sat next to my bed last night, and held me hand, and I canna say I would 'ave been sorry to die then, for I knew I was going to Heaven of a certainty. A beautiful angel, mind you. A man," she said with relish. "Ye should try nearly dyin' just once in order to see what I saw."

"That was no angel. It was Ad—the vicar."

Henny pondered the implications of this. And

then her eyes widened. "Ye're quite certain of this, now."

"Yes. Unless an angel came and joined the two of you whilst he was in here with you."

"There was only the one cove," Henny confirmed. And then it dawned on her:

"If the vicar was here, then it was . . . I was . . ." It seemed not even Henny could add "going to die."

To her horror, Evie felt her eyes beginning to well again.

Henny saw this, and her jaw dropped. She stared at Evie, so horrified and fascinated that Evie's tears evaporated instantly in indignation.

"I willna have ye weeping like a ninny over me, now," Henny ordered uncomfortably. "I lived."

Evie sniffed with great dignity. "More's the pity."

Henny patted her hand, then squeezed it hard, and they both pretended nothing of the sort was happening.

"The vicar, he held me hand?" Henny smiled dreamily. "D'ye know, I knew everything would be all right when he touched me. I just knew. I may never wash it again."

"You most certainly will if you ever hope to ride in a carriage with me again."

Funnily enough, this wasn't far different from how Evie had felt when he'd touched her. She'd been unaware of the weight of her life until his arms had gone around her, and suddenly she was . . . a river flowing into the sea. It had seemed the most natural, necessary, inevitable thing she had ever done in her life, and for the first time in her life, searing pleasure had launched her from her body.

It had been disastrous, in other words. What

now would he expect from her? What did he think of her?

What did she want from him? How could any other moment in her life compare from now on?

What could possibly happen next?

"And 'e prayed over me. I heard voices saying 'Oh, God' again and again."

"Part of your fever dream, I imagine," Evie managed steadily enough.

And there was *that.* She wasn't a shouter or moaner in the throes of passion; she left that to the men. She'd never before called upon the deity with any sincerity since she'd never before lost herself, given that her existence had depended upon ensuring that the man in question lost his own mind in passion.

Henny's eyes were narrowed now, inspecting her the way a bird inspects a worm.

"I imagine *I'm* not a picture a'tall, but *you* look dreadful. Yer eyes are red and ye've crusty bits at the corners of 'em, and a bit of a rash on yer cheek, looks like, and yer hair is like a tower of snakes. Isn't Lisle arriving today?"

Oh, God! Frederick! And a *rash*? Evie brushed the back of her hand against her cheek. Tender from where the beginnings of his whiskers had rasped her. She tasted again, relived ravaging kisses. Another little bonfire of desire lit; she ruthlessly stamped it out.

"Frederick does arrive today. I can dress myself and do my own hair. Not as well as you can, mind you," she hastened to add, "but I forbid you to leave your bed. We'll have broth and bread and tea sent up. But tell me, what shall I wear?"

Henny mulled it. "White. Wicked innocence is the trick, you see. Something a bit drifty, like fog. And be sure to wear that cross."

"You are a genius," Evie acknowledged in a rare compliment. She didn't say "And I will never take off the cross."

"I do me best with the tools what God gave me," Henny told her humbly. "Though Lord knows ye don't make it easy for me."

"I'll show myself to you before Lisle arrives."

"Verra well. I'll just sleep then, won't I?" Henny said, and promptly did just that.

HE SLEPT LIKE the dead. Or, more accurately, like the newly born.

He was already smiling when he opened his eyes. It was another few moments before he realized why: He became aware of a loose-limbed languor, the noticeable absence of the ever-present tension that had pulled the very fiber of his being so tight one could have plucked a note from him.

He'd had explosive sex with Evie Duggan the night before.

The smile grew.

He closed his eyes again, just for the pleasure of seeing only her in his mind's eye, of filling his hands with her breasts, of her gasps of pleasure, of her soft mouth crushed against his, of the way his hands slid over the silken contours of her as she rode his—

His cock was stirring to attention again.

It had been . . . a culmination, a miracle. Bloody fantastic, thoroughly satisfying, bone-melting. Though he doubted it was the sort of miracle Mrs. Sneath sought.

He simply didn't know what it meant. Had it been an extension of the moment, the dark, the fire-light, the fear of death? Did she regret it?

Did *he* regret it?

He didn't want to think it away; he only wanted to feel.

But he was never casual or careless; he was never frivolous. And he was not a coward. He would need to think about it.

He sighed and rolled over, tipped himself into an upright position, sat on the edge of his bed. And he wondered if she was still asleep, what she looked like in the morning. What it would be like to open his eyes and see *her*.

He wanted to know—he needed to know—what she was thinking this morning. She, after all, had been an experienced courtesan. Perhaps it had all been a bit of a yawn to her.

And then he smiled with smug satisfaction at his own private joke.

He knew she'd been out of her mind with plea-sure, too. And no matter what, it would remain one of the privileges of his life to know he had given that to her.

The thought of seeing her was a spiked pleasure. The freckles, eyelashes, silken spirals of hair, eyes lit with a smile . . .

He was dressed and bathed and shaved and out the door before noon.

He stole the wildflowers from the vase in the vicarage entry, the way he had before his first visit to Eve.

If he did it one more time, perhaps Mrs. Dalrym-ple would begin thinking of it as a miracle.

By noon Evie was pacing the downstairs drawing
room.

The white muslin dress she'd chosen featured
puffed sleeves, a generous but not tartish expanse of
bosom, and a single flounce. Her gold cross dangled
just above the shadow of her cleavage. The fire had
been built up high to accommodate the sheerness of
her gown, and though she might pass once or twice
before it—she wore only the one petticoat, so the line
of her body would be a delicious, tantalizing hint.

She inspected the room one final time, trying to
see it through Freddy's jaded London eyes. It was
spotless, gleaming—the maid had seen to that.

But for some reason she hadn't let them take
away the wildflowers drooping in the vase on the
mantel. The ones Adam had brought to her the first
time he'd visited. They seemed like a talisman.

Freddy was announced at half past twelve, and
he swept in, bringing London with him from the
top of his sleekly groomed hair to his ruthlessly
barbered chin to the flawless toes of his boots. His
coat was the color of chocolate, which did splendid
things for his eyes, and the buttons appeared to be
silver and stamped with his family crest. It occurred
to her that she hadn't seen anyone so scrupulously
groomed in a while. He seemed a bit out of con-
text in this room, but he was so sure of himself, so
certain of his welcome everywhere he went, that he
transferred something of his own ease to her.

"Freddy. You're looking dashing."

She held out her hands to him, and he seized
them and brought them one at a time to his mouth
to kiss lingeringly in a very French way that would
have alarmed everyone else in Pennyroyal Green.

"Alas, I know 'dashing' is the compliment you bring out when you're feeling noncommittal, my dear."

"I notice you haven't produced a compliment of your own, and you've already been here for two minutes."

"Well, then . . ." He stood back and studied her suspiciously. "I scarcely recognize you without your fashionable London pallor. The country has put roses in your cheeks. Or is that rouge? What's the occasion? My visit? I'm flattered."

She knew, by the way he faltered a little that he was not unmoved by the white muslin and the bosom display and by everything else about her he'd once claimed he *needed* to sample lest he die unfulfilled. But that was the way Freddy talked. All hyperbole interspersed with innuendo punctuated by wry moments of awareness.

"If my cheeks are rosy, I fear it's from the unbearable excitement of coming down the stairs and ordering the servants about in preparation for your visit. There's really naught else to do in Pennyroyal Green. Apart from healthful walking."

He snorted. "If God had meant us to walk, he wouldn't have made me rich enough to buy a barouche and the cattle to pull it." He lowered himself into the nearest Chippendale chair. Stiffly—the motion was in fact perilously close to a topple—and she reminded herself that they were all getting older, and Frederick's one abiding love was excess. She examined him, too: he'd thickened a bit in the few months since she'd seen him. The elegant lines of his face had blurred, his body was softer. His buttons didn't strain at all across his waistcoat, however. Oh, no: Frederick could afford a tailor to adjust his clothing to the minutest changes in measurement, and he would tolerate nothing ill-fitting.

"I must warn you, there's very little else to do here in Pennyroyal Green that doesn't involve walking. Naught that *you* would consider entertainment."

"Oh, I wouldn't say there was naught to do. I might enjoy a hand of cards this evening, for instance, particularly if an interesting wager is involved."

Freddy never leered. He simply fixed her with his admittedly fine dark eyes and his eyebrows, as lively as spaniels, gave an upward twitch.

"I've grown fond of Faro," she said cagily. "The popping sound of the box interrupts the eternal silence of the country."

He gave a short laugh and nodded, as if acknowledging a dodge and a parry. "Perhaps a game later, then. We can discuss the stakes."

"Perhaps." The smile she gave him promised both everything and nothing, which, she could tell, charmed him fully. He liked everything to be a *sport,* Freddy did. He wanted to stalk and toy, just like an overfed, bored house cat.

"Silence you say, hmmm? Do I detect dissatisfaction with your new circumstances, Eve?"

"You detect flippancy." She wouldn't like Frederick to think she could be easily had or that she was desperate for escape. "I'm quite comfortable, all in all, and the villagers haven't yet stoned me for a harlot. There's the title, you see, mine until Monty's heir marries. And they're quite afraid of Henny."

She saw no need to mention the revived scandal.

And she glanced at the wilting wildflowers and felt like a traitor.

Frederick stretched out his legs, booted in Hoby and polished to such mirrorlike brilliance, she surreptitiously tucked her skirts more snugly about her ankles lest he use them to get a peek up them. He patted his palms on the arms of the chair absently and gazed about the room, his strong Gallic nose turning this way and that like a weather vane, taking in everything—the unadorned mantel, the wilting wildflowers in the vase, the portrait of she-hadn't-the-faintest-idea-who but was likely related to the earl, the admittedly fine but a haphazard selection of furniture, much of it French, as if the earl had kept the best of his revolutionary plunder for London and stuffed the rest into this house.

"So! This is what remains of your meteoric good fortune, eh, m'dear? This . . . dear little manor?"

She saw the glint in his eye. She knew he was watching her carefully and weighing his loyalty to her versus the deliciousness of describing her new and considerably humbler circumstances to the broadsheets and the rest of the ton's vultures. He *had* said they were growing bored.

"It *is* dear, isn't it?" she agreed blandly. "Will you have a drink, Freddy?"

"I'll have *many* drinks if the evening progresses as I hope. I'll begin with a sherry, if you have it. Are you certain you wouldn't rather come over here and have a seat on my knee?"

"The settee will do for now, thank you. Though

it's tempting, given that your knee is a bit more padded than last we met."

He was amused and unperturbed. "I eat when I'm sad and lonely, dear Evie."

"You'll be happy to know I'm serving dinner fit for a tragedy. Your favorite, lamb with mint."

"Perhaps I'll achieve ecstasy before dinner and be unable to eat a bite."

She gave him another small, enigmatic smile. But a wayward surge of impatience clenched her teeth. She recalled another man threading his hands up through her hair and taking her mouth with his, without question or preamble or innuendo or bargaining.

"Eve, do you recall the evening of the opera—*Le Mistral*, I believe it was? With Signora Licari?"

"I do." After the opera—during which a young man had toppled out of the balcony into the pit when he was craning to see the dress she'd been sewn into—she had gone on with the Earl of Wareham and Lord Lisle and the friends to a decadent party. She'd perched on Frederick's knee while he'd casually wagered sums that made the other players' foreheads bead in sweat. She hadn't even sipped at the seemingly endless rivers of champagne. She'd been intoxicated by the risk and the power and the endless wealth. Evie Duggan from the slums could have had her pick of the men present; there was always a part of her that remained watchful, observant.

Last night was in fact the first time she could remember losing herself entirely.

"I remember thinking your arse felt tight as a new plum perched there, Evie," he said mistily.

"Oh, Freddy, such a beautiful sentiment. What

woman doesn't want to be remembered for her arse?"

To his credit, he laughed.

"Ah, forgive me, Evie. Now you can see how your absence has affected me. I've lost the ability to woo graciously. Perhaps we can go for one of those . . . what did you call them? . . . 'walks'—and get reacquainted properly."

"If you like. I'll just see if I can fashion a walking stick for you so you can manage it."

"I'll walk behind you and enjoy that view, which will be incentive enough to remain upright."

She couldn't help it. She did laugh, and the laugh evolved into a sigh. There was comfort in familiarity; she knew how to talk to him. She fell into the familiar rhythms of flirtation and innuendo the way she would the lines of a play or the steps involved in the Sir Roger de Coverley.

"Shall I tell you about the other parts of you I enjoy?"

"Perhaps when we've run out of other conversation. Do know when to lay a joke to rest, Freddy. I find originality erotic."

The footman arrived with sherry, and she was absurdly pleased to note Freddy inspecting the livery, his eyes registering approval. If she'd married Freddy, she wouldn't look at the poor footman and the livery and calculate how much he cost her every time he appeared in the room.

He raised his glass to her. "Do you miss him? Monty?"

"Yes. Rather," she said truthfully.

"As do I. But time and tide stops for no man or woman."

He said this meaningfully.

The footman returned to the room, hovered in the doorway.

"My lady, the vicar is here to see you."

"The *vicar*?" Freddy said on an amused hush. "Have you found religion, my dear? I didn't think things were as bad as all *that*. Or have you been very bad, and he's come to chastise you?"

Another bloody innuendo. Eve would have delightedly taken it up if she hadn't been frozen in shock.

She could hardly send Adam away.

And God help her; despite how awkward it would be, she wanted to see him. She wanted to see his eyes when he saw her again this morning. He hadn't been thrilled about Haynesworth.

She doubted he would cheer at the sight of Freddy.

"Of course. Send him in."

In a moment, his tall frame filled the doorway.

Oh, dear Lord. He was carrying a bunch of wildflowers.

And all was silence.

Frederick's swift expert glance took Adam in from his head to his feet: noted in all likelihood every pore of his face, the lean height, the dusty boots. His gaze slid to the wildflowers wilting on the mantel.

And then back to the ones Adam was holding.

He turned a malevolently amused gaze on Evie. "I thought you said you'd been *bored* here in the country, my dear."

Eve suspected her color was something approaching the white of her dress, judging from how icy her hands had gone. But she managed a steady voice when she said, "How lovely to see you, Reverend Sylvaine. Allow me to introduce my friend, Frederick Elgar, Viscount Lisle."

"How do you do, Lord Lisle?" His voice was as lovely as ever. As steady as hers.

He hadn't yet looked her in the eye yet, of course.

"How do *you* do, Reverend Sylvaine? Or should I say, *who* do you—"

"Are you here to see Henny, Vicar?" Evie interjected, with a brightness that sounded tinsel false to her own ears. "So kind of you."

Adam at last turned toward her. And here his composure faltered. And his eyes flared with a heat she felt in her very veins: She saw in them the carnal knowledge of her, the possession, the want.

But then he gave her a faint, hard, ironic smile. Imposing distance.

He was deciding, she thought, that he'd been an utter fool. And that everyone had been right about her except him.

She could feel it, the distance, like a door slamming shut.

"Yes. I thought the flowers might cheer her," he said to her, and no one would ever have guessed she'd muffled her first-ever screamed release into his smooth throat the night before, and that he'd tenderly tucked her hair behind her ear.

"Are we discussing the same Henny? *Can* she be cheered?" Frederick wondered.

Adam said nothing at all. He was watching Frederick with a faintly pleasant, detached expression. But there was a fixed brilliance in his eyes that unnervingly reminded Eve of the time she'd watched a cat peruse a rat it had just killed, deciding where it should take its first bite.

"Henny's been ill." Evie's voice seemed to hear her own voice from a peculiar distance. She tried a smile, and all the muscles of her face protested against doing something it clearly felt was unnatural under the circumstances. She finally did manage to get the corners up. "The vicar has been a great comfort to her. She's still doing marvelously well, Vicar. Marvelously. But I believe she's sleeping. But sleeping well."

And now she was babbling.

"Well, then! We're having an early supper. Perhaps you'd like to join us for it, Reverend Sylvaine?" Lord Lisle nearly purred it.

She didn't dare look at Frederick. The only look she was capable of giving him would kill him, of that she was certain. Then again, the ton already had just the perfect nickname at the ready.

Adam transferred his gaze to Frederick. His face registered only a sort of mild, pleasant curiosity. As if Freddy were an unusual species of mushroom he'd stumbled across in the forest. Evie thought, not for the first time, that he likely didn't give any visible warning at all before he threw a fist into someone's jaw.

And then he smiled, slowly, the sort of slow smile that boded no good at all.

"Thank you for your invitation, Lord Lisle. I think I will."

She wondered if she could find a moment to ask the housekeeper not to set the table with knives.

Chapter 23

So THIS WAS LORD FREDERICK LISLE, THE MAN WHO had lost the right to marry her in a card game. She hadn't mentioned she was expecting a visitor.

Then again, the night before had featured very little conversation.

Plates of steaming food were placed in front of each of them by the silent housekeeper. The chandelier overhead, Adam noticed, dripped with crystals pointed as fangs. Reflected in the silverware, in the candelabra.

"How did you come to know my dear friend Lady Wareham, Reverend Sylvaine?"

Dear friend, was it?

"She fell asleep during one of my sermons. It was rather unforgettable." He smiled politely.

Evie's dress and the color of her complexion remained a startling unison of white. She stared at her lamb chop as if she didn't know quite the way into it. She hadn't yet picked up a utensil.

"Really tremendously rude of me," she said brightly.

Lord Lisle laughed. "After the life she's led in London, she needs all the rest she can muster."

"Oh, yes," Adam said, after a moment. "I've

heard a good deal about her life in London. Her life in Sussex has been rather active, too."

Funny. He'd just discovered one of the pleasures of innuendo.

It could be used to punish. To lash out when one was wounded.

"Has it now? And Eve was telling me how very little there is to do in Sussex that doesn't require . . . healthful exercise. Perhaps you'd fancy a card game, Vicar? Or are you allowed to gamble?"

"Frederick," Evie's voice was clipped. It was unmistakably a warning.

Which meant she unmistakably understood his intent.

"I don't see the point in gambling, Lord Lisle, when what I want is simply given to me without even asking."

Adam said this easily. He chased a few peas about his plate and coaxed them onto his fork.

Eve turned her head toward him then, slowly. Her eyes were flints, and as dangerously cold and hard as the dangling shards of chandelier overhead. Imagine that. So she understood *his* meaning, too. He perhaps had rather a knack for innuendo. He was loathing himself more and more by the minute, too, but that seemed neither here nor there.

"Did you know that Evie once winked an eyelash from her eye and caused a duel, Reverend Sylvaine? Two men each thought she was winking at *them,* and jealousy ensued. It's a rare woman who can inspire that kind of primitive competition in two sane men."

"Swords or pistols?" Adam asked, as if he were

measuring Lisle for one or the other. *Perilously* like he was calling him out.

Enough so that Lisle paused. And Evie's eyes had gone wide with disbelief.

Eyes that had been so warm and vulnerable last night, then heated and slit, then closed with wild pleasure.

"Swords," Lisle said finally. "Nearly a gory end to *that* one." Implying that it was just one of many, many others. "Did they teach you how to fence at Oxford, Reverend Sylvaine? That's where I learned."

"Oh, I learned that from my brothers. And from my cousins, the Everseas. We practice rather a lot. I learned how to fence, as well as sense for what and who was worth dueling over. Very little, it seems, is *actually* worth it."

She hadn't stopped staring at him. Each word he said was a deliberate blow, and he saw her go paler as he said them, but he couldn't seem to stop himself.

"Of course. You likely haven't dueled. But then I suppose dueling is a pastime generally confined to gentlemen," Frederick said offhandedly, then flashed a brilliant smile.

"Oh, of course," Adam agreed cheerfully, sawing off a piece of lamb. "Then you don't know anything about it, either."

He said it so casually, with such an easy smile, that it took even clever Freddy a moment to hear the words.

And then his smile froze as if he'd just realized a stiletto had been slid between his ribs.

The smile drifted from his face. It was like watching a lake disappear in a thaw.

And suddenly he seemed to begin to really *see* Adam.

"Perhaps we ought to discuss something other than guns?" Evie suggested rapidly. Her hand had closed over her napkin, and she was squeezing it as though she were imagining someone's neck between her fingers instead.

"But there's not much to do in the country other than shoot things," Adam explained to Freddy.

He smiled faintly. Almost disinterestedly.

Frederick was staring thoughtfully at him. He leaned back in his chair, his elbow resting on the table. He remained in that position of repose, entirely as if he was lord of the manor.

And then he leaned toward Eve, and very familiarly lifted her cross delicately in his fingers, rested it on his thumb, which skimmed her silky skin.

Adam's knuckles went white on his knife.

Frederick smiled slowly, enjoying this. "I admit it's been too long since I've seen her, and I've never seen her looking lovelier. So fresh . . . so *deceptively* innocent. And I must compliment the necklace, Evie—how it adds that necessary flare of innocence. But she's so artful about appearing to be whatever she'd like to be. A talent all actresses share."

Adam slowly, deliberately laid the knife down next to his plate.

And then he pushed out his chair, and stood abruptly.

"Reverend, are you leaving us?" Lisle was all feigned innocence.

Despicable bastard.

"Parish business never ends, Lord Lisle. I apologize for my abrupt departure. I hope you enjoy your visit." He got the words out without spitting them like a furious animal.

"I expect I shall," Lisle said. Leaning back away from Evie, content as a cat curling up next to a fire. Satisfied he'd won. Whatever winning meant under these circumstances.

"I'll just escort you to the door, Reverend."

Evie's voice was a glacial warning as she pushed her chair back with significant force that nearly tipped it to the floor.

But he was walking so swiftly she nearly had to run to catch up to him.

"Adam . . ." she hissed. "What in God's name . . . What on earth makes you think you have the *right* to—"

He halted abruptly then and turned, with a finger to his lips.

She fell silent instantly.

They stared at each other for a moment.

And then he leaned down slowly, deliberately, and whispered in her ear:

"I hope you took the time to wash the scent of me off your body, my lady, before you rode *him*."

She reared back, eyes blank in shock.

Her breath gusted from her as though she'd fallen a great height.

For a moment they stared at each other. Pure, cold fury snapping between them.

Her eyes narrowed, and her hand flew up to slap him.

Effortlessly, he caught it in midair.

Effortlessly, he held it. To prove that he could.

And that he quite simply wouldn't allow her to hurt him. Ever again.

"Slapping me would be redundant, Eve."

And then he dropped her arm as if he were dropping the carcass of a snake and walked away.

OF COURSE, BY the time he'd returned to the vicarage, he felt like a thoroughgoing bastard, a raving infant, a spoiled innocent. All of these were entirely new sensations.

Then again, he told himself mordantly, allegedly you *like* new experiences, Sylvaine.

"I don't want to see anyone this morning," he said abruptly to Mrs. Dalrymple.

Since he'd exhausted the possibilities of the woodpile, it became plain there was simply no escaping himself. The best punishment for his despicable behavior, he thought sardonically, was to be alone with himself and really, truly dwell on it.

Such a delightful panoply of emotions she'd introduced into his life. Everything heightened and intensified, thrown into stark relief. Every emotion possible unearthed, presented to him to juggle, to absorb, to combat, to savor, to wonder at.

She was part of him now. With an intensity, an irrevocability, a sweetness, a fire, a torture, that had transformed every cell of his being until he was now and forever a different person entirely. There could be no one else for him.

This, he realized, was entirely *his* problem.

She'd given him pleasure, she'd promised him nothing, she'd asked for nothing—unless one counted a little assistance obtaining friends.

Which was just as well, as he could give her nothing, and likely Lisle could give her everything.

I thought I might never be whole again, is what Colin had said when he'd thought he lost Madeline. And he thought of Lady Fennimore, living a life divided, which wasn't far different from never being whole.

She would never again be at the mercy of any man, she'd said.

And round and round his thoughts went, chasing each other and never catching, never solidifying into any conclusion.

"Reverend Sylvaine." Mrs. Dalrymple's voice was so gentle it took some time to penetrate his emotional morass. She'd already said his name twice.

He looked up.

"Jenny has sent for you. It's Lady Fennimore's time."

"I WANT YOU to go, Freddy," Eve told him the moment she returned to the table. She didn't sit down. She stood hovering over him. She was tempted to give him a good prodding with a fork.

He looked up, genuinely shocked.

"Eve . . . why, Evie, you're upset."

"How observant you are, Freddy. I was upset all through our meal, and you've only now just begun to look at me."

"Come sit beside me . . . I'm so sorry, my dear. I didn't mean to . . . you know how I hate to lose. I could see that man—"

"Reverend Sylvaine."

"I could see he means something to you. Or you

mean something to him. And I couldn't help it, Eve. Old habits of competition die hard."

She remained icily silent.

"I couldn't help myself, Eve," he repeated. "The man is a gorgeous bastard, and my pride was abraded, I suppose I just took it a bit too far."

"*You're* hardly a gargoyle, Freddy, but that's neither here nor there. You *humiliated* me. I don't like the game anymore, Freddy. I, in fact, never did. I don't want to be a bloody pawn in *any man's game*!"

Her voice rose and rose and rose until the last three words were wince-level pitch.

Frederick eyed the candelabra, certain one was about to be hurled across the room.

"It's almost as though you don't know any other way to *be*, Freddy."

"I don't understand," he tried soothingly.

"I know, and that's the trouble."

He was flailing now. "You know I care for you. Genuinely. I'm hardly a gargoyle, as you said, and I could still have my pick of any of the eligible young ladies in the ton, and yet I'm here, with you, now."

"Ah, Freddy. Lucky, lucky me. I think I might fall in love with you any minute. Listen to how you woo me."

He did laugh. Albeit shortly.

And then he said almost tenderly, "*That's* why, Eve. When you say things like that . . . it's not the plum for an arse, or not only. That's why I can't forget *you*. It's you I care about, and that's why I'm here. I'm offering marriage, you know. You and the motley characters you call a family. I'll take them all on. From a distance, mind you."

It really only sounded like he was raising the

stakes in a game because he wasn't getting what he wanted immediately.

She sighed. "Oh, Freddy. Go."

"Are you banishing me, Eve?"

"No. I just want you gone for now. Will you go?"

He considered her. "I'll give you a fortnight to think about my offer. Come to me in London then . . . or don't come at all."

Ah. An ultimatum. Well. The man did love gambling.

But still. The moment he'd said it she'd felt a clock begin to tick on the option, and what that life would mean for her, and her family.

"Will you think about it, Eve?"

And in truth, she couldn't in good conscience say any other thing:

"I'll think about it."

He came to stand before her. Looked down somberly at her a good long moment.

And then he kissed her on her forehead.

"Then I'll go."

Chapter 24

BY NIGHTFALL, A DULL ACHE HAD SETTLED IN behind her eyes and didn't seem inclined to budge an inch.

Her housekeeper kept quite a selection of jars of ointments and unguents labeled for the complaint they were meant to alleviate, all lined up in a neat row in the pantry. Unfortunately, as none of them said "Disgust with Men" or "Ennui" or "Fear of the Future," Eve finally accepted a tisane. It made her feel cared for at the very least.

She drank the tisane, which though it didn't quite cure her headache was so vile surely it ought to frighten off any ailments before they could even think of taking hold. She kicked off her slippers and slid out of her dress, and, clad in just her shift, propped her feet up close to the fire grate, wiggling her silk-covered toes, and bleakly pondered how much longer those stockings would last and whether Frederick was worth a lifetime of silk stockings and finely sprung carriages and the health and welfare of her siblings and nieces and nephews, who were then bound to go forth and breed with the enthusiasm of rabbits.

She rubbed at her forehead, as if she could erase

the events of the day. The misery caught in her throat: The white tension about Adam's mouth, the cold disdain. And how powerfully he'd hurt her, how *skillfully* he'd lashed out. She sensed he'd never done a thing like that before in his life. Ah, what love—or desire—had taught him. *I'm always such a good influence,* she thought sardonically.

He could go to Hades, the vicar could. Share the bones of the Nemean lion. Her heart, as far as he was concerned, was a block of ice.

She leisurely unpinned her hair, stacked her pins, and shook it out. She pictured Adam pulling one strand out, tucking it behind her ear. The look on his face . . .

She shoved the thought away.

Honestly, would anything in her life ever align properly again?

She glanced out the window, thinking she wouldn't miss Sussex at all should she leave it. She turned away toward her mirror. Froze, whipped her head about toward the window again.

"Sweet Mary *Mother* of—"

She toppled from her chair, heart in her throat, crashed to her hands and knees. And then she crawled over to the window and slowly raised up on her knees, and peeked out.

Yes. There *was* a man standing just outside the gate. She stared; the figure was in shadow, all muted grays. Gooseflesh prickled her arms. Who the *devil*—?

Whoever it was came no farther than the gate. His coat rippled a bit at his knees, caught and tossed by the wind. She stared at him, wondering if she was to be haunted by—perhaps it was One-

Eyed William, the highwayman?—in addition to everything else.

And then the cloud obligingly moved away from the moon with a flourish like a magician's cape—Voila!—revealing who it was. He wasn't wearing his hat. To her weary eyes, his fair hair looked like a tiny twin of the moon.

She really ought to get a dog, she mused, as she stared at the bastard. A large savage, fetid-smelling animal, a bit like the O'Flahertys' dog, only with sharp teeth—fond of *her*, mind you, so fond it would curl up in her lap for stroking—but who would keep all men and their demands and caprices at bay.

She sighed and slid her arms into her pelisse, and stuffed her feet back into her slippers. And then she hooked the lamp over her hand and carried it down the stairs.

Odd. For a glacier, her heart seemed to be moving at an inordinate speed. Pounding, one might almost say.

SILENCE, APART FROM the crunch of her footsteps over frosted grass and pebbles and the ringing of blood in her ears sent by her pounding heart.

She stopped just short of the arbor. They stood and regarded each other in utter silence for a moment.

"I'm not really lurking," he said by way of greeting, finally. "Just experiencing a little . . . indecision."

"Oh, I never thought for a moment you were lurking. The role of brooding hero doesn't suit you."

She said it lightly, but the sentence was edged all around with thorns.

"I suspect I need to be swarthier in order to brood convincingly."

She denied him a smile.

He remained where he stood, just outside the gate, as though she were St. Peter or some other authority who could decide whether or not he would be allowed to pass.

"I behaved horribly," he said abruptly.

She remained silent, which was her way of agreeing.

"I should like to apologize," he added stiffly.

"Very well. Go right ahead."

"I apologize."

"I'm bowled over by your conviction."

He took a sustaining breath. Released it. "I . . . hadn't the right. It was unlike me."

"How do you know if it's unlike you? Have you much experience in playing the jealous swain, then, Adam?"

She enjoyed delivering the barb, and sweetly, too, mocking his inexperience. Despite the cold, which would become punishing very soon, she hadn't any intention of making it easy for him.

"None," he said evenly.

She couldn't mock him with the truth about himself.

The words came, swift and clipped and taut and strangely formal. "It was . . . unlike me because I consider all of my words and actions, I endeavor to be fair and never to hurt. I think I succeed more often than not, for which I am grateful. But . . . I wanted to hurt you."

Because I was hurt was unspoken.

A blunt and potent succession of words, even for him.

"You succeeded." Her throat was tight; the word was low; the confession cost her.

He always managed to strip her to her truest self, left her no time for strategy or consideration, only truth, and that rattled her. She was vulnerable only to him. She wondered if he truly understood how this frightened her.

And so their confessions hung taut between them: They could hurt each other, which meant they mattered to each other.

"It felt monstrous," he admitted.

She closed her eyes briefly. He'd thrown a fist at the man who'd cast aspersions upon her questionable honor, for God's sake. Of course it was killing him to know he'd hurt her. He'd been punishing himself for it ever since. And yet she knew a surge of impatience for the *innocence* of the man.

"Welcome to the life of nearly every other living, breathing human. We're all only one step away from behaving like tantrum-throwing children when we're feeling thwarted, particularly in matters between men and women. Isn't 'mine' the favorite word of tots everywhere? We wouldn't need laws against dueling and the like if we'd a prayer of being civilized."

"I've never behaved that way." *Until you,* was the unspoken accusation.

"Well, well, well. I hope you don't intend to self-flagellate."

"I intend nothing of the sort. But I do thank you for the lecture, Lady Wareham. Once again, I benefit from your . . . superior experience."

Her head jerked back a little. She was tempted to tell him this bit of irony quite canceled out his apology, except for that she rather admired it and likely deserved it.

More silence. The stars were as crisply delineated as punched tin, the night was so clear. The cold was beginning to penetrate her slippers, numb her cheeks, and suddenly it seemed absurd to stand on one side of the arbor talking to a man who stood on the other in the dead of night.

"Well then. Is that why you're here? Your tortured conscience drove you out of bed to my gate in the dead of night to apologize?"

"No."

So definitively stated she almost blinked.

"Then why are you here?"

She wanted him to say it aloud. To say "I want you" so she could refuse him. He was a man, after all, of explosive passions, and now that she'd clearly unleashed him, she suspected it would be rather like trying to stuff a hurricane back into a box. She tucked her freezing fingers into the belled sleeves of her pelisse, turning it into a muff of sorts and symbolically barring herself from him. She stared coolly up at him.

He'd brought an offering of an apology in exchange for sex. Pity she never wanted to touch him again.

If, however, he should touch *her*, she could not be held responsible for what happened next, for she wasn't fool enough to think her mind had any say in it at all.

He took a short hard breath, huffed it out at length in a white cloud.

"Lady Fennimore died tonight," he said finally.

Surprise blanked her mind for an instant. Then came welling sadness. She waited. He said nothing more. But she knew him well enough now: His voice was at its most even, most unreadable, when his emotions were at their most fierce and untenable.

"I'm sorry to hear it." She genuinely was. She hesitated. "Were you . . . with her?" she ventured gently.

"She died holding my hand. It isn't the first death I've attended, mind you," he added hurriedly, as if he wanted to spare her picturing it. "It's my duty to usher souls out of the world, and if they should want prayer and absolution and ritual, I know precisely what to do. It's always different, but there is comfort in time-honored rituals, sometimes even beauty in it, for them, for their families, even for me . . . it's all life, the births and weddings and deaths. Such a certainty, such a trust they place in me to ease them into the afterlife. I'm grateful and blessed I can give them that, that I can be a part of that, even when I feel . . . uncertain or unworthy. Which," he said ruefully, "is more of the time than I'd admit to nearly anyone."

The planes of his face were harlequined in moonlight and shadow, betraying nothing of what he felt or needed. And she did picture it, for how could she not? This big man leaning forward from a chair likely too small for his frame, pushed up close to the bed of a frail, dying woman, his lovely voice murmuring the familiar prayers that eased countless people from life into death. She thought:

Those blue eyes, the weary hollows beneath them, the beginnings of a beard faintly shadowing his jaw, his big sure hands, were the last thing Lady Fennimore saw on earth, were the last thing she touched. She'd trusted this man with something as profound as her life and the end of it.

An epiphany broke over her like a wave.

Evie had been courted by kings and pursued by princes; she'd married an earl who'd won her hand in an infamous card game.

And now . . . all of it, all of them, the men and their courtships and the flowers and jewels and duels, suddenly seemed like . . . so much Punch and Judy. Like little boys at their games. She suspected she looked upon greatness for the first time in the form of a dusty, weary, rueful vicar, who did things like hold the hand of an old woman as she breathed her last breath and throw his fist into the jaw of a man who slurred her questionable honor and come in the dead of night to sit by the bed of her maid.

"I suppose I'm sorry she's gone," he said simply. "I quite liked her." When it seemed she'd never say anything.

Awe and a terrible, beautiful fear muted Eve.

"Ah," she finally said. All emotion, that syllable, whispered and wholly inadequate.

At last he cleared his throat. "Well." His voice was almost threadbare with fatigue, and faintly, faintly ironic. "I'll just be off, then."

He bowed. And turned abruptly and began striding up the road. Lord, but the man could cover a distance rapidly with those legs.

And damned if she didn't at last unfreeze and find herself running after him like a green girl, skirts hiked in her hands.

"Adam!"

He halted. He slowly turned. But he didn't walk to meet her; he waited for her to run all the way to him. She stopped just short. And then tentatively, as though he were a skittish animal, she rested her hands flat against his chest. Apart from the sway of his breath, his body was as unyielding as the punishing backs of the pews in their little church. His hands remained in his pockets. He looked down at her; she couldn't read his expression. She drew closer to him, and closer, so that her body just brushed his, slid her hands down, slipped them through his arms, hooked her arms around his waist. And held him.

After a moment, his breathing deepened, quickened. She closed her eyes and breathed him in, woodsmoke and cigar smoke and perspiration and mist and cedar and horse, his coat a veritable travelogue of smells, because likely he had only the one winter coat and no wife or valet to polish him up.

His hands remained stubbornly in his pockets. So she held him until he surrendered, which mercifully wasn't long since, despite the fact she was pressed against a big man, the cold was insistent. He sighed, the tension eased from him, his body molded to hers. And after a moment, he rested his cheek against the top of her head, and he fished his hands out of his pockets, and his arms went around her. Surrender complete. He breathed in and out, in and out, and it felt like a gift to feel it, to ease the tension from him.

She pulled him closer. This strong man had come to *her* for strength, and she knew only gratitude that she was strong, too. She had courage and strength to spare.

Her only weakness was him, after all.

"It's all right if it's sometimes all too much," she murmured, with some difficulty since her cheek was pressed against the wall of his chest.

He wasn't about to agree with her or acknowledge anything of the sort. He had his pride, despite all that nonsense about its going before a fall.

But his arms tightened around her.

She suddenly wanted to look at him, to see him again in the wake of her epiphany. She leaned back in his arms and touched her fingers to his jaw, dragged them softly along the scrape of morning whiskers, traced the long, sensual swoop of his bottom lip. He tolerated her exploration for a moment or two, and then, with that thrilling decisiveness of his, grasped her wrists, raised them to his shoulders—she obeyed by looping them about her neck—and his mouth fell to hers.

The kiss bolted through her blood like raw whiskey; she moaned low in her throat from the sweet shock of it. He murmured something that might have been an oath or her name, and his mouth became demanding. Instantly, her universe was the silken heat and sweetness of his mouth and the rasp of whiskers over her chilled cheeks and the icy tip of his nose. The kiss was graceless, hungry; her mouth fell open beneath his, inviting him deeper in; it was never deep enough. She combed her fingers up over his icy ears and through his silky hair as his mouth traveled to the base of her throat, where her heart threatened to choke her with its pounding. He pressed his lips there, to feel her heart beat.

"You're like silk, Evie." He half laughed it, voice cracked in wonderment. As if he could scarcely believe his luck.

He made her new. Everything about her was new beneath his touch, God help her.

His hands slid hard down her back, pressed her against him, she hissed in a breath of bliss when she discovered how hard he was, how much he wanted her. His hands spanned her buttocks, and he lifted her up until she fit hard against his cock, her legs wrapped around his waist.

"I want you." He whispered it. As though it was his most precious secret.

And the woman who'd sworn she'd never have him again couldn't speak for wanting him.

So it was just as well he didn't wait for her reply.

Later she remembered the journey to the house, wrapped tightly in his arms, her legs locked around him, her face tucked against the warmth of his throat, the cold whipping past them as his long stride took him through the arbor at last, through the ajar door, where his hands fell away from him, and she slid the length of his body and her breath snagged in her throat.

A fire burned low in the drawing room where he'd first seen Frederick.

He settled her down on the settee, gently. But swiftly, purposefully, he unbuttoned his shirt, flung it aside. The casual glory of the torso he revealed shocked her. She reveled in her extraordinary good fortune as he worked open his trousers, pushed

them down, muttered a curse about his snug boots.
He was lean, sinewy, pale gold, his beautiful broad
shoulders angling down to a narrow waist, hard
thighs scattered in coarse gold hair, and buttocks
small and firm with a gorgeous scoop out of each
muscle on either side, the perfect place to fit her
hands when her legs were wrapped around him,
as he rose up over her to plunge—

"Leave the boots on," she ordered hoarsely.

She couldn't wait. She wanted to feel the entirety
of his smooth skin against her now. She wanted to
discover the terrain of him with her fingers, her
lips, her tongue. She wanted to know what it felt
like to drag her hands over those defined quad-
rants of his chest, the valley bisecting the ridge of
muscle between his ribs, to tease the coarse gold
hair that ran in a fine trail to his deliciously con-
cave belly to where his swollen cock curved up.

He dropped to his knees next to her, seized her
shift where it was bunched at her hips, and urged
it off over her head, flinging it over his shoulder to
join his shirt. She reached up for him, threaded her
hands through his hair, brought his head down to
hers for a kiss. He teased her lips with his, bumping
them gently, sliding softly, then tracing them with
his tongue until she gasped. His mouth covered
hers then, and his tongue delved, tangling with
hers. He planted his hands on either side of her
torso, tantalizing her with the promise of the touch
of his skin, hovering just a hairsbreadth above her
until she arced, her nipples brushing his chest. His
breath gratifyingly snagged in his throat. She slid
her hands over his chest, hot and smooth, traced
her finger down that delightful seam that seemed

expressly designed to point the way to his cock.
She licked his nipple, then nipped it, but he wasn't
done with her.

He slipped away from her grasp to drag his
cheek along the tender side of her breast, then
traced his fingers along the contours of it, lowered
his mouth to taste her again. Quicksilver shivers of
pleasure fanned through her body from wherever
he touched her, until she was dazed from it. The
flat of his hand followed a trail of hot kisses down
the line of her ribs, down to the curve of her belly,
to the triangle of curls springing at her legs. He
blew softly there, and her legs slipped apart, inviting him in, and, experimentally, he tasted.

"Jesus," she gasped.

Correctly interpreting this as approval, he did it
again, with the tip, then the flat, of his tongue, and
the shock of pleasure sent her arching upward.

"Good?" he whispered. Unnecessarily, she
thought. With a smile in his voice that included just
a little self-congratulation.

And again he did it. And again.

They colluded in finding a rhythm. His fingers
played lightly with that vulnerable skin between
her thighs as his tongue artfully drove her closer,
and closer, and closer to the brink of losing her
mind. She could feel it when her body began to
dissolve into pinpricks of hot pleasure. Her breath
was a savage saw now, as she writhed, beseeched
him with his name, frightened of the intensity of
the bliss and hurtling toward it inexorably. The air
spangled before her eyes, and her hips were frantic; and then nearly violent bliss bowed her body
upward.

She came apart with a cry.

She dropped again to the settee, shattered and amazed, and he left his palm against her to feel each pulse of her release before he joined her on the settee. And then he covered her with his long, hard body, fitted his cock to her, and she raised her hips, locked her legs around him, pulling him into her, and he plunged.

He tried to go slowly. His arms shook with the effort of control. And this in itself excited her nearly unbearably: His control was so extraordinary, so hard-won. She wanted him to release it to her for the evening.

"It's all right. I want you, Adam. Please. Now."

He sighed, and he moved his hips. Languidly at first, but then he abandoned attempts at leisure and moved swiftly, ever more swiftly. She clung to his shoulders and rose up to meet him, taking him deeply, reveling in the drumming of his white hips, until his release came on the harsh cry of her name.

They lay quietly wrapped together, sated. And for a peaceful, wordless time, she indulged in exploring his body the way she would any new and splendid terrain: She slid her hands over the smooth, hard contours of his shoulders, the planes of his chest, tangled them in the dusting of gold hair there, followed the seam of hair to his cock. And when it began to stir again, she slid to the floor to kneel next to him.

And she took him in her mouth.

He sighed the pleasure of it as she closed her lips around the smooth head, and followed the shaft down with her mouth, and his hands languidly tangled in her hair. She followed it up again, then traced the dome of it with her tongue, circling, circling, until he shifted, and dropped his legs wider, and tipped his head back, and his body bowed upward.

"Evie." He sighed. "Oh, God. Evie."

And in that moment, she blessed everything she'd learned in her life: She was a skilled giver of pleasure, and yet she'd never been more grateful to possess a body, to know how to use it in service of a man's bliss, to be the reason this extraordinary man who shouldered the cares of so many should entirely lose himself.

Languidly, she moved her mouth along him, with her fist following, taking him deeply into her throat, again, and then again, and again, until she felt his belly rise and fall ever swifter, until he thrashed his head back hard, arching into her, aiding her, urging her faster.

"Inside . . . you . . ." he gasped. "Please. I want . . . inside you . . ."

She rose again and straddled him, and together they fitted him to her, and she slid down over him. She paused, savoring the feel of him, and smiled wickedly down at him. Teased him a little by rising up and away from him; he swore and bucked fiercely upward.

"Mother of God . . ."

And then he held her hips fast in his hand and took her hard, bucking fiercely upward, their bodies colliding until he went rigid and cried out again.

Later, together, they got his boots all the way off, and his trousers. He had long, hairy feet, she dis-

covered, and she tangled her small ones with his
on the settee.

Quietly breathing, limbs practically braided,
they lay together, their bodies sheened in sweat,
until the cold became uncomfortable.

He stood and unself-consciously crossed the
room to tend to the fire. She dozily watched him
kneel, add logs, poke them, and reach for the flint.
How *right* his body seemed to her. How different
from the bodies of the men she'd given herself to,
men who were fit enough, but soft, too; so much of
their lives were seen to by other people, shaped by
luxury. The muscles etched in Adam told the story
of his life—the walking, the riding, tending to the
roofs, tending to his own woodpile. Taking care of
others, taking care of himself. And his body was
magnificent, but his buttocks were so small and
white, so oddly dear and vulnerable, in the half-
light.

"I didn't have sex with Freddy," she told him.

He turned to her swiftly. Surprised perhaps. He
simply knelt where he was.

"It doesn't matter," was all he said.

"Adam, I swear to you, I never have. And I didn't
while he was here."

"It doesn't matter," he repeated evenly.

"And I had naught to do with Haynesworth.
Ever."

"Eve . . ." He paused. "It *doesn't matter*. I believe
you. But even if I'd known you had . . . even if all
of those things were not true . . . would have come
to you and Henny. I would have come to you if you
were on the moon. I would have found a way. I
would have come to you."

They looked at each other from across the room. He'd said it, not with resignation, but matter-of-factly. A man surrendering to his fate.

But everything he felt was in his eyes.

I love you, too, she wanted to say.

"I know it changes nothing," he said.

And if he'd waited for her to deny it, he waited in vain. They gazed at each other across that gulf for a moment.

But they still had tonight. He rose and returned to the settee. She opened her arms, and he burrowed in. Neither of them spoke after that.

He fell asleep, and she held him while he slept.

FORTUNATELY, THE COLD woke them before the servants could stumble across the two of them, naked and entwined on the settee. He kissed her mouth, her closed eyelids. And then he stretched and gently pulled away from her, rolled down to try to start the fire again.

She watched him crouch there, loving him so fiercely it was like sunlight had replaced the blood in her veins. But it was the sort of glorious brightness and heat that could never be sustained.

And if only things were different, this might be what she saw every day for the rest of her life: his beloved back poking at the fire. Sharing homely moments like these. But she knew what she had to do, and because she was brave, she would do it now.

"I'm going to London in a fortnight, Adam."

He turned slowly around. His face was at first expressionless, as if she'd spoken in another language entirely. Slowly absorbing what she'd said.

"To . . . visit?" But he said it as though he knew the answer.

"For good," she told him gently.

He sat motionless. Stunned. He began. "You cannot . . . surely there's a way . . ."

He came to her, knelt next to her on the settee. "Eve . . . Evie."

"Listen to me," she said, and touched his face, dragging her fingers along his jaw, to his mouth. Branding the shape of him into her soul. He caught her fingers gently between his teeth, kissed them.

"It's better this way."

"No! Let me speak, please." *Before I lose my courage.*

"You know they will never accept me. Your whole livelihood depends on parishioners filling the pews, and oh, Adam, they're so lucky to have you. You're so brilliant at your job, I don't know if you even realize it. I'm just in . . . awe." Her voice cracked. "They need you. And you've a chance to be happy, Adam. Or at least content. To have a family of your own, live among the family you love in peace and contentment . . . but if I'm the spectre that prevents you from living fully . . . think of Olivia Eversea. What her life is like. I refuse to let that happen to you. I won't allow it."

He watched her, the appalling words absorbing only slowly.

"You're going to Lisle," he said flatly.

"He isn't a horrible man, Adam. He truly isn't. He will never be you. But he'll honor his commitment to me. He'll marry me. He may give me children. He has the resources to care for my family, and he will."

She heard her own words with disbelief. Even though she meant every one of them. She could hardly believe she needed to tear out her own heart and his in order to keep living.

"How can you . . . how can you talk of . . . *marriage* and children with him . . . of lying in bed with him . . . after . . ."

He was sickly pale. His breath came in swift bursts, as though he'd just run a mile. "Eve," he said softly, pleading.

She heard herself as if from a distance, as though she was separate from her body. It was the only way she could bear to break both her own heart and his. She heard her voice say the words that would free and kill both of them.

"You know there's no way, Adam. You know I'm right. When you think about it . . . and you'll be able to think about it after this morning, but now, now . . . you'll know I'm right. Perhaps you didn't expect it to be so soon, but perhaps that's for the best, too. I want this moment, this perfect moment to be good-bye. So kiss me now . . ." Her voice broke then. ". . . and tell me good-bye. And go."

He shook his head roughly. "No."

"Adam . . ."

He saw implacability in her eyes.

He leaned over and kissed her. She tasted heartbreak, and fury, and love, and infinity in that kiss. She felt the persuasion of it weave itself through her very soul, felt her body stir, felt her thoughts begin to dissolve into need. And he knew it.

So it was she who ended it.

She ducked her head into her chest. Closed her eyes. "I want you to go."

There was silence.

She listened as he dressed swiftly.

She felt him leave as much as heard him because the sound of the door's shutting seemed to snuff out the light in her heart.

Chapter 25

FIRE, AND FLOOD, AND JEALOUSY . . .

He stared uselessly out the window of the vicarage. He jerked his thoughts back to the task at hand and scrawled on the foolscap instead:

"Lilies of the field?"

He tried to stare the words into yielding an entire sermon to him.

They hatefully remained inscrutable. All he saw was Eve holding wildflowers in her arms when he'd first gone to meet with her, and suggesting lilies of the field, and . . .

He scratched them out with something approaching antipathy and wastefully bunched the single word into a ball and hurled it across the room.

And she'd be leaving Pennyroyal Green for London in less than two weeks.

I thought I'd never be whole again, Colin had said.

What if Colin was right? Adam moved and spoke and breathed and slept. But food had lost its taste. He didn't seem to notice hot or cold. Mrs. Dalrymple shoved plates beneath his nose, took them away untouched, and worried about him, but he didn't notice that, either.

Eve hadn't attended church since he'd last seen

her. Everyone *else* had, of course. For the first time, he saw Mrs. O'Flaherty and her children, who were shockingly well behaved throughout, and who wore admiral hats and swords.

Eve had made it possible for her to be there.

He'd seen them and lost his place in the sermon briefly. Stared at them so intently that a few pairs of eyes grew curious, then worried, which was enough to nudge him into speaking again.

He shook the memory away, selected another sheet of foolscap, smoothed it flat. Then did it again. As though he could stroke it like a cat into surrendering a decent sermon.

Fire and flood and jealousy. *It's not like that first Corinthians* nonsense Lady Fennimore said.

And that's when he leaned back in his chair, struck dumb.

He knew it by heart, but he thumbed his Bible open to Corinthians and read.

Well. Inspiration, you fickle visitor, that's where you were hiding. Thanks for stopping by at the eleventh hour, as usual.

Lady Fennimore, you were wise, but you didn't know *everything*, he thought.

Inspiration burned a hole through the fog, and suddenly he knew what he needed to do.

And so he set to writing. But not the sermon.

No, the sermon could wait.

Dear Freddy,

I'm coming. Don't gloat. Will be pleased to see you. Perhaps you should see about a special license?

Evie

He would appreciate the pithiness of it, Freddy would.

And he *would* gloat.

Eve had given it to Henny to take to Postlethwaite's Emporium. The mail coach took it to Lord Lisle. Likely he'd had it framed, knowing Freddy.

And now Henny was supervising the packing of Eve's wardrobe in readiness for their departure to London.

"Ah, this white muslin . . . this is what you wore the first day the reverend came to visit." She held it up. "Do you recall?"

Evie stared at her suspiciously. "I recall."

"You were a picture in it. "And *this* . . . the green silk. You wore this to the Assembly."

"I *recall*, Henny."

But Eve stepped toward her and took the green silk in her arms for a moment. Cradling it like she would a wounded thing.

"What will you wear to church tomorrow?"

Eve stared at her incredulously. "We're . . . not *going* to church tomorrow."

"I'd say ye was a coward if ye didna go in one last time."

"You do like to call me names," she said to Henny. And sighed. Not taking her seriously.

"If the shoe fits, m'lady. Wouldn't you like to go out in triumph? Wouldn't you like to see all of them one last time before you become the wife of a viscount, hold your head high, and never look at them again? And shouldn't you do it for the reverend? 'e saved my life, after all."

"More's the pity," Eve muttered.

It was a very unfair card for Henny to play.

Henny said nothing for a time, just watched Eve. Who was holding the green silk gown, her face as rapt as someone waltzing with a big vicar.

"He was very kind to you, m'lady," Henny said softly.

And to her horror, tears started up in Eve's eyes.

She turned abruptly away and walked toward the window. She put her hand up to her throat, covering the cross.

She didn't want to go to church because she didn't want to have to see him. She was just getting *accustomed* to the idea of never seeing him again. It would be reopening a wound.

Then again, she would have a lifetime to heal from it. And once the idea of seeing him insinuated itself, it was powerfully difficult to release it.

And avoiding it was for *cowards*. Henny was right. Evie despised showing weakness.

"All right," she said quietly. "We'll go. On our way out of town, we'll stop for church. And we'll leave for London *immediately* thereafter, do you hear me?"

"Splendid," Henny said cheerfully. "Now, I think ye should wear this lavender, and the hat with the dark purple silk ribbon, and . . ."

And it was then Eve saw two women who seemed to be moving virtually on tiptoe toward her arbor.

They were followed by a little boy and a brown dog with a whip of a tail.

She dropped the curtain and scrambled downstairs.

It was Margaret Lanford and Josephine Charing, along with Paulie and his dog, Wednesday. Who smiled up at her with the usual impartial, world-loving dog smile.

Margaret Lanford was carrying a basket.

"We heard you were leaving and wanted to say good-bye," Josephine whispered. "We've missed you."

"You needn't whisper, Josephine. I missed you, too."

"Oh, of course. It's just that if the other ladies saw us here, you see . . ."

"I do see." Eve couldn't stop her heart from sinking just a little.

"I will never, never forget your kindness, Lady Wareham. And I know how you enjoyed my tea cakes." Margaret Lanford thrust the basket at her. "So I wanted you to have them as a farewell gift."

Eve was touched speechless.

"Although . . ." And then Margaret Lanford flushed. "I fear this batch may have turned out a trifle harder than I'd prefer."

"They're like rocks!" Paulie expounded cheerfully.

Evie looked at Margaret for confirmation. She nodded dismally.

She bit her lip thoughtfully. And then she brightened.

"I know what we can do!"

And so for the next hour, the four of them spent a delightful hour hurling tea cakes across her garden at a target she drew against the back wall, while Wednesday the dog chased them, barking.

And thus she said farewell to Pennyroyal Green very much the way she'd greeted it.

AFTER HOURS OF exhausting the fronts and backs of most of his foolscap and stacking a whole cannonade of crushed drafts, he'd arrived at a sermon about brotherhood. It was a topic as well-worn as his boots. If ever Evie Duggan wanted a nap, this was the sermon to use.

But it would do for his purposes.

He was in church well before Liam Plum began ringing the bells. Much like any other morning, sunlight shafted in through the windows of the altar as it had for centuries, illuminating clergyman after clergyman.

Although . . . it could very well turn out to be a morning unlike any *he'd* ever had.

Or ever would again.

"Good morning." He smiled at his congregation.

They smiled sleepily back at him.

"It's such a pleasure to see you all gathered here. Each of us, in a sense, is family. And we all know that the strength of a family lies in unity." He found the O'Flaherty children and their mother; his eyes warmed. "As Matthew tells us, 'Any kingdom divided against itself is laid waste and any city or house divided against itself will not stand.' And though we may be sorely chal . . ."

The church door pushed open, and Eve, followed by Henny, sidled in and slid into the last pew.

Henny nodded to him, very, very subtly.

Nearly two weeks. He'd been Moses wandering in the desert without a glimpse of Eve for two weeks.

His parched eyes drank her in.

They stared at each other long enough for it to become awkward.

And then for impatient rustles to begin.

The rustles seeded whispers.

Which is when with a long, long breath he tore his gaze away and looked down at his sermon again.

But he'd suddenly forgotten how to read English. His eyes burned. The words swam before them, meaningless, elusive.

Someone coughed into the awkward silence.

And then he crushed the foolscap sermon and hurled it over his shoulder.

Which made a few of the parishioners jump.

No one moved. No one spoke. They seemed to be riveted by whatever it was they saw in his eyes.

"Place me like a seal over your heart, like a seal on your arm; for love is as strong as death, its jealousy unyielding as the grave."

A few gasps erupted.

His voice rang out, bold, clear.

"It burns like blazing fire, like a mighty flame. Many waters cannot quench love; rivers cannot wash it away."

It was safe to say everyone was awake now. He'd startled most of his parishioners and aroused the rest of them.

"Evie Duggan . . ."

And all the heads officially swiveled to follow the beam of the reverend's gaze. Then swiveled back to him.

Then back to Eve.

Whose heart was in her eyes.

" . . . You are the seal upon my heart. You are the fire and flame that warms me, heals me, burns me. You are the river that cools me and carries me. I love you. And love may *be* as strong as death, but *you* . . . I know now you are my life."

A pin would have echoed like a dropped kettle in the church then.

Eve was absolutely riveted. Frozen, her eyes burning into his.

"And though I wish I could have protected you and kept you safe from some of the storms of your life, I find I cannot regret any part of your past. For it has made you who you are. Loyal, passionate, brave, kind, remarkable. You need repent *nothing*."

The last word fell like a gavel.

Not a single person moved or breathed.

"There are those who think good is a *pastime*, to engage in like embroidery or target shooting. There are those who think beauty is a thing of surface, and forget that it's really of the soul. But good is something you are, not something you *do*. And by that definition, I stand before you today and declare that Evie Duggan is one of the best people I have ever had the privilege of knowing."

He could see her breathing quicken as she warred with tears. She shook her head slowly, in disbelief.

"And yes. Love is fire and flood and flame. Love can be a beautiful suffering, as a wise woman once told me. But she was wrong about one thing: The answers for *us*, Eve, are in First Corinthians. It says—"

Mrs. Sneath stood up abruptly. Her cheeks were scarlet, and her voice trembled.

"Pardon me, Reverend. I feel I must *speak* to everyone before you go any further." She folded her hands tightly before her. "'Love rejoiceth not in iniquity, but rejoiceth in the truth,'" she quoted. "*That* is Corinthians, too. And the truth is, something you said to me made me realize that the countess has been a true friend to us all. I believe we have been unfair. I would like to apologize, and humbly offer my friendship."

Adam was as stunned as the rest of the parishioners.

Eve nodded once, regally.

Suddenly nobody seemed to know where to look next. A moment of absolute silence gave way to the whoosh of heads swiveling about like weather vanes.

Miss Amy Pitney stood abruptly, which caused another little excited intake of breath. Parishioners clutched their seats, now in a fever of anticipation to see who would leap up next.

And for a moment all was silent. Her hands in her fine gloves twisted in the folds of her dress, nervously.

And then she squared her shoulders and turned to Eve.

"Corinthians also says 'Love suffereth long, and is kind; love envieth not.'" She inhaled deeply, blew the air out of her cheeks before she spoke again. "I . . . didn't want to see the truth of something; envy blinded me to it. I understand now the courage it took for Lady Wareham to show it to me. To show myself to *me*. To make me like what I saw. I know now how much she risked to do it. Love may suffereth long, but I now know it is patient, too, and so will I be patient. I can never thank you enough, Lady Wareham. But I hope to repay you, by being as good a friend to you as you've been to me, if you'll allow it."

Eve's eyes were glittering now with unshed tears.

Henny had gripped Evie's arm with one hand. With the other she fished out a handkerchief to have at the ready. And she whispered to Eve, ". . . by the way, I never sent the letter to Lord Lisle."

Eve whipped about to stare at her.

And then turned again when another hush fell.

And then Miss Josephine Charing stood slowly.

So that's where all the heads turned next.

And then smiled, as though she was surprised to have actually stood up in church and was enjoying the attention a bit.

" 'For now we see through a glass, darkly; but then face to face.' That's Corinthians! I do read my scripture, you know. I confess I didn't see things *clearly* at all; my glass was quite dark. I was blinded to what was right before my eyes. Because Lady Wareham knows how to be a friend, she returned a friend to me." She exchanged smiles with Amy Pitney. "And I'm indebted to her forever, for she helped me to realize what I was missing by not looking clearly at people. And when I really looked . . . I found a face I'll never, never tire of."

It was what she'd first said to Eve about the vicar. But she wasn't looking at the vicar.

She and Simon Covington were exchanging dreamy stares.

She slipped back down into her seat in the pew. And then he saw, to his astonishment, Olivia

Eversea rise. The hush took on a different quality then.

"When I was a child, I spoke as a child, I understood as a child, I thought as a child: but when I became a woman, I put away childish things."

It was all she said.

She sat down again. And it might have sounded like a non sequitur to anyone else but him. But Adam thought she knew what she meant.

And he was glad.

She nodded once to him.

And that was when the door of the church swung open, and a great swath of sunlight stampeded in and blinded everyone for an instant.

When people were able to focus again, they realized a man was standing in the doorway. A *handsome* man, it was immediately noted, with hair as dark and curly as Eve's, eyes a snapping green, the fair skin of an Irishman, a rakish shadow tracing his jaw.

And as he came into focus, Eve stood slowly, in disbelief.

"Seamus! The *dev*—"

"The devil himself," he confirmed, cheerily.

"About time, ye show yer face 'ere, ye 'andsome mongrel," Henny muttered.

Seamus grinned at her. "I love you, too, Henny."

"Obviously, you share a sense of theatrical timing with your sister. Tell her, Seamus," Adam ordered. "Tell her why you're here now."

It was an order that brooked no argument.

Seamus, apparently, had no qualms about orating to a church of strangers. Evie wasn't the only one with a flare for drama in her family. "It was

Henny who told *him* how to write to me." Him was apparently Adam. He jerked a thumb in his direction.

"But . . ."

Seamus, contriving to look hopelessly dashing in the cheap new clothes he'd apparently bought with the money she'd sent, said, "Yon Reverend wrote to me. A persuasive man, he is. Ought to be a lawyer. Bloody difficult to refuse a man of God! Very good strategy, I'll grant you that, Eve, finding *him*! He put the shame into Seamus first, the fear of God in me next, then he put this proposition to me: I'll live in Damask Manor and help work the land there and at the vicarage, take a share in the profits. There's room enough for Cora and the children to stay as long as need be."

Eve's face blanked. "Cora and the childr . . ."

There was the sound of scuffling of a dozen or so feet, the sound of a woman shushing, then a woman peered in behind Seamus. Petite and dark-haired and light-eyed. In her arms a baby was swaddled. Little boys and girls pushed into view, nudging and jostling each other, grinning shyly, staring somberly, mouths stuffed with thumbs or open in gap-toothed grins.

"Cora . . . !"

Cora smiled at her, wearily and joyfully.

Eve turned back to Adam. She shook her head in wonderment. Tears were falling unchecked now. "How . . ." She put her hands to her face.

"How? Well, we're back to Corinthians. And it's now clear we all know it so well, because love is everything to us, isn't it?" he said to his parishioners. "And this is what it tells us: Love bears all things, believes all things, hopes all things, endures all things. And when I released the idea of *suffering* and decided to *believe* all things, I found a way for us, Eve. I sent for them. And it was a risk, I grant you. But that's where 'believes all things' comes in. I believed in you. I believe we were meant to be. I never stopped believing."

And he moved slowly away from the altar. He walked down the steps.

Apart from a bit of soft weeping and dabbing of eyes, the church fell absolutely silent, so silent they could hear each of his footsteps as he set them down in the aisle, every one bringing him closer to her and forever.

Eve would remember the sound of his footsteps for the rest of her life.

She rose to stand in the aisle, and waited for him to come to her, and brushed impatiently at her tears, lest she miss one second of the look in his eyes.

"I love you, Eve. Marry me. Be my wife. Live here with me, have a family with me."

He said it softly, but such were the acoustics of the old church, everyone heard it. Everyone sucked in a breath.

She could barely choke out the words. Joy and tears husked her voice.

"I love you more than I can say, Adam."

"You can say it with a single word. Say 'yes.' "

She reached up her hands to touch his face. Cradled it in her hands. Brought her face close to his. "Yes," she whispered.

"Kiss her!" Mrs. Sneath bellowed.

He didn't need the encouragement, but he appreciated the enthusiasm.

He kissed her. And all around them jaws dropped, hearts soared and broke, friendships mended, but above all, love ruled.

"Love thy neighbor, *indeed*, Reverend!" Mr. Eldred approved. "*That's* showing us how it's done!"

Epilogue

✦

THEY IMPORTED A VICAR FROM A NEARBY TOWN TO marry them as soon as the banns were cried.

Literally cried, in the case of a number of female parishioners, who softly wet their handkerchiefs for the three consecutive Sundays but would never dream of staying away from church as long as Reverend Sylvaine gave the sermon. Besides, his story was so desperately romantic, they found it inspirational.

Fortunately, novelty is a wonderful opiate, and Adam had also thoughtfully imported Seamus Duggan, and one look at him dried the tears and set the lashes to batting. But Adam made sure Seamus was so busy working the land at both Damask Manor and the vicarage that Seamus fell into bed at night *much* too spent to break any of the hearts he collected.

For now.

Mrs. Sneath believes Seamus Duggan would make a *wonderful* project, and this keeps Seamus rather looking over his shoulder, too.

Cora and Mary O'Flaherty struck up a fast friendship, and Damask Manor is now often over-run by a dozen or so redheaded children, all wearing wooden swords and admiral hats. Henny is their devoted slave, and is worshipped in turn, as she often obliges them by playing the role of Sea Monster. She happily divides her time between the vicarage and Damask Manor, though Mrs. Dalrymple, whose nerves had never been tensile strength, always arranged to be out when Henny was in.

By the end of the year, with a little help from the town, the O'Flahertys had a new roof, a new fence, a new barn, three cows, a fat mule, well-plowed land, a few sheep, and puppies. Because Molly the dog really was a bit of a slut.

John O'Flaherty was never seen in Pennyroyal Green again.

Jacob Eversea congratulated Adam on "making it right" in an inimitable Eversea way. As did Colin and Ian. Colin insisted he'd warned him about Evie by way of encouragement since the only way a member of their family ever did what they were supposed to do was by being told not to do it.

Adam read the banns for Josephine Charing and Simon Covington the week after he read his own.

As it so happened, Mr. Bartholomew Tolliver was discovered to be genuinely passionate about botany, and he and Miss Amy Pitney struck up a lively correspondence. Mr. Tolliver harbors secret romantic hopes about Amy. Amy harbors secret romantic hopes, too.

For Seamus Duggan.

The town watches and waits.

A WEEK AFTER their wedding, Adam and Evie stopped by the churchyard to lay Sussex wildflowers on Lady Fennimore's grave.

Eve leaned back against the great wall of his chest, secure in the loop of his arms, and tucked her head beneath his chin, where she fit perfectly. They admired Lady Fennimore's headstone. Her epitaph read:

DON'T THINK IT WON'T HAPPEN TO YOU

"I used to think my epitaph would read 'Here lies Evie Duggan. No one ever got the better of her.'"

"And what do you think it should read now?"

"Here lies Evie Sylvaine. Better because of Adam Sylvaine."

He pulled her tightly against his body and she pressed against him, arced her throat so he could kiss it. Evie felt that familiar languor of want begin to take hold of them both. The sort that usually required them to rush back to the house at odd hours of the day.

"Lady Fennimore wouldn't mind if we did it here," Adam murmured in her ear.

"But we've a living audience, of sorts."

He followed her gaze out toward the road, where in the lowering light two people were walking together.

"It's my cousin Olivia. And . . . by God, if that isn't Lord Landsdowne she's walking with."

They beheld the miracle in silence.

"Landsdowne might just win that wager yet," Adam said on a hush.

Next month, don't miss these exciting new love stories only from Avon Books

Kiss of Surrender by Sandra Hill

Trond is a thousand-year-old Viking vampire angel who's undercover as a Navy SEAL. But it's not all bad. Working out with SEALs like Nicole Tasso is a perk. Nicole knows Trond is hiding something strange, but it's not easy figuring out a man she finds as attractive as she does annoying. Will Trond and Nicole get their stories straight . . . before it's too late?

King of the Damned by Juliana Stone

Given a chance to atone for his past, Azaiel, the Fallen, must find out if the League has been breached. What he doesn't foresee is the lovely Rowan James, a powerful witch out for vengeance and in need of an ally. Wanting Rowan means risking salvation, but will these desperate souls find love...or be forever damned?

The Importance of Being Wicked by Miranda Neville

Thomas, Duke of Castleton, has every intention of wedding a prim and proper heiress. That is, until he sets eyes on the heiress's troublesome cousin. Caroline Townsend has no patience for the oh-so-suitable men of the *ton*. Suddenly Caro finds herself falling for a stuffy duke . . . while Thomas discovers there's a great deal of fun in a little wickedness.

How to Deceive a Duke by Lecia Cornwall

When her sister runs off the night before her arranged marriage, Meg Lynton saves her family by marrying the devilish Nicholas Hartley herself. Nicholas never wanted to change his wicked ways for a wife—until he discovers Meg's deception. Now, the Duke will have to teach the scheming beauty how to be a duchess, kiss by devastating kiss . . .